FROM THE ACCLAIMED AUTHOR OF *JIM KANE, THE OUTFIT,* AND *THE FORESTS OF THE NIGHT* COMES THIS STIRRING SAGA THAT CAPTURES THE REAL SPIRIT OF THE SOUTHWEST THROUGH THE LIFE AND TIMES OF THE UNFORGETTABLE MEN AND WOMEN WHO CARVED THEIR DESTINY FROM A MAGNIFICENT LAND OF SANDSTONE CANYONS AND SUN-PAINTED HILLS . . .

A. B. COWDEN—With his clear vision and unshakable values, this brawny, straight-shooting rancher made the brand of the El Durazno ranch stand for strength and pride. But can one family stand against the thieves and gunfighters preying on the innocent and the raiding Apaches scourging the earth with arrows and fire?

VINEY COWDEN—The dark-haired, beautiful wife of A.B., she stood beside her husband through every hardship, running their sprawling household with courage and skill. Now the perils of the harsh frontier threatened to take all she loved from her . . . especially the child of her heart.

BEN COWDEN—Like a river running deep, the oldest Cowden son hid the swift currents of his passion beneath a calm surface, but he would face down any man without fear or hesitation—even when a crooked lawman put a price on his head.

LES COWDEN—Second son of the Cowden clan, his wild streak and brooding temper made him a brawler and a scrapper by nature, but there was no better man with a gun—and n watch your back.

DUNCAN VINCENT—Dude owner of the vast VO spread, he plotted to fence in the range and make his white-faced cattle king of Arizona's steers—even if he had to hire an army of renegades and killers to do it.

HOOZY BRIGGS—The worse of the ruthless Briggs brothers, he was slow of wit, fast on the draw, and sneaky as a coyote. Natives of Sonora, he and his brother were natural enemies of the Cowdens, who they swore to kill.

LORRIE BRIGGS—Pretty as a picture in calico and lace, she was as different from her brothers as silk from a sow's ear, but when she set out to win Ben Cowden, was it love—or her brothers' coldhearted trap?

CHE CHE—He called himself a Mexican, but he handled a knife and tracked like an Apache. Solemn, mean, and mysterious, no one knew where his loyalties lay or whether his thirst for vengeance would make him a killer . . . or a hero.

PAULA MARY—An irrepressible tomboy and daredevil, she was A.B.'s youngest daughter and undeniably all Cowden, but her love of mischief and adventure threatened to sweep her into the arms of a danger from which not even the Cowden clan could save her.

MAUDY JANE PENDLETON—Long-legged and lovely, this Arizona cowgirl would be a catch for any young rancher, but she had eyes for only one man, Ben Cowden— and she'd wrest him from the grip of death itself to make him her own.

THE YAWNER—Unsmiling, clench-jawed, and undeniably the greatest Apache warrior the West had ever known, he was ironically called "the Yawner," but his violence spoke louder than any words as he set out to win back the land for his people.

**THE ARIZONA SAGA
BOOK 1
THE BLOODED STOCK**

Bantam Books by J.P.S. Brown
Ask your bookseller for the books you have missed.

THE OUTFIT

THE ARIZONA SAGA, BOOK I

THE BLOODED STOCK

J. P. S. Brown

BANTAM BOOKS
NEW YORK · TORONTO · LONDON · SYDNEY · AUCKLAND

THE BLOODED STOCK
A Bantam Book / September 1990

ISBN 0-553-28068-6

Published simultaneously in the United States and Canada

Bantam Books are published by Bantam Books, a division of Bantam Doubleday
Dell Publishing Group, Inc. Its trademark, consisting of the words "Bantam
Books" and the portrayal of a rooster, is Registered in U.S. Patent and
Trademark Office and in other countries. Marca Registrada. Bantam Books, 666
Fifth Avenue, New York, New York 10103.

PRINTED IN THE UNITED STATES OF AMERICA

OPM   0 9 8 7 6 5 4 3 2 1

For Aunt Laura Mary Sorrells Bergier,
who was born in Harshaw one hundred years ago and still
lives in Santa Cruz County, Arizona. She told me about
chucking the walnuts at Chris Wilson's mules and other
stories that inspired this first book of *The Arizona Saga*.

*When blooded stock is introduced to a country, it must
adapt as well as the native stock if it is to thrive. The
husbandman of blooded stock must pick sires and dams
through generations in order to breed a line that is as suited
to a country as the natives. Good stock must thrive on a
country's feed, water, and shelter and then give back more
than it used.*

*Sonorans say that the stock from different families and
bloodlines become* de la misma mata, *as sprigs from the
same bush, stock of the same blood, when it has been bred
in the same country through generations.*

CHAPTER 1

Paula Mary Cowden heard the mules coming. The twenty-mule team that pulled Chris Wilson's ore wagon was Paula Mary's quarry. She had a terrible obsession for pestering Chris Wilson's mules. Most of the time she was ready and laying for them, but today Chris surprised her, and she only had a few minutes to prepare her ambuscade. She ran for her walnut tree, scampered up the trunk and out on a thick limb that stretched over the road. She gave no thought at all to the danger of falling. Her bare feet found the way quickly over the same steps she had taken on that limb every day of half the summertimes of her life.

The mules were not yet in sight. She could see their dust, but they had not come around the bend to start their climb up Harshaw Canyon. She gathered a handful of green walnuts, lay along her limb, and waited. People were always saying, "An Apache can hide where a white man cannot." Well, what about Paula Mary Cowden? She could hide as well as any Indian. No one ever saw her when she didn't want them to. She'd been harassing mule teams on the road to the Harshaw mine her whole life, and she'd never been caught because only the mules knew she was doing it, and they never saw her either. They couldn't tell on her, even if they could talk. Well, not her whole life, but half her life, and that was half a dozen years.

Paula Mary knew by the echo of the ore wagon in the canyon that she had time to wait. Three riders came around the bend, ahead of the wagon, and she recognized them right away because they made her eyes sore every time she saw them. The main one was Dick Martin. He was always trying to let on that he was a cowboy. Whenever he was around Paula Mary's brothers, he tried to talk "cow," and he didn't know which end the plops came out of a cow.

Dick was riding a skinny paint horse. Somebody ought to tell him any cowboy knew how to stay off his horse enough to feed and rest him. Look at him, riding along with a turkey feather in his hat. Somebody'd probably sold it to him for an eagle feather—probably that Mexican riding with him.

The Mexican riding with Dick was really an Indian. He rode a naked Mexican saddletree with a blanket over it like an Indian, only he wanted people to think he was a Mexican. Anyone could tell by the way he handled a horse that he was an Indian. Probably an Apache, too. He was riding a thin dun horse he never shod. Paula Mary's brothers said Mexicans didn't ride barefoot horses. Her brother Ben was ten years older than she, and he was always right about men and their horses.

She made herself smaller on the limb. That Indian was a hard case if she ever saw one. Dick had stopped at her father's barn the other day, and the Indian had stood back while Dick did the talking. Paula Mary was holding her father's hand, and that Indian kept looking at her like he would like to eat her.

The Indian called himself Che Che. He and Dick were sure having a time. Old Dick rode with his big feet hanging so long in his stirrups they almost bumped the ground.

Listen to that Indian laugh, thought Paula Mary. He wasn't fooling anybody that he was a Mexican. Paula Mary's brothers told her his voice was too low in his throat to be a Mexican's. Those black eyes he used for looking at a person showed her he didn't have any more feeling in him than a reptile.

The third rider called himself Hoozy. His name was Horace, or Hoozier, or something. Hoozier Briggs. He was riding along on his fanny with his feet hanging down like most miners did. This one dearly loved his guns. Everybody carried guns this spring of 1885 in southern Arizona, because Geronimo's Apaches were killing people again, but Hoozy loaded himself down with guns and knives. Anybody that scared ought to stay down in a mine, but he wanted to be out where he might get to shoot somebody. He was packing a butcher knife in a sheath, a .4570 rifle in his saddle scabbard, and pistols on each hip with crossed gunbelts. Paula Mary's brother Mark said the rifle was so big it took more than one miner Hoozy's size to handle it and would blow his foot off someday.

They were passing underneath her now, and she realized she'd missed a lot of the talk because she was criticizing them so much. She allowed she missed a lot that way, talking to herself and not listening to anything else. Look at them. Now wouldn't anyone say these three belonged to the rough set?

"Tastes good," the Apache Che Che was saying. "*Sabe a tesguin*. It tastes like *tesguino*." Paula Mary guessed they were talking about saloon beer tasting like the *tesguino* beer that the Indians made out of corn.

"*Para la cruda*," Dick said. Paula Mary knew that meant "for the hangover." That Dick, and everybody he ran with, was always getting drunk. She bet they were headed straight for Harshaw's twenty-seven saloons. Paula Mary was under strict orders never to look to the left or to the right when she walked past the twenty-seven saloons on her way to school in Harshaw. Her folks would be surprised how much she could see out of the corner of her eye.

"How about it, Hoozy? You ready for a drink?" Dick Martin looked back over his shoulder and almost caught Paula Mary's face out in the open.

"I guess a beer'd taste good," Hoozy said.

Che Che grinned at Hoozy. Paula Mary bet that between them, Dick and Che Che couldn't raise the price of a two-bit cone of brown-sugar *panocha*. Couldn't buy a stalk of raw sugarcane. Hoozy probably could. He worked his own mine when he felt like it. The mining companies were hiring. They'd hire anybody. Miners were leaving the country, afraid of Geronimo. Hoozy could get hold of a little money now and then whenever he felt like working. Dick was fooling Hoozy along, telling him he'd teach him how to be a cowboy so he'd pay for the drinks.

Paula Mary couldn't think why he carried the Indian. She guessed he must like mean Indians. Hoozy was waiting to shoot somebody, and Che Che would do any darned thing he could to be mean. Paula Mary felt like bouncing a walnut off Dick Martin's dumb head, but she sure did not want to risk hitting that Indian or the other one with the guns. Her brother Mark said Dick showed some manners when he could be cut away from the trash he ran with.

Dick and his trash went on, and Paula Mary turned back at the very moment Chris Wilson's sorrel lead mules rounded the bend and came on. Her heart sprang like a racehorse, but she lay quiet while her limb swayed in a breeze and the rough bark held her still. She listened to the mules' shod hooves, the rattle of the tracechains, and the ring of the steel tires on the empty wagon's wheels. She watched twenty pairs of long ears sway back and forth in line. She could tell if a wagon was full or empty by the sound. The loaded wagons crushed the rocks against the road on the way to the railroad. The empty ones bounced and took back the punishment the whole rocks gave on the way back to the mine. You always get back what you give, Paula Mary's mama said.

Paula Mary watched and timed the pace of the mules. She would not strike until Chris Wilson's hat was beneath her and the wheel team was a rod beyond her. Even if Chris saw the walnut streak past him and smite his mule, he would not be able to turn and see her unless his neck had hinges on it. Her ambuscade was foolproof.

The heads of the wheel team passed under Paula Mary's limb and pulled on by. The top of Chris Wilson's head passed so directly beneath her, she could have spit on his hat if she dared. She raised up and pegged a walnut straight past his ear into the off wheel-mule's hip. The mule flicked an ear and went on as though the nut was less than a fly, less than a clod that flies off a wheel. Paula Mary sat up because the team was now on a short, steep downgrade into Harshaw Creek. She was behind Chris. He would never in a hundred years be able to turn and see her. She pegged three more nuts, rapid-fire, at the team. The second one bounced off Chris Wilson's hat. She flattened against the limb and held her breath. Chris' hands were full holding the mules on the grade, but he looked up into the tree he was passing, and that squeezed a scared giggle out of Paula Mary. That proved it: Her ambuscade was foolproof.

"Paula Mary, where are you?" her mother called.

Paula Mary pressed her face against the bark of her limb and let her breath out carefully, silently. She ought to know better than to gloat over a successful ambush. She must not be caught, must not be seen.

"Paula Mary, I know where you are! Come down out of that tree this minute."

Paula Mary went cold. She was discovered.

"Paula Mary, answer me."

Paula Mary waited an instant longer to see if her mother was bluffing, then decided any delay would be truly dangerous. She started to climb down.

Chris Wilson's wagon and team crossed the creek, climbed the opposite bank, and headed around another bend. Chris now probably knew who had been bouncing walnuts off his mules.

"There you are. Why don't you answer when I call, young lady?"

"I needed another minute, Mother."

"Well, come on, now. I don't know what you're doing up a tree when your very best friend is coming to see you. What keeps you in that tree, Paula Mary?"

"Nothing, Mother."

"I bet Chris Wilson's mules wish that was true. Aren't you afraid you'll cause a wreck?"

"No, they don't mind."

"You hit one in the eye, and I bet he'll mind. I wonder how many times you've pestered those poor mules. It's a good thing Chris keeps a good hold on them when he goes by our house."

"I guess so, Mother."

"Come in now, and take your bath before your brothers come home. I'll swear, the boys don't get as dirty working cattle as you do when you're supposed to be watering my flowers. What do you do in that tree besides devil Chris Wilson's poor mules?"

Paula Mary saw her mother was smiling at her from the screen door on the back porch. She was a tiny woman with shiny black hair combed neatly in a bun. Her name was Viney. Paula Mary always thought that was such a pretty name for a mother.

"I do a lot of *thinking* up there, Mother," said Paula Mary.

"Don't try to tell me that, Paula Mary. You're always too busy pestering people when you're in that walnut tree to do any thinking."

"Now, Mama. I'm practicing for war. I'm better'n an Apache at hiding and watching. What do you think would happen to us if I didn't keep a lookout for Apaches?"

"Lordy, Lord, I'd hate to think. However, your water's hot in the tub, so get a move on. Your friend Maudy'll be here any minute, and your father is taking us for a drive before the dance."

Paula Mary was standing in the tub drying herself when her father, A. B. Cowden, walked into the kitchen. He was straight and lean and wore a great white brush of a mustache. Paula Mary was sure his blue eyes could see through a thundercloud, but not through the curtains of the alcove that sheltered her bath.

"Are you done outside, Mr. Cowden?" asked Viney.

A. B.'s El Durazno ranch was on the road between the Duquesne, the Mowry, and the Harshaw mines and the railhead in Patagonia. He was undersheriff for that part of Pima County, and he did a good business selling teams and saddle horses. The family's cattle work was done by his boys.

"All through," A. B. answered. "Chris Wilson just went by, and that's the last wagon today. The mine is shut down now for the celebration. I hear a mouse splashing her feet. Who is that mouse in our tub?"

"That's your smallest daughter," Viney said. "I wish you'd talk to her. She'd rather climb trees and terrorize Chris Wilson's mules than water my flowers. What do you think of a girl who does that?"

"I think she's awful."

Paula Mary peeked through the alcove at him. His hat was on the table, and he was reading a newspaper.

"I think the newspapers ought to hear about it," A. B. said, looking over his paper and catching her face in the open. Thunder rolled down the canyon from the south. "Listen to the thunder. Better get out of that tub, Paula Mary. Lightning strikes the wicked."

"I'm out, Papa." Paula Mary stepped out of the alcove dressed. She kissed her father's big mustache, sat down, and drew on her best cream-colored stockings. She buttoned on her shoes and climbed into his lap.

"Do you like my dress, Papa?" she asked.

"Has a toady got warts?"

"It's a brand-new percale Mama made me."

"Yes, I see it, daughter."

"Do you like my high lace collar?"

"Oh, yes."

"Papa, do you think I'll just look a picture after Betty combs my hair?"

Viney walked into the room with comb and brush. "Here, I'm combing that hair this time," she declared.

The little girl's hair was long and straight. She held up a handful to study the black shine of it while her head bobbed with the tug of her mother's brush.

"I've been wondering, Papa. Is Dick Martin trash?"

"What makes you ask a thing like that, daughter?"

"Well, I've heard you say trash runs with trash, and mules don't run with racehorses. Are Indians trash? Dick Martin acts like he's friends with that Che Che, the one you said was an Indian."

"Some Indians are trash; some are not. That one is."

"What did he do?"

"For one thing, he tries to pass for a Mexican. That proves to me he's an Apache."

"And Dick Martin and Hoozy Hoozisface are trash?"

"They act like trash, I guess."

Paula Mary endured her mother's tugs on her hair awhile. Then, keeping her head down, she said, "Am I an Indian?"

Viney gasped, then laughed, so Paula Mary looked to her papa's eye for the truth. She found no answer there.

Her father was the best poker player in the territory. He could use that eye when he committed to nothing, and he could use it to lay down a gentleman's deadly warning to an enemy and never say a word.

"Nobody else but an Indian and my brother Ben has hair black as mine. My hair shines even when it's dirty, like an Indian's, and I can hide as good as any Indian in the country."

"Well, you're no Indian, little daughter. You're a Cowden."

"But I'm a Porter, too. I could be an Indian from the Porters. Mama's a Porter, and her hair is black as mine."

"Yes, and you and all your brothers and sisters have blue eyes. No Indian has blue eyes. My, my, the things you come up with," A. B. said.

"Well, I'd feel better not being an Indian."

"You don't ever have to be ashamed of who you are, Paula Mary," said her mother. "I'm finished brushing you. Go sit still a little while so you won't get mussed."

Paula Mary dragged herself off her papa's lap.

Eileen, the oldest daughter, came in carrying Paula Mary's comb and brush. "Oh, I was going to take care of Paula Mary's hair, Mama. Did you hear what Hoozy Briggs and his brother Whitey did?"

"Don't tell me they finally shot somebody," Viney said.

"No, they did something worse. They advertised for wives in the newspapers back east."

"Well, that's nothing new," Viney said. "This country isn't exactly running over with womenfolk."

"Mama, they advertised themselves in Kansas like seed bulls. That's terrible."

A. B. threw back his head and laughed. "That pair ought to be saved for seed, all right."

"Terrible is as terrible does, maybe, but that shouldn't bother you, daughter," Viney said.

"Besides that, the girls are already in Patagonia."

"Now, who in the world told you all this? You're better informed than the *Tucson Star*. What about it, Mr. Cowden? Did you see anything in the paper about Hoozy and Whitey Briggs and the arrival from Kansas of their brides-to-be?"

"Not one thing," A. B. said.

"Sarah Farley told me all about it when she came by this morning with her papa. The girls are sisters, and they're both pretty."

"I always say, if there's anything that will keep a fellow from shooting another, it's the full attention of a pretty girl," Viney said. "Thank God for gullible Kansas girls."

"Isn't that something?" Eileen said. "Two pretty girls coming all that way sight unseen for the Briggses to wed."

"Not anything like the hardship your beau endures courting you, Eileen," A. B. said from behind his paper. "John Bonner has ridden unescorted a hundred and twenty miles twice a month for two years through the most thickly infested Apache country in Arizona to see you, and you don't think that's something?"

"I don't know, Papa. Old John never gets excited, and so I never get excited. I love him dearly, and I'm going to marry him, but he's never even been late coming through all that country that's supposed to be dangerous with Apaches."

"Mr. Cowden, are we still going on a drive before we head for the dance?" Viney asked.

"Of course," A.B. said. "Is everybody ready?"

"See, Papa, nobody in my own family even noticed my new dress," Eileen said. "Old John's not much different. When he gets here, he'll say, 'You sure look good, Eileen.' Then he'll say, 'Yes, you do, you sure do.' And that's all he'll ever say until he comes back two more Thursdays later."

"I guess I better hurry and hitch the team," A. B. said. "I can see how much we need excitement, and the most exciting thing I can do is take us on a drive with Brooks and Joe."

Outside, the first thing A. B. did as always was search the sky for rain. A breeze was stirring in from the east, a good sign. The prevailing winds were from the southwest and the Sea of Cortez, but when they brought rain, they usually went on by further south, then hooked back in from the east. Anyone inside that eastern hook might get rained on. A breeze out of the east meant water for somebody and was as promising for a stockman as the prospect of finding pure gold.

A. B. started toward the barn and came face-to-face with another figure of promise, Maudy Jane Pendleton. Maudy was Paula Mary's best friend. She was the daughter of Will Pendleton, a rancher from the Canelo Hills northeast of Harshaw.

Maudy carried the dress and shoes she would wear to the Harshaw dance that evening. She was dressed in a faded yellow dress, but she looked pretty enough to go straight to the dance.

A. B. often hinted to his sons that this young person showed promise. She was small, but she was long-legged and high behind, as good stock should be. She was redheaded and enjoyed the clear complexion of the redhead without a freckle on her face. She also carried a light in her eye that showed she could love anything she looked at but would never be fooled by anything she loved. She always seemed full of quick, graceful energy and great good humor.

"Well, howdydo, Mr. Cowden," Maudy said, bouncing in front of A. B., smiling into his face and shaking his hand.

"My, you look fresh as a little daffodil, Maudy," said A. B.

"I'm going in to visit with your girls and change my dress for the dance."

"You make yourself at home. Come here any time you need us. Maybe one of my big old boys will encourage you to stay."

Maudy blushed, but she was still smiling as she went in the house.

The forge was cooling in the blacksmith's corner in the barn, a sign that Bill Knox was still sleeping his siesta. Guilo Soto, the stableboy, was resting, too.

Will Pendleton was waiting for A. B. in his office. He stood up when A. B. walked in, his hat on the back of his head.

"Well, young man, how long have you been here?" A. B. asked. "Let's go to the house so Viney can give you pie and coffee."

"No, no, my family is expecting me to come right back to Harshaw," Will Pendleton said. "I came by to bring Maudy and maybe do some business."

"Then, what can I do for you, young man?"

"I need a good team. They don't have to match, but they do have to be sound and gentle. I'm sending my wife and children down to the Macarena ranch to stay while Geronimo is loose."

"Have you looked at my horses? I have six teams and thirty saddle horses for sale."

"I like the brown and the bay. I've seen them work."

"You have a good eye."

"Sometimes my eye is richer than my pocketbook."

"Did you look at the matched sorrels?"

"Oh, well, yes. I've been looking at those sorrels ever since you drove them to Patagonia Easter Sunday. I admire them, but I can't buy horseflesh that fine."

"You want your family to be safe with their team, don't you?"

"Well, yes, A. B., but I can get along with the brown and the bay. If I buy the sorrels, I'll only be paying extra for more looks than I need."

"Did you ever see two horses better matched for looks and disposition than the sorrels?"

"Gosh, A. B., that's your own team. How could I afford the best horses in Arizona?"

"What do you think a good team is worth? Mind you, I have a price on my horses, and I know what they're worth. I want to know how much you'll pay for your family's safety when you know Geronimo might come after it."

Will Pendleton laughed as he followed A. B. outside to look at the horses. He was thinking the old devil was trying to shame him, so he could trade him out of his last dollar. A. B. stopped at a spot by the corrals where they could see all the horses.

"Well, I know you're asking a hundred and twenty-five dollars a team," Will said. "That's a shade above the ordinary price, but the brown and the bay are a lot better than ordinary."

"What would you pay if the sorrels were the only horses that suited you for moving your family to the Macarena?"

"Well, I'd have to give you what you asked, I guess."

"My price is a hundred and twenty-five for the sorrels."

"No, A. B., don't say that. I'm ready to pay a hundred twenty-five for the brown and the bay."

"You're taking the sorrels. Did you bring halters?"

"I won't let you do it."

"Bring your halters." A. B. headed back to the barn.

Guilo came out to see if he was needed. "*Guilo, por favor traiga martigones para el tiro alazan,*" A. B. said in his soft voice. "Bring halters for the sorrel team."

"No, I won't let you do this, A. B.," Will Pendleton said.

"I want to do it. From now on they belong to you. Give your halters to Guilo so he can catch them, and you can be on your way. You've been dickering with me so long Wilma will think Geronimo is drying your scalp on his horse's mane."

"Darn it, I didn't bring my halters. I didn't figure on taking them now. I didn't even bring my money. I didn't intend to pay for them until after the celebration when I headed for home."

"Come for them anytime. They'll be fed and watered and ready to go."

"A. B.," Will said, frustrated. "You make me feel like a piker."

"Believe me, no man's a piker who's ready to buy the best for his family. I'm happy the team suits you. You go on and enjoy yourself. I'm taking my girls in after a while, and we'll see you at the dance."

Guilo came out carrying halters, and A. B. decided to harness the sorrels one more time to say goodbye. His eyes were soft when he looked at them. They were looking at him, too. They had long been his pet team. A. B. esteemed them, and they knew to expect the best from him. The way he looked at it, with the Pendletons, they had a better reason for being good horses.

Guilo hitched the sorrels to a buggy, and A. B. circled them on the road to warm them, then waited in front of the barn. Viney and Paula Mary climbed into the front seat beside him. Maudy, Eileen, and Paula Mary's middle sister, Betty, sat in the back. A. B. started up the road toward Washington Camp.

"Mr. Cowden, the sorrels are shining like new pennies. They're handsomer every day," Viney said.

"Joe's the off horse again today, isn't he, Papa?" said Paula Mary. "Is old Brooks going to be the near horse from now on?"

A. B. enjoyed talking to Paula Mary about his horses. "How do you know Joe's the off horse, daughter?"

"I just know. I can tell them apart by the way they look at me. Are they twins, Papa?"

"No, but they look enough alike to be twins, don't they? They're full brothers."

"Can I take the lines?"

"After they've lined out a bit. We'll see if we can meet your brothers. They ought to be close to home by now. Ben said they'd try to be back in time for the dance."

Thunderheads were high in the south, marking the farthest reaches of the sky over Sonora. The day was hot. The *bellotas*, the black oaks, by the road were weighted down with white dust.

This part of southern Arizona had been U.S. territory for thirty-two years, since the Gadsden Purchase, but Americans had only been showing enough interest in it to settle it for about twenty years.

During the Civil War, Jefferson Davis annexed Arizona into the Confederacy, and no one in Arizona objected enough. That made the Union unsympathetic to Arizona's need for military protection, and the army abandoned it to Apaches and bandits. Confederate sympathizers in Arizona never did the Union a particle of harm unless Viney Porter's father could be counted as a guerrilla. William Henry Porter was jailed in Phoenix once for cussing the Union in public.

When the soldiers left Arizona, the Apaches began trying to kill everybody who stayed. Even so, people like the Cowdens did not feel they were fighting a war against an Apache nation. They were protecting their lives, homes, and livestock against predators. The Apaches preyed on everybody else who was trying to make a living in the country—Mexicans, Americans, and the other Indian tribes alike.

Killing and stealing was the Apache way. They did not make war to defend their land. War was their way of accumulating loot. Before the white man came, they preyed on all the other Indians. The white settlers were richer prey. A careless settler they caught alone forty miles from his nearest neighbor, trying to do a day's work, was no enemy warrior to an Apache. He was a juicy windfall.

People like the Cowdens and Porters who had been in Arizona since 1850 respected the Apaches the way they did the wolves. They held open season on them and were careful not to get cornered and hamstrung by them.

Apaches could be encountered on any family excursion like the one A. B. Cowden's family was taking that day before San Juan's Day 1885. The Cowden family was not careless or foolhardy, though. They knew that likely as not, if Apaches were seen, they would be in small force and in a hurry to get out of sight. The army at Ft. Huachuca thirty-five miles away patrolled the country with cavalry. The Cowdens saw Apaches about as often as they saw wolves. They avoided excursions when those predators were not hiding what they did.

Being confined to the road in a buggy with his women-folk limited A. B.'s ability to fight, but he was a veteran teamster. He had driven the Overland Stage between Carson City and Sacramento for three years before he came to Arizona and married Viney. He learned to handle teams from his father, a sutler for the army at Ft. Smith, Arkansas.

A. B. Cowden knew how to defend against road agents of all kinds. On the Overland across the Sierra Nevada, he had driven routinely on the edges of precipices and ravines, and around switchbacks that were more deadly than road agents or hostile Indians.

That road across the Sierra Nevada was worked by more road agents than any other in the world, but A. B. was only stopped twice in three years. He was driver enough to keep his coaches out of range of bandits. Most agents tried to commit their robberies alone and were no match for a determined driver with a good shotgun man by his side.

A. B. remembered the bandit who stepped in front of his horses to hold him up and then stumbled, his feet skating over loose round rocks until he fell under the horses. A. B. drove the stage over him and took his passengers out of range before the man could peel himself off the ground. That day, A. B. had been able to handle six horses and a coach loaded with passengers better than the bandit could maneuver his own feet.

"Papa, do you think Uncle Billy Porter and his family are back from San Francisco?" Betty asked.

Betty was the most beautiful of A. B.'s three daughters. Eileen was the highfalutin daughter, and she was a pretty girl, but Betty's face, figure, and carriage made men and women, girls and boys, turn back for a second look when she passed by.

"Yes, I think so, Betty," A. B. said. "In their letter they said they'd be home in time to celebrate *Día de San Juan* with us."

Betty subsided. She might not say another word for the rest of the drive. She was as good a poker player as A. B., and she would not be telling anyone why she wanted to see her cousins. A. B. knew she was craving to hear the Porters tell about their trip to San Francisco. She would rather travel than marry, be famous, or get rich. Even this short drive away from the house was like a tonic to her. She bloomed when a man put wheels under her. She seldom let on when she felt good, though, and she never told anyone when she felt bad.

"I can't wait for the Porter girls to tell us about the ocean," Paula Mary said. "I want to hear about the fishing smackers. I want to know why they call them smackers. Probably that's the sound the fish make when they fall out of the net, don't you think so, Mama?"

Viney shook the buggy with silent laughter. "Oh, yes, I'm sure that's right, daughter. They just go 'smacker, smacker.'"

"Well, isn't that right?" asked Paula Mary.

"I think they're called fishing *smacks*, Paula Mary," Eileen said. "I want to hear about the concerts they went to. If I ever go, I'll spend all my time listening to good music."

"Well, what other kind of music can a body listen to?" said Paula Mary.

"I mean fine music. Classical music. Beethoven, Mozart, Handel."

"Hansel and Gretel, you mean."

"No, Paula Mary. Tell her, Mama. Tell about the concerts."

A. B. looked at Betty. She was not letting on that she desired anything in the world, intent on a dream of a place far away that she knew better than anyone else.

"What would you like to do if you ever found yourself in San Francisco, Maudy?" A. B. asked.

Maudy was happy to have company. She was responsible for the care of her two little sisters, for all the housework in her home, and for much of the cowboy work her father needed done.

"I'd just like to be able to sit and watch somebody else wash and dry and put away the dishes," Maudy said.

"Never mind, Maudy," Viney said. "Someday we'll all go to the coast together. My favorite places are the museums and restaurants. When I was a little girl and we lived on the Russian River . . ."

CHAPTER 2

The day before Paula Mary was caught ambushing Chris Wilson's mules, her brothers were prowling the southern edge of their home range. They rode upon the tracks of someone driving a bunch of their cattle toward Mexico and hurried after them.

Ben Cowden was glad he and his brothers were riding fresh horses. The Cowdens raised good horses, so they would be well mounted in this situation. They often extended their prowling for days into unfriendly country. The Cowden horses would not quit a man in a tight spot.

At noon, Ben left the tracks and climbed a hill to look across the main draw of the Buena Vista range into Mexico. He stopped his horse so only his hat and his eyes cleared the top of the hill, and he saw the dust of the cattle. Mexican riders were moving them.

"Well, there they are," Ben said. "No use hurrying. We'll catch them in the Santa Barbara foothills. They must be *vaqueros* from the Maria Macarena ranch. They'll stop to water at La Acequia."

"Good, now we can go straight to them and quit this tracking," said Les, the second oldest brother. "I don't want any more *tracking*. It makes me *tired*."

"How can anybody complain about tracking a herd this

big?" asked Mark, the youngest brother. "Paula Mary could do it." He was laughing at his brother.

"You ought to have the kink in your neck that I do. I've been the one had to do all the looking down for tracks."

That was the end of the fun for Mark. Les was serious. Mark looked away after the cattle and forgot about tracks and discussions.

Ben was surprised when Mark opened his mouth to talk. Mark usually did not say much. He was always at the right place at the right time in his work, but he was usually quiet and reserved. He followed his brothers with quiet good humor and did whatever they decided to do, but every once in a while Les brought an argument out of him. Les' judgments amused Mark. Les was extremely hot-tempered and quick to attack anything that made him angry, and Mark knew he was lucky Les was gentle with his family. Sometimes he just could not help laughing at him, though.

Ben and Mark were seldom angry with Les. He ran himself with his feelings, but he had good reasons for being emotional. He was only nineteen, and he was out trying to retrieve cattle that might kill him when he took hold of them. He did his work looking over his shoulder for Apaches who might run a wooden shaft through him and cattle thieves who might shoot him and cut off his ears so his mama would not know him.

Mark was only seventeen, but he gave each task a lot of thought before he took hold of it, and he was as good a cowboy as Les. Ben was twenty-one. The brothers were born after the Civil War and in the middle of the Apache war. They went horseback before they could walk and had never known a time without conflict. Their mother and father taught them to find peace inside their family.

"What'll we do when we catch them, Ben?" Les asked. "Can we teach them a lesson this time?"

Ben laughed softly. "What can we teach them? They own the school today. We'll own it tomorrow. They tracked some of their cattle over here and are driving some of ours back with them. We'll get ours back if we can and might have to bring some of theirs home. Where's the lesson in that?"

"Well, we should make them sorry for taking our cattle."

"Papa says we'd have to do something sorry to make them sorry."

"Well, let's at least bring back some of their horses and leave them afoot for a while."

"No, we won't take anybody's horses. Take a man's horse, or shoot his dog, or steal his wife, and he never lets you live it down. Anyway, what would we do with those dinks the Maria Macarena *vaqueros* ride?"

"Fatten them up and sell them, I guess. That's what I'd do."

"We have too many *good* horses to feed. What could we do by stealing a few dinks, except cause a hardship on the Mexicans by putting them afoot and on ourselves by having to pour a lot of feed into them? How would we explain to Papa when somebody told him Les went crazy and tried to sell someone a Maria Macarena dink? We'd have to sell them. Which one of us would want to be seen riding one?"

"I sure wouldn't let Papa know. I'd keep them in Temporal Canyon until they looked good and the brands haired over. Then I'd sell them to the army at Fort Bowie. No horsemen from this country would ever see them."

Ben was leading the way around the crest of the hill so he would not be silhouetted against the sky. A horseman might not live long after he showed himself on top a hill in Arizona. The only time the Cowdens ever saw the silhouette of a horseman was when somebody drew a pretty picture of one and published it back east for all the world to see.

The Cowden brothers rode south through cedar, piñon, and white oak beside the open draws of the Buena Vista and across the Mexican border. They did not talk. They kept their horses at a high trot a good distance apart and concentrated on seeing what they had to see. They watched the ground for tracks, even though they were keeping the dust of the cattle in sight. They looked closely at any shape that was within range of a rifle, a pistol, or the flight of an arrow.

They saw the spring grass was better on the Mexican side of the Buena Vista because not many cattle were running there. Apaches liked to take Mexican beef with them when they returned to their haunts in the Sierra Madre. They were decimating the Maria Macarena cattle. They did not take many Cowden cattle. The Cowdens stayed on the prowl to keep their stock from drifting south.

All humans and warm-blooded animals were prey to the Apache, but when an Apache thought about his enemies, he thought about Mexicans. His hate for Mexicans was in his blood. Mexicans had taught the Apaches awful ways of getting even with enemies. They gave the Apaches back what the Apaches gave them with more imagination and pleasure than Americans ever did.

Ben Cowden looked down and saw the smooth print of a *tegua*, the Apache footwear. He slowed his horse and coursed away from the trail, looking for more. He found the tracks of five Apaches. He looked to the other side of the trail, and Les was holding up four fingers. Nine Indians had walked across the cattle tracks, then split to overtake the herd. They probably planned to hook in and attack the *vaqueros* from both flanks and be in position to hold the cattle. The brothers heard shots, then, four or five pops that sounded harmless with no echo in the open distance. They climbed the side of the Santa Barbara Hills so they could study the camp at La Acequia a mile away. The dust of the herd was going on past the camp.

"Now, that's not right. The *vaqueros* should have stopped and rested the cattle at La Acequia." Ben watched the dust. "Look, the cattle are going on."

The cattle were crossing an open rise.

"I don't see horsemen with them," Les said.

"We better get ourselves down to that camp," Ben said.

The brothers split apart, drew their pistols, and made a run across the side of a hill above the camp for a good look. They ran off the hill through the camp and stopped at a stream beyond it to let their horses blow. Ben and Les looked into each others' faces. They had ridden so close by the bodies of two *vaqueros* that their horses had shied from them.

"I only saw two carcasses," said Les. "We've been following three *vaqueros*, haven't we?"

The brothers rode back to the bodies and examined them a moment without dismounting. Both men had been shot with arrows, stripped, and lanced. The sight of them made the brothers look around at the hills for Apaches again. They felt they could be taking their last look at their mother earth. The staring eyes of the *vaqueros* had certainly not enjoyed their last sight of God's creatures.

Ben said, "This one's going to raise a wail. He's Pedro Elias, Don Juan Pedro's son. I wonder why he rode all the way to our side of the Buena Vista and then slowed himself with cattle on the way home. He must have known Apaches might get him. I guess he felt like taking chances today. I know one thing; he was a working son of a gun."

"This one over here is José Romero," Mark said quietly. "He and I pardnered playing fiddles at the last Patagonia dance. Nice feller. He's married to Margarita, Don Juan Pedro's daughter. He sure could sing."

"Well, we better hush up and keep our eyes open. Don't relax," Ben said. Then he saw the track of small bare feet by the body of Pedro Elias. "Here's our other *vaquero*." He followed the track.

"I guess we'd better move them out of the sun," said Les. He rode to look inside the camp's adobe house.

A ramada shaded the front of the house. Ben followed the barefoot tracks to the back of the adobe and saw that the child had climbed to the roof.

"*Bajate. Somos amigos. No te vamos a lastimar,*" Ben said, quietly. "Come down. We're friends. We won't hurt you."

Someone on top of the roof gave voice to his tears then.

"Bring yourself down," Ben said.

The top of a small black head showed above the parapet on the roof. "Let me see you, *buqui,*" said Ben. "Come on."

A pale face, muddy with dirt and tears, showed over the parapet.

"*Ai,* poor little fellow," Ben said.

"*Tengo miedo,*" the boy said. "I'm afraid. It's too high."

Ben moved his horse against the building, stood on top his saddle and offered his arms for the child. The boy stepped off the roof into his arms. Ben rode to show him to his brothers. He was about twelve.

Ben handed him down, and Les sat him in the shade while Mark brought him water in a gourd.

"*¿Como te llamas?*" asked Les. "How are you called?"

"His name is Pepe," Ben said. "He's José Romero's son. We know each other, don't we, boy?"

"*Sí*," the boy whispered with an intake of breath.

"This is the boy who worked the roundup on the Buena Vista with us last fall and made such a good hand," Ben said. "He's growing so big I didn't know him."

Les and Mark picked up a body to carry it into the house, and the boy started to cry. "My father," he said. His grief pressed a squeak out of him when he tried to speak again.

Ben gripped his bare toes in both his hands to steady him. "It's all right. We'll put your people in the house and take you home to your mother."

The boy made himself stop crying, but he looked miserably away from Ben. "*Gracias.*"

"Drink water so you can tell me what happened," Ben said. "How did you escape the Apaches?"

"They didn't see me."

"Tell me. Where were you when they attacked your people?"

"I don't know. The *partida* we were driving was on the stream. A cow had stopped in the mesquite thicket when we passed through. I missed her at the stream and went back for her. She faced me in the thicket and armed herself to fight. I went in after her afoot. She broke out and trotted toward the other cattle, and I remounted my horse.

"I was still riding in the cover of the *mesquital* when I heard the shots and the Apaches screaming. My horse ducked back from the noise and threw me. I was riding bareback, and as I flew over his head, I snatched my bridle off. The horse jumped over the top of me and trampled my ankle.

"He ran away, and I crawled into the thicket and hid. My uncle Pedro was screaming, but my father never made a sound. After my uncle was quiet, I heard the Apaches move away with the *partida*. When they were gone, I went out and found my father's body."

"What did they take, besides the cattle?" asked Les.

"All the cattle and horses, the clothing, arms, and provisions."

"Didn't they look for you?"

"No, they would have found me. I did not have a good place to hide. They could have tracked me."

"I wonder why they didn't look for you," said Les. He smiled. "Was your guardian angel with you?"

"Maybe they didn't realize my horse was carrying a rider. I left no saddle marks on him, and he carried no bridle."

"It's a good thing you didn't run after him," Les said.

"I tried, but my ankle hurt so bad, I sat down, and then my uncle started to scream. He suffered an agony with those screams. I couldn't go any closer."

The boy bowed his head and began to cry.

"You're a brave boy," Ben said.

The boy controlled himself again. "I didn't cry until I saw my father's dead eyes."

Ben watched him another minute, then shook his feet gently and said, "We'll hurry to the Maria Macarena now, so you can be with your mother and so your grandfather can send someone for the people."

Ben picked the boy up and sat him behind his saddle. Mark had watered the horses at the stream. The brothers rode for the Maria Macarena and reached a hill above the hacienda at dusk.

The main building was built like a fort, in a square with an open patio in the center. All doors opened indoors on the patio except the front entrance. Four horsemen could enter abreast through this archway. It was high enough to accommodate a wagon and team and was secured by an iron gate and a heavy wooden door.

Aged cottonwood and mesquite trees shaded the hacienda. The only windows on the outside of the main building were long narrow slits that served as rifle ports high in the walls. Ben gave out a cowboy call so the hacienda would hear them coming and have time to recognize them.

Juan Pedro Elias, the elderly don who owned the Maria Macarena, came out the front archway to greet them. He recognized the boy riding behind Ben and did not smile. Ben looked over his head and saw Margarita, the boy's mother, lean against a wall, stricken with fear to see her son return without her husband and brother.

"*Hola, Benjamín,*" said Don Juan Pedro. "What happened?"

"Bad news, Don Juan," Ben said. "Your son and your *yerno* were attacked by Apaches. Your little grandson only escaped by chance and the intercession of his patron saint."

Ben gave the boy his arm and swung him off the horse to Don Juan, but waited for an invitation to dismount. Everyone in the community came to the front of the main building. Margarita fainted against the wall, and another woman hurried to catch her. Ben had danced at fiestas with Margarita before she married.

"Dismount, please, gentlemen," Don Juan said.

The Cowden brothers stepped off their horses. They were ready to sit in the shade with a drink of water.

"Please, hand your reins to these boys. Let my people put up your horses. Please come inside." Don Juan was embracing Pepe with one arm. He took Mark's arm and escorted them both toward his front door. His daughter was lying with her head in the lap of the woman who caught her. He turned to his workers and family. "Here— you, men—you, Genoveva—you, Chata—help this poor woman. Carry her inside."

Pepe stopped beside his mother. The Cowden brothers passed through the wide, cool archway to the open patio inside the hacienda. Lamps and candles were lighted, and the place smelled of fresh flowers and moist earth. The floor of the enclosure was worn adobe brick, newly swept and sprinkled with water to cool it and settle the dust.

Don Juan asked that chairs be brought for the brothers. Les did not wait to be served water. He stepped up to an *olla*, a pot sweating with cool water that was hanging under the ramada. He scooped out a drink with a gourd that was floating inside. He quickly sucked all the water out of the gourd. He drank another gourdful. He scooped out another and held it a moment. "I'll tell you," he said. "I dry up like a corncob every time I even smell an Apache." He sipped half of the water, scattered the rest over the patio brick, then gently floated the gourd in the *olla*.

"Here, Chata, you women," Don Juan ordered. "Bring clean cups so these men can drink water. Bring them coffee. You, *muchachita.*" He pointed to a young *gata de casa,* a girl employed in his household. "Bring my *demajuana* of mescal. These men have come a long way under great stress. They're tired and hungry. Here, Chata, see to their supper and then tend to their bedding in the guest room. They'll want to be together in the same room when they sleep."

Ben was amused. Don Juan was always good to the Cowden brothers when they came to his house. The usual reason they were there was to retrieve cattle Don Juan's *vaqueros* had driven away from the Buena Vista range. The only sign the old don ever showed that he might have differences with the brothers was to give them the same room, so they could be sure they would not be separated and betrayed.

Mark was smiling for the same reason, but Les was not. Les was busy accepting a cup of coffee and spooning sugar into it from a bowl held for him by a servant. He took a small cup of mescal when it was offered him, swallowed the stuff quickly, and looked around for more. He uttered no sound of appreciation, even though he heard his brothers thank the servant softly and politely. He was seldom polite unless he suspected A. B. or his mother was watching.

Don Juan was busy attending to the grief of his household and the care of his grandson. His wife had been sick in bed for many months, and after a while he went into her room and quietly shut the door. For a few moments, no sound came through the thick walls. Then all of a sudden a long, high wail of agony came through as if nothing would ever silence the woman's grief. Ben wondered how long Sonora and Arizona women had been screaming with sorrow because of the Apaches. The cry was not weakening.

The brothers walked to relax their legs while they sipped mescal from Don Juan's clay demijohn and waited for him to come back. Cowhorns were mortared into the walls, so horses could be tied to them inside the enclosure. The hacienda's tack was kept under the ramada that sheltered the walls and doorways.

During the day, the *talabartero* who tanned and finished the ranch's hides did his leather work at a table in the patio. The saddles were astraddle individual stands in a line against a wall with every braided horsehair cinch neatly caught up to a keeper by the horn. Every reata was tallowed and coiled and hanging on the near side of each saddle below the cantle. A tallowed quirt of braided rawhide hung from each saddle horn.

No more sounds came out of the mother's bedroom, and after a while, Don Juan came out and went straight to the demijohn. He poured stout measures of mescal for himself and the Cowden brothers.

"Doña Tili will never survive this illness now," Don Juan said. His eyes were red. "No one completely survives the loss of a son. And to lose a son to the knives and lances of murderers . . ."

Ben could see the man was cornering most of his grief inside himself, but part was escaping and having great effect on his eyes. He was about fifty years old, straight and physically strong like A. B., dressed plainly as people did who lived hundreds of miles across desert and ambush from a store. "We are fortunate that you and your brothers did not catch up to my son sooner, I suppose," Don Juan was saying. "You might also have been killed."

"I'm sorry we didn't catch up before they reached La Acequia. We'd have been honored to help them in the fight," Ben said.

"It's true the Apaches might never have attacked if you had been with my people." Don Juan smiled. "But then, you and my son might have argued over your reason for coming after him."

"We expected no argument from Pedro. Our errands to the Maria Macarena are always friendly. We have never been shown anything but friendship on this ranch."

"Ah, gentlemen must be kind, must they not?"

"Our father wants us to be good neighbors."

"The world is full of evil, Benjamin. We have to fight the savage. Let's not bring harm to a neighbor. What made you follow my son?"

"He crossed the Buena Vista and picked up cattle on the edge of our Harshaw range. He cleaned out an area where your cattle and ours share a spring. That spring is a long way from the Maria Macarena. We wanted to help him separate our cattle from his and bring them home. We're always ready to help you round up stock on range we share in common."

"As any neighbor should," said Don Juan. "I'm glad you're here. Your friendship is a comfort to me. Ah, now see, your supper is ready."

Don Juan led the way into the candlelight of his dining room. The floor was worn brick, like the patio, but every other surface in the room was shining with polish. Thick, ax-hewn mesquite beams spanned the ceiling, their old hardness reflecting the fire on the candles. A white linen tablecloth covered the table. Napkins and old silver were laid by old chinaware.

The meal was simple—stewed corn, broiled beef loin, beans whipped and fried with cheese, and white sheets of flour tortillas were served. The black coffee had been ground at home and sugar roasted on an open fire. The dessert was wild honey and butter on hot tortillas.

After supper Don Juan left his guests and went to look after his household. The brothers were sitting quietly in the darkness of the patio, smoking. Two *vaqueros* came in with a priest from Santa Cruz. One of the women showed him into Doña Tili's bedchamber. He was in the room a few moments when the brothers heard the mother's scream— "*aaayyy!*"—once again, and then no more.

The brothers were ready to sleep, and they trooped to their room. Their beds had been formally turned down, their *tendidos*, the places for their resting, prepared according to strict and generous rules of Sonoran hospitality. The beds were laid on heavy sailcloth cots with Yaqui blankets and flannel sheets over cotton mattresses. The cots were large and easily accommodated the tall Cowdens. Each cot was against a wall with its own bedstand and lamp. A pitcher of water with a clay cup was placed under each stand. The brothers undressed and lay down to sleep without conversation.

They went out to saddle their horses in the morning and found them inside the patio tied to the cowhorns. The horses had been bathed with yucca soap and brushed from their foretops to their hocks. They were feeding at mangers full of fresh sacaton hay. Don Juan had given orders that they be fed corn at dawn so the brothers could leave early if they wanted to.

Don Juan stood by while the brothers were saddling. Les and Mark mounted their horses as Ben turned to say good-bye.

"We know you won't be celebrating your saint's day tomorrow, but we wish you happiness on all your future San Juan days," Ben said, and he embraced Don Juan. Then he mounted and turned his horse toward home with his brothers.

As A. B. drove his sorrels up the Washington Camp road, Paula Mary saw her brothers appear in the canyon below on their way home from the Buena Vista. She threw up her hand, waved, and sang out, "Adiós, big brothers," using the Mexican custom of saying good-bye instead of hello to someone passing by.

The brothers looked up and smiled at her. "Adiós, Paula Mary," they called. They climbed up to the road and waited while A. B. turned the buggy around and came back.

On the way home, Ben told his family about the visit to the Maria Macarena, but left out the Apache killings. He only said that Geronimo was raiding in Mexico again.

The brothers turned their horses out to pasture at home and took turns carrying hot water to the barn for their baths. When they were shaved and dressed for the Harshaw dance they went to the kitchen for supper.

Ben was sitting on the back porch after supper, smoking. He liked to watch the swallows feed at twilight and the saddle horses roll before they left the house. If they had not been ridden too hard, the horses would use the last light to find better grass, so they could eat their fill before they slept. They were grazing along, but they kept looking up, trying to make the decision to move away to taller feed.

Finally, they lined out and walked away. They would rest better on full stomachs, and the feed was always short near the house. They were good horses and always made an effort to stay full and well rested when they were on their own. Ben was proud of the Cowden brothers' horsemanship that evening. Those mounts could have been too leg-weary to move out to pasture.

Paula Mary slipped out of the kitchen while her sisters were doing dishes. Ben saw she was growing as long-legged as the rest of the Cowden kids when she stepped up onto his lap. She hugged him around the neck and kissed him on the cheek.

"Well, Paula Mary, you're sure nice to do that," Ben said.

"Nice as Lorrie Briggs?" Paula Mary watched his face for the pleasure he always showed when he heard Lorrie's name.

"Do I know anyone called Lorrie Briggs?" he asked.

A. B. and Viney were coming out the back door as he said that. They usually sat on the porch in the evenings after supper while A. B. smoked a cigar, but when A. B. heard Lorrie's name, he straightened like a soldier and stopped, still holding the screen door open. "I guess I'll smoke on the way to town this evening," he said. "We should get started. The boys still have fresh horses to saddle, and we promised to visit the Farleys before the dance."

Paula Mary would not be distracted. "Did I say Lorrie Briggs? I meant Maudy P. What made me mention Lorrie Briggs?"

"Plain old orneriness, and you're in no position to tease me, ticklish as you are," Ben said.

"Oh, well, your face always lights up when I say 'Lorrie Briggs,' and the twilight was almost gone and I wanted you to see my new earrings. Did you see them when your face lit up?"

"Oh, yes." Ben watched his mother turn back into the kitchen and his father walk alone toward the barn.

"Papa heard us talking, didn't he?" said Paula Mary.

"I believe so."

"He sure doesn't approve of Lorrie Briggs, does he?"

"No, he sure doesn't."

"Do you love Lorrie Briggs, Ben?"

"My, my, you sure dig in, don't you, Paula Mary?"

"Well, for a long time I've been wanting to know if you did. It's getting so it bothers me. I'd feel awful if I was to find out you loved her, with Papa disapproving the way he does."

"My, my, such a fuss as people make over the way they feel," Ben said.

CHAPTER 3

A. B. Cowden's sorrel team rounded the curve by the cemetery and headed into the town. Paula Mary always watched the horses when they first turned into the lamplight. The smell of mesquite smoke from cooking fires, the shouts and laughter of children, the quiet mumble of sin in the saloons, and the sounds of roosters, burros, and other livestock were enough to make a team balk when it rounded that curve.

That spring was drouthy, but the evening air was freshening the town and settling the dust of the day. The thunderheads of the early afternoon had blustered awhile, then turned to wisp and disappeared. The sky was clear and starry. Harshaw was built at the head of a box canyon. A deep pond of water was dammed in the center of town, and every sound in the saloons was carried clearly across the water to the silent Cowdens: every cussword, old jade's laugh, glutton's roar, and gambler's whine.

A. B. and his ladies were in the buggy. Ben, Les, and Mark were riding horses they used when they held a herd at night. Paula Mary was holding Mark's fiddle case. Mark was a good fiddler, and he would be playing for the dance.

The Cowdens' home was only three miles from town, and they were not as lonesome for company as most families in that country. Plenty of visitors stopped at El Durazno to do business with A. B. Still, the last hundred yards of their approach to Harshaw was a happy time for the Cowdens. This was the place where all the other people they liked would be.

A. B. drove to the Farley home, where the boys unhitched and unharnessed the team and unsaddled the horses. Danny and Donny Farley, twin brothers Mark's age, came out carrying a bottle of mescal. They were as alike as a matched yoke of brother oxen. Sometimes they even turned and cocked their heads toward a new sight or sound in unison, as though they were yoked. They liked mescal too much, and it made them cross. They would soon be too full of drink to dance with the girls. They were arguing over the names of the horses the Cowdens had ridden into town.

"Anybody can see that's Dan, Ben's night horse that he named after me," Danny said.

"No, it ain't Dan," Donny said. "Ben's night horse is a buckskin. That ain't no buckskin."

"The hell he ain't. That's Ben's Dan. I'd know him day or night. How many drinks you had? You been drinking ahead of me?"

"That's a dun horse. Can't you tell a dun from a buckskin?"

"You poor fart. That's Dan. Ain't it, Ben?"

"Yes, that's the horse I call Dan," Ben said. He was having his own troubles. He'd known the twins all their lives, and he still could not always tell them apart.

"There you are," Danny said. "I'll swear, Donny, you couldn't tell one horse from another, even if you were riding one and packing the other. You're as liable to throw your saddle on your packhorse as you are a burro. Hell, you wouldn't know your own self from somebody like me if you happened to look up and see yourself in a strange mirror."

"The hell you say," Donny said, his head down.

"Think, Donny, is it really you, or are you Danny?" Les said, laughing.

Mark headed for the town hall with his fiddle case. Ben, Les, and the twins started after him, and then Danny stopped. "Where's the jug, Donny?" he said. "Better go back and get it."

Donny turned back and headed for the house. Danny watched him a moment. "I have to do all his thinking for him," he said.

"He ain't so dumb, Danny," Les said.

"How's that?" asked Danny.

"He can drink it all now."

Danny hurried after his twin.

"Hell, Les, he doesn't need you to send him after his brother," Ben said. "He'd have gone all by himself in another minute."

"I know, but I like to tease him. I never saw them that far apart before."

"I've seen them apart working cattle. They're always in the right place at the right time when they're cowboying."

"Well, the Cowden brothers work damned good together, and we don't set up a howl when we get separated like the twins do," Les said. "I'll tell you, I worry their hearts will break when they lose sight of one another. If they could nicker like a horse, they'd be screaming for each other all the time."

"Well, I guess that's right." Ben walked through the crowd of men at the door and into the dance hall. He stopped at the edge of the dance floor to look for Lorrie. The place was lighted by lanterns placed high on the walls. A buffet of roast beef, fried chicken, potato salad, beans, sourdough bread, flour tortillas, cakes, pies, and coffee was spread on oak tables.

More mothers and grandmothers had come to chaperone than girls to dance. Lorrie Briggs was sitting with two new girls near the back door of the hall. The newcomers were probably the Briggs brothers' imports from Kansas. They were nice-looking.

Someone called Ben's name from the front door. The crowd stepped back, and a cowman named Duncan Vincent walked toward him. The men in that country always stood inside the front door at the dances, as though they felt a need to bunch up like bulls in a winter pasture. The women used the chairs, and the men stood around the door as though they needed to be ready to flee. If a stampede occurred, it would be out the front door, away from all females.

These dances attracted everybody in the country, and if a girl didn't come, it was because her parents did not permit her to dance or worked her so hard that she never had a chance to learn and was too shy to be taught in front of other people. The most awful trauma that could befall a body was to be caught out on the dance floor with no knowledge of where to put the next foot. A boy or girl could die of that, even though he or she had run a forty-mile gauntlet through Apaches to arrive there.

Everybody was dressed in best clothes. Ben was wearing his suit, his gold watch chain with a fob on the front of his vest, and a ring with an emerald stone his grandfather wore through the Civil War. Duncan Vincent stepped up in one of the three-piece suits he wore every day of his life with the trouserlegs stuffed into the tops of high laced boots. He wore a heavy brown hat with a railroader's crease in it, no curve to the brim, and no style in the angle it shaded his face. The hat was only sitting up there on the top of his head, which was wrong, because everybody else in the place, miner and cowboy alike, had left his hat at home or at the dance-hall door.

Two weathered cowboys were with Vincent. The man was not there to enjoy the dance, and he did not give a damn that everybody else in the place was trying to act civil. He had his business to attend to. "There you are, Cowden," he said. "I figured you'd probably show up here. I gambled on it and rode all the way from the San Rafael to catch you."

"I wish I'd known you wanted to see me, Mr. Vincent," Ben answered. "I was near your place a few days ago. Where's Dorothy? My sisters are waiting for her in the schoolhouse."

"You know I'm not here to talk to you about my daughter. My men saw you at La Noria the other day. I'm here to ask what you were doing there."

"Why, that must have been plain for your men to see. I wasn't hiding."

"I want to know what you and Will Pendleton were doing on my range." Vincent looked around to make sure his bodyguard was close and the people were listening.

Vincent's cowboys were anglo strangers. He imported

them as he did his livestock. The native cowboys of southern Arizona were as good as any in the world, but they spoke Spanish, and Vincent did not trust them because of it. Some of them even spoke Yaqui, Pima, Papago, and Apache.

"I guess anyone who knows cattle would know what we were doing," Ben said.

"My men saw you and Pendleton branding calves."

"That's right. We branded some calves in Will's corral there."

"You branded three whiteface calves."

"You got that right, too."

"Well, you broke the law. Those calves belong to me. These men who are standing right here with me said you branded two with Pendleton's brand and one with the 7–X. Since I don't recall selling the cattle to you, I want an explanation."

"Your spies are wrong. They saw no Vincent cattle in that corral. Those calves were out of Pendleton and Cowden cows. Instead of sneaking around, your men should have come down to the corral for a better look. We'd have given them a cold drink of water and a piece of jerky to ride home on, and they wouldn't have carried tales that worried you."

Ben looked around. Every man, woman, and child in the place was looking at him. Branding another man's calves was as serious a crime as murder. Every cattleman at that dance was trying to build a herd for himself on the public land. Gentle cattle were scarce. Vincent had brought in the only white-faced Hereford cattle in that country. Nobody else owned good beef cattle. People with no backing from the banks were starting their herds on the native wild cattle that ran in the Huachucas, the Whetstones, the Patagonias, and the Santa Rita Mountains.

Vincent thought he was cornering a wrongdoer, but he was sensible enough not to call Ben a cow thief. Ben might kill him on the spot.

"Cowden, did you or did you not brand three whiteface calves at La Noria the other day?" Vincent demanded.

"I most certainly did, and good calves they are," Ben said. "They were sired by your Hereford bulls. Your bulls are good breeders, and they're toning the raciness out of our natives. If you're here to find out if I'm grateful that you brought them to the country, then thank you."

"I'm not here to be thanked, Cowden," Vincent said. "One reason I have Hereford cattle is so I can tell they belong to me without looking at their brands. My bulls mark a white face on every calf they throw. No native bull marks his calves that way. You and your accomplice Pendleton put your brands on my cattle."

Ben laughed. "Since when does the sire of a calf establish ownership of him? That might be the way it's done in New York where you come from, but not here. In Arizona, the brand on the mother goes on the calf."

"My men didn't see the brands on the cows, but if you haven't broken a written law, you've broken an unwritten one. I didn't bring those good bulls all the way out here at great expense so you could reap their profits. You owe me for those calves."

The crowd laughed at Vincent. His cowboys were embarrassed. Vincent's stand was ridiculous. An owner could not claim his bull's bastard calves anywhere in any cattle country in the world.

Ben said, "Your bulls are on open range. At first I didn't appreciate them mixing with my cows, but as long as we were sharing the country and the nature of the beasts that populate it, I decided to accept them. I have to say I like the kind of stock your big old bulls throw.

"Now, if you don't want us to have calves by your bulls, I guess you'll have to pull in your bulls. Because the law, as it stands, protects the man who owns the cow, not the man who turned his bull loose."

Ben was surprised he was not angry. He did not like Vincent's high-handed ways and had been expecting this confrontation for a year, but now he could see Vincent's stand was ridiculous.

Vincent had bought private land from the Romeros, who owned a Spanish grant on the Arizona side of the border in the San Rafael valley. With that ranch as a base for a few Hereford cows, he was importing thousands of big steers and taking more than his share of grass on the public land. The more steers Vincent's eastern syndicate ran, the fewer cows his neighbors could run.

"I'm starting a breeding program that will change the shape of the beef industry in Arizona," Vincent was saying. "I'm doing something for the common good here, and I'm serving notice that from now on, my cowboys will be shooting any unbranded native or mustang cattle they find. We don't want to make a mistake and kill any of your stock, but we have to keep those common cattle off VO range."

Ben spoke slowly and quietly. "Mr. Vincent, if you've got it in your head now that you can start killing our cattle, you're making a bad mistake. Your neighbors are building their herds on wild cattle. You're a stranger here. We helped you when you first came to the country, and we've been trying to be good to you, but now you're threatening us."

"I'm not threatening anybody. I'm only warning you that you can't stand in the way of progress. Ten years from now, you won't see a native cow in this whole country. You people will have to sell your herds and buy cows that yield more beef. The wild cattle you've been catching in order to call yourselves cattlemen won't be worth a nickel."

Vincent turned to leave, but he was blocked by the crowd. His cowboys moved ahead to make way for him, but nobody moved until Mark struck up the "Processional" from *Aida* on his fiddle. The crowd was amused enough by that to allow Vincent to leave, but he was forced to walk around some of them on his way out. Then a path opened as A. B. Cowden walked in. Vincent nodded to A. B., stepped aside for him, and walked out.

Will Pendleton stepped up and shook Ben's hand, and the band started playing the "Varsoviana," then "Put Your Little Foot." Ben watched Paula Mary, dainty as a fawn, step out to dance with Chris Wilson, the muleskinner. She attached herself lightly to Chris at arm's length and smiled up at his face from the level of his watch pocket. One of Chris' brogan shoes weighed more than she did.

Les was already wooing one of the Kansas sisters who were supposed to marry the Briggs brothers. Les did not care that striking a spark in the girl would cause an explosion in the Briggses. Les did not give a damn about a thing in the world when it was time for him to socialize, and Mark was fiddling with a grin on his face as though he liked that socializing a whole lot too.

Ben did not like to dance the "Put Your Little Foot." He went to find Lew Porter and found him by the door talking to the Farley twins. The twins were Lew's cousins on their mother's side, and Ben was Lew's cousin on his mother's side. Lew's horses were almost as good as Ben's, and he had matched Ben a horserace that would be run down the main street of Harshaw the next day.

Lew was happy to turn away from the twins when he saw Ben. "They're drunker'n goats again," Lew said.

"Well, I guess that's what they set out to do," Ben said.

"I wish someday they'd decide to stay sober and waltz with the girls at one of these dances. I'll swear, how will they ever tear loose from each other and the mescal long enough to marry?"

"Darned if I can tell you."

"Who've you picked to start the race?"

"Let's see if Juan Heredia will do it."

"He's just right. What time do you want to run, sunrise or sunset?"

"I think sunrise is too early, don't you? If we run that early, a lot of people will miss it."

"I think so too. Sunset?"

"Fine with me. Who's holding the stakes?"

"I have no idea. How about your papa? Would he do it?"

"He's fine with me."

"Then nobody will have to worry. Your daddy would pay the winner if it was Geronimo."

"Fine with me."

"It's settled then. Unless you can think of something else."

"I can't think of anything that can go wrong, unless my horse gets outrun," said Ben, smiling.

"Oh, well, you're gonna get outrun, all right," said Lew and he did not smile. "I'm taking your money this time."

The band was playing "Cuatro Milpas," Ben's favorite Mexican waltz. Lorrie Briggs was dancing with a miner. Ben wished he knew if that big miner had danced "Put Your Little Foot" with her. He decided he did not care; he was not ever going to dance that step. Anybody could have all of Lorrie's "Put Your Little Foot" they wanted.

"Mr. Cowden?" said a short pale man beside Ben.

"Yes, sir," said Ben.

"I'm Walter Jarboe, from Kansas." The man offered his hand.

"Looks like the country's filling up with Kansans," said Ben.

"I know what you mean," said Jarboe, nodding toward the Kansas girls. "Our state really couldn't spare those pretty girls. I traveled to Arizona on the train with them. They're nice girls."

"They're sure stouthearted," Ben said.

"Mr. Cowden, I've come to find some cattle an associate of mine bought here last fall and was unable to receive."

"Who do the cattle belong to, Mr. Jarboe?"

"They belonged to a man named Kosterlinsky, but now they belong to me."

"Kosterlinsky the Mexican *rural*?"

"Yes, sir, that's his name, but I didn't know his title."

"That's the man you want. There isn't anybody else by that name in the country." Mister, you're in trouble, Ben said to himself.

"I was told you might help me locate Mr. Kosterlinsky."

"Well, Mr. Jarboe, it's easy to find out where he is when you're as far away from him as we are now, but it'll get harder as you get closer."

"Am I getting closer? Do you know him?"

"Every man in this room knows him, but you're only a little bit closer to meeting him now than you were in Kansas."

"Mr. Cowden, I know how hard it is to locate that man. I've written him several letters and sent him wires and even paid to have them delivered by messenger. My messages might as well have slipped off the edge of the earth."

"He's impossible to find that way. He waters at night like the *ladino* he is. He gets wilder when he suspects somebody he owes is closing in on him."

"Can you help me find him so I can talk to him?"

"I can almost bet a new hat he'll be here tomorrow."

"How is that? Do you have business with him too?"

"In a way. My cousin and I are running a horserace tomorrow. Kosterlinsky comes to horseraces the way coyotes come to chicken yards."

"I'm sure," said Jarboe, but his smile showed he was not sure at all. "How can I get to meet him?"

"Come to me at the celebration tomorrow, and we'll look him up."

"You know him well then?"

"I can truthfully say me and my brothers know him better than his own mother does," said Ben, then he thought, if he has a mother.

"I understand you might be able to sell me some big steers yourself," Jarboe said.

"My brothers and I can put a little bunch together for you."

"How many steers could you deliver next fall?"

"I think we can put three hundred together."

"Do you think you could help me buy a thousand head?"

"You mean with my cattle and my neighbors' cattle?"

"Yes, I'm looking for someone like you to buy cattle for me."

"I only know what me and my brothers can deliver."

"Mr. Cowden, let me make myself clear. I'd like to put up the money and partner with you in the purchase of one thousand steers. I'm sure you can buy the cattle cheaper than I can and make us both some money."

"No, Mr. Jarboe. I'm not interested in making money that way, but if you're fair with me, I'll introduce you to my neighbors. Your trade will be between you and them."

"Well, that's as straight as a man can be. I wish you'd take some time to think about it, though. I'd furnish all the money and pay you well for buying and shipping cattle to Kansas. You'd be saving me trips to Arizona."

"Mr. Jarboe, I hate to turn you down, but I'm no trader. I only know what cattle belonging to my family are worth. If you and I can agree on a price, you can have them."

"Well, if I can't make a partner of you, I'll do business with you any way I can."

Jarboe offered his hand, and Ben shook it.

CHAPTER 4

Ben looked for Lorrie Briggs again. This time Les was dancing with her. Ben and the Farley twins were the only ones who were not dancing a cloud of dust off the floor or filling up with supper at the buffet. Mark had abandoned his fiddle for the buffet. The Salazar brothers were making music with guitar, trumpet, accordian, and the *guitarron*, a bass guitar.

After a while, if he didn't fall over in a faint from the mescal first, Donny Farley might join the band with his harmonica. Playing the mouth harp was a talent he enjoyed all by himself. Danny could not carry a tune. He made noise with the Jew's harp, but his pitch was so bad he made trash of the tunes he joined and wiped out all surrounding accompanists.

Ben looked for the twins and found them outside with their jug under a tree. He drank a few swallows with them, listened to them rave awhile, and made himself late for another set. He went inside in time to see Les walking out on the floor with the Kansas girl he'd been wooing. Lorrie was nowhere in sight. Hoozy was hovering near the other Kansas girl, but she was ignoring him.

Ben looked around for someone he could ask to dance. Maudy Jane Pendleton was giving him the eye. Ben was surprised. The girl was only two or three years older than

Paula Mary, and she was giving him a look. She had decided she was grown-up enough to ride the river with somebody. Ben took her hand and sashayed forth to dance.

Maudy was growing so fast, she was prettier every time Ben saw her. Her eyes were the greenest he'd ever seen. Months ago, maybe years ago, he'd seen her standing in the sun and noticed a golden sheen in her thick sorrel mane. Now, her look was calm and bold, the kind a man searched for in the eyes of a woman. He was happy for her. She was enjoying growing up.

Maudy Jane was good stock and always did her best to be a responsible lady. She did not climb trees, and she did not giggle. Young as she was, she could dance and visit with any man. She could work as hard and as capably as any woman. As soon as the beauty of her figure caught up to that face, Maudy would bloom, and all the men would see the woman A. B. bragged about.

When the set was over, Ben took Maudy back to her folks and asked Lorrie to dance. He stopped her in the middle of the floor and put his arm around her waist, waiting for the music to start.

Hoozy was looking mean. He could not stand to see Ben and his sister together. He resented all Cowdens. He had paid court to Betty and been run off like a fool. He had little to say to any Cowden, so he never let on that he did not want Ben near his sister, but when he was angry at anything, he gave the Cowdens dirty looks.

Hoozy was careful Les did not see him do it. No one who knew Les ever showed him animosity. He was easily provoked, and crazy in a fight. He always fought to kill or at least to maim. Everybody in the country knew it was not safe to give him dirty looks at a dance.

Ben was sorry Hoozy felt so put out, but the poor feller never could have interested Betty. She found all suitors inferior to the men in her family.

Ben and A. B. were the men Betty admired most. Mark was her favorite brother. Les was her warrior. She wanted a gentleman for a suitor, not some pistol-packing thug like Hoozy. Betty ran him off because she caught him picking his nose in her mother's parlor.

Before that, she had resolved to ask him nicely not to

come to see her anymore. He was too much in the way, and she had work to do.

After she caught him picking his nose, she told him plainly that she did not like to look at his face anymore, so he should take it home and never bring it back. He was terribly surprised. All the Cowdens had been nice to him, and he thought Betty was convinced he was much of a man.

Lorrie Briggs was making Ben smile. She was bright, nice, and fine-looking. As far as he knew, no sister in history was as different from her brothers as Lorrie was from Hoozy and Whitey Briggs.

Ben would have liked to dance every set with Lorrie. They enjoyed being together so much, they could be sweethearts, but people were always watching them. Ben was not courting Lorrie, but he knew people thought he should be.

They had never enjoyed one intimate moment together, never said anything personal or endearing to one another. They only saw each other once in a while at gatherings with their folks and were naturally drawn to one another.

Every time Ben thought of taking Lorrie away from a gathering, he looked up and saw a dozen people watching him, reading his mind. He was well liked, and Lorrie was the best-looking girl in the country, and people watched to see if they would mate.

Hoozy would not be ignored. He was thinking if Ben Cowden could step out with Lorrie to everyone's approval, then he had a right to court Betty.

Hoozy tended to forget his humiliations, especially if they were not made public. Betty had not told anyone she put the run on him, so he was entertaining thoughts of courting her again.

A whole year had gone by since Betty had run him off. He was more mature now, a seasoned frontiersman. He was smarter about women. He was being schooled by the bordello girls of Santa Cruz.

No other men called on Betty as far as he knew. She had smiled at him on his first visit to her house. She did not seem to be interested in anyone else. She was not even at the dance yet. She, Eileen, and the Farley girls were listening to the phonograph in the schoolhouse. Hoozy had watched them light the lamp and crank the machine.

Any filly worth owning kicked hell out of a stud before she gave in to him. Fillies were especially bad about that when they first came in season and discovered they needed a stud. Betty was coming in season. The stud with the audacity to dive in first and take a nip out of her flank would be the one who got her.

Miners knew that nothing worth having ever showed itself clearly to a man. A miner might work himself to death digging hard rock and shoring boulders when he could poke a hole a few inches in a different direction and find pure gold.

Hoozy decided to give Betty another chance. By now she must know about the Kansas girls. She could be worrying she'd been too mean to him and be sorry he was marrying someone else.

Hoozy quit being mad and went out the back door of the dance hall. He never let anybody see him drink whiskey, but he always kept a jug in a bush by the schoolhouse during a dance. He found it in the dark and drank from it, then went over and stood behind a tree and watched the Cowden and Farley girls. They were having a great time trying out their dance-steps with one another, but Hoozy could see they needed a man to take hold of them and show them real dancing.

He put down his jug, chewed on a mint leaf he'd been saving in his shirtpocket, wiped his mustache with it, and walked in on the girls. They turned their faces toward him. By hell, if he could believe their expressions, they did not like him. That's the way females acted when a man tried to be nice to them. He kept grinning at them, and they quit dancing and turned away.

"Here I am, girls," he announced. "Hoozy Briggs, dancing master, at your service."

The Farley girls looked at the Cowdens and giggled. Eileen Cowden turned to see what he wanted. Highfalutin was what she was. She thought she was better'n anybody else because she was a Cowden.

Hoozy walked up to Eileen, wrapped both arms around her waist, and pulled her to him the way he'd been doing the bordello women. He lifted her off her feet, held her against himself, and looked over at Betty to see what she thought of that.

Betty's look was bloodthirsty. She picked the needle off the phonograph and stopped the music.

Hoozy tried to jiggle up a dance with Eileen, but she had gone stiff as a plank. He let her down. She didn't take a backward step. He was taller than she, but she was looking down at him.

"Did you get all of that you wanted, Mr. Briggs?" she asked.

"Well, no. I can see you girls need a man to practice with." He reached for her waist again, remembering the bump of her strong thighs against his. Women in the bawdy houses did not have thighs like that. This decent stuff was firmer, stronger, longer. She'd been knee-to-knee with him. She stepped away, out of his reach.

"Who asked for you?" said Eileen. "We know where to find men. The women who want to dance are all over at the dance hall. What's the matter, are the men too much competition for you?"

"My fiancée is amusing herself with your brother. Turnabout is fair play. Anyway, I'm not here for you. I came for Betty."

Betty walked up to him, slapped him on the chest with both hands, and shoved him away from Eileen. "You came for me? It's me you want?" She was making him scramble to keep his big feet moving. "I thought you had enough of me when I caught you with your finger in your nose and made you slither home."

Hoozy saw the same mean heat, the high temper glowing out of Betty's eyes that had scared him in her mother's parlor. That heat took all the temper out of him and made him feel he was a fake.

Hoozy brought forth his purple face to show Betty he could be mean too. The Farley girls looked scared enough, but the Cowden girls laughed.

"Run for your life, Hooz-your-face," Betty said. "Take your baboon's face, and hide it in a cave."

The Farley girls laughed uncontrollably at that, and Hoozy felt his face turn gaunt and pale.

"I'm going," Hoozy said. He was so miserable, he could not swallow. He could barely talk. "All I wanted to do was invite you to the dance. I thought you'd appreciate me coming over and looking after you like a gentleman."

"Gentleman—you?" Eileen said quietly. She looked down at the phonograph. She was through with him. He was Betty's responsibility.

"Yes, a gentleman," said Hoozy. "I didn't mean anything wrong. I only wanted to join your fun. Don't you know I'm getting married? Tomorrow at this time I'll be married to Ann Burr. That girl came all the way out from Kansas to be my wife."

"Poor girl," said Betty. She was still standing in front of him. "I'd hate to be this far from home, and my only hope was for you to let me in your tribe."

That was the end of Hoozy. He left before she could say more.

Hoozy was lucky he left when he did. John Bonner, Eileen's fiancé, showed up at the schoolhouse a few minutes later. He was late for the first time in all the years of their courtship. He had been in a running gunfight with eight Apaches in the Canelo Hills and almost killed his horse escaping them.

Bonner walked the girls to the dance. They did not tell anybody about Hoozy because they did not want to cause trouble for their brothers.

The dance was almost over when someone yelled, "fight!" and most of the men ran out the front door. Ben and Lorrie stepped out the back door. They walked around the schoolhouse, and Ben carefully drew her close and kissed her.

"Well, it's about time," Lorrie said softly. She put both arms around his waist and gave him a husky squeeze.

Ben laughed. "I didn't think we'd ever get to do this unless the whole town was watching."

"Will I have to wait until somebody has a fight before you kiss me again?"

"Not another minute." He kissed her again.

"Ben Cowden!" somebody yelled.

"Dammit," said Ben.

"Ben Cowden!"

"That's Hoozy," said Lorrie. "And he's headed this way. I don't want anybody to see me."

"Hide. Go through the schoolroom and back to the dance. I'll stand in the door," Ben said.

Lorrie was passing through the dark schoolhouse when Hoozy came around the corner leading a crowd.

Ben lit his pipe so they could see his face.

"Here he is!" yelled Hoozy. "Hiding by the schoolhouse."

Hoozy's yelling was emptying the dance hall, and the crowd was growing.

"Who's fighting?" asked Ben when Hoozy stopped in front of him.

"Your cousins started a fight with peace officers," said Hoozy.

"Which cousins?"

"The Farley twins."

Les and Mark walked around the crowd to stand by their brother.

A man wearing a star on his shirt came to the front. "Ben Cowden?"

"That's my name, I guess. Everybody ought to know it by now, as much as this man's been hollering it."

Another man stepped up. "You're under arrest, Cowden."

"And who in the hell are you?" Les asked.

"We're rangers."

"What's a ranger?"

"We've been appointed by the cattlemen to stop the rustling in this county."

"Me and my brothers are cattlemen, and we sure didn't hire any 'rangers,'" Les said.

"Nevertheless, we carry constables' badges, and we're arresting this man for being a cow thief."

"What's your name, feller?" Les demanded.

"*Constable* Broderick."

"I thought so. You work for Vincent on the VO."

"Yeah, so what? I'm carrying a ranger's badge."

Les struck a match and held it under the face of the

other man. "Thomas; I know you. You're no sheriff, you're just another VO waddy."

"Tonight we're both working for the law." Thomas stuck his thumb behind his badge to show it off in the light of the match. "We're taking Ben Cowden to the Tucson jail."

"How will you do that?" Ben asked softly.

"Any way we have to," Broderick said. "I just fed my pistol barrel to one of your cousins. I don't mind making you eat it too."

Ben hit the man with a straight right hand that knocked him out from under his hat, then stepped in and hit him another. Broderick's face was wide and fleshy, a target Ben could not miss in the light from the dance hall. His hard fist connected twice with the man's nose cartilage and assured him he was on target. The sound of Broderick's head landing on the bottom step of the schoolhouse made him worry he might have killed him.

Nobody in the crowd offered to take Broderick's place in front of Ben. Hoozy disappeared. Most of the crowd knew Ben would not stand and argue with anyone who accused him of being a cow thief.

"You sundayed him. That will go hard on you," said Thomas.

Ben stepped in to hit him. Thomas threw up his hands to protect his face and ran backwards out of range. "Damn, don't hit me, too. I won't try to arrest you by myself."

"Who is calling Ben Cowden a cow thief?" A. B. Cowden pushed his way through the crowd.

"Sheriff, this son of yours assaulted an officer of the law," said Thomas.

"Who is calling himself an officer of the law?"

Broderick was not even quivering, but no one seemed to care. Mark stepped over to look down at him and prod him gently with his toe.

"We're here to stop Ben Cowden from branding VO calves," Thomas said.

"Who gave you the authority to arrest anyone?" A. B. said.

"Well, we're constables."

"Yeah, you're constables. You're brand inspectors assigned to the San Rafael, that's all. You can't arrest anyone.

Tell Mr. Vincent to try some other way to put my son in jail. You can pick up your partner and get on back to the VO now. Next time you come to Harshaw, leave your badges in the bunkhouse."

The Cowdens went home, put up their horses, and went in to have bread and milk at Viney's kitchen table.

Paula Mary said, "How can it be that Lorrie Briggs is so delicate and pretty and curly-headed, and Hoozy is so ugly with that big snout and eyes way back in his head like they're peering out of a cave?"

Eileen and Betty looked at each other, stood up from the table, gathered bowls and spoons, and started washing dishes.

"John Bonner says old Yawner was leading the Apaches that jumped him this afternoon," Ben said. He did not want to talk about Hoozy. His father might ask him why he hit a constable. "John said he was in sight of the Canelo ranch when they started relaying him. He was riding that Bob horse Eileen gave him and had to run farther every time a fresh Indian fell in after him. They ran him clear to the Vaca ranch. Somebody finally made him late for courting you, didn't they, Eileen?"

"*Apaches* did," Eileen said. She did not look up from the sink. "But after the fight started, we never even got to dance anymore."

"If John's ever later than he was this evening, you can figure they caught him." Les was trying to steer the talk back to Apaches.

A. B. looked up at Ben. "You should not have hit that man, son, especially after he told you he was an officer."

"I know it, Papa."

"Vincent sent those men to make you lose your temper and get you in trouble. They succeeded."

"I guess they did, Papa."

"Now they have fifty witnesses who can say you hit the man after you knew he was an officer. They'll surely use that against you and have a warrant issued. They can make me arrest my own son."

"I've been thinking the same thing. What should we do now, Papa?"

"You're smart enough to know you're in a pickle. I wish

you'd been smart enough to know they wanted to put you in the jar when they cornered you. You should have waited for me to handle them."

"I lost my temper, Papa."

"I thought I taught you to control your temper."

"What can I do now?"

"After the celebration, you and your brothers go up and work Temporal Canyon. If a warrant is issued, I'll have to come and get you, but until then you'll be out of reach."

"Can't I stay at Temporal? Nobody has to know I'm there, do they?"

"If they issue a warrant, you'll have to come down for my sake. Vincent is buying the law. If he can get me fired as undersheriff, he'll replace me with somebody on his payroll."

"Ben can hide, can't he, Papa? Not even you can find him if he doesn't want to be found," Les said.

"If a warrant is issued, I'll want Ben to come down—that's final. The best way to avoid a war with Vincent is to abide by the law."

"How long do they have to be in Temporal?" asked Viney. She worried when her boys were away camping on wild cattle. "I think they should stay home. Apaches almost killed John today. Do they have to take a remuda of good horses up to the Temporal and attract more Apaches? Why can't they wait until after that old Yawner is caught and taken back to the reservation?"

"Apaches don't bother us, Mama," said Les, smiling. "We can outrun them, outride them, and outshoot them."

"Just be careful, Leslie, for your mother's sake," A. B. said.

"Why do they have to go now?" asked Viney. "That is entirely beyond my understanding."

"Aside from Ben's having to get out of sight awhile, a Kansas buyer has given him an order," said A. B. "The boys need to camp on their traps in the Santa Ritas awhile, so they can bring down some cattle."

"Why can't they work country closer to home?"

"Mama, there's big cattle in the Santa Ritas because nobody but us goes up there when Apaches are running," Les said. "The cattle up there have wild water and feed, and nobody bothers them. The Kansas man wants big old cattle."

Viney stood up from the table and smoothed her apron. "Well," she sighed. "I guess I shouldn't worry about Apaches getting you. Why should they waste their time lancing you when they can sit on a hill and watch an old *ladino* run a horn through you? I'll swear, sometimes I wish I raised miners."

"You know, come to think of it, nearly all miners look like Hoozy," Paula Mary said, and the whole family knew she was about to say something smart and be put to bed. "Great big shoulders, great big necks, and purple faces."

"Paula Mary, that's enough," Viney said.

"Well, did you ever notice that cowmen and cowboys are all long-legged and good-looking? Hoozy Briggs looks like a baboon."

"Paula Mary—"

"Well, he does, Mama. I'll bring in the encyclopedia and show you. There's a picture of Hoozy right there under 'Baboon.'"

Ben and Viney were not amused by this at all, but all the rest of the family was.

Paula Mary took heart when she sensed a smile in her father's poker look. "I really shouldn't say that, I know," she said, looking into her father's eyes. "Lorrie's real pretty. She doesn't look like a baboon, so all the Briggses aren't ugly. Lorrie could be one of our sisters, she's so pretty. She might even be our sister someday. Don't you think she'd make a good daughter, Papa?"

A. B. stiffened and turned away from the table. "I'm afraid it's time this outfit went to bed." He stood up and walked out of the room.

Paula Mary looked up, and her mother's arm was sticking straight out behind her finger, pointing to the bed. Paula Mary knew she'd better move. She went off to bed, and her sisters silently followed her. She fell asleep listening to the soft voices of her brothers and thinking she had never known an unhappy day in her life, and now she knew the formula for never ever having any.

CHAPTER 5

Paula Mary watched the foam rise over the edge of the bucket as her brother Mark squeezed milk in thick streams out of Gussy the cow. He was sitting on a stool and pressing his head with his hat on it into Gussy's flank. Paula Mary squatted with her chin on her knees on the other side of Gussy and peered under her belly at Mark's face. She put her hand on the side of the bucket to feel the smooth warmth of the milk.

Les was leaving the corral horseback, driving a fat steer on the end of his *reata*. He gave the steer slack to make him think he was getting away and headed him up the road. The steer was to be butchered and barbecued under the cottonwood grove in Harshaw that evening.

Paula Mary watched Les ride away in his shirtsleeves. She knew he was happy. He liked to get off by himself in Vince Farley's saloon. Vince was in charge of the barbecue and was furnishing free beer. Les' suit-jacket was tied on his saddle behind him, and he was wearing a necktie for the San Juan's Day celebration.

Paula Mary turned back to Mark. "You know that I never learned how to milk, Marky?"

"Is that right?" asked Mark. He did not seem much affected by that news.

Paula Mary cocked her head between her knees in

order to see Mark's eyes. He would not look at her. "You'd think a ranch girl like me would know how to milk, wouldn't you?"

"You're too pretty to milk a cow, aren't you, Paula Mary? That's it, isn't it?"

"No, I don't think that's the reason. Maybe not, anyway. Eileen knows how to milk, doesn't she?"

"I expect she does."

"She had to learn how to do outside chores like that, being the second oldest child growing up on a ranch, didn't she?"

"I expect she did."

Mark stood up and put the full bucket on a shelf. He spread a clean floursack over it to protect the milk from dust and flies. He picked up another clean bucket and returned to his stool to finish milking Gussy.

"Did Garbie Burr do the milking at her house?" Paula Mary asked innocently. She was laying a snare to see if Mark would admit he knew all there was to know about Garbie Burr, the youngest of the two Kansas girls.

"I'm sure I wouldn't know what Garbie Burr can do at all."

"Well, why not? You danced four sets with her last night. You talked-talked-talked and smiled-smiled-smiled through every set. I never saw you talk so much and smile so big. Aren't your jaws sore this morning?"

"Garbie's a good dancer," said Mark with only the glint of a smile in his eye.

"She sure is pretty, isn't she?"

"I expect she's pretty enough."

"I think she'd make a good sister. If you marry Garbie Burr and Ben marries Lorrie Briggs and Les marries Garbie's sister Ann, whom he took charge of last night at the dance, and Eileen marries Johnny Bonner, then that'll only leave Betty and me. There won't be a soul left on this outfit to milk the cow."

"My, my, Paula Mary. You sure can find problems to multiply, can't you?"

"Well, that is a problem for you to think about, isn't it?"

Paula Mary watched Mark strip the last of the milk from Gussy's bag. When he could not squeeze out another drop, he put aside his stool, picked up the full bucket, handed Paula Mary the half-empty one, and headed for the house.

Paula Mary watched his feet and matched him stride for stride. He began taking longer steps and hiding the extra effort. Paula Mary worked harder to keep up with him, stretching her legs and biting her tongue, but not complaining. He kept lengthening his stride until she laughed and broke into a lope.

Mark stopped at the back porch, let out his breath in a rush, and laughed. That showed Paula Mary he'd been holding it to hide the effort he had to make to beat her to the house.

Guilo Soto, A. B.'s stableboy, came out the door. Guilo was sixteen, the oldest of six children. His father was Gilbert Soto, a blacksmith in Harshaw. Paula Mary gave Mark her bucket and abandoned him and headed back toward the barn with Guilo.

Guilo was counting his money. Les had paid him a dollar for a six-strand, sixty-foot *reata* that one of Guilo's uncles made. Part of the money was in Mexican coins, and part was in scrip issued by the Harshaw mine. Guilo was separating his scrip and centavos from his American money.

Paula Mary tried to see how much he had. He was prospering. He was good at protecting his money and making it grow. He liked to count it and calculate what it would do for him. He bought all his own clothes and never looked shabby.

Paula Mary's mother was trying to teach her not to be nosy about other people's money, but she could not help herself. "You rich yet?"

"Not yet." Guilo spoke with a thick Mexican accent.

"When, Guilo? When you gonna get rich?"

"Someday, maybe."

"What we gonna do now?"

"We harness Sam and Cat for your papa."

Paula Mary helped lead the black team into the barn and harness them. She took the lines, climbed to the driver's seat, and held the team while Guilo hitched them. Guilo climbed up beside her and drove the horses up the road until they settled down, then handed the lines back to Paula Mary.

The sun was not shining on the bottom of the canyon yet, and the team was fresh and anxious to move. Guilo's musty smell that Paula Mary was not supposed to notice because she wanted to be a lady was also good, and she could not see how she could ever be happier.

At a wide spot in the road, she wheeled the blacks in a circle without shortening their stride and headed back toward the barn. They rounded a bend where the road narrowed against the canyon wall out of sight of the house. They came face-to-face with Dick Martin, Che Che the Indian, and a tall Indian known as the Yaqui.

Paula Mary was headed downhill with momentum. She expected Martin and his partners to move aside, so she would not have to stop, but Che Che only smirked like a cutthroat and held his horse in the road, blocking her path. Guilo had to help her stop the team.

"Good morning, Paula Mary," Dick Martin said. "Where you going? The barbecue and whiskey is all back the other way." He laughed and turned to see if the Indians liked his joke.

Che Che stared at Paula Mary like a reptile on the hunt. Guilo tried to drive the blacks past him, but the Indian snatched Cat's checkrein and snubbed him to his saddle horn.

"Hold your team, Guilo," said Dick Martin. "You don't want to run over us, do you?"

Paula Mary looked to see what Guilo would do. He was sitting beside her with dignity. That was all he was doing. For a boy, he sure set great store by his dignity.

"Dick Martin, if you don't have sense enough to get out of the way of a team on a downhill run, you *ought* to get run over." Paula Mary whirled toward Che Che but did not look him in the eye. "Let go that checkrein," she yelled.

Che Che yanked Cat's head from side to side, then backed him up, to show he controlled both horses.

"Now, Paula Mary, don't give Che Che orders," said Martin. "He wants to visit awhile, that's all."

"This is the *hembrita*, the little female, who spies on travelers from up in the trees," Che Che said in Spanish. "I stare face-to-face, not hiding in a tree. Ask her how she likes me."

"*Haste un lado*," Guilo said. "Move aside, or I'll use this whip."

Che Che jerked Cat's head into his lap with one hand and pointed a finger at Guilo's heart. "Use the whip. Use it," he commanded. He was twisting the snaffle in Cat's mouth.

Dick Martin looked around to see if anyone was coming. He would be in trouble if he was caught helping an Indian waylay a white girl. He was bound to get caught if Che Che badgered the girl much longer. A lot of traffic moved on that road on fiesta days.

"Ricardo, tell him to let go of the team," Guilo ordered Martin. "*Portate bien.* Behave yourself."

"Behave myself?" Martin spurred his horse up to Guilo's side of the buggy. "Since when does a Mexican manure-gatherer like you tell me to behave? You don't get to be a Cowden by shoveling their turds. You're just another one of their turds."

He snapped the poppers of his quirt on Guilo's hat and made the boy flinch and duck his head. He laughed, jerked the buggy whip out of Guilo's hand, and lashed Cat on the hips with it.

Cat tried to lunge, but Che Che held him fast and twisted his muzzle so tightly his eyes rolled. "What's the matter with you, Mexican, you think this horse can move without his head?"

Martin laughed and whacked Cat's rump with the buggy whip again.

"Here!" The shout from up the road was like a drill sergeant's. "Get away from the team."

Martin turned to see Les Cowden riding toward him and building a loop in his *reata*. He dropped the buggy whip behind the dash at Paula Mary's feet.

Les swung his loop alongside his horse and brought it down between Martin's horse's ears. The horse spun away and ran down the road with Martin hauling on his reins to stop him. Les kept swinging the loop. He whipped Che Che's hat down over his ears. Cat lunged against Che Che's horse. Che Che's horse lunged away from the *reata*.

Les said, "Let's see what comes apart now, you son of a bitch." He lashed the Indian across the back of the neck.

Che Che's horse jumped away and stretched him to the end of his stirrups, broke his grip on Cat's head in midair, and dropped him on his back in front of the team.

Guilo shouted and whipped the team and buggy over the top of Che Che. Martin and the Yaqui spurred their horses wildly to get out of the way. Les rode to them.

"Everybody all right?" he asked. "You all right, Martin, or do you want the double of my *reata* between your horns?"

"No, Les. We were just playing around."

"I like that game. Be sure and invite me the next time you play."

Martin rode away to catch Che Che's horse. Che Che was down on his butt with his head between his legs. The back of his shirt and his hat were covered with the dust of the road.

"Keep your head down, Che Che," laughed Les. "Somebody else might want to come along and ride his horse over your ears." He rode after Paula Mary and Guilo. At the barn, Guilo jumped down and tied Sam and Cat to a rail. Les dismounted and loosened his cinches.

"Whew, Lessie," said Paula Mary. "I sure was glad to see you come back. I thought you were gone for the day."

Les looked across his saddle at her. "Now, Paula Mary, why would I want to leave my family and run off to play in Harshaw all day?"

"Well, you wore your tie and took your suitcoat with you. What else was a body to think?"

"A body should think her brother was absent-minded and put on his coat when he shouldn't have and then decided to tie it on his saddle so he wouldn't sweat through it while driving a steer to town."

The sun was warming the rocky bottom of the canyon when Paula Mary walked into the kitchen for breakfast. The family ate a late Mexican-style *almuerzo* on holidays or when everyone was working around the house. They only ate an early breakfast when the work took some of them away from the house.

Eileen and Betty were setting the kitchen table. A. B. and Ben were working on their tally books in the front room. A. B.'s pen was poised over a ledger. "Now give me the figures on each camp," he said.

Ben was sitting on the polished oak floor by A. B.'s desk with his back against the wall. He read his tallies and A. B. made entries in his ledger for the different cow camps the Cowdens worked. Ben kept dictating until A. B. tallied all the cattle the brothers had branded at the Canelo Hills, the Porter Canyon, the Buena Vista, and the Mowry camps. A. B. then totaled the count.

"You'll probably be able to sell three hundred big steers to Mr. Jarboe, then?" he asked.

"I could bet a new hat we'll have over four hundred, but I haven't promised him that many."

"I'll buy new hats for all my sons if you sell him more than three hundred."

"Better watch it, Papa. We've got it cinched."

"That would tickle me to death."

The camps the Cowdens were talking about were in mountains where wild cattle ran. The Canelo Hills camp was the only one that lay in country that was easy to work. It lay below the Huachucas in a draw, where cattle could be held in the open. The Cowdens shared this camp with their cousins, the Porters.

These camps were sore spots for absentee syndicates that were trying to run big herds on this public land. The syndicates were buying up homesteads and mining claims in the country to control the public range around them. The camps would someday force them to fence their ranches, not to keep their cattle in but to keep their neighbors' cattle out.

The camps lay on small parcels of deeded homestead land in the middle of public range. Cowmen like Ben Cowden were using them as bases for catching wild cattle and building their herds.

Mexicans abandoned a lot of country to the Apaches before the Gadsden Purchase in 1853 and had not reclaimed it. Title to that land was in dispute for many years.

The wild bulls that ran in the mountains established their own herd boundaries. When Ben Cowden tallied thirty head of cows, he was talking about thirty head he had caught in the traps he set in the canyons, ravines, and water holes of an area a camp served. The Cowdens shared camps everywhere in the country with their cousins the Porters and other neighbors. These families had been in the country for so long they claimed all the grass and cattle near their camps. They did not invite strangers to work their camps. They discouraged interlopers but tried not to shoot them.

Newcomers who moved into the country and established their homesites were welcomed and helped. Cattlemen were traditionally hospitable and God-fearing. The first of them had been welcomed and helped with generous hospitality by the Mexican ranchers who settled the country first. They had no government or law, and no neighbors except the Pimas and Papagos. The Mexicans gave the Americans a *muestra*, a fine example of the proper way good people welcomed strangers to a frontier. Newcomers were celebrated with fiestas of thanksgiving.

Ranchers set high standards for work and play, courting their girls, and dealing with one another. They tried to provide visitors with some pleasure that was always hard to come by in the land. Good stock in cattle and people was scarce, so business and courting had to be conducted with decency.

By June 24, 1885, the Cowdens owned clear title to the Durazno ranch at Harshaw where they lived. That ranch owned patents on the stock water that controlled fifty square miles of grass. Their Yerba Buena camp on the southern edge of the ranch was on the border of another ranch, the Spanish land grant called the Buena Vista. The owners of the Buena Vista had been run out in the 1860s by the Apaches. The Cowdens shared the use of that range with the Mexican Elias family on the south, the Pendletons and the VO on the east, and the Salazars and Gandaras on the west.

The Buena Vista grant covered a million acres, but no one knew where it started or where it ended. No one paid attention to formal boundaries. The only people who used the country were cowmen who did so in peril of Apaches, bandits, and wild cattle. In close combat, the native cattle were as savage and dangerous as Apaches.

The Cowdens drove into Harshaw at midday. Ben rode

ahead of A. B.'s buggy leading Prim Pete, the bay horse he was running against Lew Porter. The family unloaded at the Farleys'.

A. B., as undersheriff, set out on a round of the saloons. Ben turned Prim Pete into a shady pen and went to look for Lew Porter. Les hustled over to Vince Farley's saloon for free beer. Mark looked for the Salazar brothers so he could practice his fiddle.

Paula Mary and the Farley girls were to have their picture taken with Mrs. Chance, their teacher. Myrtle Farley was Paula Mary's best friend. As they were walking toward the schoolhouse, Paula Mary noticed Myrtle had acquired a gold ruby ring.

"My, isn't that a nice ring," Paula Mary said.

Myrtle stopped and held up her hand so Paula Mary could have a better look. "My aunt May gave it to me this morning," she said. "She's my favorite aunt, and I'm her favorite niece."

"Can I try it on?" asked Paula Mary. Myrtle took it off and handed it over. The ring was tight on Paula Mary's finger, but she made it go on. It was adorned with a cluster of rubies in the shape of a heart. "Why, that's the prettiest thing I ever saw," she said. "Can I wear it in the picture?"

She realized that Myrtle probably wanted to wear the ring herself, but she didn't care. Myrtle would have other chances.

"All right, but I want it back right after the picture," Myrtle said. Myrtle didn't have to give in to all of Paula Mary's wishes, but she usually did.

Mrs. Chance was the tall lady who had taught all the Cowden children. She formed her students in ranks in front of the schoolhouse for the photographer. She placed Myrtle and Paula Mary in front of Guilo Soto and his sister. The Sotos were acting stiff and dignified in their dress clothes. Guilo wore his formal frown as though worried everyone might not give this event the importance it deserved. He wiped sweat off his temples with the heels of his hands. He and his sister, Elogia, were impressed with the seriousness of being photographed. This was a milestone in their lives, a record for all time.

"Steady," ordered the photographer from underneath a

heavy black cloth draped over the camera. "Hold your positions and don't move." He came out from under the cloth and stepped up beside his lens, picked up his shutter button, and looked at the children. "Keep your eyes open, now. Look at the camera, and hold very, very still."

Paula Mary smiled and posed with her hand on her chest to show off Myrtle's ring. The photographer clicked open his shutter, then it closed and the picture was made.

Myrtle asked for her ring. Paula Mary was having trouble getting it off.

"All right, Paula Mary, take it off," Myrtle demanded.

Paula Mary screwed up her face and pulled on the ring until the end of her finger turned purple. "Look, my finger is black, and it still won't come off. I don't know what else to do."

"Oh, don't start carrying on, it's only purple. That'll go away," said Myrtle.

Paula Mary sucked on her finger and pulled on the ring with her teeth, but it would not budge past her knuckle. To relieve her pain and worry, she shook her hand, put it behind her, held it away from her body, and walked in circles.

She bore to the east until she was inside the schoolhouse. Her schoolmates crowded through the door with her. They could see the ring had taken hold of her.

Mrs. Chance came into the room with Mrs. Hopkins, a sweet and beautiful widow lady. Paula Mary was so awed by the lady she went mute whenever she came near. Mrs. Hopkins was a nurse. A. B. admired her greatly and said she had been a spy for the Confederacy during the War of Northern Aggression.

Paula Mary was holding her hand out behind her and walking in circles again. Her fellow pupils stayed close, observing her, alarmed. She began to cry, and Mrs. Hopkins put an arm over her shoulders. Myrtle turned away, disassociating herself from the scene Paula Mary was making.

"What in the world happened to you, Paula Mary?" asked Mrs. Hopkins.

Mrs. Hopkins lifted the hand so Paula Mary could feel her breath on it. Her face was beautiful and untroubled.

She asked Guilo to bring soap and cold water. While he was gone, she smiled into Paula Mary's eyes and spoke softly to her.

"You're Ahira Cowden's little daughter, aren't you?"

"Yes," said Paula Mary, transfixed by the lady's perfume and the gaze of her green eyes.

"How many daughters like you does your handsome father have?"

"Three."

"Are you the prettiest? You must be. How could anyone be prettier than you?"

"I don't know."

Guilo came in with the soap and water.

"Now watch this, and remember how easy it is," said Mrs. Hopkins. "I've rid myself of many a tight old ring this way."

Paula Mary was aware of the bright gold-and-amber sheen on Mrs. Hopkins's hair as the lady gently bathed her hand with soap and helped the ring slide off. The ring slipped into the soapy water and disappeared. Mrs. Hopkins kissed Paula Mary's cheek to help her forget the ordeal.

"Remember how we did that," said Mrs. Hopkins. Paula Mary watched her walk away with Mrs. Chance. Mrs. Chance called her pupils to her, and Guilo walked away with the washpan. Paula Mary joined the line to order her picture.

Myrtle was mad at her. Paula Mary had used her ring to get attention. Myrtle was not going to ask for it back while everybody was looking. She gave Mrs. Chance the order for her picture, stepped outside to wait for Paula Mary, and saw something that completely distracted her from the ring.

When Paula Mary caught up to her, Myrtle asked, "Are those the two Indians you said held up your team this morning?"

Paula Mary looked into the hateful stare of Che Che. He was squatting with the Yaqui under a tree at the edge of the playground. "That's them! Run!"

The girls ran all the way back to the Farleys', but the Indians did not follow them and they soon forgot to be afraid. The twins hitched gentle Stokey to a cart so Paula Mary and Myrtle could drive around town.

They drove away from the house and picked up Guilo in front of his father's shop. He was excited about the race, and he was being allowed to hold stakes. Hoozy and Whitey Briggs called to him when they were in front of the saloons, and the girls stopped the cart and let him off.

Hoozy and Whitey were betting against Ben's horse. Paula Mary followed them down the main street. Every time they made a bet, the stakes were handed to Guilo, and he recorded the names of the bettors and the amounts of the wagers in a notebook.

Miners came out of the saloons and joined Hoozy's crowd, looking for cattlemen who wanted to bet on Ben's horse. Ben had been winning miners' money so long, they wanted revenge. Some of them were even angered if a cowboy refused to bet against them.

Most of the American cattlemen in the country were related to the Cowdens. Twenty of the Porter men, uncles and cousins of Ben's, were in town. The Farley twins and their father and uncles, the Pendletons, and other cattlemen crowded around Ben to support him. Most of the miners were full of whiskey and as ready to fight as they were to bet. Eleven of the VO cowboys who worked for Duncan Vincent came to stand with the miners and bet against Ben's horse.

Ben and Lew stood in front of the crowd and handed A. B. $250 apiece to stake the wager. Guilo was holding a heavy amount of cash, coin, and scrip. The miners and *vaqueros* were pressing more money on him. Gilbert Soto, Guilo's father, went up and spoke quietly to A. B.

"Somebody take Guilo's stakes," A. B. ordered. "This is too much responsibility for the boy."

"Wait a minute; he's the one we agreed on," said Hoozy. "We're not switching stakeholders. He's made the record of our bets, and he's our man."

A. B. could see Guilo would be disappointed if he lost the prestige of being a stakeholder.

"All right, but get away from him. Give him room so I can see him until after the race has been run and all bets paid. Come up here, Guilo."

Guilo walked up and stood close to A. B., his eyes bright with pleasure. Paula Mary and Myrtle had stopped Stokey under an oak tree behind the crowd, and her father and brothers were facing her. Che Che walked up, leaned against Stokey, and draped an arm across his hips. He was sporting a wide, watery scratch across the side of his face, souvenir of his wearing the Cowden buggy and team for a hat that day. He began tormenting Stokey by pinching the hair off one spot on his hip. The horse turned his head and rolled a nervous eye at him.

The Indian watched the bettors hand large quantities of money to Guilo, growling to himself at the sight. Guilo held the money tight in his fists overhead to show it to the bettors before he put it away and recorded the wager.

Paula Mary was proud of the way Ben looked every hostile face calmly in the eye and still kept his good nature. The banter between the sides was more like fighting than gaming. Ben was the center of attention, and he deserved to be as far as Paula Mary was concerned. He was taller, broader of shoulder, blacker-headed, bluer-eyed, and handsomer than any other man in the country. Today she could be sure of it because every man in the country was in Harshaw.

Stokey jerked uncomfortably and switched his tail at Che Che's hand lying innocently on his hip. Paula Mary knew the Indian had tortured him in some new way while she was admiring her brother. She danced the popper of her buggy whip on the back of Che Che's hand.

The Indian turned his face and stared at her.

"How ugly," said Myrtle and giggled.

"Just quit tormenting the horse," Paula Mary said in Spanish.

Che Che pinched more hair off Stokey's hip.

"I thought you understood Spanish," Paula Mary said. "Aren't you the Apache who says he's a Mexican?"

Che Che nudged his hip against the horse and let his arm slide down until he was hugging the rump. He bit the tip of his tongue to show his contempt for the horse and the driver. Then he shoved away from the horse, turned toward Paula Mary, leaned against the cart's dash, and reached for the whip. Paula Mary jerked it away.

He stuck his chin out and made quick snatching grabs for the whip, not looking closely at it and not really trying to grab it but lunging closer to Paula Mary as he reached farther over the dash. Then he grabbed Paula Mary's knee and pulled her to him so he could have the whip.

Paula Mary could not escape him, so she poked the fist that held the whip into his flat nose and pounded the butt of the handle down on the top of his hat. She lashed Stokey across the hips, and the cart lurched forward, brushing the man aside.

She stood up to hold Stokey as he lunged into the back of the crowd. He reared and fell back toward the cart when a man cursed and slapped his head. Another man caught a line and held him. Paula Mary looked for Che Che. He was not staying to show his face after causing the trouble. He was loping away, limping on one *tegua*.

"You ran over his toe, Paula Mary. I saw this big iron cartwheel bounce right down on his toe," Myrtle said.

"You'd think he'd learn. That's the second time he made me run over him today."

Paula Mary drove back to the Farley house and parked the cart; she and Myrtle put Stokey away. She washed, rested awhile, and then got up, brushed her hair, and headed for the picnic with her mother, aunts, sisters, and cousins.

Myrtle was walking by her side when she said, "Paula Mary, can I have my ring back now?"

CHAPTER 6

When Myrtle found out that Paula Mary had lost her ring, she accused her of being selfish, careless, and devious. Paula Mary knew she should add "inconsiderate." She bowed her head and took the scolding she deserved.

Myrtle asked if it ever occurred to Paula Mary that a body might want to be photographed wearing her own ring. Paula Mary admitted that since the photographer was only taking one picture, she had wanted to be the one wearing the ring.

Myrtle was so mad she walked away. Paula Mary did not suffer long because the picnic was at hand. The food was laid out in the solid shade of the *alameda*, the cottonwood grove. A breeze showed the silver sides of the leaves in the sun and spread the odors of braised beef and mesquite smoke from the coals of the barbecue pit. No one was playing music, though, because Duncan Vincent was in the pavilion making a speech. The only people paying attention to him were his own henchmen, who did not dare eat barbecue and drink beer while their boss was expounding on his great principles.

Paula Mary saw that her little brother Freddie Lee was having a runaway, as usual. He had been staying with the Farleys in Harshaw, sick with the chicken pox. Today was his first day out of bed. He and the Farley boys his age had gone to the picnic early. He was difficult to control at public gatherings; now, he was flying in and out of the picnickers in a fever of lawlessness.

Viney stopped to listen to Vincent. "Hold up a minute, girls," she said. "It's not polite to walk right under the nose of a man and disrupt his audience. Let's at least see if Mr. Vincent has anything good to say this time."

Vincent was proclaiming that "immigrants" were spoiling this frontier of great opportunity.

"Well, there you are, that's what he said in the last speech he gave," Viney said, and she moved on.

Paula Mary and Betty stopped to watch Freddie Lee. The boy was the fastest runner they knew, even though he was small for his age. Viney was giving him his schooling at home because he was so wild Mrs. Chance could not handle him. The boy was shy as a wolf cub and seldom came out when visitors stopped at El Durazno. He was growing lawless as an Apache and was prone to savage all peaceful gatherings of whites such as this. He usually picked a downhill path through a gathering and launched himself like a projectile. His game was to dash as close as possible to the dangerous public without being caught. If he found he was still alive after a headlong run, he slowed to a lope and circled until he felt the craving to run again.

Because this was his first day out of his sickbed, Freddie Lee's fever for running had reached an early peak. His face was hot, flushed, and sweaty; his movements too anxious, his eyes too bright. Paula Mary knew someone should catch him and hold him down before he made himself sick again, but only a whole gang of footracers chasing him in relays would ever stop him.

A procession of the Catholic community of Harshaw, carrying a statue of *San Juan Bautista*, filed by the picnic toward the church. The priest leading the procession was attended by two altar boys dressed in cassocks and surplices. The boys were Freddie Lee's age. To keep from being distracted by the fun of their peers, they frowned and pursed their lips in their most pious expressions.

Behind the priest, bobbing on the shoulders of four men, came a statue of Saint John the Baptist. Saint John's face was painted brown as an Indian's. Behind the statue walked most of the Mexican families of Harshaw, the women's faces shrouded by black *mantillas*, the unmarried señoritas in white dresses and white mantillas, young men in dark trousers and white shirts, and older men sweating in their best suits.

The procession was singing a hymn in Spanish. This did not deter Duncan Vincent's speechmaking. He trekked on about the great western migration. Paula Mary worried that he might rave all afternoon and everyone would have to eat the barbecue without the music.

Freddie Lee paused a moment, trotting in place, surveying the field from a slope at the edge of the picnic. While Paula Mary and Betty watched, he let himself fly straight toward the pavilion. Duncan Vincent had begun to expound on the honor of the territory's illustrious bankers.

"My God," said Betty. "He's taking dead aim for Mr. Vincent."

Freddie Lee darted through the picnickers like a baby quail. He did not turn away when he reached the pavilion. He flew up the stairs to the platform, shied away from the grasp of a Vincent henchman, and streaked on toward the great man. Vincent gestured with his hat and let it sweep behind his back. Freddie Lee collided with it, clapped it over his head, and ran on without breaking stride. The hat seemed to have sprouted legs as the henchmen grabbed to retrieve it. Duncan Vincent stopped raving in midsentence and turned to watch his hat run away.

When he turned back and saw the picnickers were finally giving him their attention but were laughing at him, he looked as though his life was ruined. Hardly anyone had been paying attention to Vincent. Everyone had been keeping track of Freddie Lee and was happy he was finally leaving the picnic and falling in step with the procession for *San Juan Bautista*, cousin of Jesus. He caused no stir in that parade, but the laughter stopped Vincent's speech.

Betty and Paula Mary watched the hat bob up the hill with the procession to the door of the church where Mrs. De La Ossa picked it off. One of Vincent's henchmen retrieved it from her as Freddie Lee took sanctuary in the church.

In the late afternoon, cowboys showed off their roping

and riding in an arena walled in by ore wagons and the cliffs of Harshaw canyon. They roped big steers, busted them down, and tied them like calves. The Porter brothers provided bronc horses for testing the riding skill of young hardtwists. Ben Cowden led each bronc into the middle of the arena and snubbed him close to his horse as the bronc was blindfolded and saddled. The rider climbed up behind Ben and mounted the bronc from the back of Ben's horse. Ben handed the bronc's lead shank to the rider, removed the blindfold, and the wreck was on.

The men contested well-known broncos mature in years and smart in ways of hurting men. Their reputations were so bad they discouraged anyone who was not so reckless he could be called suicidal. They were incorrigibly mean and set in their ways, and that was the only reason the Porters allowed them to be contested. They were not good for anything else, there being no market for horsemeat. On that San Juan's Day, the celebration did not bring rain from the sky, but the Porter broncs made it rain cowboys.

The miners would not be outdone. Between each cowboy event they showed off their prowess with double-jack and drill, crushing rock and loading ore cars by strong arms and shovels.

Near sundown, the ore wagons were moved aside, and the street was cleared for the race between Lew Porter's horse, China, and Ben Cowden's Prim Pete. Ben and Lew rode their horses the length of the street past the saloons and the alameda to the head of the canyon where the race was to begin. The finish line was drawn in front of Vince Farley's saloon in the center of town. The race would be run down the straightaway of the one hard-rock street.

Ben took his first look at China. Lew had not allowed him to see the horse. He was a small, Berber type stud horse, a bay with a curly mane and tail and three white stockings. He was well shod, but Prim Pete had the advantage in hooves: White feet were soft feet.

Because of the coronary band, an artery that encircles a horse's foot at the hairline above each hoof, horsemen said a horse had five hearts: the great heart in his breast and a heart for each of his feet. Ben figured if that Arab, Spanish, and Mexican tradition was true, three-fifths of China's courage would be lacking in the race.

None of Prim Pete's feet were white. His feet were big and gave him great balance. They were hard and thick in a country where a man might lose his life if his horse's feet were not like stone. The Harshaw street was a layer of dust on bedrock.

Ben decided that old China probably came from Mexico. Some Mexicans liked their top horses to be dancers. This horse had not been taught to remain quiet and save his energy when he was carrying a rider. He pranced, danced, struck sparks off his shoes, and made Lew jockey every step.

The band was playing, and China was in rhythm with the music. The whole town was watching him, and Ben could see that Lew was enjoying the attention. His China was a fine-looking stallion. Ben was glad Lew was having a high moment on his stud while he could, because he was about to be fed hardrock off Prim Pete's heels. Prim Pete was Steel Dust bred on his sire's side and gave Ben the sprint speed and maneuverability a cowboy needed. He was all thoroughbred running horse on his mother's side. Nobody could tell he was a racehorse by watching him in this moment before the race, though. Ben let him have a slack rein, and he shuffled along, raising dust with his head down.

Ben dismounted and reset his saddle. Both horses were ready to run. Ben and Lew would ride side-by-side past the starting line, turn back head-to-head toward each other, and let their horses run back to the line for a lap and tap start.

If he could see no daylight between the two horses when they crossed the line, Juan would shout "Santiago," and the race would be on. If he could see daylight between the tail of the leading horse and the head of the trailing horse, he would call them back and try again. The best jockey would be in the lead at the start, but no matter how good he was, he would be called back if he crossed the starting line more than one length ahead of the other horse.

Ben knew he was as good a jockey as Lew, and Prim Pete was a smooth and businesslike starter. China was prancing so high he might never come back to earth in time to run the race. Ben took his time cinching Prim Pete, then stepped on him and let him shuffle along to the start. Lew had to take hold of China with both hands to keep him in step with Prim Pete.

Ben and Lew rode past Juan and went on five more lengths. Then they spoke to one another, turned their horses back toward the starting line, and let them run. Prim Pete sprinted away, but China hobbyhorsed in place and was lagging four lengths behind when Prim crossed the starting line. Juan Heredia called them back.

Ben wanted to run the horserace. He was sure his horse could outrun China dragging an anchor if the race ever got started. He decided not to jockey for a big advantage at the start.

He rode past the starting line with Lew again, turned with him, then held Prim Pete back and let China hobby-horse ahead a jump or two. When Lew saw he was ahead, he pitched China the slack and let him run. Ben leaned over and shouted in Prim's ear. Prim's nose was on China's hip at the starting line.

"*Santiago!*" Juan Heredia shouted.

Lew's scheme to win the start succeeded, but Prim Pete stretched out close to the ground and passed China like a freight train passing a ricksha. When Ben saw he was ahead by two lengths and still going away, he straightened up, looked back, and grinned at Lew. His hat blew off into the street and made Lew's stud horse look where he was going for the first time that day. Prim Pete crossed the finish line ten lengths in the lead.

Ben stopped his horse and started him pacing back up the street. Lew had been outrun so far he pulled up before he even crossed the finish line. He grinned as China hobbyhorsed toward Ben, sidling and blowing as though he had been in a race.

"Look at this counterfeit son of a gun," Lew said. "He thinks he still has me fooled into believing he's a race-horse."

Ben smiled back at him. "There must be something he can do, but he sure can't run, can he?"

"Yeah, but what *can* he do? I've been hoping like hell he

could run. Being a racehorse was going to hide all his other sins."

"Take him to a dance. He knows some fancy steps. I was thinking before the race that if he could run like he can dance, me and Prim Pete would bog in his dust."

"Hell," Lew said. "I guess I'll never find a horse that can outrun you."

Ben saw Walter Jarboe standing by the hotel and realized Kosterlinsky must not have come to the race after all. He rode over and received his congratulations. "No Kosterlinsky, Mr. Jarboe?" he asked.

"I've asked several people to watch for him, but so far no luck," Jarboe said.

"I'm riding into his country in two weeks. Want to go with me?"

"No, but I can't go anywhere else until I've found the cattle we bought from that man."

"If you haven't found him by the Fourth of July, I'll help you hunt him down."

"I'll stay in the hotel and pay you to go find him. I'm not much of a horsebacker."

"All right, then, in the meantime I'll make you acquainted with folks who might help you, and I'll introduce you to my father. He can find your man sooner than anybody."

Jarboe saluted and his thanks were lost in the noise of a crowd of cowmen that closed in on Ben. Will Pendleton walked up to Ben's stirrup with Gilbert Soto. The crowd was not celebrating as it should be. Ben looked into the face of his friend Abel De La Ossa.

"What's the matter, Abel, did you bet on the wrong horse?" Ben asked.

"No, I bet on the right horse, but we can't find our stakeholder," Abel said.

"Who was holding your stakes?"

"Guilo was holding for all these men," Gilbert said.

Ben looked for Hoozy and Whitey Briggs. They were not in sight.

"He'll show," Ben said. "He's probably with my papa."

"A. B. was called to the back of the Noche de Ronda

saloon," said Will. "They sent for Mrs. Hopkins, too. Somebody was hurt in a fight back there."

"If somebody'll take this horse and walk him, I'll go see what I can find out," Ben said.

He dismounted. Abel took Prim Pete's reins and led him away from the crowd. "Get on him, if you want to, Abel," Ben said, and he watched the careful way the good hand checked his cinch, turned the horse around and looked him over, then quietly slipped the bridle reins over his head and stepped on him without burdening him.

Ben walked around to the back of the Noche de Ronda and saw A. B.'s hat in the center of a crowd gathered there. Les turned to him when he walked up behind the crowd. Mrs. Hopkins was kneeling by someone lying still on the ground.

"Who's hurt?" Ben asked.

"He's dead," Les said.

"Who?"

"Guilo."

"Our Guilo?"

Les's chin wrinkled like a sad child's, and his eyes filled with tears. Ben patted his shoulder. For all his meanness, Les was the softest-hearted of them all.

"How can Guilo be dead?"

"Somebody stabbed him," Les said angrily.

"Why would anyone kill Guilo?"

"I don't know, but they haven't found the stakes he was holding. I can't understand what he was doing behind the saloons."

Ben saw Will Pendleton and Gilbert Soto coming.

"Another thing I can't understand," Les said.

"Yeah?"

"He was killed by an *estocada*, a knife punch that severed his spine at the base of his skull."

CHAPTER 7

Guilo Soto was the first dead human Paula Mary had ever seen. The corpse was covered to the waist with a sheet and blanket and laid out in the Soto front room. The border of the sheet was folded neatly over the top of the blanket, the hands crossed on the breast. The skin on the brown hands was clear and looked as clean as it would be from a long soaking. The nails on the lifeless hands looked as though they had never been used.

A. B. paused to speak to Mrs. Hopkins. That lady had been with Mrs. Soto since the body was brought from behind the saloon. Her face lighted when she looked into A. B.'s eyes; then she smiled at Viney and took her hand. She finished being nice to Viney right quick and turned back to A. B. She was not able to look at A. B. Cowden without smiling.

"You have such a nice family, Ahira," Mrs. Hopkins said.

Paula Mary thought that was funny. She hardly ever heard her father called Ahira. Everybody called him A. B. or Mr. Cowden. Even Viney called him Mr. Cowden.

A. B. took both Mrs. Hopkins's hands in his. "It's wonderful of you to help out like this," he said. He looked the woman briefly and sternly in the eye and barely paused, but she did not take her eyes off him while he was close.

"I'm happy to help this family," she said. "I can't believe the little fellow's gone. He looks so sweet lying there, so natural."

Paula Mary didn't think there was a thing natural about the way Guilo's poor carcass looked. Four ornate church candles on brass stands stood at the corners of the bed, tall as her sister Betty. All the curtains were drawn, and the room was close.

Candlelight in the warm room put a flush on the faces of the mourners, but it sure did not raise life in Guilo's face as far as Paula Mary was concerned. She did not gaze at Guilo long because, as she expected, the close sight of the cadaver scared the pee-wadding out of her. She wanted to run away from there. Now she understood why they had to bury everybody.

Paula Mary remembered that once, a long time ago, she had dreamed her mother died and her grandfather Porter and her Porter uncles came to bury her. She could not stand the thought of anyone putting her mother in the ground and tamping dirt on top of her like a fencepost. The dream made her worry about what she would do if someone ever came to bury her mother and father, or her brothers and sisters. She decided she could not allow it. She would get a butcher knife or her Papa's pistol and keep everyone away from her family's bodies if they ever died.

She was trembling to the very ends of her limbs. She reached for Betty's hand.

"Dear Lord, Paula Mary, why are you shaking?" Betty whispered.

A. B. and Viney were seated with other heads of families along a wall. Youngsters and bachelors remained standing. Families were arriving to be in attendance for the *velorio*, the wake. Every man would take his turn to stand watch a few minutes at the head of the bed or at the foot, before the body was carried to the church for the funeral mass.

"Mama," Betty whispered. "I think Paula Mary's sick."

Viney looked into Paula Mary's face and reached out to her. Paula Mary buried her face in her mother's bosom and started crying. "Why, my little girl is *mortified*," Viney said. "That's awful, that old mortification, isn't it?" She held

Paula Mary away and wiped the tears off her cheeks with her fingers. The girl nodded, agreeing about the nature of the trouble.

"Betty'll take you back to the Farleys' and put you to bed, so you can sleep a little and forget this," Viney said.

Paula Mary quit shaking before she reached the Farleys', but Betty put her to bed anyway. She tried to lie still after Betty left, but she was out of the bed inside an hour. She hated naps. She was bathing her face with cool water when Myrtle came in. By that time the wake was over, and the body was at the church. Myrtle had suffered sunstroke when she was two, and her mother made her lie down for a nap every day, but she did not like being forced to lie still in the daytime either.

The girls sat in their underwear for a while, trying to figure how they could go back to the funeral without getting into trouble. Paula Mary had seen all of the cadaver she ever wanted to see, but she wanted to see more of the show of mourning and sorrow.

The girls began to play with the clothes in the closets. They tried on Aunt Edna Farley's hats and shoes and twirled her silk purse by its drawstring. They put on Vince Farley's silk hat and looked at themselves in the mirror. They put on the white shirts and three-piece suits with knickers the twins had worn when they graduated from Mrs. Chance's school. Paula Mary and Myrtle laughed and posed for each other. They looked in the closet again and came out with another box, full of old hats. Among them were matching cloth caps. They put these on, and they fit; the caps went with the suits. The girls stuffed their long hair under the caps and went outside to try their disguise on the funeral procession.

They practiced walking like boys and laughed about that. They were strutting and traipsing in front of the house when the funeral procession came out of the church. They knew they would be recognized if they stayed close to the Farley house, so they composed themselves and crossed the street in front of the procession. They stood under the cottonwoods by the pavilion to watch the mourners go by on their way to the cemetery.

The priest and his altar boys were in the lead. The boys

were Onofre De La Ossa and Fermin Heredia, the same two who had served for the procession of San Juan. They only wore semipious looks on their faces this time. Their piety was having trouble surviving two long public processions. They looked up and saw two strange boys standing under the cottonwoods in cloth caps and fancy suits. Their piety vanished as they showed their contempt for the gringo kids in the sissy suits.

Paula Mary decided the best protection for her disguise was audacity. Onofre and Fermin did not recognize her, so she gave them back the Cowdens' transparent stare. She outlasted them because they were forced to look to the front again when they passed her.

Guilo's brothers came next, bearing his pine coffin on their shoulders. After that, the Soto family passed. Myrtle's mother and sisters walked by with only a glance at the miscreants, but the twins looked them over, recognized them at the same instant, turned to each other, and grinned. They went on without saying anything but turned back once and winked.

Paula Mary's family was coming, and all of a sudden she felt an awful dread; her audacity deserted her. She knew that her papa was bound to discover her and pin her to the ground for capture with one glance. She hid her face against a tree. Myrtle knew she could never stand alone under the Cowden scrutiny, so she hid her face beside Paula Mary's. They did not look up until the Salazar brothers went by singing "*La Golondrina.*"

"*Adonde vas, los pajarillos cantan,*" sang the Salazars. "Where you're going, the birds are singing."

The girls climbed into the pavilion and watched the procession pass the saloons. The mourners drew shouting and laughter out of one saloon. The bartender came out and called for A. B., who left the procession to follow him back inside.

"Now why would my papa leave the funeral and go into a saloon?" asked Paula Mary.

"To have a beer?" asked Myrtle.

"No. My papa only drinks his own kind of whiskey. He gets a new barrel straight from Tennessee every time he runs out."

"Let's go home now," Myrtle said.

"No, let's see what my papa's doing." Paula Mary headed for the back of the saloon. Myrtle followed her but balked at the door when Paula Mary opened it.

"I'm not going in there. You better not either."

"Come on," said Paula Mary. "We can't see anything out here. Maybe Papa's arresting a hurdy girl."

"I don't need to see your papa arrest anybody. Just think what will happen to us if we get caught in a saloon dressed like boys."

"I don't care. I have to see." Paula Mary went in and left the door open. Myrtle stayed outside, shut the door, and backed away to give herself a good head start toward home if someone besides Paula Mary came out.

Paula Mary heard her papa's voice right away. She tiptoed through a cool room that smelled pleasantly of sawdust and whiskey. She peeked through a hole in a curtain hanging over a door and saw him in the barroom talking to Whitey Briggs.

A. B. always talked softly, but his deep voice was reverberating off the boards in the place. All the ranch families who came for the San Juan's Day celebration were headed home already or were at the funeral. Most of the miners were at work. Whitey, Hoozy, and Dick Martin were sitting at a table in front of the bar, the only customers in the place.

"You're awful rowdy, aren't you, Whitey?" A. B. asked good-naturedly. "Didn't you know a funeral procession was going by?"

"That was a funeral, was it? I thought so. That's why I was singing 'Bury Me out on the Lone Prairie' when they went by. Didn't them Mexicans appreciate my singing?"

"It's not their way, to pay attention to drunks when they're grieving," A. B. said. "I noticed you, though."

"Oh, you noticed, did you?" said Whitey. "You fellers hear that? Old A. B. noticed."

"Come on, straighten up, Whitey," said Hoozy. "We've been trying to get him out of here, Mr. Cowden. He hasn't been to bed."

"Pay attention to your brother, Whitey," said A. B. "Go

home and sleep. Quiet down now, so everybody can forget you disrupted the poor folks' grief."

"Now *there's* something I can't understand. What's a dead Mexican matter to anybody?" Whitey said.

"What?" A. B. said.

"Who gives a damn? So, one Mexican stabbed another. Who cares?"

"Oh, damn!" said Hoozy. He knew Whitey was not so drunk he did not know what he was saying.

"Stand up," A. B. said.

Whitey's head lolled back, and he let out a yell, trying to fool A. B. that he was too drunk to comply.

A. B. knocked his hat off, drew a pistol, grabbed a handful of his hair, and jerked his head down between his legs. Whitey started off the chair, and A. B. jerked him forward and speared his head into the bar. Whitey bounced back, straightened, and staggered against A. B. A. B. shoved him against the bar, poked his pistol into his spine, and pulled his head back by the hair. Whitey's eyes were starting out of his head and staring right at Paula Mary's peephole. She recoiled, shocked at the violence in her papa and afraid Whitey had seen her.

"Empty your pockets on the bar, Whitey." A. B. was not out of breath.

Whitey stuck one hand into a pocket.

"Both at once," said A. B.

Whitey pulled everything out of both pockets and laid coins, a pocketknife, and a derringer on the bar.

"Turn them inside out," A. B. ordered.

Whitey complied, then emptied his back pockets. "Hands on the bar." A. B. reached around and separated two $20 goldpieces from the coins on the bar. "Whitey, I arrest you for the murder of Guillermo Soto."

"Wait a minute, A. B. I got drunk, that's all. I didn't kill anybody," Whitey said.

"You either killed the boy, or you connived with somebody else to do it."

"What makes you think that? What proof have you got?"

A. B. held up the goldpieces. "These coins belong to me," he said. "I gave them to Guilo to carry when you made him your stakeholder. My initials are scratched on them.

Since the murder, every saloonkeeper in town has been watching for them."

He showed the coins to the bartender. "Buff, are these the coins you saw Whitey take out of his pocket when he paid for his drinks?"

"Yes, sir," said the bartender.

"How do you know?"

"I saw him take them out of his pocket again when you ordered him to."

"Will you testify to that in court?"

"Yes, sir."

"Don't you want to know where I got them?" asked Whitey.

"Tell me."

"Well, I didn't kill the Meskin for them, I'll tell you that. Won't you let me tell you who killed him?"

"Speak."

"Che Che did it."

"Is that right?"

"I got the coins from him."

"You're trying to tell me another sneak turned up with two twenty-dollar goldpieces, and he gave them to you and then told you he committed murder for them?"

"Well, yes, he told me he killed the Meskin."

"So instead of reporting it, you came in here and got drunk. Why would Che Che give you forty dollars in gold?"

"He owed Hoozy and me money. We sold him some horses."

"Where did you and Hoozy get any horses?"

"We bought them in Tombstone."

"Well, don't bother telling me a story. You can tell it to His Honor in Tucson. Right now I'm locking you in a shady spot so you can sober up for the trip."

"You're not taking me anywhere." Whitey tore away from A. B. and backed down the bar. A. B. shook Whitey's sweaty hair off his fingers, calmly cocked his pistol, and took aim at Whitey's foot.

"You can travel with me on two healthy feet, or you can go on one with a hole in it if you'd like that better. It's all the same to me."

Whitey looked down at his foot. "I don't want to go to jail," he said.

"Nevertheless, that's where you're going," A. B. said. "But don't worry, it won't be so bad unless you're nursing a hole in your foot."

"Listen, it's all right, Whitey," said Hoozy. "We'll get you out of this."

"Who's *we*?" asked Dick Martin. "I hope you're not trying to include me in another scheme."

"Do you want to wear chains with your brother, Hoozy?" A. B. asked. "If you do, I'll yoke you to him neck-and-neck right now."

"No, sir, but my brother didn't kill anybody. He told you who killed the Meskin."

"Do you think you can take my prisoner away from me?"

"No, sir, I didn't mean that."

"Then get out of my sight."

Dick Martin knocked over a chair in his hurry to leave the place. Hoozy kept his dignity but left immediately, too.

"Put your hands in your pockets and make fists," A. B. ordered Whitey. "Keep them jammed in your pockets. Make any move other than a beeline for the jail, and I'll shoot you in the butt."

Paula Mary slipped out the back door and ran with Myrtle to get ahead and cross the street to the Farleys' without being seen by her papa. In her heart she knew she was sunk. Her papa saw everything. She pulled up near the pavilion and looked for A. B. She had not moved fast enough. A. B. was close enough to recognize her. She and Myrtle hid behind a cottonwood tree.

The jail was on the edge of the cottonwoods between the church and the pavilion. Its one room had a dirt floor, a brick and beam ceiling, and adobe walls twenty inches thick. The door was a slab of half-inch steel with a barred window. A. B. moored Whitey to a seven-foot length of chain anchored to an oak post in the center of the room, gave him water, and locked the door on him.

Two of the Salazar brothers who lived on the Buena Vista range stopped to talk to A. B. on their way home. Paula Mary saw this as her only chance to cross the street. She stood up straight, saw to it that Myrtle did the same, boy-walked out from behind the tree, and started across. She listened to her father explaining his reasons for jailing Whitey and assuring the Salazars he did not need their help. She hoped the Salazars and their horses would hide her, but when she glanced toward them, she looked straight into her papa's eyes.

"Well, I guess I shall have to call you Tom from now on, Paula Mary," A. B. said softly and then went right on talking to the Salazars.

A. B. never again mentioned to Paula Mary that he saw her dressed as a boy. He never found out that she followed him into the saloon and watched him arrest Whitey Briggs. She and Myrtle Farley kept that secret all their lives, but that evening Viney sent everybody out of the kitchen and asked Paula Mary to stay. The little girl looked into her mother's stern face. Viney seldom disciplined her children, but the Cowdens knew the rules she expected them to follow every minute of the day.

"Who was that boy called Tom your father saw this morning, Paula Mary?" Viney asked.

"That was me, Mama," said Paula Mary.

"You dressed up like a boy? Where did you get the clothes?"

"They were old clothes of the twins'."

"So you're turning into a person who has no modesty, sneaking around in trousers whenever you please? You think you can act like a hurdy girl in a saloon? Is that how you're turning out?"

My gosh, does my mother know I was in the saloon? thought Paula Mary. "No, Mama, we were just playing."

"I realize that, Paula Mary, but I thought you knew that the ladies in this family do not show off in trousers for all the world to see."

"I didn't think I was being immodest, Mama. I wore a three-piece suit and a cloth cap, and no one recognized me."

"Your father recognized you. Why do you think you do not have one pair of trousers in your wardrobe? Is it only because we don't like you disguising yourself, Paula Mary?"

"I don't know, Mama."

"You don't know? Well, I'll tell you. Ladies do not wear

men's trousers in this family because it is unnatural and immodest. You are not a boy, don't look like a boy, do not walk like one, sound like one, or smell like one. Does a blackbird hen have a red wing?"

"No, Mama."

"All right, from now on you will keep your body out of boys' clothes. I don't ever want to hear of you painting your face, or showing your limbs, or wearing trousers again as long as you live. Do you understand, Paula Mary?"

"Yes, ma'am." Paula Mary began to cry.

Viney hugged her close until she stopped. When she squirmed a bit to be free, Viney wiped her face.

"Now you're the second one in this family to cry over this," Viney said.

"Who else cried?"

"Your papa's eyes were full of tears when he told me his little daughter had taken to impersonating boys."

"I didn't mean to do anything bad, Mama. We were just playing."

"Well, I know, but play does not excuse anything, daughter."

The next day, the family was up at 4:00 A.M. to help the boys load a wagon with equipment and provisions. Ben, Les, and Mark were going to their camp in Temporal Canyon in the Santa Rita Mountains to brand cattle.

After breakfast, A. B. left for Harshaw to attend the inquest into Guilo Soto's death. Paula Mary went to the barn and watched Mark braiding the end of a rope around an iron ring for a *mancuerna*. Cowboys used the rope and ring to neck cattle together so they could control them when they drove them out of rough country.

"When is Papa taking Whitey Briggs to Tucson?" Paula Mary asked Mark.

Mark looked up from his braid. "Who told you Papa was taking Whitey Briggs to Tucson, Paula Mary?"

"Didn't you know he arrested Whitey for killing Guilo? I thought the whole town knew it."

"No, when did Papa do that?" Mark's look was not warm.

Ben and Les were saddling horses only a few feet away. They did not look up.

"Why, yesterday morning, while everybody was at the cemetery, Papa went in a saloon and arrested Whitey Briggs, didn't he?"

"I wonder how you know all this, Paula Mary," said Mark.

"Well, uh, I was at the Farleys' with Myrtle and saw him put Whitey in jail."

"How do you know Papa arrested Whitey for killing Guilo?"

"Oh, well, I don't know why I thought that. I guess I'm wrong. . . ." Paula Mary took a deep breath. "Do you know, Mark, I'll *never* be able to eat Frank Wong's pies again."

Mark was still giving her the cold look that he seldom gave his sisters or other children, only grownups. He did not like her to gossip. Changing a subject usually warmed him up sooner or later, though.

"Why is that, Paula Mary?"

"You know how pretty, brown, crisp, and tasty the crusps of Frank's pies are?"

"Yes," said the cold-stone stare. "You mean the *crusts*?"

"Yes, well, Myrtle told me that Emily Porter told her the way Chinamen get those crusps on their pies is, they fill their mouths with milk and spray it on their pies just before they put them in the oven to bake. Can you imagine that? I don't think I'll ever eat a piece of Frank Wong's pie again."

"Frank's pie never hurt you before, did it?"

"No."

"It can't hurt the pie if he spits milk on it before he puts it in the oven. The fire in the oven would burn up anything bad that came out of Frank Wong's mouth, or anybody else's mouth, even some old Gila monster's."

"Oh. Would you eat a pie after somebody spit milk on it?"

"No," said Mark, and he almost smiled. He finished braiding the rope onto the ring. He whirled it over his head and tossed it into the wagon. The wagon was hitched to A. B.'s bay team.

When they were ready to leave, the brothers went to

the house and kissed their mother and sisters good-bye. Outside again, Ben picked up Paula Mary and kissed her. "Paula Mary, how come you're prettier every day? By the time we get back from the Temporal, you'll be so beautiful, we'll have to sell the ranch and buy you a crown of diamonds. You'll be queen of the Santa Cruz."

Paula Mary could never say anything when her brothers made over her like that. Ben handed her to Les without putting her down.

"Little sister, we'll be thinking of you every minute, worrying you're causing a wreck," Les said.

He handed her to Mark. Mark kissed her cheek. "I expect you'll be in charge while we're gone, won't you, sister?"

"Yeah," said Paula Mary with a husky breath, liking what she saw in Mark's eyes now.

"Then I won't worry. Our poor mother's in good hands."

Mark put her down. Ben mounted his horse to stand in front of the team while Mark climbed up to take the lines. Les mounted, and the brothers waved and rode away. Paula Mary watched them cross the creek and go out of sight around a hill in the horse pasture. As she turned and started toward the house, she remembered Guilo would not be there to keep her company, and she began to grieve.

CHAPTER 8

A sense of urgency bothered the Cowden brothers as they started toward Temporal Canyon. They did not want to isolate themselves from their family now. Their little sister had worried them about their father.

Work on the frontier was often dangerous. The brothers worried about their parents when they traveled away from El Durazno and Harshaw. Now, the brothers were so worried about A. B. that they kept looking over their shoulders, as though something on their back trail would give them a clue that he was safe. They wanted to turn back and ride straight to Harshaw to help him, but their cattle traps at Temporal needed inspection. Cattle would run out of feed and starve if they were not taken out of the traps promptly.

Paula Mary's story about A. B. arresting Whitey Briggs was bad news. The brothers thought A. B. had only left the funeral to stop Whitey from jeering at the mourners. They did not know he had taken Whitey into custody for murder. A. B. always kept his undersheriff business to himself. The brothers were surprised Paula Mary knew about the arrest. Now they were glad she was such a gossip. If she had been as close-mouthed as all the rest of the Cowdens, they would still be ignorant of A. B.'s danger. The brothers knew A. B.

usually transported a prisoner to Tucson for arraignment the next day after an arrest, and he always went alone.

The brothers hurried on to set up camp quickly so they could double back and make sure Hoozy did not pull some coward's trick to free Whitey and get even with A. B. Temporal was a deep, steep, wide canyon on the eastern slope of the Santa Rita Mountains. A tender alkali *sacaton* grass grew stirrup-high in good years on its slopes, bottoms, and rims. The slopes were studded with black, white, and Emory oak. The black oak yielded sweet scorns. A sugary mescal that was good for making spirits grew on the steeper slopes that provided longer shade.

The brothers kept a permanent camp under cottonwoods in a narrow bottom of the canyon that was walled by high sheer cliffs. Ben and Les corralled their remuda at the camp and rode out again in opposite directions. They spent an hour looking for Indian sign before deciding to let Mark take the wagon down to camp. The camp was not in close arrow range of the canyon walls. The brothers never rolled out their beds until after dark, and they slept in different places every night.

When they were working the country, the Cowdens kept their mouths shut more often than they used them for speaking. That gave them an advantage over adversaries who rode through the country talking and laughing instead of listening. A man could find out a lot that was important to him if he could keep quiet and ride with men who did the same.

The trigger trap at Temporal was holding thirteen head of marketable cattle and several sucking calves. The trap covered a quarter-section of ground. Before the brothers set a trap and went home, they always cut grass outside and stacked it inside to sustain the trapped cattle.

Water was not plentiful in the canyon during June, the hottest, driest month of the year. The brothers kept salt inside the trap to keep drawing cattle to it all year round. During wet seasons, when cattle were scattered, the brothers left the gates wide open. Cattle went in and out to the salt without being bothered. That way, in the dry season when cattle were forced to come to the camp for water in greater numbers, they were not shy of the gates.

The ladino cattle never went through the gates unless they were desperate for salt or starving for water. Ben had watched these outlaw cattle stay outside when other cattle were passing in and out at will. Most ladinos had come close to capture at least once. Some had been caught, branded, and castrated but escaped before they could be taken to market.

Ladinos kept away from man and lived on the high points. They walked the cliffs and tried to keep their enemies at their feet and upwind, where they could sense them when they came in range. These cattle were so outlawed they no longer even trusted their herd instinct and they ran alone.

The Cowdens enclosed their traps with spiney brush piled high in stretches where canyon walls were not sheer enough to contain cattle. Gates were built on the entrance trails. Poles were lashed together and hung in a gate to form a chute and a lane into the compound. The poles were sharpened on the ends that hung inside the compound. The two sides of the chute were hung like rail gates that swung into the trap. Rock weights were wired to the ground under the sharpened ends to hold the ends of the chute open or shut.

During the rainy season, the weights held the chute wide open, so cattle could go in and out at will. When the Cowdens wanted to set a trap, they swung the sharpened ends closed and weighted them down, so the cattle could see their way in and walk through the chute by pushing it open with their sides. When they tried to leave, they found they were facing the sharp ends of the poles that had closed behind them.

The brothers made camp, ate supper, and relaxed against their bedrolls. They had not talked much about their worry for A. B. He seldom asked them for help and never deputized them, so they were sure he did not think he needed them.

They listened to the canyon awhile and smoked their pipes. When Ben decided all sounds were normal and the brothers could talk, he quietly spoke up. "I'm sure Papa didn't leave for Tucson today. He would have left the house earlier than he did this morning. He always tries to reach the Andrade ranch by noon. He went to the inquest today. He'll start to Tucson with Whitey in the morning."

The brothers rested in silence again. They never slept under the trees or near running water or near a corral full of livestock. They needed silence. Sometimes they slept a hundred yards from the place they laid their fire. If any creature threatened them, the horses would give them a sign. When they talked, their voices were half heard and half felt. Because they were brothers, they could talk so softly to one another that someone else could be standing at their elbows and not understand a word.

Their father did his sheriffing on his own. He usually caught his miscreants by himself and took them to the judge without help. He did not endanger his family when he policed criminals. He prided himself on his good style—driving the best horses in the country, wearing a three-piece suit, and not breaking a sweat. Having to show style was a vice he allowed himself, like drinking whiskey; he kept his family out of his law enforcement and his whiskey drinking.

"Papa told me he would be at the inquest, or at the jail making sure Whitey was fed and watered," Mark said.

"Who's guarding Whitey?" Les asked.

"Guilo's daddy might not be a deputy, but I bet he's got his eye on him," said Ben. "Gilbert only lives fifty paces from the door of the jail."

"Yeah, I bet Gilbert's watching him." Les laughed. "He's hoping Whitey will run for it."

"Gilbert and his relatives would remedy him being a fugitive right quick," Ben said. "Papa'll be taking Whitey to a safe jail in Tucson in the morning. Me and you, Les, will ride down to the road and watch for him. I'll stay awake until midnight."

"I'll stay awake after that," Mark said.

"Lordy, I get to sleep," said Les. "Smite me if I snore." He rolled over and went right to sleep.

After his first sleep, Ben lifted his head and located the *guia*, the star in the east that rose about 2:00 A.M. He rolled out and built a small fire. Before he set the coffeepot where he wanted it by the flames, Les was on his way to the corral to grain the horses, and Mark was making bread in a wooden bowl. Ben carried buckets to the spring for water.

The brothers breakfasted on turkey eggs, bacon, fresh sourdough bread, and coffee. While Ben and Les were gone, Mark would brand the calves and mavericks in the trap. The cows were already branded.

Mark banked coals around a pot of beans. He could tend the pot while he worked the cattle in the trap. After the beans were cooked, he would ride out to check other traps.

Ben knew A. B. would leave Harshaw early and keep moving. The drive was mostly downhill from Harshaw to the Andrade ranch, from five thousand to three thousand feet and about thirty miles, enough haul for one day in warm weather. Ben and Les lined out at a high trot and found him by a place called Monkey Springs. Hoozy Briggs and Dick Martin were a half mile behind him. The brothers were relieved to locate A. B. before he needed help. They stayed off the road in a position to ride in on Hoozy if he threatened A. B.

"Ben, you suppose Hoozy and Martin are dumb enough to think they can take Whitey away from Papa?" Les said.

"That Hoozy'd backshoot Papa if he could. He's close enough with that Sharps rifle, but he's too much a coward."

"I guess he's seen us," Les said.

"I hope so. If he sees us, he'll stay away from Papa."

"Maybe we ought to go on down and keep Hoozy and Dick company. Strike some damned old fear in their gizzards."

"Let's stay away and watch as long as Papa stays ahead. Maybe they'll go back to Harshaw when they see us."

"Oh, well, maybe they're only going along to make sure Whitey gets his cigarettes in jail," said Les.

"Sure, or maybe they're watching to make sure Papa does his duty," Ben said, smiling.

"Yeah, they're good citizens. Hoozy and Martin probably only want to make sure law and order is upheld," said Les.

Ben stopped his horse to examine tracks on the ground. "*Teguas*," he said softly.

Les stopped instantly. He did not see the tracks, and he did not want to walk his horse over them. He watched the hills for new enemies.

"A bunch!" Ben said. He rode on, keeping the tracks on the uphill side of his horse. "A *big* bunch!"

Les rode up. The tracks had made a batter of fresh dust through a tall stand of dry sacaton grass toward the peaks of the Santa Ritas. The brothers could not tell how many Apaches had gone by, but the dust was so thick and powdery it was splashed onto the grass beside the track.

"I bet they came through here about the time we rolled out of bed this morning," Les said.

"This is a migration, or a renegade bunch. Been a long time since this many came through."

"I hoped all the mean ones were in Mexico."

"This is a wartrail, and they're not so far away they can't look back and see us."

Ben looked into the Santa Ritas. He needed better eyes. More than fifty Apaches were probably looking at the Cowdens on their backtrail. He imagined the Apaches with their women and children filing up the slope in the cool darkness of that morning with the *guia* star rising behind them; moving in a spare, silent, unhurried pace as they sought high ground and concealment before daylight.

"They're watching you and me, but they can't get us," Les said. "Mark's up there by himself."

"I bet this bunch broke away from the San Carlos reservation and is headed for Mexico," said Ben. "This could be the old Yawner's bunch. They might go right on over the Santa Ritas and not even come close to our camp."

"What if Mark runs into them? He said he'd try to ride up to the peaks today."

"This is a big party, and some are mounted," Ben said. "They could relay him up there and hamstring him. What do you think we ought to do?"

"What do I think? We've been worried about Papa since we left home. We know two sneaks are following him. We'd better stay with Papa."

"That's what I'm thinking. The Apaches might see Mark, but he'll have the same chance to see them. He'll be all right."

"He has all that stock to brand and a pot of beans to cook before he leaves Temporal," said Les. "Maybe he'll stay in camp today."

"These Indians probably stopped to rest at daylight. They won't move again until tonight. Papa'll be at the Andrade by noon. We'll go on and have a talk with Hoozy at the Andrade, and I bet we can get back to the Temporal tomorrow. Then we'd better see where those Apaches go before we try to do any work up there."

"You know what?" Les said, smiling.

"No," said Ben.

"I bet these are the Apaches that relayed Johnny Bonner and made him late to take Eileen to the dance."

Ben laughed quietly.

"That was forty miles from here," said Les. "It's all uphill from the Canelo Hills to here. They're too wore out to catch Mark unless he closes his eyes and stumbles into their fire."

The brothers rode on without looking back. Apaches watching them would never guess they were leaving a brother and a remuda of horses behind.

To be light and mobile, A. B. was driving his black team on his Carter buggy. Anybody coming after him would sure have to be riding good horses. He already knew Hoozy Briggs and Dick Martin were behind him. Their horses were having trouble keeping sight of the black team's dust.

The black team was only warming up, but A. B. felt he might have to slow down. Whitey the hoodlum had not shut his mouth for ten miles, and he was becoming more abusive every step.

A. B. turned around to look at Whitey. The prisoner was on the backseat wearing manacles on a light chain that was attached to the rear of the buggy. He was also wearing leg-irons. The contraption would not allow a man to take a full stride, but he could shuffle. Another chain was moored in the floor under the rear seat and snapped into a ring on the back of a belt on Whitey's waist. Another chain connected the belt with the manacles and the leg-irons. A. B. allowed himself to listen to Whitey's abuse a moment longer.

". . . and after all I have my rights. Didn't our goverment buy this country from the Meskins to keep from killing them for it? Over in Texas we whipped the crap out of them and took it. Nobody gets in trouble for killing a Meskin over in Texas. We're all white men against the Meskins, ain't we? No jury of white men will ever convict me of killing that Meskin."

Whitey stamped both feet down on the good hickory floor of A. B.'s Carter buggy. "Dammit, Cowden, you're nothing but a Meskin-lover, and you're using me as a scapegoat. You know damned well I'm innocent."

"You're guilty as hell," A. B. said and stopped his team. He climbed down and unsnapped the belt chain that was moored to the floor. "Get off your rump and stand down on the ground, murderer."

"What?"

A. B. brought the butt of his buggy whip down on Whitey's hat.

Whitey quickly covered his ears and face with his arms. "Dammit, are you going to whip me now?" he yelled angrily.

"I am unless you move your butt off that seat and stand down on this road right quick."

Whitey showed his face. "All right, I'll get down, but I can't walk in these irons. I don't have to go to the bathroom, either, if that's what you're thinking."

"Get down here!" A. B. whacked the top of Whitey's head again.

"You want me, do you? Here I come, old fool." Whitey launched himself at A. B.

A. B. stepped aside as the chain on the manacles went taut and Whitey's own fists hit him between the eyes. He stretched out feet first in midair and landed on his back beside A. B. He grunted as all his breath was slammed out of him.

A. B. was holding the team by the lines, but the horses jumped ahead a step and tangled Whitey under a wheel. A. B. backed the team and rolled the wheel off him. He calmed the horses while he waited for Whitey to recover.

"Now, get up from there," A. B. said when Whitey was breathing again. He picked up Whitey's hat and put it in the buggy for him.

Whitey sulled. "By the great lord, you mean old devil,

you can't make me. I'm going to lay right here until my
brother catches up. When he sees what you're doing, he'll
kill you." He rolled over on his side with his back to A. B.

"Stand or be dragged."

"Drag and be damned."

A. B. climbed into the buggy. Whitey's eyes rolled
around and watched him. A. B. wheeled the team in their
tracks. Whitey flinched away from the rear wheel. "All
right, all right," he cried. "Let me get up."

A. B. whistled and started the team briskly. Whitey was
jerked upright by his manacles and forced to hop and
shuffle behind the buggy as the horses moved on. He was
an athletic and well-coordinated young man and did not
fall. He started howling, but he soon found that was wasted
on A. B., and he needed the breath to keep his feet.

A. B. looked at his watch and timed him. He seldom
made a prisoner go afoot. Most of his charges believed he
would drag them all the way to Tucson if they tried his
patience. A. B. called this treatment of his prisoners the
shuffle. He could gauge a prisoner's meanness, defiance,
and antagonism by the length of time he sustained a shuffle
before he gave up, fell over, and begged for relief. Whitey
was probably a fifteen-minute shuffler; because he was a
good athlete and thought he was mean.

When A. B. could see that the exercise was using up all
the heart in a man, he pulled up. He did not care how long
a man's meanness kept him going, but when his defiance
was gone and heart was all that kept him trying to keep up,
A. B. stopped the exercise. He respected the heart of a
man, no matter how mean he was.

After ten minutes Whitey Briggs gasped, "I can't keep
up anymore."

"Don't worry, you'll keep up. I won't go off and leave
you."

"Ain't you ever gonna stop?"

"That's what I've been wondering, Whitey. How much
shuffling do you require?"

Whitey did not understand the question too well, so he
did not waste his breath answering.

"We're about an hour from the Andrade," said A. B.
"But it's almost all downhill."

He heard a thump as Whitey gave up and let himself be dragged awhile. The horses leaned into their harness to pull the carcass. A. B. slowed the team and allowed Whitey to regain his feet, but he did not stop and he did not look back.

He went on until Whitey groaned and fell again. This time he stopped the team, set the brake, took a swallow of whiskey from his flask, and waited for Whitey to recover. He looked back.

Whitey was on his back measuring his length upon the ground. He found his voice and said, "Don't start up again, sir, please."

"Do you want to ride in the buggy, Whitey?" asked A. B.

"Yes, please."

"I want that too. Why do you suppose you had to shuffle all that way?"

Whitey thought a moment. He wanted to give the right answer.

"I complained too much?"

"Exactly. Will you relieve us of your complaining?"

"Yes."

"You can mount and ride now."

Whitey climbed stiffly into the backseat again. "I'm tied up; my muscles cramped," he said.

"Is that a complaint, Whitey?"

"No, sir. Not at all. Just telling you what happened to make me ask you to stop."

"Are you going to start complaining again, Whitey?"

"No, sir, I just—"

A. B. stepped down and snapped Whitey back into his seat by the belt chain. "Maybe you better not risk saying anything at all, Whitey. That way I won't think you're complaining."

"Yes, sir."

A. B. looked back and saw Hoozy and Dick Martin sitting their horses within rifle range. "We'll go on now. But be quiet. We make better time when I don't have to listen to you."

A. B. drove on at a trot and soon outdistanced Hoozy and Martin. He reached the Andrade ranch at noon, unloaded Whitey under a giant cottonwood, and chained

him to the trunk. The cottonwood would shade Whitey that
afternoon and shelter him that night. A. B. had let him tend
to his washing and toilet at a spring on the way in. He paid
the Andrade family with government vouchers for his own
bed and board and the meals of his prisoners. The Andrades
did not charge for the meager comfort the prisoners could
find among the roots of the cottonwood. Before leaving
Harshaw, A. B. had allowed Whitey to send one of the Soto
boys, one of Guilo's brothers, to his shack for a blanket.

Hoozy Briggs and Dick Martin were resting behind a
hill near the Andrade ranch with a dense mesquite thicket
at their backs. A dry wind was gusting from the west. The
noise of the wind through the thicket helped Ben and Les
stalk to within fifty feet of the badmen. Hoozy was lying on
his stomach. He raised his head and began talking loudly,
so that Martin could hear him in the wind.

"I don't imagine we'll have much trouble with the old
man," he said.

"I don't imagine we will either," said Martin, yawning.

"I never understood how he got that sheriff's job.
Nothing about him scares me."

Dick Martin was sitting profiled to Ben and Les. He
looked as though he wished he were someplace else.

"Does he scare you?" Hoozy asked.

Martin did not answer.

"Well, does he?"

"Naw," said Martin, looking down at the ground between his feet. "He's kind of a nice old gentleman,
but . . ."

"But what?"

"But the old man ain't all a feller has to deal with. You
do something to A. B., you get to deal with the whole
outfit."

"A bunch of cowboys with their noses in the air. How
heavy can they be? I've got a two sixty-grain forty-five slug
that weighs as much as any of them."

"Then you've got that Porter tribe, about twenty more
cowboys all the same size."

"Twenty more slugs is all that means."

"I'd sooner go home and beg my mama to take me back

than get in a fight with the Cowden-Porter clan. Then there's their partners, the Sotos, Romeros, De La Ossas, and Heredias."

"What are you doing here, then?" Hoozy demanded. "You're yellow. If you can't help me get my brother back, why don't you just get the hell on out of here. I don't need you."

"You know, I've been *wondering* what I'm doing here. If you think you can kill A. B. Cowden and get away with it, I *know* I don't belong here."

"Get on out, then. Get gone."

Martin stood up. "Just give me my share, and I will."

"Your share of what?"

"My share of the stakes the Indian took off the Soto boy."

"Your share? I've got a brother down there on the way to hang and I'm supposed to give you money so you can run out on me?"

"Listen, I was in that deal from the start, and I never heard anybody say anything about killing the boy. The Indian was only supposed to take the money away from him, give it to us, and run."

"Is it my fault the Meskin fought back and I had to step in and kill him?"

"It's all your fault."

"Get on out of here. I'm gonna kill Cowden tomorrow morning after he leaves this ranch, and I'm gonna use the stakes money to take my brother to Texas."

"Well, damn your luck when you find yourself in range of that old man's double-barreled shotgun." Martin turned and took one step and had to stop. Ben and Les were walking out of the thicket in front of him.

Ben's pistol was drawn, cocked, and pointed at the ground by his side. He wanted that counterfeit Hoozy to look him in the eye and say again he was going to kill his papa before he pointed it at his sonofabitching mouth and pulled the trigger.

Les walked straight toward Martin.

"Hoo-Hoozy . . ." Martin stammered.

"I always knew you'd tuck your tail between your legs when it came to a real fight," Hoozy whined.

He was lying on his stomach and propping himself up with his forearms. His pistol was on the ground between his hands. His tune had changed to a whine because Martin was quitting. He did not want to spend a night all alone in the open worrying he was not man enough to kill A. B. Cowden.

"Hoozy," Martin said, staring at Les. Les walked up and split his nose with his right fist. Martin was uphill from Les, and he fell forward, embracing Les as he collapsed toward the ground.

Poor Hoozy still did not know he was in trouble. He heard the sound of Martin's nose burst asunder and turned his head. Les carried Martin another step and stamped the heel of his boot down on Hoozy's neck. Ben winced.

Les shoved Martin away. Martin swiped at his nose with both hands, looked at his blood, and swooned.

Les lifted his boot over Hoozy's head.

"Wait, Les. Don't," Ben said. He rolled Hoozy over with the toe of his boot and picked up the pistol. Les had stomped Hoozy's nose into the pistol. His front teeth had taken a big bite out of the ground. Blood from his nose and a split lip was making mud of the dirt in his mouth, but he did not know it. He was unconscious.

"Badmen," Les said. His anger was gone. He was almost sad. "Hoozy should have been packing a pumpkin pie instead of that pistol. It would have been easier to eat."

Ben and Les delivered Hoozy and Martin to A. B. A. B. deputized three Andrade cowboys to help him take the prisoners to Tucson. Ben and Les stayed overnight to be with their father. They headed back to Temporal Canyon as the *guia* star rose in the east again the next morning.

CHAPTER 9

Ben hoped the Cowden luck would hold. Catching Hoozy and Dick Martin before they hurt A. B. had been lucky. Now, as he and Les were nearing Temporal, he hoped Mark was still in business and not drawn and quartered with his hide stretching on a wagon wheel. The horses Ben and Les were riding were still tough, but Ben would be glad to catch a fresh one, if there were any left at Temporal.

The brothers stopped on the rim to examine the canyon. Their camp was good bait for a trap, so they always approached it carefully. A dry wind was gusting out of the west again and they were downwind from their remuda of saddlehorses. The brothers hoped the horses would not start nickering and draw every cutthroat within earshot to their camp. The remuda was hobbled and grazing in sight. The cattle in the trap were all branded and lying under the trees chewing their cuds. Mark had gathered more cattle.

"What's that spilled on the ground by the front wheel of the wagon?" asked Les. "Everything looks good but that."

"I don't know," said Ben. "Apaches and wolves don't spill anything. What spills our stuff?"

"Coons, dammit. Bears."

"I bet it was the coons, or a *solitario*."

"Well, that's good if only coons or coatis been in our

camp. Our horses and wagon are still here. That means maybe nothing wilder's been bothering it."

"Maybe," said Ben.

Les rode into the canyon. Ben waited until he was halfway down, then rode down on another trail the brothers kept hidden. They used it to sneak up on their own camp. They always wiped out their tracks, cluttered it, and hid its upper and lower entrances after they used it.

Mark and Les were lying in the shade drinking coffee when Ben rode into camp. He unsaddled his horse, hobbled him, and hung a morral full of grain on his muzzle. He poured himself coffee and found some leftover biscuits and bacon in the chuck box. The coons had overturned Mark's bread bowl, and played with the strainer, and spilled flour and dough lumps on the ground. Nothing else was disturbed.

"Our brother saw the hostiles," said Les.

Mark was sitting with his back against the trunk of a cottonwood, his hat tilted over his eyes. He was whittling on a tiny stick, pulling off a long shaving with the razor edge of his stock knife. He was not one to show his face if he thought someone might be wanting him to show his feelings.

"What did you see, Marcus?" asked Ben.

"Apaches," Mark said, not excited, in no hurry to talk about it, carefully shaving his toothpick.

"He saw twenty-two braves," Les said.

"Where?" asked Ben.

"First, I saw four hunters in American Boy Canyon."

"Did they see you?"

"One spoke and one laughed, and I heard them before they could see me. They were down in the sycamores. I watched them load their meat on a packhorse."

Mark pointed over his shoulder with the blade of his knife. "They hit a high trot up American Boy Trail and never looked back."

"They never saw you?"

"I was lucky. There's no rock on that flat above the canyon, so my horse hadn't made any noise. I stayed on the rim until they started climbing out toward the saddle. Then

I rode into the canyon and watched them ride over the skyline before I followed them again. They were hunters for a big party."

"I told him we saw their tracks on the way to the Andrade," Les said.

"How many more did you see?" Ben asked.

"I followed the hunters until they joined the main party on that saddle below Mount Wrightson. I counted twenty-two braves, but they had a lot of women, old folks, and youngsters with them."

"Why did you follow the hunters, Marcus?" asked Ben. "That could have turned out bad."

"I figured I ought to find out all I could about them."

"That scares me. How close did you get?"

"About from here to the rim of the canyon."

Ben and Les both looked up to the nearest rim to see how close their little brother had come to being caught and skinned. Mark kept whittling.

"Were they on the march? Were they drunk to let you get so close, or what?"

"No. They made camp." Mark let out a sigh as he remembered being close to the Apaches. His brothers were making him see he should have been more bothered than he was.

"Did you get off your horse?" Ben asked.

"No, I sure didn't want to give them a chance to catch me afoot."

"Well, how did you get so close horseback?"

"Dumb luck," Mark said. "I didn't know about the rest of the tribe until I climbed above the saddle to see what I could see. The hunters were the only ones I was worried about. I didn't figure they could hear me while they were making the climb."

"Hell, that slope's not a hard climb for an Apache," said Les.

"No, but they were in a hurry, and I figured the way their horses were blowing, they wouldn't hear any sound I made. I was riding old Jack and I'll tell you, neither one of us was even breathing. You should have seen his ears. He was straining so hard to keep track of the Apaches the tips almost touched. If the Indians'd made one little move in our direction, all the rope in Tucson couldn't have held him on that mountain."

"Well," said Ben. "He knew they could kill you, that's all. They could have shot you both."

"They all had rifles, but I never got in close rifle range during the day. I had to worry about their sentries. I stayed back and out of sight of the high points. I never went real close until they lit their fires after dark."

"My God, Mark, you stayed with them until after dark?" Ben said.

Les laughed, shook his head, and looked all around. "Lordy, now I feel I have to watch for spooks."

"After dark, they lit a signal fire, and I rode way around and got above them," Mark said quietly. "That was when I got close. I was scared then. I kept having to move to stay hidden, but then I saw they were feasting on fresh meat. The way they were chewing the bones, they couldn't hear a thing. I was having trouble holding still, I'll tell you, until I finally rode up behind some boulders that hid me good."

"Anybody else would have come home when the sun went down and called it good," Ben said.

"After dark was the best time to get close, wasn't it?" said Mark. "What could they do to me? Their signal fire blinded them, so they weren't able to see any better than me. They were afoot and I was horseback."

"What did you see that made it so worthwhile?" asked Les. "I would have seen a bunch of savages eating meat with both hands and me without supper myself."

"What did I see? I saw the old Yawner himself."

"Are you sure, Mark?" asked Ben.

"The very old wolf himself. They'd been talking while they were eating. Then they quieted down, and I was thinking of moving off because it got so quiet. *That* was scary. I didn't know why they shut up.

"Then one voice spoke up, and they all paid attention. I kept old Jack's head behind our big rock, so they couldn't see the reflection of the fire on his eyes. I watched everything through a crack between two rocks. Old Jack didn't even want to look. He didn't steal one peek.

"The Yawner was sitting in shadow with his side to me.

When he finished talking, they all got up to leave. He walked around the fire, and I saw who he was."

"Are you sure it was him? How are you sure?" asked Les.

"Hell, we stared at him for an hour that time the soldiers brought him through Santa Cruz when they were taking him to San Carlos with all his people and his cattle and horses. I'll never forget him. You know how he kinda grins with his teeth clenched? His mouth is a straight slit across his whole face like a snake's and looks wide enough to swallow a quarter of a beef. Nobody else in the whole world has jaws like that.

"Then they left. Horses and Apaches went off into Madera Canyon. They didn't make another sound. I hit for camp."

"Boy, I don't know," said Les, shaking his head. "That's too close for me. I like to stay away from a bunch like that with their knives and their terrible dislike for *nice people*. I don't know. They'd have snared me sure as hell."

"They did exactly the right thing to draw you in and snare you near their camp," Ben said. "They couldn't chase you, so they could have been luring you. Didn't you think of that?"

"I knew they weren't luring me. I saw them before they could see me. I heard them before I saw them. If they'd heard me first, I wouldn't be here, but I heard them first."

"Gosh, the only feeling I ever get when something like that happens to me is *run*, or *fight*, or *drop your drawers before you get them dirty*," said Les. "I think if I'd been lucky enough to hear Indians like you did, I'd have made it all the way home to my bed with Papa and Mama last night."

"They headed west?" asked Ben.

"West," sighed Mark.

"I wish there was a way to warn people down at Tubac and Amado."

"Let's eat," said Les. "If they're bothering folks at Tubac and Amado, they can't bother us."

The next day, Les and Mark rode out to bring cattle from other traps back to Temporal. Ben rode to the

American Boy country to look for an AB-Bar cow he had seen up there. She was a good high-horned blue-roan cow with a blue heifer calf. She had a big two-year-old blue heifer running with her, probably her daughter. The last time Ben had seen them it was too late in the day for him to brand the calves, and he was riding a tired horse.

Ben knew where the cow was watering. Those three females were worth riding across an Apache wartrail to find. With luck they might have attracted a young bull or two.

Ben was happy to be alone. The brothers liked to ride by themselves and work alone whenever they could. Ben did some all-around thinking while he kept an eye on the country.

He was riding a horse he called Star, a solid dark brown with long thoroughbred ears and a black mane so thick it parted in the middle and covered both sides of his neck. The only white mark on him was a small star squarely between his eyes.

Ben had promised Will Pendleton he would look at the traps they shared in American Boy Canyon. The roan cow was running on a mesa near American Boy. He found two cows with baby calves by their sides in the first trap. He found the Pendleton branding iron in its hiding place, and branded, castrated, and earmarked the calves, and then let them go.

He was on his way to the next trap, rimming high so he could watch the country and protect himself. He rode onto a line of fenceposts someone had unloaded off a wagon across a grassy foothill. He knew the Pendletons were not planning to build a fence there. They shared the country with the Cowdens and would not fence the country without telling Ben. Ben stopped his horse in the shade of a juniper to study the line of posts. A fence here would cut Cowden cattle off the American Boy water. The wagon tracks told him the posts were brought about the time everybody was celebrating *Dia de San Juan*.

He rode down to another trap. Thirsty cattle were waiting outside because someone had fenced it off with barbwire and closed the gate. Now he could be positive the Pendletons were not doing this fencing. No one ever shut the gates on traps and went away. Cattlemen wanted cattle always to be able to reach water. Somebody who did not give a damn about the Cowden and Pendleton cattle was claiming ownership of this water.

Ben opened the gate and rode inside the half-section trap and found cattle walking the fence looking for a way out. He drove them to the corral, branded the calves, and turned them out. He cut big stretches out of the fence and hid the wire, so cattle could water. The brush fences of the old trap were ruined. They could be repaired after the Cowdens and Pendletons found the fencers and dealt with them.

Ben headed for camp, hoping he would find his blue cow on the way. He felt good about cutting down the barbwire before the cattle suffered. That was what cowboys called being horseback at the right place at the right time. He still had time to prowl for the blue cow. He had caught twelve pairs of heels without missing a loop that day. He was proud of Star's quiet work in the corral. Star was making a good horse.

Ben struck the tracks of the blue cow where he expected to find them. The country was dry, and she was not hard to track. Inside a half hour he found her in a grassy swale. She, her overgrown daughter, and her sucking calf were so full of milk and grass they were groaning. He shook out a loop in his Manila and rode up on them from the downhill side. The sight of him did not excite the cow; she had seen him before, and she was so used to having her own way she did not figure on him changing her status.

Ben cut the big heifer off the cow and calf, headed her uphill, and rode to catch her. When Star cruised up close, Ben saw she was a lot bigger than he had realized.

He held Star in her wake and rated her, keeping pace with her as she began to duck to give herself a different look at him with each eye. Then she dove into a narrow wash to shake him off. Ben stayed out of the wash and let her run. She lunged up the opposite bank. Ben jumped Star into the wash and roped her by the horns as she scrambled on the bank. He checked her there, then rode off and jerked her over backward into the sand.

Star dragged her on her backbone, and Ben jumped off, tied a front leg and hind leg together, and rolled her over on that side, so she could not get up. He did not take time for a long breath. He took his rope off, coiled it as he remounted, and ran to catch up to the cow. She was out of the swale and lining out for higher country. She was out to escape Ben, but she was probably glad for the chance to leave the big heifer behind for good. If the cow could have told Ben her troubles, she would probably complain that her big old daughter was sucking her tits raw and not leaving the calf enough milk to fill a teacup.

She was making deep tracks and covering them with thin manure to show Ben how she felt. He caught up on an open mesa, roped and tied the calf, and rode away quickly, so the cow would come back to the calf.

The big heifer was tied down only about a quarter mile away, so he rode back, put his rope on her horns again, let her up, and drove her to the calf so he could brand both animals with one fire.

The cow decided she'd been wronged and came back to sling her horns and threaten Ben.

He busted the heifer down and tied her beside the calf. He led Star to the shade, hobbled him and loosened his cinches, then built a branding fire. Ben would have liked to unsaddle Star, but he did not know what kind of attention he might have attracted with the dust he raised. He never felt much in danger when he was at a dead run after cattle, but he was always careful to look around for any changes in the country after the stock settled down and before he loosened his cinches.

He screwed the pipe handle on his running iron, put it in the fire, and noticed another line of fenceposts littering the brow of a hill nearby. If those posts were set in the ground and wired together, they would cut the grass of this mesa off the Temporal water. The Cowdens and Pendletons had been catching cattle and driving them home from this grass for ten years.

The mesa was so broad that no one could ride up on Ben without showing himself for several minutes. The mother cow was fifty yards away in the open, watching and waiting for her calf, far enough away that she would not be hooking at Ben's britches when he branded the calf and made her bawl.

Ben was thinking he had the country all to himself when Star looked back over his shoulder and nickered. Two men were riding toward him across the mesa. Ben figured they were VO cowboys, Vincent's fencers. This was the first time Ben had seen Vincent cowboys in the Temporal country, but he was not surprised they were there. Vincent was a barbwire hog. Ben guessed he was starting another of his legal-paper frauds. He was always enlisting bureaucrats in the territorial government to issue paper that would help him take public range away from people like the Cowdens. He coveted any range the Cowdens used. Vincent was determined to take over the whole country by juggling titles in the territorial offices.

Ben was glad to see the two VO culprits riding to him. This pair was flesh and blood, not permits, mortgages, warrants, quitclaims, false titles, charges, suits, bonds, or written demands. These two had ears, would hear him, feel his wrath about barbwire, and save him a trip to the VO headquarters.

He lit his pipe on a coal from the branding fire, drew his pistol, checked his cartridges, put it back, and did not latch the safety strap over the hammer. He did not figure on shooting anybody, but none of the good people he knew ever figured on shooting anybody, and every once in a while somebody got shot anyway.

One of the cowboys was Sid Thomas who had been with Vincent at the dance. The other was Campana, a Mexican from Santa Cruz. The Campanas had been preying on the Elias family for so long they looked like them. Campana was not much of a cowboy, but he was mean enough to kill a man without even saying hello. Ben located the big knives and guns on both men when they rode up.

Campana was the more dangerous of the two. Vincent's gringos called him Campino, the Spanish pronunciation being too much for the intolerant Anglo tongue. The last time Ben had seen him, he was accompanied by a black dog that was so thin every bone in his carcass showed, and he was covered with ticks. Campana stopped at El Durazno to ask A. B. for a job cleaning stalls. A. B. told him to ask Ben if he needed help with the cattle. Ben asked him what he could do. He said he was a cowboy. Ben asked him whose dog he was traveling with, and he said the dog was his, he'd raised him from a pup.

Ben figured anybody who would let ticks get fat on a lifelong friend would never make a cowboy. He told the man he could not use him. Campana knew he could not fool Ben, and every time he saw him now, he gave him dirty looks. Here he was again, but now he was prosperous, riding a VO horse and drawing Duncan Vincent's pay.

Campana stopped his horse at a respectful distance, but Thomas rode to the fire and stood his horse between Ben and Star. He positioned himself so that if Ben faced one VO man, he would have to turn his side to the other. Ben did not turn to look at Thomas. Campana was the dangerous one.

"Get down and visit awhile," Ben said. "Thomas, you ought to come around in front of me where I can see you. You're standing between me and my horse."

"Look at me," said Thomas, and he laughed. "I'm being impolite."

Thomas yanked on his horse and moved him so Ben could see him. "Now this looks like an awful mess you're in here, Cowden. Me and Campino have caught you with your hands in the sugar bowl, haven't we."

Ben banked the coals over his running iron. The tool was white hot. "Get down and rest your bones. I haven't got coffee and I haven't got a drink, but I can set and visit a little if you want to."

"I don't set with cow thieves," said Thomas. "And I don't need an invitation from you if I want to set here. This mesa belongs to the VO. Can't you see we're fencing it?"

"Be neighborly," Ben said. "Get down and cool off."

"You hand over your pistol. I'm an authorized ranger and constable, and I'm taking you in for thievery and for using a running iron."

Ben picked his iron out of the fire and walked to the calf.

"You better think twice before you brand that calf, mister. Stop right now!" Thomas barked.

Ben branded his father's AB–Bar on the calf's left ribs. The calf bawled like the eagles were carrying her home. Ben fit the iron carefully into the coals again. The roan cow brandished her horns and moved in for conflict. She wanted a fight so bad her eyes bugged. She shook her head, streamed slobbers, spurted hot manure, then pawed the ground to make sure she was getting Ben's attention.

Campana was wearing a veiled expression that said I'm not committing. I'll wait to get behind you if I can. No hard feelings until I do. I'm waiting until I see what the bigshot who is doing all the talking is able to do to you.

Ben knew the look. The coward was weighing advantages. Ben always wondered why cowards could not keep from letting that expression show. He took out his stock knife and earmarked the calf with the Cowden *balazo*, which looked like a bullet hole, in the center of the left ear. The operation caused another fit of bawling. Ben straightened up and folded his knife, watching the cow.

He heard the scuff of Thomas's boot behind him, and suddenly the cow shifted her gaze, backed up a step, and shook her horns at Thomas. Ben turned in time to set himself as Thomas swung a fencepost at his head. The wood bumped hard against his skull, but he caught most of the blow on his shoulder and arm, his knife flying out of his hand.

Thomas's momentum and the weight of the post carried him past Ben toward the calf. The cow charged. Thomas saw her coming and let go of the heavy post. The cow lowered her head, skipped over the calf, and hooked the post. It arched high over her back toward Campana and made his horse shy and dance away. The cow bumped Thomas with a shoulder and knocked him down, then lowered her head and headed for Ben, scooping the brush with her horns, lunging and bawling and lapping at the ground with her tongue. Ben stepped aside, and she barreled on. She veered toward Campana's horse and made him scatter away with Campana snatching at his head and digging with his spurs to keep from falling off. The blue cow trotted after the horse with her head up, her manures spurting and her tail writhing over her back, clearing the field.

Ben picked up his running iron and turned in time to see Thomas raise the post again. The pipe handle was cool and handy in Ben's grip. Thomas was big enough to swing the post like a pick handle. He held it by one end overhead and launched himself at Ben. Two steps before he would have let it fall, Ben stepped in with the running iron and cowkilled him between the horns like an ox in a slaughterhouse. Thomas followed his nose to the ground. Ben straddled him and slapped his hat off.

The iron was still glowing. Ben laid it across the top of Thomas's head and seared a clean white part down the middle of his scalp. Smoke rose from tiny flames that licked the hair on both sides of the crease. Ben patted it to keep the fire from spreading, but Thomas did not feel it. He was in a swoon.

Ben looked and caught Campana reaching for his pistol. Campana was being so careful and watchful that he stopped moving in time and his hand relaxed and settled on the saddle horn.

"*No te busco pleito.* I'm not looking for a fight with you," Campana said, his mouth barely moving, his voice barely sounding.

Ben laid the branding iron in the fire, banked the coals again, and walked to his horse. He carried several kinds of medicine in a boot-top tied behind the cantle of his saddle. He took out a flask of Little's Sheep Dip he used for antiseptic and doused the calf's brand with it; he doused some on Thomas's scalp, too. He untied the calf and let her up. She ran to her mother, and they hit a trot for higher country.

Ben kept track of the pair until they were out of sight. He wanted to give the old sister a chance to get away before he branded the two-year-old and let her go. The big heifer would be smarting so much from the branding she might forget about her mama, and the cow could be shed of her for good.

Ben branded and earmarked the heifer, and let her lie while he watched Thomas come out of his faint. Ben was still angry, and he was not through with the man. He took Thomas's pistol and knife from his belt. Fat bulged over the belt. Vincent's cowboys were doing well. He took Thomas's rifle off his horse, laid all the weapons in a pile, and motioned Campana to drop his weapons on the same pile. Campana complied quickly. Ben looked for his stock knife but could not find it.

Thomas's leg jerked as he began to revive. The color returned to his face, and he began to sweat. After a while he sat up and looked for his hat. Ben kicked it to him, and he picked it up. He put it on his head but made no sign he was affected by the new part in his hair.

"You sonofabitch," he said.

"What?" Ben asked. He stepped up and kicked Thomas in the ribs, and when he rolled over on his side, Ben stomped the side of his head gently, not hard enough to make him faint again, only enough to remind him to be careful what he said.

"Did you want to call me a cow thief again, too?" Ben asked.

"No," Thomas grunted and sat up. "Don't kick me again, either. I'm not a dog." He put both hands on his hat to straighten it, and this time he winced.

"I don't kick dogs," said Ben. "Get up."

Thomas rose to his feet and gave Ben an evil look.

"I slap barbwire fencers, though." Ben slapped Thomas across both jaws and warmed to it. He measured him and slapped him with both hands across the ears, and then across the mouth.

"Damn, man. Stop it now," Thomas groaned.

"All right, I'm through now." Ben pushed the man back, stepped away and gave him room. "Get on your horse and get agoin," he said quietly. "If I ever hear you say to anybody, even to yourself, that a Cowden is a cow thief, I won't let you off with a slapping. I won't complain to everybody in the country like your boss does, either. I'll find you, and I'll kill you. Do you believe it, or do you need more convincing?"

"Yes, dammit, I believe it."

"All right. Remember it. Now get on your horse."

"Give us back our weapons. We can't ride in this country without our pistols and rifles."

"You can come back and get them after I leave. Now, ride out of my sight, and tell Vincent to forget about fencing this country, unless he wants a war."

The sun was setting when Ben reached the rim of Temporal Canyon. He looked down from the cliff and saw his brothers. He rode down and dismounted at the corral, and Mark handed him a morral for his horse. Mark looked at Ben's face, smiled, and went back to making biscuits. Les was chopping firewood.

Ben unsaddled and led Star down to the spring to drink, then led him back to the shade, hobbled him, and gave him the morral. He took off his hat, lay by the spring, drank his fill, washed blood off his face, then stuck his whole head in the pool. He took off his shirt, rinsed the blood out, and put it back on. A breeze stirred through the cottonwood shade and cooled him. Les walked into camp with an armload of wood.

"My brother's got the blackest hair in Arizona Territory," Les called when he saw Ben's wet head. Then he looked closer. "Your horse run you under a limb?"

"You might say that. Limb about the size of a fencepost." Ben showed how big Thomas's post was.

"Knock you off your horse?" Les asked.

"I got off to brand the blue cow's calves." Ben told his brothers the story of Thomas and Campana, the fencepost, the blue cow, and the running iron. That entertained Mark and brought a long smile to his face while he made biscuits and laid them in a pan.

"I'd have laid their bones to rest for good if they'd called me a cow thief," Les said. "You're too big and easy, brother."

"Well, we'll always be able to tell which one hit me with the fencepost," Ben said. He went to his saddle, got his running iron, and showed it to his brothers. "Look what his head did to my running iron."

Mark and Les grinned when they saw a bend in the iron. "It must have been hot at the time," Les said.

"Hot as hell. Had to be. Look how he bent it."

"Scorch him a little, did it?"

"Damned right it did. He'll look at the bar in the AB–Bar every time he combs his hair the rest of his life. This time I branded him. Next time, I'll vent him."

Les was laughing. "Well, that tickles me. Does this mean when you vent him you'll be dispatching him from this life?"

"No, just from this range," Ben said.

CHAPTER 10

The Yawner was far ahead of his pursuit and feeling strong. His band was lean, hard, and light of foot after six weeks on the trail. The country was full of game and wild cattle. He could always find meat. He did not have to raid to eat; he raided because raiding was in him, like the poison in a scorpion's stinger.

The Apaches' "Enchanted Land" was teeming with prey. While the Yawner was being held at San Carlos, Americans had been riding in on good horses and fattening. Now they would depend on the soldiers for protection. The soldiers could not catch the Yawner, even though he was only moving at the pace of his children and old people. How could they stop him from preying now that he was lean again?

The Yawner and his people were happy as a wolf pack in a chicken yard. When he became too heavy and tired for coursing and raiding, he would put on his sad face and tell the soldiers he was *triste*, sad, from fighting. He would tell them the women were keening for the dead and the children hungry. That would allow the soldiers to puff out their chests and brag they had ruined his will to fight, even though they knew it was a lie. He would remain quiet while they reminded him of their rules. After that, he would require them to let him keep his booty if he went back to

San Carlos. As a prisoner of war, he would march back to the reservation, and the soldiers could take care of his people the way they did before. He would rest there and eat beef until his stinger hurt him again.

Now he was in a cool cottonwood thicket watching the Canelo ranch on the Santa Cruz River. The Huachuca soldiers were based only a few hours away. The Mexican soldiers were only a day ahead of him, but they would never bother him. He would have peace in Mexico.

Like an old wolf on the prowl, he had been coursing every day and choosing his prey. All he had to do now was show himself, and the fat people ran. They were sometimes so full of panic when they saw him they threw away their goods before he could catch them to cut their throats. When he was loose in the country, whites ran for town and left the ranches to him. Sometimes he found ranches had been deserted for weeks because someone heard him coming. He did not like to steal that way. He liked to terrorize them, run them, catch them, bring them back, and clutch their goods while he was killing them.

The Apache, the wolf, the *leon pardo*, the cougar, liked to catch their prey in flight as much as they liked eating it. Long after the old *tigre*, the jaguar, lost his desire to eat and procreate, he lived on to kill. The Yawner was like that.

The rancher who lived on the Canelo ranch and his red-haired daughter had ridden out of sight toward El Durazno. This rancher would not go away for long and leave his woman and small children unprotected. He would probably soon be back. The fat white mother, another white woman, and two little girls were loading a wagon with provisions in front of the house. Two fleet-looking sorrel horses were harnessed and tied to a rail by the wagon. The first hour they were made to keep pace with Apaches would melt the tallow off these sleek horses, but their hearts would have to bear it.

The Yawner was waiting for Eligio and his brother to come back. Eligio and his brother were after the father and the red-haired girl to kill them for the brown horse and the buckskin they were riding. The Yawner was contented. The whites were loading the wagon with fat bundles for him to take.

"Yawner. Let's show ourselves now while the father is away," said Chato. He was always impatient.

"Show yourself, then, if you have to," said the Yawner.

"Don't you recognize that man who harnessed the sorrels?"

The Yawner looked at the man he would kill. "Isn't he the same man with the two arms and two legs and one head with the black hat we all know?"

"He looks like the one who raises pigs at *Puerto de Nogales*."

"You see that one everywhere we go."

"See his big rifle by the horses? I think that is the one he fired at us to protect his pigs," Chato said.

The Yawner showed a glimmer of his teeth in a straight line across the bottom of his face, almost like a smile. "Maybe it is," he said.

"Yes, it is."

"Maybe he still knows how to shoot it."

"If this is the man who shot us to protect his pigs, he knows how to shoot it."

"Maybe he can shoot it better now. That fat woman probably told him she would choke him if he did not protect her."

"Let's show ourselves, then, while the other man and the red-haired girl are away. Let Eligio and his brother have those horses. These and the bundles can be ours."

"I want Eligio to kill the father first. That white man has been here a long time. His kind puts up houses to make the women comfortable but live outside themselves and fight like *tigres*."

"You think he's a good fighter?"

"I know he is. I would be a fool if I thought he was a weakling. He won't make us a gift of his lives and his horses."

Two shots sounded together from the pasture. The shots were from different guns that were fired in the same instant. Then the Yawner and Chato heard a shout and two more shots.

"Eligio showed himself," said Chato.

The Yawner only grinned. The Mexicans had perversely nicknamed him *El Bostezador*, because he never opened his mouth. He yawned, smiled, and spoke with his jaws clenched. He often stretched his lips from side to side but almost never in good humor.

El Bostezador, the Yawner, sighted his rifle on the white man in front of the house. "Let's see," he said.

He took a deep breath, found the black hat, and squeezed the trigger as he brought the shiny bead of the sight down to the shirt. The round went off when the bead reached the fifth button, and the bullet pierced the man in midstride. The man plunged onto the hitchrail and flailed at the horses' heads as he collapsed. The sorrels fell away from the dying man and jerked the rail out of the ground. They whirled as the rail rattled and splintered, and the man clawed at their legs. They kicked the body free, stampeded out of the yard, and headed straight for the Yawner and Chato with the rail bounding between them.

"Catch them," said the Yawner. "I want them."

Chato turned and looked at him. They were good horses, but the Yawner must be getting old to "want" two stampeding horses so much he "wanted" somebody to get in front of them and be run over so he could have them. "Let them go," said Chato, running toward the house. "Who wants them like that?"

The Yawner watched the two pretty sorrels tear through a split-rail fence and across a pasture, trampling, smashing, and battering a swath with the rail. He looked back toward the house. The young son of Vinagroso was running through the open front door. The white father and the red-haired daughter were in sight, their horses running and stretching for the house.

The Yawner saw a flash of red fire through a front window caused by a large explosion in the house. Vinagroso's son sprinted out the door and hurdled the small neat fence in the woman's yard. The woman appeared at the door with a shotgun. She fired the second charge and shook the windows of the house again. The stuff that erupted with the second explosion did no harm to the boy. He kicked up his heels and laughed when the concussion smacked him from behind.

The red-haired girl's buckskin outran the father's brown horse to the house. The girl's hair was like a wing flowing behind her and was pulling the corners of her eyes back at the temples. She was pale, but her face was determined and unafraid. "Mother!" she shouted. She dismounted in the backyard without reining the buckskin to a stop. He was still sliding on his hind feet as she flew through the back door of the house.

Chato knelt and pointed his rifle at the spot where he expected the father to appear at the front corner of the house, but he did not take aim. The father came around fast, slid his horse to a stop, and sighted on the running son of Vinagroso. The boy would be in the open yet for half as far as a man could throw a rock. The father took aim without dismounting. Chato began shouting advice as the boy dove and ducked to reach cover. The boy instinctively let himself fall and flattened on the ground as the father fired the shot. The bullet missed him and tore into the ground beyond him. The horse whirled under the man before he could take another shot.

The Yawner raised his rifle and sighted quickly on horse and man. His bullet missed the man, but drilled through the saddle and struck the brown horse in the spine. The horse dropped. The man rolled clear and ran to the house with the Yawner's, Chato's, and Vinagroso's bullets fanning his ears and his rump.

The Yawner's grin showed only a thread of his teeth. "Missed," he said.

Chato had fired only one shot. The sight of the man shooting at the boy had entertained him. The Yawner knew Chato was jealous of Vinagroso. Chato had no sons. He enjoyed seeing Vinagroso's son as a target.

The boy ran to the Yawner. His sweaty face and healthy young smell showed he was happy in his games.

The fat mother was screaming in the house.

"How did she miss you inside her own house?" the Yawner asked the boy.

"Nooo." The boy was breathing hard. "She shot her little daughter. I was moving, and she didn't lead me enough. As I ran by the girl, she shot her in the face."

The Yawner's lips peeped open across his face. A new volume of fire made Chato jump up from his cover and run. The Yawner saw the smoke of weapons rising from behind a rock *trinchera*, a wall beyond the house.

"Mexicans," Chato yelled.

The Yawner saw he was in the range of sharpshooters.

"Shooters!" Chato said. "With .30's"

The Yawner turned away, picked up his reins, and mounted his horse. "Let's go. *Ya estuvo.* This is no good now."

Later, Vinagroso's son caught up to him after helping cover the retreat. "Where's Eligio?" the Yawner asked them.

"Running, or dead with his brother," said the boy. "The father could shoot."

"Go back and find them."

"Maybe they're both dead now."

"Take horses, so you can bring them if they're dead."

Mrs. Donovan was having another fit in Harshaw. She drank. Her hair was in her face, head thrown back, her dress wide open at the throat. She was in the middle of the street in front of the saloons, waving her arms and wailing like a banshee.

She was using the whole street. Betty and Paula Mary were trying to get home. They dodged her and hurried by to give her room but did not look at her. At the end of the street, Buff the bartender told them Mrs. Donovan had been saying she was going down the canyon to tell Mrs. Cowden her troubles.

At home, the girls told Viney about Mrs. Donovan, and she said, "If the poor woman comes here, I'll give her a cup of coffee and help her calm down."

Freddie Lee quietly took one of his papa's pistols and a chair out to the front gate to sit and wait for Mrs. Donovan. Viney followed him, took the pistol from him, saw it was not loaded, and handed it back.

"You wouldn't shoot the poor woman, would you, Freddie Lee?"

"Well, we don't dare take any chances, Mama," he said.

Freddie was still in his chair an hour later when two cowboys came by driving a small herd of steers. A. B. had taken a fresno and team, scraped up the bottom of the creek, and built a dam with a spillway so he would have a pond for irrigation.

Usually, when anyone stopped to water cattle at the pond, they were careful to keep them off the dam. Anyone could see it was soft. It was only used in the spring before the summer rains. The rains always washed it away, but it was not needed after the rains started. No one but the Cowdens depended on the creek for water.

Freddie was not surprised to see cowboys driving big steers toward the mining camps. The camps used a lot of beef. Besides Harshaw, there were big camps up the mountain at the Washington, Duquesne, and Mowry mines. He was surprised when the cowboys let the cattle mill on the dam and spillway. The cowboys kept looking toward the house and barn until they saw that Freddie was their only witness.

"Where's your daddy, boy?" asked one of the riders.

"My papa's gone to Tucson to take a murderer to jail. I think you better not let those steers tromp our dam anymore."

The other rider saw the pistol in Freddie's hand then. He put his hand on the handle of his own pistol and watched Freddie a long moment, speculating.

The rider who had spoken to Freddie laughed and said, "Get it off your mind, Ted, he's just a little boy."

"Maybe he's a little boy, but his finger's big enough to pull a trigger," said Ted.

"Forget it. He's watching for Indians, aren't you, boy?"

"I'm watching for Mrs. Donovan," said Freddie, but he was thinking he better leave the pistol in the house next time. In the face of the rider called Ted, he saw how people got themselves shot.

"Where's all the rest of the Cowden men?" the first rider called to Freddie.

"My brothers've been at Temporal, but they'll be home today."

The rider laughed and ran his horse at the cattle. The other cowboy charged from his side, and the heavy steers swelled over the dam. The water broke through their tracks and began washing the dam away.

Paula Mary came out and saw the pond was draining

and shouted for her mother. Viney came outside with Eileen and Betty, in time to watch the dam collapse in the current. Paula Mary saw her mother's face was set hard against her feelings. The riders turned their backs on the Cowden women and started the cattle up the canyon.

"Our brothers and our papa will be home today," Paula Mary called to them. They did not turn back and show their faces again. "Who are they, Mama?" she asked.

"I don't know, but I know who they work for," said Viney. "Those are VO steers."

"One of them is named Ted, Mama," said Freddie.

"Your papa will tend to them. That's the end of our garden, though, unless it rains."

"Papa and the boys can scrape the dam back up in one day, Mama," said Eileen.

"Yes, but it'll take two weeks for it to fill enough so we can irrigate. Our garden will dry up in that time."

"Don't worry, Mama; it'll probably rain early," said Eileen.

"Yeah, it'll probably rain," said Paula Mary. "If it doesn't, Mama, I'll carry water to your flowers."

Bill Knox, the blacksmith, came out of the barn and looked toward the house. Freddie Lee stood and laid the pistol down on the chair. Paula Mary headed for the barn to tell Bill what happened. Viney picked up the pistol.

"I'd hate to think what would happen to us if we didn't have Freddie and Bill Knox to look after us," Viney said.

Later, Viney called Paula Mary to the kitchen, handed her a small pail, and asked her to bring drinking water from the well. Paula Mary hurried to fill the pail. That was a lady's chore, not so much a labor. She came back, gave a small gasp, and heaved the full pail up to the counter. She wiped perspiration off her temples with the tips of her fingers the way she had seen her mother do. She hoped she could have this job and her mother would not ask her to carry water all the way up from the creek for the acre of flower beds.

Viney lowered her dipper carefully into the water, as though she did not want to disturb it, brought out a portion, and tasted it. She gave Paula Mary a serious look. "My, that's the best water I ever tasted, daughter. How did you ever find it? Did you put sugar in it?"

This made Paula Mary her mother's water carrier for life. "I'll get more, Mama," said she.

"Well, maybe you could find more of that best water for washing your papa's handkerchiefs," Viney said.

Paula Mary had long been assigned the office of laundering her father's handkerchiefs after he complained they smelled sour when they were boiled in the big wash. He paid her ten cents for each batch of clean handkerchiefs because he said her hands gave them a good smell.

Paula Mary was at the tub in the orchard scrubbing a handkerchief when she saw the Pendletons' spring wagon coming. Brooks and Joe, the sorrel team, looked sweaty and jaded. She waved to Maudy, but none of the Pendletons smiled when Maudy waved back. She ran to tell her mother and then ran with Freddie Lee to the barn to help the Pendletons unload.

Gordo Soto, Guilo's older brother who had taken his place at the stable, took hold of the team while Will and his family stepped down.

"Where's Carly?" asked Freddie Lee. Carly Pendleton was Freddie's age. Paula Mary could see the Pendletons were sad. Maudy hugged Freddie Lee and told him Carly was dead. Paula Mary looked for Carly in the spring wagon to see if it was really true and saw only Pearl, the other little sister. She saw some hair sticking out from a bundle and all of a sudden realized a dead man was lying in the back of the wagon, wrapped in a canvas tarp.

Will helped Mrs. Pendleton down from the wagon. She was carrying Carly's body wrapped in a blanket. Gordo put up the team, and the family went to the house. Maudy and Pearl walked to the orchard with Paula Mary to help her finish the wash. Maudy told her the Apaches raided the Canelo ranch and killed Carly and Wiley Kitchen. Mrs. Pendleton was taking Pearl and leaving the country.

"Where's your mama going?" asked Paula Mary.

"She has a homestead on the ocean in California," said Maudy. "She's been wanting to go back for a long time. Her brother and sister live there."

"Aren't you going too, Maudy?"

"No, I have to take care of Father and my brothers."

"Where were your brothers during the raid?"

"Ray was up on the Hard Luck with Herb Valenzuela gathering cattle. Pete was working his homestead."

"Did you see the Apaches, Maudy?"

"You bet I did. Father and I were riding when Father looked back and saw two Apaches. He fired at them, and they fired at us. They were afoot, and Father chased them to shoot them. I put Little Buck right in behind him and stayed with him. Then we heard shots at the house, and we hit for home.

"I jumped off and ran into the house, and the Apaches shot Big'un out from under father and he ran in. Mother was in a terrible state. I picked up the shotgun and charged it with powder and shot. Then Don Juan Pedro Elias and his vaqueros came and put the run on the Apaches and killed one with their rifles."

"What was Don Juan Pedro doing there?" asked Paula Mary.

"Don Juan Pedro was coming to take Mama and my little sisters home with him to stay while the Yawner was loose. That's why we bought Joe and Brooks from your Papa, so my Mama would have them in Mexico. Now she's going away on the train and taking Pearl, and I might not ever see her again."

"But you can go with her, can't you?"

"I don't want to go. I want to stay home."

The three girls began hanging A. B.'s handkerchiefs in a peach tree. "I want to stay in Arr-zona, but I have to go because I'm little and I don't know how to work hard like Maudy," Pearl said.

"Well, I think you ought to be able to stay if you want to, Pearl," said Paula Mary. "Let's go and ask if you can stay with us."

The girls trooped away to the kitchen. Paula Mary expected they would be given a collation of biscuits and milk. Viney, Betty, and Eileen were in the bedroom consoling Mrs. Pendleton, who looked as though she had taken a shotgun blast in the face herself.

"Why we ever chose this godforsaken country as a place to raise children is beyond me," Mrs. Pendleton was saying. Carly's body was still inside its blanket on Viney's bed.

Viney was combing Mrs. Pendleton's hair and putting it in place. Paula Mary had never seen Mrs. Pendleton when she did not have every hair in place and wearing a fresh outfit with her cameo pin on her breast.

Now, her voice was too high, too soft, and absolutely defeated. Her outfit was mussed, and she looked and sounded like a child.

"You need to get away now," soothed Viney. "I know how hard it's been for you to live so far away from your neighbors."

"We've had such bad luck," said Mrs. Pendleton. She put out her arms for Maudy and hugged her close. "I don't know what I'm going to do without this girl."

"Don't go, Mama," said Maudy in the same voice as her mother's. "I'll work harder. I'll do for everybody if you'll stay."

"I can't stay another minute. I just can't. I don't even know how I'll stay alive long enough to bury my child and get to the train with Pearl."

Maudy began crying so hard and so silently that Paula Mary was afraid she would suffocate. Her own eyes were filling with tears and her breast was aching; Freddie Lee was crying. Pearl laid her head in her mother's lap, and Paula Mary took Freddie outside.

They walked blindly away from the house, crying. They stumbled along until they subsided. Paula Mary felt a terrible hate for Apaches then.

"I ought to get a gun and kill that old Yawner," she said.

"You think it was old Yawner who killed Carly and Wiley?" asked Freddie.

"It's always old Yawner."

They looked toward the barn and saw A. B. climbing down from his buggy. They started running for the barn but stopped when they saw their three big brothers ride around a bend in the road, coming home.

"Now, we'll see about old Mr. Yawner," said Paula Mary.

"Yeah," said Freddie. "Old Mr. Yawner better look out now."

CHAPTER 11

Carly Pendleton and Wiley Kitchen were buried in Harshaw the next day, the Fourth of July 1885. A. B. Cowden moved his family into Harshaw with the Farleys. Many families were coming to the safety of the community to stay until Geronimo, the Yawner, and other bands of Apaches stopped raiding.

Every man in the country was armed. The Mexican colonel Bustamante was in town, his troop bivouacked under the cottonwoods by the cemetery. His officers were quartered in the hotel.

Duncan Vincent leased the top floor of the two-story Harshaw Hotel for his family. He was circulating in town complaining about "depradations." He was saying the Apaches were not the only ones committing them. The scrub cattle of certain "squatters" were using up precious grass and water that he needed for his purebred cattle. He complained that until these squatters were fenced inside legal boundaries, he would not be able to continue his work of bringing progress to the cattle industry of Arizona.

A patrol of the Fourth Cavalry was also in town. Ben went to a meeting in the town hall to hear the military reports on Geronimo. The townsmen complained a lot about the threat of Indians. Townsmen were about as threatened by Apaches as Ben and the other ranchers were threatened by train wrecks.

Ben listened awhile to the loud and strident voices in the meeting hall, then stepped outside for air. He watched the bivouac of American soldiers on the edge of town. The soldiers were staying by their fires, listening to the loud proclamations of the townsmen. The troopers' voices were so soft Ben could not hear what they were saying. They knew the value of a quiet voice on the frontier. They were staying in the shade, smoking their pipes and Mexican cigars and relaxing. Their horses were standing with their sleek, polished butts side-by-side on a picket line. The cavalry was always moving in the country, trying to keep the peace and never asking a favor. They were trying to learn more about their business all the time, and they rode good horses. That was the most a Cowden could say in any man's favor.

A man stepped up beside Ben while he was watching the soldiers. "Excuse me, Mr. Cowden, I'm Walter Jarboe, remember me?" He offered his hand. "From Kansas?"

Ben took the man's hand with embarrassment. He had promised Jarboe his help and then forgotten him. "Nice to see you, sir."

"Well, you sure aren't hard to find when you come to town," said Jarboe. "Everybody seems to know the minute you ride in."

"Did anyone tell you where to find Kosterlinsky?"

"I hoped he'd be here at the meeting."

"No, if I know him, he's gambling in one of the saloons, laid up in a crib, or trying to match a horserace."

"Well, I'm sure he'll turn up sooner or later. Then maybe I'll have the privilege of meeting him."

"Mr. Jarboe, if we wait for him to turn up, we'll miss him again. Let's unearth the sonofagun."

"I don't want to take you away from your meeting. You might miss something important."

"When that bunch in there is talking, they're not doing, Mr. Jarboe. When they're not doing, they're not important. Let's go find Kosterlinsky."

Ben took Jarboe over to Vince Farley's Shamrock Saloon. Mark and Les were sitting in a corner with their hats cocked on the sides of their heads, drinking beer with their uncle Vince. Ben surprised them. His brothers were not used to him showing up in bars. They always hit for the Shamrock the first minute they were free in town. They had never been carried out of any bar, but when they were in town, they made themselves available for any game in the saloons and had fun until time to feed the horses.

A bargirl glided off Les's lap with great instinct for self-preservation when she saw Ben's hat appear over the top of the swinging door. Ben caught her straightening up as she coasted away from his brother without looking back. Her departure brought a mean glint to Les's eye, but it faded when he saw the intruder was his brother. Mark laughed softly.

"As Paula Mary would say, 'my, my,'" said Les. "I almost got caught with a hand on the brown-sugar *panocha*."

"Is that beer cool?" Ben asked. He introduced Jarboe to his brothers, asked for another pitcher of beer, and sat down with them. He could see Jarboe would nurse one glass of beer for as long as he sat there.

"Mr. Jarboe's looking for Kosterlinsky," Ben said.

"He's right next door in the Glass Slipper." Les pointed his forefinger and dropped his thumb on it like the hammer of a six-shooter. "Breaking the bank."

Mark and Les listened politely while Ben explained Jarboe's problem to them. The Cowdens knew Kosterlinsky well and were sure he was not planning to give Mr. Jarboe his money back, or his cattle. Mark and Les believed Jarboe's money was lost. Ben believed Kosterlinsky should be made to deliver the cattle. The country needed cattle buyers who would come back every year, and it did not need Kosterlinsky.

"We're gong to help Mr. Jarboe get his cattle," Ben said.

"Now, that'll be the day," said Vince Farley. He left the table to bring a pitcher of beer.

"Mr. Jarboe and I will go talk to Mr. Kosterlinsky," Ben said. "You fellers come over in ten minutes, and we'll see how much of his winnings he wants to put into cattle for Mr. Jarboe."

"He has been winning," said Les. "He's undoubtedly in a generous mood."

Lt. Gabriel Kosterlinsky was in a corner with his back to the wall, playing baccarat. His stack of blue chips looked tall enough to finance the Mexican army's campaign against Geronimo. A band of musicians was standing over him playing a *diana*, the short song of accolade for a wager he had won. A saloon-girl was draped across him with her head on his breast and a lush pout on her lips. A brand-new cigar was clamped in his golden molars. His hair was in his eyes, and his campaign hat was on the back of his head. All the music and most of the laughter, theater, smoke, and roar of the joint was happening in Kosterlinsky's corner. He reared back and let out a joyful yell when he saw Ben.

"*Benjamin, mi amigo*," he shouted. "*Cueva de vaca.* Cow Den. Come *here*, my friend."

Jarboe's feet began to falter at his first sight of the man he was begging to see.

"Come *on*," shouted Kosterlinsky. "Have a drink with me."

The man was sleek in starched khakis. His olive face was shiny with good humor because he was winning at cards. Ben shook his hand and submitted to an *abrazo*, the Mexican's formal embrace of greeting with slaps on the back. Kosterlinsky was a pirate, but he was always friendly with Ben.

"What brings you here to see me, Benjamin?" Kosterlinsky asked.

"See this man, Gabriel?" Ben pointed to Jarboe.

"Yes?" Kosterlinsky shook Jarboe's hand and turned back to Ben without letting it go.

"His name is Walter Jarboe, and he wants to talk to you."

"But I am *winning*," Kosterlinsky said. He stuck out his chest and grinned, his cigar jutting. "Come back when I'm no longer *winning*."

Ben handed the musicians a $10 chip from Kosterlinsky's stack. They broke ranks and walked away.

"Wait, what have you done? Don't send away my music."

Ben handed a $10 chip to the girl. She resumed her

workaday face and faded away from the table. Kosterlinsky made a grab for her, but she gave him only an impersonal smile and slipped by.

"My girl," Kosterlinsky said, sorrowfully. He watched her walk away. "*Adios, Chulita*, you *little cutie*," he called.

The dealer put away his box of cards, ceremoniously spread his hands over the table, clapped them, and backed away. Ben handed him a blue chip.

"My *cards*," said Kosterlinsky. "My lucky *dealer*."

Ben swept all the chips into his hat and headed toward the cashier's cage.

"My *money*," said Kosterlinsky, hurrying to catch up. "All right, *cueva de vaca*, I'm at your service. Take me where you will."

Ben unloaded the chips at the cage and asked the cashier to bring the money to a corner table.

"What are you doing to me, Ben?" asked Kosterlinsky when Ben sat down at the table. "I was *winning*."

Ben motioned for Kosterlinsky and Jarboe to sit with him.

"I know you want to get back to your fun, Gabriel," said Ben. "But you owe this man a thousand steers. He's been waiting a year to hear from you. He's come a long way, and he can't wait any longer."

"And how could I owe anyone a thousand steers?" asked Kosterlinsky. "I am not in the *cattle* business. I am in the business of hunting *Apaches*. In the business of hanging *Yaquis*. I don't know the business of one thousand steers or even two cows."

Jarboe took out a contract, unfolded it, laid it on the table, and showed the last page to Kosterlinsky. "Is that your signature, Mr. Kosterlinsky?" he asked.

Kosterlinsky looked at the signature, an elaborate, arty, and complicated mark composed of twirling lines and pickets, dots, and whorls. He picked up the contract and scanned each page. He lifted it delicately before him and let it drop off his fingertips to the table when he was through with it.

"That's the contract you signed with Mr. Jarboe's representative. His name was Pete Rosser. Do you remember him?" asked Ben.

"Pete Rosser, Pete Rosser," said Kosterlinsky.

"Don't stall and don't lie, Gabriel."

"All right. I remember signing the contract, though I would not remember for anyone but you. After all, why should I lie? It would not change anything. I don't have one thousand cattle."

"Then tell Mr. Jarboe how you plan to deliver the cattle."

"How, Ben, how? Tell me, because I want to know. These are phantom cattle you are looking for."

"All right, I'll tell you. You contact Juan Pedro Elias who is a good, honest cattleman and give him the money Mr. Rosser gave you and he'll round up one thousand head of Maria Macarena steers for you. Mr. Jarboe and I will go down to the ranch to receive the cattle, and you will *complir* and become sufficient to that millionaire's signature you left on this contract.

"After that, Mr. Jarboe and I will come down every year and buy cattle from you. Gabriel Kosterlinsky's brand will be known all the way to Kansas, and he will be known as a man of his word."

"I am already a man of my word. I am an honorable man, Benjamin."

"I expected you to say that. I believe you are a good man in your own way."

"But I don't have the money Señor Rosser gave me. I did not spend Mr. Jarboe's money, and I don't have one heads of the cattle."

"Ah. Where are they?"

"El Señor Vincent owes me for them."

"You sold the cattle to Duncan Vincent?"

Kosterlinsky began speaking slowly and loudly, as though Jarboe was dim-witted and deaf. "Señor Rosser, he no come. You, Señor Jarboe, you no come. Months and months going by. Señor Vincent, he come. He offer to see what he can do with cattle. He take that thousand. He sell and come back with the moneys. I buy more, and he sell that and—"

"So you've been using Mr. Jarboe's money to finance steers for Vincent."

"No, Ben. Vincent no come back for months. Three,

four months ago he take seventeen hundred heads, and he no come back. He *hide* from Kosterlinsky. I send my sergeant with a squad of soldiers to his ranch. No find Vincent. I'm still look for him. Imagine it yourself, if you can."

"Imagine this, Gabriel. Vincent is here in town."

"No, how fortunate." Kosterlinsky looked out the window and swallowed.

"You're lucky. We're all here in town today, Gabriel," said Ben. "We'll help you corner Vincent and settle this for Mr. Jarboe."

Les and Mark came to the table and Ben put a brother on each side of Kosterlinsky and trooped him over to the hotel. Vincent was sitting in a corner of the lobby with John McClintock and Jack Akin, two more cattle barons who represented companies that were turning out herds of big steers on public land.

"Well, well, well—Ben Cowden," said McClintock. He was likable and good-natured, but he was too big a glutton for grass to suit Ben. The man spent a lot of time horseback, though. A man could not be the kind of husbandman he was and be a bad man. He ran thousands of native steers that he bought from smaller cattlemen like the Cowdens, so he was a good neighbor and easy to deal with.

Akin was more like Vincent, but smarter. He was seldom in the country and was not interested in being accepted socially. He kept an office staff in Tucson, making title searches and buying deeded land. He was using that private land as bases for his cow camps on the edge of public land.

Akin's word was good and he was honest, but he was greedy and ill-tempered. He paid for everything he took and did not try to steal, but he never helped a neighbor or paid a bonus in gratitude to a man who worked for him. He had done the country one good turn. He turned a hundred good Durham bulls out on the open range, and his neighbors' native cows were giving birth to beefy red-roan calves.

McClintock and Akin both stood up and shook Ben's hand.

"We were talking about you, Cowden," said Vincent.

He did not stand up for anybody. He kept his rump in his easy chair and puffed on a cigar. He was trying to smile and keep his poise, but he did not like McClintock and Akin being cordial to Ben and liked it even less that Ben did not offer to shake his hand.

"Imagine this," said Ben. "I came over here looking for Vincent the Hereford, and I found the Durham and the *corriente*, the native, too."

"What brings you here, Ben?" asked McClintock. "You look full of business. Let me order drinks. You and your brothers and Lieutenant Kosterlinsky sit yourselves down."

Les and Mark escorted Kosterlinsky to a chair, saw him seated, and left the room.

"I was about to propose a drink, myself," Ben said.

"What is it you want here, Cowden?" asked Vincent. "I don't think I have time to sit in on this. My family is waiting for me."

"This won't take long, Mr. Vincent. Mr. Jarboe has come to us for help. I guess you know Mr. Jarboe."

"Yes, he's been here several days," said McClintock. "I understand he's been trying to bring us some business."

"Mr. Vincent, do you know the reason Mr. Jarboe is here?" Ben asked.

Vincent was not looking anybody in the eye. "I think so, but I'm not quite sure I understand it all."

"Well, I'll be glad to explain it to you," said Ben. "You've been using Mr. Jarboe's money to buy and sell steers. Lieutenant Kosterlinsky and Mr. Jarboe are here to settle that account with you. I don't know much about Lieutenant Kosterlinsky's business with you, but I know Mr. Jarboe wants his steers."

Jarboe spoke up. "I'm surprised, Mr. Vincent, that you never mentioned your part in this deal to me. I've spent hours talking to you here in this lobby."

"How do you figure in this, Cowden?" asked Vincent. "I made a deal with Kosterlinsky. I didn't know he was selling me cattle that belonged to somebody else. I do know I didn't make my deal with any squatter, so I don't see what you have to do with this. I've been paying Kosterlinsky for the cattle I got from him."

"Is that right, Gabriel?" Ben turned to the Mexican.

Kosterlinsky chewed up the last of his cigar and threw it out the front door of the hotel. He was pale. "I let the man take the cattle. The man sells the cattle, buys more. Sells those cattle, buys more . . . then never comes back. I've been searching for the man." He waved at Vincent. "Hello, man," he said.

"All right, here I am," said Vincent. "We can settle this as soon as Cowden leaves the room. I don't deal with squatters."

"Mr. Cowden will be assisting me until this matter is settled," Jarboe said.

"I'm here to settle some accounts with you, myself," Ben said.

"I don't really want to discuss business with you, Cowden. I'm sure Mr. Jarboe and I can come to terms without you," Vincent said.

"Mr. Jarboe asked me to help him. He's been in the country weeks, and he's asked a lot of other people to help him, including you. He only found out today that you're the one who's been using his money."

"I don't see what the problem is. If Kosterlinsky owes Jarboe for cattle, he'd better pay."

"Mr. Vincent, you have the man's money, not me," Kosterlinsky said.

"You mean for the last bunch of cattle I bought from you?"

"You have all the money. I haven't seen it since you drove away the seventeen hundred heads."

"You and I agreed I did not have to pay until the cattle were sold. That last bunch has not been sold. I paid you for the two bunches, and they're long gone. This last seventeen hundred that you let me take on the credit are still on my ranch."

"When will you be selling them?" asked Ben.

"I have to see," said Vincent. "I was discussing the matter with these two gentlemen when you barged in, but I want to tell you, I'm not prepared to sell. I still have plenty of grass in my country. Those cattle will continue to grow and make money for some time."

"Your country, Mr. Vincent? Your grass?"

"What's your point, Cowden? I don't see how anybody

can tell me how I ought to run my steers on my own ranch."

"That brings us to the reason I'm here putting myself in the big middle of this, Mr. Vincent. You're running seventeen hundred steers that don't belong to you, along with at least three thousand more that do, on grass that doesn't belong to you."

"I own the country where those steers are running."

"You lay claim to ten times more country than you hold deeds to. You are still in contention over those deeds. You bribe your cronies in Washington to get patents, but they haven't been able to come up with the legal papers you need to prove you own all the land you're claiming."

"I have deeds to two hundred thousand acres and have a right to put cattle out on the public land that borders me, the same as everybody else."

"You have a deed to twenty thousand acres, and part of that is in Mexico. My father and I looked up your titles at the recorder's office. You have no right to run more cattle than your neighbors. We've been shipping all our male cattle to keep good range for our cows. You and Mr. Akin and Mr. McClintock have been bringing in thousands of steers from outside to clean up the grass we're trying to save for our cows."

"Until you take me to court and prove I'm doing anything illegal, I'm afraid you and all the rest of the squatters will just have to hump up and take it."

"We might not be able to do anything about the three thousand steers that belong to you without drawing your blood, but we can do something about the steers that belong to Mr. Jarboe. I believe the seventeen hundred are branded with Kosterlinsky's KY."

"Yes, you said it, they're wearing Kosterlinsky's brand. I don't see how that establishes ownership for Jarboe. I'm the agent for the cattle, and I'll do anything I want with them. As far as I'm concerned, Jarboe hasn't any right to interfere, and neither do you."

"You are mistaken, sir," said Walter Jarboe. "The KY brand is registered in Sonora to Kosterlinsky, Jarboe, and Moore. The brand is registered in Arizona only to Jarboe and Moore. You've been selling our cattle and keeping the money; there's no other way to describe your operation.

"However, you've managed the money well. Our original herd of one thousand has apparently grown into seventeen hundred. We'll settle for immediate delivery of seventeen hundred KY cattle to avoid litigation."

"Litigate with my brother, who is my lawyer. His name is Royal Vincent, and his office is in Tucson," said Vincent. "I'm sure your assistant, Cowden here, can tell you how to find him."

"Well, Mr. Vincent, I'm a lawyer myself," said Jarboe. "And I happen to be carrying all the legal documents I need to take immediate possession of my company's cattle. I already have federal authorization to search the territory and take possession of my property, wherever it may be."

"May I see the documents?" asked Vincent.

Jarboe handed Vincent the proof of his authority. Ben was astounded. For weeks, Jarboe had seemed to be a meek little greenhorn, begging to talk to an elusive Mexican who had stolen his money. All that time he had been holding the cards that gave him the power to take back his money and put the thieves in jail without any help at all.

Vincent put on his eyeglasses and examined Jarboe's credentials, then examined them again. Finally he put away his glasses, looked up, and handed back the documents. "Who is going to pay me for the pasture, time, and money I've put into these cattle?" Vincent asked. "I conditioned more than four thousand KY cattle for market this past year."

"How many times have you bought and sold cattle with our money and made a profit?" Jarboe said. "We might investigate that and find you owe us more than seventeen hundred. If you haven't paid yourself for feed and care while you've been handling the money, I have no idea who will pay you. You'll have to deal with Mr. Kosterlinsky. He is the one with whom you were conniving. When can I expect delivery of these cattle?"

"I don't know," said Vincent. He looked into Jarboe's eyes now because he wanted mercy. "My crew is busy. I'll have to ask my foreman when he can help you."

"Oh, well then, if you can't get to it, I'll hire my own crew."

"I don't want a foreign crew on my range."

"Mr. Vincent, you read those documents well. You saw that I carry the office of United States Marshal empowered to recover this property. I will deputize my crew and gather the cattle."

"You'll stay off my property."

"The titles to your property are in dispute and have not been established. We'll probably stay on public land. I doubt we'll ever be on your land at all."

"I've surveyed my land, and I'm in the process of fencing it."

"Now, that's another of your sins I want to talk to you about," Ben said. "You will not fence the American Boy and the Temporal range. The private land up there belongs to the Pendletons, the Cowdens, and the Englishman Sparks. We have clear titles to it."

"I have a deed, and I'm fencing it," Vincent said.

"Bring an army that's ready to die."

"I'll have the firepower and the law in my favor."

"You'll be as much a target as your army, law or no law."

"Wait a minute, gentlemen. Let's get back to the KY cattle for a moment. There is a way I can take delivery without further dispute," said Jarboe.

"And how will that be?" asked Vincent.

"I can wait until the next roundup, when everybody comes together to work the country."

"We haven't planned to hold a roundup until the fall," said Ben. "We've held off this spring because we wanted some moisture to start the green feed and strengthen the stock."

"Fine," said Jarboe. "We'll do that. We won't be putting Mr. Vincent out, and I won't have to hire an extra crew."

"Let's hold our roundup in September," said Mc-Clintock. "I've sold my steers to Mr. Jarboe, too."

"September it is." Ben stood up and shook hands with McClintock and Akin. Akin was not friendly.

"I haven't said anything about it, but I have to tell you, I think you're being awful high-handed, Ben," Akin said.

"Jack, you don't know what high-handed is until you've tried to neighbor with Duncan Vincent," Ben said.

Akin turned away to talk to Vincent. Jarboe was talking

to McClintock, having his own way now and doing business.

Ben and Kosterlinsky shook hands, and Kosterlinsky headed for the hotel bar. Ben walked out to the hotel's veranda. His brothers were sitting in rockers, chewing on toothpicks, removed from all contention. They were wearing new black hats. All three brothers liked black hats. Their everyday hats were black, and their dress hats were the same, only newer.

Ben smiled at his brothers. How could a banker, a cow buyer, or a cattle baron like those four bigshots in the lobby take the Cowden brothers seriously? Only workingmen wore black hats. Businessmen, lawyers, capitalists, the men who made the big deals in the front offices, wore silverbelly hats.

Les and Mark were relaxed and indolent as colts lying in the sun. They had no more interest in business than Ben did in the Bessemer process, and that was the way life should be. Cowdens should only worry about how to keep their livestock fat and their horses shiny. Instead of that, Ben's stomach was burning from contention with people like Vincent, Kosterlinsky, McClintock, Akin . . . and Jarboe.

He realized he could have turned Jarboe loose on his own, and everything would have come out a lot better. He would not have made a worse enemy of Vincent, and his stomach would not be hurting him. He should have gone with his brothers to dinner and then to a chair on the veranda to whittle, chew on a toothpick, and watch the people go by.

"All through with Kosterlinsky?" asked Les.

"All through," said Ben.

"Did Mr. Jarboe get what he came for?"

"He got double what he came for."

"You get what *you* came for?"

"Damned right."

"I didn't get but a little bit of what I came to town for. Did you, Marky?"

Mark smiled, shook his head, and kept his eyes on a sliver he was whittling.

"We want a little more beer, but before that, we want to go walking with those girls from Kansas," said Les.

"I thought the Kansas girls intended to marry the Briggs brothers," Ben said. "You ought not to be sparking them."

"Anybody can spark them, now that the Briggses are jailbirds. The girls hired out waiting tables here in the hotel dining room. Me and Marky just came from there."

"My, my, you fellers sure work fast when you're not being supervised," Ben said.

Mark was watching somebody come up the front stairs of the hotel. He said, "You know, brothers, it doesn't look like we'll go sparking today."

Hoozy, Whitey Briggs, and Dick Martin stepped up to the veranda and grinned at the Cowdens.

The sight of them drained all the blood out of Les's face. Mark resumed his whittling.

"I thought you fellers would be on the way to the penitentiary by now," Ben said to Hoozy Briggs.

"Hell, Ben, we almost beat your daddy back to Harshaw," said Whitey.

"Your daddy didn't take along any evidence to use against us," said Hoozy. "Our uncle Malcolm Briggs is a *lawyer*, didn't you know that? Your daddy had no more than walked out the courthouse door when our uncle Malcolm traipsed us by the judge and out another door. Your daddy probably thinks we're still in jail waiting for a hearing."

"Well, congratulations. You probably think you got away with murder," Ben said.

Whitey walked up, stood over Ben, and pointed his finger at him. "We're not going to the pen; we're going to get even, hotshot."

Les stomped both feet on the floor and started out of his chair as though he would hit Whitey. Whitey and Hoozy both sprang away from him, ready to flee. "Get your finger out of my brother's face, Whitey," Les said.

"That's OK," said Hoozy, holding up his hands and showing the palms. "Everything's OK. Whitey had to shuffle ten miles, and I got stomped, and you knocked all the snot out of Dick, but it's OK. It's all over now. We're only here to have a few drinks and a nice dinner in the hotel."

"Yeah, you know how it is. We have to celebrate a little," said Whitey.

"Besides, your daddy would not like you starting trouble with us again. That would only add to your mama's heartache," said Hoozy.

"Whose heartache?" asked Les quietly.

"Hasn't anybody told you? I guess not." The Briggs brothers walked on through the door into the lobby. Martin followed, but turned back at the door.

"Yeah, Ben, you do have your, er, troubles, now." Martin flushed when he heard his own voice telling off Ben Cowden.

"You're not one of my troubles, are you, Dick?" asked Ben kindly.

"N-n-no. But the high sheriff in Tucson is. He's issued a w-w-warrant for your arrest. So, you ain't so s-s-smart after all."

CHAPTER 12

As Hoozy Briggs passed Duncan Vincent in the lobby of the hotel, the great man saluted him with a finger over his brow. That made Hoozy glow. He was still beaming when he took a table in the dining room with Whitey and Dick.

Hoozy was not surprised when Vincent stopped by the table later. "Well, Messers Briggs, and you too, Mr., uh, Martin, I'm glad you're back," Vincent said. "We all heard you'd been arrested by old Cowden. I must say I'm glad to see our legal system is working. I've been wondering when someone would show everybody our undersheriff is an incompetent fool."

"You're calling that right, Mr. Vincent," said Hoozy.

"As I understand it, he arrested all three of you for the murder of a Mexican that worked for him."

"A man's accuser better have evidence," said Hoozy. "We proved that. We weren't guilty."

"That's what I thought," said Vincent. "I'm glad you're back. Listen, Mr. Briggs, as soon as you can spare a few minutes, I'd like to talk to you about your mine."

Ann Burr, one of the Kansas girls, was passing by the table, and Hoozy motioned for her to stop and wait on him. He wanted her to know how grand a man he was.

"Why, sure, Mr. Vincent, anytime." said Hoozy. "We're about to have our dinner. Let me order you a drink."

"No, I still have business with Mr. McClintock and Mr. Akin. I'd like to meet with you as soon as possible, though. Listen, when you're finished with your dinner, come up to Room one-twenty-eight. That's my office. I'll give you a good cigar."

"I'll be honored to smoke a cigar with you, Mr. Vincent. I believe you'll find we have much in common."

"I'm sure." Vincent moved away toward the lobby.

Hoozy sat back, pushed the menu away, and gave Ann Burr his order for dinner. "Tell that cook to hurry up. I have business with Duncan Vincent," he added.

Hoozy ate his dinner and hurried upstairs. The door to Room 128 was open. Vincent was writing at his desk with his head down. Hoozy knocked, and Vincent put his pen into the inkwell, stood up, and motioned to a chair.

"Let's talk about the mining business, first," Vincent said. "What I have to say might be a bit distasteful, but nevertheless I want to straighten out a problem I'm having. How legal is your claim to the mine you call The Squeezings?"

Hoozy was as wide-eyed and alert for business as he would ever be in his life. This might be his chance to get ahead. "How legal? Sir, it's as legal as any claim can be."

"What I mean is, have you filed for the title?"

"Oh, yes. I've been working that mine for a year and a half."

Vincent looked down at the pages in front of him. He penciled a number on a page, smiling. He sobered and looked up. "You haven't taken out much real silver, have you?"

"Oh, yes, I've taken out quite a lot of silver."

"No, I think most of the silver you've realized from that mine has been in coin you've taken from California investors provided by the lawyer Malcolm Briggs. You and he have been running a confidence game."

All of a sudden Hoozy's neck was hot. He had never even admitted to himself that he and his uncle Malcolm were running a confidence game on The Squeezings. How could Vincent know anything about it? Hoozy had not taken fifty cents worth of silver out of that mine. He received money regularly from Malcolm because he was supposed to be working the mine, but he had not brought out a shovelful of ore.

"Our investors believe in us, Mr. Vincent."

"Well, I don't really care how many poor city folks you're bilking. They can probably afford it. However, I can't afford to be bilked and won't stand for it."

"Sir, we have no intention of asking you to invest in our mine. What made you think we did?"

"No one asked me to invest in your worthless little salt mine, but the thing is in the middle of my range. You don't own it, and you're using water that belongs to me, and I want that to stop."

Hoozy was thinking his fortunes sure could turn sour in a hurry. He had been hoping Vincent would ask him for advice on mining or hire him as a ranger for the Cattleman's Association. Instead, he was being accused of stealing water. He said, "Well . . . I . . . I'm pretty sure our claim is legal. I'll have to ask Uncle Malcolm to look into this."

"It's not legal, and there's not a thing you can do to make it legal, Briggs. When can you get off my range? That's all I want to know."

Hoozy could not answer. Every single time he had reason to hope he was taking a new step toward success, something like this happened.

"Look, Briggs, I don't care it you're working a confidence game, but why did you have to do it on my land? Didn't you know it might sooner or later involve me? No, I can see you didn't think about that. I suspect the one who's been running the game is that lawyer uncle of yours. Isn't that right? I always thought you were a sensible, hardworking young man."

Hoozy quickly put on his workingman's face. "I'll swear, Mr. Vincent, I've been waiting for my uncle Malcolm to provide the money so I can work that mine."

"How much money are you talking about, a hundred dollars?"

"Thousands, Mr. Vincent." Hoozy was ready to bare the truth. "Let me tell you, my uncle Malcolm doesn't deal in hundreds. In his business he deals in tens of thousands of dollars. Someone made a bad mistake in his calculations is about all I can say to you without looking at the records and the documents available at this time."

"Fiddle-faddle. Don't con me. I'm wise to every con ever invented by four-flushers like you. That mine's salted. However, that's not the reason I asked you here. I like your audacity and your opportunism. How would you like to work for me?"

Hoozy could stand setbacks. He could never stand sudden favorable changes in his fortunes. It always made him talk big. "What makes you think you can afford me?" he said.

"If that's your attitude, I might not be able to. You might think you're so smart that nobody can afford you. Maybe if I let you hang, you'll realize how much you're worth. Believe me, I can find you a gallows if you prefer hanging by your neck to working for me. You are only free today because of a telegram I sent to certain lawmen in Tucson."

Hoozy looked at Vincent's cigar box and decided he would try to keep his mouth shut.

Vincent continued. "The job I have in mind for you, as an alternative to jail, is very simple and probably one you'll enjoy."

Hoozy was hopeful again.

"All I want you to do, plainly and simply, is to keep those Cowdens occupied. I don't want to know how you do it, but I want those Cowdens, Porters, and Pendletons kept so distracted and riding so hard, they won't have time to interfere with my work."

Hoozy figured he must be sufficient to the task if Mr. Vincent thought he was.

Vincent went on. "My banker will send you a periodic check for cleaning up The Squeezings mine. That will be a steady wage you can depend on. He'll send you a bonus whenever I hear of special mischief you've done the Cowdens, or any of the squatters for that matter. However, I want full title to your mine. That means you must relinquish your claim to that holding."

"How can I do that without asking my uncle Malcolm?"

"Just sign your name to this quitclaim." Vincent took the

document from a basket on his desk and handed it over with pen and ink.

Hoozy signed it. "My Uncle Malcolm is not going to like this, but I guess I can handle him," he said.

"Malcolm Briggs, you say? Your uncle Malcolm Briggs is also being retained by my company at this time."

"Pardon me, Mr. Vincent, but I'd like you to make it clear what kind of mischief you want."

"Listen, Briggs, I leave the mischief to you. I gather you've been pestering people all your life. I'm sure you're imaginative and clever enough to damage property and stock, to keep from being caught, and to leave me out of it if you are. For this you will be well paid."

"How much will I be paid?"

"Never question my generosity. I won't question what you do, either. I pay well for good work."

"What's to keep old Cowden from shackling me again and shuffling me off to jail?"

"Later on I'll see about making you a constable and ranger for the Cattleman's Association. That will legalize your work."

"The Cowdens have every local lawman and judge on their side," said Hoozy. "Old A. B. is the law here, not your constables. The only law you can buy is seventy miles away."

"We own Cowden's boss. Enough of that," said Vincent. He took a fresh cigar out of the box on his desk and carved off the end with a small penknife.

Hoozy remembered he'd been promised a cigar when he was being wooed to this office, but the great man didn't seem to have any recollection of that now.

"Mr. Vincent, I have an idea," said Hoozy. "If I can start today, I know what I can do first."

"Don't tell me about it," said Vincent. "I don't want to know. I want to talk about something else now. I understand your sister is sweet on Ben Cowden and vice versa. What kind of problems will that cause? I don't want you changing sides on me if you become Ben Cowden's brother-in-law. What'll your sister say about the mischief you do if she finds out about it?"

"My sister takes care of herself in the same way Whitey

and I do. She's a good-looking girl, out for what she can get, and she's tougher in the way she uses her looks than I am with a gun."

"What if she gets a hold on Ben Cowden's affections? Will she help us?"

"I don't know if she'll help us, but she'll put an end to him. She's so full of poison, the day he starts caring for her is the day he might as well curl his toes and give up the ghost."

After the noon dinner at the Farleys', Ben went out to sit in the shade and smoke his pipe. Paula Mary followed him and climbed into his lap.

"Don't you help Mrs. Farley?" Ben asked her, annoyed by her, even though she was making him smile with her puffy breaths. "You smell like a puppy dog."

"Well, you smell like a javelina," Paula Mary said.

"Do I smell that bad?"

"No, but don't you think you ought to bathe and shave your whiskers before you go sparking Lorrie Briggs this evening?"

"And what makes you think I'll be sparking Lorrie Briggs?"

"I saw her this morning, and she said for you to come see her."

"Oh, she did, did she?"

"Yes, she's going to *pasear* around the pavilion with the Burr girls when they get off work. She told me she'd be expecting you to come walk with her."

"Oh, and I suppose you told her I'd be there."

"Huh! I'm not in the habit of telling anybody where my brothers will be during *paseo*. My brothers are liable to be out chasing Geronimo, or venting a VO cowboy, or visiting those nice Campana girls down in Santa Cruz."

Ben laughed. "Paula Mary, you're stuck-up. Why didn't you tell her you'd give me the message?"

"Huh! I don't tell nobody nothin. They can wish, hope, and guess before I'll tell them anything. They have to know me awful darned good to get any help from me. Anyway, I don't know if I approve of Lorrie Briggs."

"Well, why not?"

"Don't you know what she does?"

"No, what does she do?"

"Papa says she's from people who make biscuits in the morning before they wash their hands."

"Papa said that?"

"He did."

Ben knew his father did not approve of Lorrie, but he always thought that was because of her brothers' behavior. Now he learned A. B. did not like the stock. A. B. was a southerner, and he had unfathomable criteria for the stock his sons and daughters should marry.

Ben put Paula Mary down and went to talk to his father. He found him with Viney on the Farleys' veranda, watching the people go by. Ben pulled up a chair and sat beside his parents.

He listened to their talk about the dryness of the year. They did not imagine how he felt about Lorrie because they never went against their principles. They were as opposed to a marriage between Ben and Lorrie as they were against drought, disease, straying animals, bad language, barbwire, preaching, actions governed by emotion, and elopement or any other kind of unauthorized mating.

"Papa, I need to know why you don't like Lorrie Briggs," said Ben.

A. B. did not hesitate. He said, "Son, I like Lorrie Briggs, but I'm concerned you might choose her for a wife."

"Why shouldn't I, Papa?"

"She is not from the same stock you are. You know her brothers. They are dishonest, and bent on becoming outlaws. They have an uncle in Tucson who is as well educated and acts as highborn as any duke of the ruling class, and he is as crooked as a dog's hind leg."

"Is there any other reason you wouldn't like to have her for a daughter?"

Viney stopped mending socks and looked straight into Ben's eyes to show she agreed with A. B.

"The reason I gave is reason enough. Stock inherits its disposition, conformation, nature, and temperament. Your girl's brothers and her uncle are all untrustworthy. Her sweet, fun-loving front makes me believe she's devious.

Deviousness would be prevalent in the females of that stock."

A. B. was compassionate and no bigot. He treated all men with reserve and courtesy, even when they had broken the law. He never defamed another man or professed hatred for another man.

Certain words were as forbidden as blasphemies and obscenities in the Cowden household. Among these were the expletives used in a common manner in streets and corrals that denigrated people because of their race. Ben had grown up with a fear of even thinking those words. Woe to the Cowden or Porter child who made fun of a Pole, Irishman, German, Jew, or Negro by calling him a name that insulted his race, religion, or nationality. A. B. said most people came to the frontier to work hard and raise families. Nobody was better than anybody else. The Cowden children learned most of their manners by watching their parents and were seldom lectured on how they should treat other people. A. B. never called Sam Porter, a black man who came to Arizona with the Porters, a colored man. He called him Sam Porter.

Ben knew his father was against Lorrie because he was suspicious of her as a person. He knew this because A. B. said so. A. B. could never say anything worse about a stock of people than they made biscuits in the morning before they washed their hands.

"Are you against me courting Lorrie, Papa?" asked Ben.

"You can do as you please, son," said A. B. "However, you and this girl are not a good match for each other."

"I wanted to invite her to the Farleys' for supper this evening. I like her, and she has no friends. I already mentioned that I wanted her to meet you."

"Do as you like, son," A. B. said.

"Ask the girl to supper this evening, if you want to, but we don't want you getting serious about her, son," said Viney.

"If you'll be nice to her and make her feel at home, I will ask her," Ben said. "If you don't like her, I'll break it off."

"We'd like to meet her, son," said A. B.

After the supper with his family, Ben walked Lorrie to the *paseo* at the pavilion. The *paseo* was an evening promenade of young men and women.

Even though his family had been nice to her, Ben could see she did not like them. She could not be warm and friendly to the family of the man who arrested her brothers for murder.

Lorrie only became lighthearted again after Ben walked her away from the Farleys'. He took her hand and joined the current of people in the *paseo*. He made the remark under his breath that if the *paseo* was a parade of the stock, Lorrie's step was the lightest and her conformation the best. Lorrie collapsed in mirth against him, and her easy grace made Ben happy to be with her again.

They walked until late, then took a trail toward the house Lorrie shared with her brothers. At a place everyone called *La Arboleda*, a grove of big willows, Lorrie guided Ben off the trail into a dark thicket, put her arms around his neck, and kissed him.

They were warm from walking close together. Ben could not see a thing wrong with Lorrie's stock. The girl was strong, pretty, shapely, and straight-limbed. She had a glint of strong character in her eye, a laugh that moved him and made him happy, and a grip that held him fast. They kissed again.

That was as far as Ben Cowden was ready to go, only that far, with a little more quiet conversation. He was too used to being watchful when he found himself in thickets and unable to see very far. Lorrie's brothers were only about fifty yards away. If they found him hiding in the brush with their sister after dark, they might take him the way owls took roosters when they caught them in the trees. They would break his grip on Lorrie and pluck his feathers before he could run home.

He found a great need for the girl's kisses. He moved closer to Lorrie. They were finally alone after a year of wanting each other. They embraced so tightly they could not move. Ben could not stand that very long. He moved a hand lower to see if that would do something to relieve their aching. Lorrie arched her back and spread her knees against him, as though readying herself for anything he wanted to do. Then she broke away from him and laughed. She laughed so hard, her hands fell dead on the back of his neck. The thicket was so dark Ben could barely see her face. He worried her brothers would hear but did not try to quiet her.

At first, Ben thought Lorrie was laughing because she was happy and relieved they were finally enjoying some intimacy. Then she spoke, and he found out she was laughing at him.

"I didn't know you thought you could handle me that way, Ben," she said. He moved toward her to hold her again. She quit laughing, stretched as though suddenly drowsy, and stiffened her arms against his chest.

Ben moved clear away from her, so she would not think he was trying to force himself on her. She leaned back against a tree and feigned a yawn.

"You weren't the only one being handled in that lashup," Ben said. "I guess we just weren't doing it right."

"Have you ever gone that far with a girl before?"

Now, if that isn't something, Ben thought. She wants to talk now.

"Are you all right?" she asked. "You're not hurting anywhere, are you?"

"No, Lorrie."

"This is no place for us to let things get out of hand."

Ben looked at the lights in her brothers' house. They were too close.

"I wish we could do what you want, though," Lorrie said softly, warmly, wooing him in the dark again. "I really wish we could." Sincerely. "When are you going to Tucson? Maybe I could go at the same time. We could do it then."

"Would you like to do that, Lorrie?" Ben had not been surprised when she did not let the kissing go on. He was surprised when she suggested they sneak away for something that could develop into a marathon fornication.

"Sure. I think about doing things with you all the time. If you feel about me the way I feel about you, we ought to elope."

"What do you feel, Lorrie?"

"A lot of love," she said warmly. "A lot of passion." She was enunciating softly. "You too?"

"Me too, Lorrie."

"You know what I wish you would do?"

"Tell me."

"Find a reason to go to California. Say you're going out there on business. Say you want to buy some horses."

"That's a good idea. I wonder why I didn't think of it. How would my going out to California for horses keep our love and passion alive?"

"Aha, that's where it all would come together. You could get on the train in Patagonia, and then I could get on the train in Tucson. You could get a compartment, and we could do as we pleased all the way out there and all the way back. How does that sound? We might even come back married."

"Oh, that sounds hunky-dory," said a voice close in the dark.

Lorrie jumped to her feet. "Dick Martin, you sneak," she shouted.

"Lorrie Briggs, you little sweetie," mocked Martin. "What you got there this time—a miner, a cowboy, a soldier, or a gambler? Who you got there?"

"You better get on back to the house before you make the worst mistake of your life and find out who it is," said Lorrie. Then she started laughing.

"I'm not the one who cares," Dick Martin said. "If I cared about every miner and cowboy you took to the bushes, you'd be making a fool out of me too."

Lorrie went to Martin in the dark, took him by the arm, and turned him toward the house. "Believe me, you don't want to know who that is. He's already mad at you. He doesn't like you at all."

"I know where you've been," said Martin. "You think I can't guess who that is?"

Lorrie laughed and was gone. Martin followed her, razzing her every step. Ben did not wait to see if she would come back. He did not know whether to act jealous, rejected, or disgusted. He did know his breast was hurting.

Betty's favorite old doll with the real hair was scalped and hanging in a tree. Apaches had cut off her porcelain hands and hanged her dead. When the Cowdens saw the doll, they knew their house had been ravaged. They rode up to the house without stopping at the barn. Monique the doll always adorned Betty's bed.

Ben, Les, and Mark drew their pistols and rode around the house, then dismounted and went in through different doors. Bill Knox and Gordo Soto were still in town.

A. B. and Viney kept the children in the buggy until the brothers came out. Maudy was with the Cowdens, too. Will had ridden on the train as far as Tucson with Mrs. Pendleton and Pearl. He would be there a week on business.

Viney, Freddie Lee, and the girls went in to take stock of the house while A. B. and the boys put up the horses. Windows and lamps were broken. Mirrors were broken. The Apaches had not set fire to the house, but Viney's velvet drapes, some dresses, and A. B.'s boiled shirts and top hat were gone.

Viney figured the Apaches had worried about traffic on the road and did the stealing and vandalizing on the run. They had come to El Durazno to steal horses. The Cowdens turned their horses out to pasture every time they went to town.

After Monique was relieved of her rawhide noose and Viney realized her house was still intact and her family safe, she laughed and said she wished she could see those savages when they dressed up in A. B.'s boiled shirts and top hat. Coffee was brewing on the stove by the time all the broken glass was swept up.

Mark stayed with the family. Les and Ben rode into the mares' pasture first and found them grazing with the stud. The shiny stud arched his neck and made his breath explode as he examined the riders from the top of a hill. Any Apache who tried to steal that band might as well be trying to drive a pride of lions away from their den. They might corral the band, but they would not find anything they could ride.

The brothers searched the headquarters pasture and discovered their saddlehorses and teams had been run through a back gate and driven away. Four of the thieves were riding shod horses. Les followed the tracks away from the pasture while Ben stopped to examine the sign at the gate. The rider who had dismounted to open the gate was wearing *teguas*. His horse was shod in rawhide.

Les came back, and Ben closed the gate. They made

plans for the pursuit while they rode back to the house. At the meeting in Harshaw, the commander of the Sixth Cavalry patrol had told everyone a troop of the Fourth was patroling southwest from La Noria in Mexico. That troop hoped to head off the Yawner if he crossed the border. Ben and Les decided they would track their horses and hope the soldiers stopped the thieves somewhere and held them at bay.

The brothers figured they could handle five Apaches if they caught up to them before they made it to a larger band. Two of the Cowden horses would not travel very far. Prim Pete was not shod, and he would be sorefooted by tomorrow evening unless the thieves took time to shoe him.

The other horse was a palomino pet the Cowdens called Lemon. He was spoiled as he could be. He never went anyplace he did not want to go. When he did not want to go, he did not let anybody else go. He would be trying to turn the whole bunch back to El Durazno. The thieves would be so mad at him they would want to cut his throat and hang his flesh to dry on their saddle strings. Before long, they would be so mad at him they would be able to eat him without salt, but they would want to keep him because he was a palomino.

As soon as they reached home, Ben and Les started packing their camp. Mark was staying home. He was only seventeen, and Viney would not let him go. He was needed at home anyway. He and A. B. could protect El Durazno from any horde of badmen, white or Apache.

Viney came into the room while Ben and Les were packing their clothes. "Now, just what in the world do you two think you're doing?" she demanded. She did not care how obvious it was that they needed to go after their horses. Her love for her boys was so great she never gave up trying to keep them away from dangerous work.

"We're going after our horses, Mama," said Les. He gave his mother his most charming smile.

"No, you *are* not. You can, by gosh, leave the savages to the soldiers this time."

Les dropped a clean pair of socks into his warbag. Ben closed the drawstring on his bag. A. B. came in and sat on the bed. He was bareheaded; he only took off his hat when he was resting. Ben looked at him closely. His cheeks were flushed and he looked like a fierce old tribal chief himself. He had swallowed a strong toddy or two in the last few minutes.

"We're not going after Apaches, Mama," said Ben. "This time I don't think Apaches are to blame. Somebody else stole our horses."

Ben did not care who the thieves were. He would never tell his mother he might have to fight an Apache raiding party.

"I don't care if the thieves are red, brown, black, or white. Any kind of savage is as bad as the red kind," said Viney. "What are we going to do if something happens to you? We can live without those horses. I can't live without my sons."

"Mama," said Les, "we're only riding out to see what we can do. We're not going to tackle every badman in the country."

"I don't see why you have to go. We have hundreds of men on the government payroll who are qualified to chase horse thieves. Just ride into Harshaw and send them a telegram and tell them our place has been raided and our stock run off."

"Mama, by the time anyone answers a telegram, the trail will be so cold we'll never catch up." Ben set aside his sack of cartridges and closed the drawstrings. "I'm ready," he said to Les.

Les said, "Mama, don't worry. We can outfight, outride, and outshoot anybody in Arizona, and if that don't work, we'll charm them." He hugged her.

Viney held him a moment, then pushed him back and looked in his face. "Pshaw!" she said.

Ben's eyes met Maudy's. She and Paula Mary were peeking around the doorsill with deeply loving and concerned looks on their faces. Maudy was always looking at him that way. He winked at her. She straightened, pursed her lips, puffed a little air his way, and said, "Pshaw!" Then she took her stately self away.

CHAPTER 13

Ben and Les were riding the horses they had ridden to
town the day before. They always rode their best-looking
horses in town to show them off, so they had saved two good
horses from the thieves. Ben was riding a horse he called
Toots, a long-legged chestnut sorrel. Les was riding Moon,
a tall, smooth-traveling sorrel with a mean eye. Both horses
were fast, deep-hearted, and tough. Moon was Les's top
horse. Star and Prim Pete, Ben's top horses, were with the
stolen remuda.

Les was leading Moon through the barn, ready to leave,
when he heard the click of a loose shoe. He pulled the shoe
off, rasped the hoof, and began tacking the shoe back on.
Paula Mary was watching. Ben lit his pipe; he did not have
another thing to do but hold his horse and wait. He
remembered pulling Prim Pete's shoes off before he turned
him out to rest in the pasture after the race.

"Do you boys think you'll get in a fight?" Paula Mary
asked innocently.

"No, sister, we're only going after the horses," said Ben.

"I wonder what made them leave. You suppose old
Yawner drove them off?"

Ben was always wary of Paula Mary's snares. She was
wearing her little tot's face, as though she did not know
there was such a thing as a horse thief in the whole world.

"Oh, every once in a while horses, just get it in their heads to strike out for new country."

"How are you going to find them?"

"Oh, we'll track them. Their tracks'll run right up under them wherever they are."

"What do you do when the rain washes out their tracks, or you just lose them, or it gets too dark to see them?"

"When it's day again, I get up high and look."

"What happens when you get tired of looking and your horse is dead tired, you're both thirsty and hungry and out of tobacco, you're getting lonesome for your family, want your bed, and still have no idea where the horses are?"

Ben laughed. "Then I guess it's time to pray."

"Will God help you find the horses?"

"Sometimes God might feel sorry for you and put you on the right track. So it usually helps to pray when you need help bad."

"What if your prayers fail?"

"You have to keep looking. You can't ever come home without the horses."

"What if you don't find them where they're supposed to be and have to ride clear on out of the country and camp night after night on their tracks? What if you find out you won't ever get them back unless you fight for them? Will you pray?"

"You bet I will, little sister. Les will, too."

Les straightened up from his chore. "We better take another packhorse and a keg of shoes, just in case," he said.

"Just in case of what?" asked Paula Mary.

Les fixed a stern eye on the girl. "Just in case we wear all the iron off our horses traveling to all the places and suffering all the hardship you're talking about."

The brothers went by the house, kissed their mother, their sisters, and Maudy Jane, shook hands with their father, and were gone. They hit a high trot for the first half mile, then a lope. They would close the gap fast at that pace. The thieves could not make good time because they were busy pointing and driving a remuda of using horses that did not want to leave home. They were also watching over their shoulders for Cowdens.

Thirty-five horses left a wide trail. The tracks were so

fresh Ben sometimes thought he could smell horse sweat on the breeze. Horse sweat and horse-thief sweat.

These horse thieves were dumb. The most successful ones stole only a horse or two per man and scattered. A man who rode one of his stolen horses and led another had a chance to choose his routes and hide his tracks. A gang of men who stole a whole remuda of horses like this and stayed together would never make horse theft a financial success. As long as horses left tracks, this gang was prey for the Cowdens.

Ben would never want Les Cowden on his trail for stealing his horse. These horse thieves were strangers in the country who did not know Les and Ben, Apaches who did not care who came after them, or gunsels who thought a fight with the Cowdens would be fun. The more the brothers trailed their horses, the more they were sure Apaches were not driving them. The only thieves they knew who were dumb enough to try to steal the Cowden horses and move them this way were the Briggs brothers. If the Briggses were up ahead, the *tegua* track Ben saw at the gate probably belonged to Che Che.

Two of the horses in the remuda would be working to turn around and go home. The thieves would never stop long enough to shoe Prim Pete. Prim would be balking and trying to stop and rest, and they would want to keep him because he would bring a better price than any of the others in Mexico. Ben wanted him back, too. He was the best of them all. Toots might be as good as Prim someday. He was young and needed training, though. More than that, he needed a few life-and-death runs like the one he was making today before he would be the horse Prim Pete was. This Toots had the equipment, though, and would be given his share of trials.

Lemon would be working hard to turn around and go home. The palomino had served fifteen years as number-one pet horse for the Cowden children. He was not much taller than a pony, but he was a fighting, balking, bawling, spoiled, sour little crank when he was loose in a herd of horses. He thought he was as tough as a stud and was a demon of a bully. Lemon did not travel well. He would not leave home if he did not want to, not under spur, whip, or bludgeon. If he decided to go, he bit, kicked, and struck the other horses every step of the way to make them as miserable as he was. The last time the Cowden brothers had driven him away from home with the remuda, he had made it so miserable for everybody they swore never to take him again.

They did not need him. They only took him because they knew how much he would grieve if he was left at home alone. Lemon had been left to grieve one time when the remuda was taken away for spring roundup. For some reason, not one other horse was left in the pasture with him. He nearly starved walking the fence on the side where he last saw his fellows. The children thought he was with the remuda, so they did not miss him. Mark found him by accident when he rode on that side of the pasture and heard him nickering as though his heart would break. He had worn a deep trail along the fence, pawed a hole in a corner, and left scraps of his hair and hide on stretches of wire where he tried to get through. He was only a skeleton with a hard dry hide stretched over the bones when Mark found him and took him back to the barn.

Lemon had been a pet so long he thought he ran the Cowden outfit. He was so tormented in those fifteen years by the capricious behavior of the seven Cowden children that he finally revolted against all human endeavor. Now, his spoiled nature was making him useful again. His treatment of horse thieves would be awful.

Hoozy Briggs was thinking he would like to kill the little sonofabitch. Hoozy knew Lemon well. Lemon had been the cause of his suffering the worst humiliation of his life.

One day when Hoozy was at El Durazno trying to make Betty notice him, Paula Mary and Freddie Lee had put on their forlorn faces and begged him to saddle Lemon for them. That was when he was first learning about horses and Cowdens. At that time he didn't own a horse; he hitched rides on the ore wagons or walked when he went anywhere. He didn't know much about saddling and bridling horses but would not admit it. Cowboy Hoozy. The Cowden kids were hands enough to saddle the worst bronc on the place, and he didn't know it.

Lemon stood still for the bridling. He lay in wait while Hoozy threw on the saddle. When Hoozy reached under his belly for the cinch, he clamped his teeth shut on a cheek of Hoozy's rump and jerked his head away with all his might. When his teeth came off Hoozy's flesh, they clashed together like a steel trap, and Hoozy learned how it felt to be torn limb from limb.

Betty was standing only a few steps away, observing. He spent a lot of time vieing for her attention, but that was one time he did not need it. He wanted to express his pain with terrible groans, but he did not dare even rub his butt in front of Betty. He couldn't cuss either. He knew the Cowdens didn't particularly want him visiting there, and they would banish him for good if he cussed.

Paula Mary and Freddie never made one sound of sympathy. They were suffering as much as he—from hiding their supreme mirth. They knew how much he had been violated, were afraid he was angry enough to kill, and that helped them keep from laughing out loud. They could have laughed. That would have been more decent than not showing any expression at all for his misfortune. He saw a smile flit at the corners of Betty's mouth. What a pretty mouth. But she controlled herself and did not show him one bit of compassion.

He could understand their not feeling sorry for him. After all, he was a grown man, and those kids believed any man should be able to saddle a pet horse without getting himself torn limb from limb. He could not understand why they did not laugh with him, though. They could have given him a chance to rub his sore places and laugh with them, but they didn't, and that hurt his feelings. They would rather watch him squirm. The clear, blue gaze that Betty gave him when he looked to her for concern was as icy, speculative, and impersonal as a card shark's.

At last he finished saddling Lemon, and the kids mounted him double. Paula Mary was in the saddle, and Freddie was behind her, carrying a switch. Lemon wrung his tail and started away from the barn with his ears laid back. Then Freddie tickled his flank with the switch, and he balked.

Hoozy did not know the boy could make the horse do

ornery things on signal with the switch. Freddie provoked him so he hung his head between his front legs, opened his his mouth, ran backward, and bawled. The kids then started hollering for Hoozy to save them. He reached over Lemon's hips to lift Freddie off, and the boy stung the horse with the switch as though to make him behave. Lemon kicked up with both legs like a mule. One leg caught Hoozy in the belly and knocked all the wind out of him. The other caught him up between his legs and smashed his most tender parts.

Luckily, Hoozy was close against the horse when he was kicked. His arms were reaching high for Freddie, and he was open to the blows, but he was so close Lemon hit him with his hocks, the elbowlike joints on his hind legs. If Hoozy had been standing farther away, Lemon would have caught him with shod hooves. The hocks only punched him like short uppercuts in the belly and the groin.

Still, Hoozy was cowkilled. He writhed on his face, hoping his breath would return. He could not show anyone that he was hurt in the groin. Being in agony over his groin would be indecent. He could only grit his teeth, roll on the ground, and hope for relief. The kids were so scared by what they'd done to him they jumped off Lemon and ran to the house.

Betty did not come close to him, did not say anything to comfort him. She cast a quick shadow over him and asked coldly if he was all right.

That should have been the end of Hoozy as far as his courtship of Betty was concerned. He'd been dreaming he might be injured doing something heroic, so she could hold his noble head in her lap, soothe him, and give him kisses while he suffered. However, no such dream came true for Hoozy. She would have done better to go away and leave him completely alone. She was cruel to stay and watch him because he could not stroke his own hurt places to find out how badly he was damaged.

Now Lemon was biting and kicking at the other horses to keep them from passing him on the trail. He was holding down the pace and preventing Hoozy from escaping with the Durazno remuda.

Hoozy glared at the yellow horse. "Lemon, you sonofabitch, I'm getting even now," he shouted and he brought the double of his rope down on Lemon's butt. Che Che showed he disapproved of the unnecessary noise and commotion. "I don't care. I hate that sonofabitch," Hoozy said. "You don't know what he did to me."

Thomas and Campana were helping Hoozy, Whitey and Che Che. For the past hour, Campana had been advising him they should head back to Harshaw and let the horses go because the Cowdens would soon be overtaking them. If they stayed with the horses, they would only make sure the Cowdens found out who stole them. Nothing else could be realized from it. Every horse the Cowdens rode was a racehorse for speed. Nobody could drive that many horses away from their home ground fast enough to outrun horsemen like the Cowdens.

Whitey was lagging behind, leading Prim Pete. Hoozy was telling himself he should have remembered he had no luck with horses. Pete was the one horse that could be sold quickly in Mexico, but he was so lame he would probably never get there.

Hoozy was sure of only one thing now. If he was forced to turn these horses loose and run for it, he was at least going to take the time to execute Lemon. Now Lemon was responsible for his failure as a horse thief.

Campana and Thomas rode up and fell in step with Hoozy. "This ain't aworkin," said Thomas. "We have to pull out, now, Hoozy."

"It's that palomino sonofabitch," said Hoozy. "He's the one holding us up."

"It ain't only the palomino. I don't think much of the squatters, but them Cowdens are horsemen and they're fighters. You can't run off their horses and leave a track a fat girl could follow and think you've done something. What do you think?"

"We could ambush them. We *should*, by dang," Hoozy said.

"Not me—it's too damned late," Thomas said. He stopped his horse. "This is where me and Campana pull up. It's even too late to take the racehorse. We better head for the home ranch and hope we make it."

"All right, somebody ride up to the lead and tell Che Che, and I'll go back for Whitey and the racehorse."

"Listen, turn that racehorse loose and come on," said Thomas. "We're going to have hell riding away from this mess."

Ben and Les stopped and let their horses blow. Ahead of them was the narrowest part of Medal Canyon, *El Cañon de la Medalla*. High rock and good cover overlooked both sides of the notchlike entrance to the canyon. The brothers could hear the clatter of their remuda's hooves and the voices of the thieves. They could see Whitey poking along with Prim Pete.

Whitey began jerking on Prim Pete and cussing him, trying to make him lead faster. Prim planted all four feet and stopped. He was looking at Whitey as though he thought the man was daft for not being able to see that he was lame.

Ben dismounted, handed his reins to Les, and climbed up the side of the canyon to have a look at the thieves. The notch was a good place for an ambush.

Ben watched Hoozy ride back to Whitey and begin arguing with him. He was about to climb down when five Apaches swarmed onto a rock above the Briggses.

Ben always felt privileged when he saw Apaches out in the country, the way he felt when he saw wild horses, lions, or wolves. They always seemed to be more vividly present on mother earth, the colors of their hides and clothes brighter, their outlines more defined. He felt especially privileged when he saw them before they saw him.

Four were carrying normal-sized bows and quivers of arrows. One, carrying a longer, thicker bow, climbed onto a smooth rock that sloped toward Hoozy and Whitey. He stayed in plain sight of the Briggses, as though he did not care if they saw him. He sat in the shade with his back against the high side of the sloping rock.

He notched an arrow, put both feet against the bow, drew the string against his chest, sighted down the arrow, eased off, and drew it again, testing the bow. He was sighting along the angle of the rock he was sitting on. It sloped toward the bottom of the canyon.

The other Apaches were making low comments and laughing while the bowman concentrated on his preparations. The bowman intended to show off his archery, and the Briggs brothers were his targets. His partners were plainly happy, anticipating Apache fun. Hoozy and Whitey were cooperating perfectly, giving the bowman time to ready himself to kill them.

Prim Pete was intent on the Apaches, and so were the Briggses' saddlehorses. Finally, Hoozy looked up and saw the Apaches. Whitey saw what his brother was staring at and began spurring his horse and bicycling his legs to get away from there. He did not look at the Apaches again, but fixed on his horse's ears as he tried to urge him past Hoozy on the narrow trail. Hoozy was blocking the way while he stared at the Apaches.

"Hoo-aah!" screamed an Apache, and he ended it with ecstatic little yips as he and his partners arched a flight of arrows toward the Briggs brothers. The arrows were flying as though let go by lazy children. They wobbled up high, strained a moment to go on, failed, dropped their heads, and started gaining momentum toward the Briggses again. Their trajectory would not prove accurate if Hoozy and Whitey moved themselves off the target spot before sunset. The Apaches seemed only to want the flight of arrows to untrack them and start them running down the canyon.

"Aah-haa!" screamed the Apache. An arrow stuck in the ground under Hoozy's stirrup. He looked up at another flight of arrows waggling their tails high overhead, then jerked his horse around and whipped him over and under down the canyon as fast as he could go.

Whitey spurred frantically to catch up. He was still holding Prim Pete's lead rope, but Prim was standing still. Whitey was almost jerked out of his saddle when he hit the end of the rope. He lost his hat but recovered his seat, cussed, threw Prim's rope away, and let his horse run.

Prim Pete cocked his head to the side so he would not step on his lead rope and ran after Whitey as though his feet had never been sore. The lead rope whipped and popped and seldom touched the ground.

Hoozy was lying over his running horse's ears like a jockey. Whitey's horse was leaving the country. A heavy-caliber rifle spoke up from the notch, and the Apaches above the bowman ducked their heads under a shower of rock.

The bowman stretched the big bow with his legs. Flat on his back and sighting down the arrow between his feet, he swung his feet along with Whitey, leading him, using the slope of the rock to steady his line of sight. He led Whitey past a sandy, level stretch, and let the arrow fly.

The arrow was so big, so visible, it seemed a long time overtaking the target. It seemed to labor, to have trouble keeping straight and catching up. Whitey was running a good race to get away, and the arrow had to come a long way to catch him. It gained on the downward slope of its arc, and its falling weight enabled it to strike with heavy impact. It pinned Whitey's thigh to his saddle, and the horse went down with a foot of the shaft through his heart.

Whitey screamed. The Apaches screamed back at him—starting with the same last note of Whitey's voice and continuing with it until they were shrieking, then ending the breath of it with high, mocking little moans.

Hoozy did not look back, did not pull up. The Apaches jeered him loudly, praising his show of great speed, urging him to show more, encouraging him to do better because he was doing so well. The big rifle answered the Apaches.

The bowman was laughing as he climbed off the smooth rock and followed his partners into the canyon. He started across the canyon floor toward Whitey, and a bullet from the big rifle exploded against the canyon wall beside him. He ran to hide behind a big rock, turned and grinned at his fellows. He turned back to gauge the distance to Whitey. He settled on his haunches behind the rock content to hide from the big rifle and wait.

The marksman with the big rifle laid a ball on the rock about a foot from the bowman's head. Shattered rock burst into the side of his face and knocked him over. He recovered, laughed out loud, and sprinted to his friends with blood streaming on his face.

Ben climbed down and mounted Toots. "We just missed a chance to shoot five Apaches and one horse thief," he told Les. "I saw an Apache stick an arrow big as a shovel handle into Whitey, though, so I don't feel so bad."

"Nice of you to finally come back and give me a report," Les said.

Gunfire began popping and booming down the canyon. Ben examined the mountains overhead. "Let's see if we can get around the notch. Maybe we can turn our remuda back toward home while everybody down there is shooting at each other."

"Where's Prim Pete?"

"He ran after Hoozy like he belonged to him. He sure didn't want to stay behind while the stickbirds with the rock beaks were flying."

Ben and Les climbed out of the canyon on the Apaches' side. They worked cattle in Medal Canyon all the time. They knew all the trails, knew every oak, cedar, and piñon tree they could use for concealment. They rode above the fight and stayed clear of it.

When they reached a good vantage point, they looked down to see if Whitey was alive. He and his horse were lying flat, settled into the ground. The horse was still between Whitey's legs and its carcass was his barricade. Ben guessed the big arrow had pulverized the artery in Whitey's thigh, and he did not need more arrows.

The Cowdens rode to the crest of a high ridge and looked down at the notch. The canyon flared out below the notch into a wide draw that stretched to Sonoita Creek. Nine Apache riflemen were spread out in rocks overlooking the draw. Hoozy's outfit was pinned down on the creek with water, shade, and a high bank of the creek for protection. Ben and Les could see their saddlehorses hobbled below the bank. Prim Pete was there too, standing with his head up and his eyes big, safe from the shooting.

The marksman with the big rifle and several other white men were in the rocks on the other side of the notch, firing across the canyon at the Apaches. Three wagons and teams were down on the creek behind them, the teams hobbled and tied to cottonwoods, the wagons loaded with Emory oak the men had probably cut for shoring in the mines. Hoozy and his outfit would all be as dead as Whitey if these teamsters and lumbermen had not come on to help them.

The fight was at a standoff. Ben did not think the Apaches would be staying much longer. He saw the

Durazno horses being driven in a hurry down Sonoita Creek by more Apaches.

"What shall we do, Les? If we stay here and help Hoozy, those Apaches'll run off with our horses."

"Let's go after our stock and let 'em kill Hoozy if they can," said Les. "He might hold out long enough so we can get our horses back."

CHAPTER 14

The brothers made Toots and Moon stretch their legs to catch the remuda. The Apaches were driving the Durazno horses away from Sonoita Creek to higher, harder ground. As horsemen, they would not want to slow them down and tire them in the sand or soften their feet in the water.

Ben and Les rode up behind the remuda. The Apaches were watching them over their shoulders like coyotes running from a henhouse. Two of them began waving blankets and screaming to start the horses running. The other two were mounted bareback on Cowden horses. They jumped down, turned their horses loose to run with the herd, and ran for cover to hold off the Cowdens. Ben and Les each chose an Apache and ran to close with them before they lost sight of them.

Ben drew his pistol and gave Toots his head. Toots did not need reining in the brush. The Indian was between Ben and the Cowden horses, and Toots headed straight for his friends in the remuda.

Ben fired two pistol shots at the running Apache, leading him in the brush. He turned Toots up a deep wash that hid him as he ran parallel to the Indian's path, then charged out of the wash to head him off.

The Indian had stopped and squatted down in a stand of saplings, and Toots almost ran him over. Ben burst on him so suddenly he caught him looking the wrong way. The Apache spun around and looked straight into Ben's eyes as Toots took flight above him. He did not flinch or duck his head as the horse hurdled him.

He was an old man, his hair gray, carrying a bow and a light quiver of arrows. He stayed low and quartered away as Toots came to ground beyond him in the thick willow brush. For a moment, Ben's back was to the Apache as Toots tore into the wall of the thicket. A bundle of broken branches stacked up in front of Ben's saddle horn while he hauled back to stop the horse.

Ben rolled Toots back on his heels and fired twice at the old fellow as he dodged and scampered through the brush like a rooster quail. Then Ben pulled up and let him go. He hurried back toward Les, changing course behind the trees so the old man could not lead him with an arrow.

He slowed Toots to a trot when he heard rifle shots. He rode on, and after a while, Les came in sight on a hill. The brothers met under cottonwoods by the creek, dismounted, and loosened their cinches. They could see the dust of the remuda a mile away.

"Let's blow a minute," Ben said.

"Well, our remuda only has two savages with it, now," Les said. "They probably heard our shots, so I'm guessing they won't stay with it much longer. My Indian wasn't armed very well, was yours?"

"Mine had a bow."

"So did mine. Those two up ahead have bows. If they heard our weapons firing, I bet they quit the remuda and hit for the high country. We can take our horses home now if we can catch up to them and turn them back before dark."

The brothers examined their mounts, watching their breathing, looking into their eyes, pressing their necks to be sure they were cooling, their heartbeats slowing down. The Cowdens would not ride jaded horses. They would not leave the creek without resting them, unless they rode at a walk or went afoot.

The sun was setting. "I've been thinking," Ben said. "It might be all right to leave Hoozy and his partners back there for the Apaches to skin alive, but those other men don't deserve it."

"What do you want to do?"

"We're almost out of daylight. I'll ride back to Medal Canyon to see what I can do, if you'll go and keep track of our horses. Don't pick a fight, but stay close until dark. I'll meet you at Valenzuela's ranch at Tubac tonight."

"All right, if that's what you want to do, brother, but you don't have to worry that you'll be helping Hoozy. I saw him leave the fight and head south."

"Well, the ungrateful *cabrón* quit the lumbermen, did he?"

"It sure looked like it."

"Why the sonofabitch. Did he still have Prim?"

"I saw three riders leave there leading a horse. They were pretty far away, but I'm sure I could see Hoozy leading Prim. The other two riders were behind Prim, whipping his butt with their ropes to keep him going."

"The sonsabitches."

The brothers mixed *pinole*, sweetened cornmeal, with creek water and drank the thin paste while their horses rested. They split up, and Ben headed back to Medal Canyon.

He was worried that he and Les had done wrong by riding away and not helping the lumbermen. He could no longer hear firing in Medal Canyon. He kept a ridge between himself and the canyon as he rode closer.

When he was near enough, he looked over the crest and saw a new mass of horses in the cottonwood shade by the wagons. The fight seemed to be over. He could not see anyone in the rocks on either side of the notch, and men were moving freely around the wagons. He kept his cover until he recognized army uniforms on figures by the wagons. He rode over the ridge into the open so they could see him coming.

Cavalry horses were picketed under the trees with the lumbermen's teams. Some of the troopers were standing barefooted out in the creek, their trousers rolled up and their galluses over their bare backs, bathing their horses.

Ben rode toward an officer standing at the tailgate of a wagon with a sergeant and another man. They were doctoring the hand of a wounded teamster. Whitey's horse was still lying up the canyon, but Ben could not see Whitey.

He stopped Toots close enough to the men so he could talk without raising his voice.

The soldiers said hello and went on bandaging the teamster. Ben counted five teamsters and lumbermen still healthy after the fight. Then he saw the Farley twins coming toward him.

"*Valgame!*" Ben said. "*Y vengo hallando a los cuates locos*. Bless me and give me real value, for I've found the crazy twins!"

"I told Donny I saw you and Les on that ridge behind the Apaches, and he didn't believe me," said Danny. "Why didn't you shoot those Indians for us, Ben? We thought you would, but you just kept agoin. We couldn't see them good enough to hit them."

"We saw you were keeping them busy enough, so we ran to catch up with our horses. What are you cowboys doing here?"

"We didn't have anything to do, so we brought these fellers down here and showed them the Emory oak they needed and then got conscripted to protect them from savages," said Donny. "Didn't you hear our daddy's Sharps go off?"

"Why, I never dreamed that was your Sharps. I saw it pulverize the rock where an Indian was hiding though."

"Get off your horse," Danny said. "Donny's going to make some bread. The real cook got himself winged by old Yawner."

Donny reached into a wagon, dragged out a five-gallon demijohn, and handed it up to Ben. Ben noticed he knew exactly where to find it without looking inside the wagon. The jug was easy to handle on the horse because its mescal was half gone.

"Someone told me you twins might be out here somewhere cutting timbers, but I forgot to look for you." Ben lifted the jug to his saddle horn and then hefted it high for a swallow. The stuff was clear, pure, and potent enough to bring the spirit back in any living creature far from home.

"Hoozy Briggs was traveling *palla* with your remuda," said Donny. "I looked up, and there came old Lemon swingfooting down the canyon big as you please. There ain't another like him this side of Hermosillo, and I knew you hadn't sold him."

"Lemon was harassing Apaches last time I saw him," Ben said. "Where'd Hoozy go?

"Him and two others ran toward Mexico when the soldiers got here."

"The lieutenant in charge of the troop came over to Ben and shook hands. "Mr. Cowden, I'm Sam Little. I met you at the meeting in the town hall the other day."

"Sure, Lieutenant. You and your troop have been seeing the country since then, haven't you?" Ben did not ask the man why he wasn't chasing the Apaches. He could see his horses were finished for the day.

"That was old Yawner," said Lieutenant Little. "We've been after him since May when he snuck away from San Carlos. We lost him three times. We thought we were gaining on him after he raided the Pendletons, but our superiors called us off and made us go to Harshaw for the damned policy meeting with Colonel Bustamante.

"When we saw you in Harshaw, our horses were fresh. We came on in a hurry when we heard they ransacked your ranch house and drove off your horses. We could use a change of horses now."

Ben shrugged and did not bother telling Lieutenant Little that Hoozy was the horse thief this time, even though Indians were driving the Cowden horses away when the cavalry arrived. Ben and Les would both have to admit they saw Apaches driving their horses away. Hoozy's tracks from the Cowden gate to Medal Canyon could not be taken as evidence to a courtroom.

"Where's Whitey Briggs? We saw him go down," Ben said.

"He's over there in the wagon," said Danny. "He's dead."

"I think he broke his neck when his horse went down, then bled to death from the arrow wound," said Lieutenant Little. "I have the arrow with my kit. You want to see it? It's almost big as a spear."

"I saw it when it was on its way to Whitey," Ben said. He turned to the twins. "Did you bring your saddlehorses?"

"Sure, they're down on the creek," said Danny.

"Good. You can drive our remuda home. Me and Les want to go on after Hoozy."

"What you want Hoozy for?" asked Donny, joking.

"Huh!" Ben snorted. "Didn't you see him? He's got our top horse."

Les came in sight, driving the Durazno remuda. The horses were strung out for home, with Lemon in the lead. Ben rode in front of them and stopped them. Les and the twins held them while Ben and the soldiers stretched a rope corral for them. At dark Ben picketed each one. Ben and Les camped with the twins and the teamsters that night.

The next morning, Ben and Les were back on Hoozy's trail early, and Les was telling Ben how the Apaches had left the remuda and run when they saw him, probably figuring he was not alone.

"Did you see any more savages besides the two we saw with the horses?" Ben asked.

"No, just Che Che," said Les.

"Che Che? Where did you see him?"

"He was the one riding the horse that was booted in rawhide, the one we tracked all the way down Medao Canyon. He was still in the lead when I caught up to the remuda. He didn't stay to talk to me, though. He and the other Apache took off when they saw me coming."

"You mean he's riding with the Yawner now?"

"That's it."

"Lordy, Lord. You suppose he was wrangling for the Yawner and got Hoozy to help him?"

"There's no telling. He sure fit in with those Apaches quick."

Ben's fresh mount was a blue horse he called Passport, and Les changed to a horse named Top. Every time Ben had to go to Mexico, it seemed it was Passport's turn to work. He was a dappled blue, the color the Mexicans called *azulejo*, or *moro azul*. He had a star on his forehead and four black stockings, was catty and quick on his feet, and could absolutely run a hole in the wind.

Top was Les's *consentido*, his pet horse. Les seldom showed affection for animals. He did not abuse them, but he used them hard, took it personally if they let him down.

and never seemed to be sorry if he had to let them go. However, every horseman sooner or later caught a passion for one special horse, and Les's eye lit up every time he got to travel astride old Top.

The brothers tracked Hoozy and the VO cowboys through the Buena Vista range and lost the tracks in the roads and trails that converged at the town of Nogales. They rode down to rest under walnut trees at a spring by an ancient rock corral. A troop of Mexican cavalry was encamped there.

The soldiers were busy at their supper fires. The brothers stopped their horses when a sentry stepped away from his fire and waved to them with a tortilla in one hand and a spoon in the other. His barracks hat was riding on top of his thick black thatch of hair. His tunic and fly were open, his boots unlaced, and he was dragging them so they would not fall off.

The sentry was a Lopez from the Sonora river, and Ben knew him. The Lopezes were good cattlemen. This one had been impressed into army service by his family for his bad behavior.

"*Que húbo, Lopez*? What's been going on?" asked Ben. "I see they finally found a way to keep you out of trouble. They made a soldier out of you."

"I'm glad to see you, Benjamin," said Lopez. "Alas, look now you find me, in uniform, because of a foolish act of love. It was the only way I could fit myself with new boots after I was forced to flee barefooted through a bedroom window."

"A fine motive for you to join a campaign against savages," Ben said.

"Kosterlinsky is here," Lopez announced.

"Oh, he is? Is this his troop?"

"Yes, we were with Bustamante in Harshaw the other day. I saw you with your family. It made me recall my own family, our fine horses, our pretty women. *Ay*, it hurts!" He grinned at Ben. "Let me take your horses to water. The lieutenant is almost a general now. He will be happy to see you. Get down."

Ben dismounted, shook Lopez's hand, and handed him his reins. "Here is Les, your friend. He'll go with you."

"Ah, Leslie," Lopez said. "*Mi amigo*. I haven't seen you since we chased the kitties that night in Santa Cruz. You remember that? *Ay!*"

"Those kitties were dressed in feathers, weren't they?" said Les, laughing. "Those were fast kitties."

Ben loosened Passport's cinches and went to find Kosterlinsky. Another soldier Ben knew greeted him and invited him to share his campfire. Ben became aware of a figure standing still and apart, watching him. The Yaqui, sometime companion of Hoozy and Che Che, picked up his rifle and moved behind a tree when Ben turned to look at him. Ben knew he served as a scout for both the Mexican army and the American army from time to time. Now that Ben knew Che Che was with the Yawner, he wondered if the Yaqui served the Yawner too from time to time.

Ben found Kosterlinsky in the only tent on the campground, a ten-by-ten with a cot, a table, two chairs, and candlelight. He stopped outside the light and watched Kosterlinsky a moment. The lieutenant who would be a general was writing in his journal.

"*Buenas noches*," Ben growled. "If I was an Apache, I would pierce your hide with an arrow and display your head on the end of my lance."

Kosterlinsky continued writing. "Come in, then," he said without looking up.

Ben lit his pipe at a fire in front of the tent. Kosterlinsky put away his pen and journal, leaned back in his canvas chair, and smiled. "Come in, *Benjamin Cueva de Vaca*. I'm glad to see you. Imagine, I have brandy."

He reached into a knapsack and pulled out a full quart of French brandy. "Cucho!" he shouted. "Bring cups and water."

"Cucho!" echoed the troopers outside, making fun of Kosterlinsky's valet.

"Sit, Ben," said Kosterlinsky. "What brings you here?"

"I'm tracking a horse thief."

"Who is with you?"

"My brother, Les."

"Ah, he's my favorite. Now that's a wildman, is it not?"

"I agree."

"Are there any tame Cowdens?"

"Oh, yes."

"Your father, is he well?"

"Yes."

"Your mother and your pretty sisters are well?"

"Yes, and so are my little brothers."

"Listen, I heard about the Yawner's raid on your ranch. Did he do much damage? Was anyone hurt?"

"Not much. No one was home."

"It's too bad your father didn't catch the cutthroat. He would be a good Indian today, and I wouldn't be on this campaign."

"Have you been riding hard to catch the Yawner, Gabriel?"

"This time we are launching a dedicated campaign to wipe him out. He has gone too far."

"That's what enemies do in a war, isn't it?"

"No, this time I'm after him with vengeance. He raided some ranches near La Noria after he was at your father's place. He scattered cattle from the VO ranch to Santa Cruz. They are awful, the depradations of this *canalla*, this fiend."

"Where do you expect to engage him."

"I'm waiting for my commandant to provide me with orders and fresh horses. This will be my main camp from now on."

"Where's the Yawner?"

"I am sure he's probably somewhere between here and Tubac. What do you think? I chased him that way."

"Oh, so that's why he's in Tubac? I thought Lieutenant Little's soldiers chased him there."

"I have not seen an American soldier since I left Harshaw two days ago. Was it two days ago? I lose track of the days."

"I left the troop of the Sixth today, and they were on his track. They're like you; their horses are ridden down."

"Listen, Ben, you're in the field a lot. Tell me what you've seen since you were with me in Harshaw the other day. What do you think our armies should do in this campaign?"

"Send a messenger to Medal Canyon. Lieutenant Little is camped there, resting his horses, too. Coordinate with him. The Yawner will be coming your way now."

"Lieutenant Little's troop?" Kosterlinsky said uninterestedly. The thought of making that kind of effort made his eyes go blank. He could not even coordinate with Cucho, his valet.

Cucho came in with tin cups for the brandy. Kosterlinsky filled them. The fumes of the spirit were sharp in the close tent. Ben sipped the brandy carefully. He had not eaten much solid food in two days, and his stomach was no place to put brandy.

"What really brings you down here, Benjamin?"

"You know why I'm here, Gabriel. I'm tracking Hoozy Briggs. He stole my racehorse."

"I know Hoozy."

"Of course you do, but you're not going to tell me you saw him, are you?"

"I know his sister, too." Kosterlinsky moaned. "*Ay, Mamacita*! What a woman, no?"

Ben was certain Kosterlinsky had seen Hoozy. Every traveler who came through Nogales Pass watered his horse at this spring.

Ben stood up to leave. He did not feel like prying information out of Kosterlinsky. Everybody in southern Arizona and northern Sonora knew Prim Pete belonged to the Cowdens, and the horse would turn up. Hoozy might find ready buyers for Prim Pete farther south, but not in Sonora. Prim was known in Sonora as El Majo, the fine and the gallant. Ben did not need Kosterlinsky's help to find his horse, and he did not need Kosterlinsky to tell him how much a woman Lorrie Briggs was.

"I'm going to find some supper and then roll up in my blanket," said Ben.

"Listen, Ben. I'll watch out for your horse. I know how much you love him. A beautiful animal. He's worth you riding all the way down here, but you could have sent me a wire. If he's down here, I'll find him and return him."

"Well, good night, Gabriel."

"No, you and Les bring your blankets in here and share my tent. Cucho!"

"Cucho!" echoed the troopers, laughing.

Cucho appeared in the doorway. "*Sí, mi Jefe*," said he. His face was fleshy and oily, but his carcass was lean. His face was oily from being too close to the campfire, its fat rendered into his collar by the flames.

"Cucho, where have you been? Bring water and another cup. This man and his brother will be supping with me. Where have you been, man? My guests are hungry. Go and find this man's brother and bring him here. Bring their saddles and blankets, also. Be sure their horses are grained."

"Sí, mi Jefe," said Cucho. He shook hands with Ben. "I'm glad to see you, *Don Benjamin*. The chief acts as though I didn't know to bring you water and prepare your supper. Your supper is already cooking."

"Then why didn't you bring water when I asked for it?" demanded Kosterlinsky.

"Ah, I didn't want to interrupt you while you were making plans to capture the *robabestias*, the horse thief who has El Majo," said Cucho.

Kosterlinsky dismissed Cucho quickly. "Don't stand there arguing. Hurry and do what I told you to do. And don't be listening at my tent. Go now."

Cucho saluted, and as he went out, he looked Ben straight in the eye; that look told Ben that Kosterlinsky was protecting Hoozy.

Ben and Les were not able to leave Kosterlinsky's camp as early as they wished the next morning. Kosterlinsky required them to fill out a report on the theft of their horse and their reasons for traveling in Mexico. The proper forms could not readily be found. Kosterlinsky stalled and would not issue the orders necessary to help the brothers get back on the trail. When they complained that they were in a hurry, Kosterlinsky admitted he did not like his visitors to leave him before he had shown them proper hospitality. He said he was honor-bound to keep Ben and Les that day and another night in order that he fulfill his duties as a host.

After pouring the Cowdens three cups of brandy by 8:00 A.M., Kosterlinsky said he decided he would coordinate his campaign against the Apaches with the gringos as Ben suggested. The first program he wanted to coordinate would be one of entertainment for the coordinating parties. He would send a military escort to Nogales to conscript *soldaderas*, a fighting force of females who would serve temporary duty in the Army of Coordination. With this female task force he would coordinate a dance. With this kind of talk and clowning, Kosterlinsky delayed the brothers' departure so long and gained so much time for Hoozy that Ben suspected he was partnering in the theft of Prim Pete.

When they were finally able to ride away, Les said, "Ben, that Yaqui who runs with Hoozy's bunch was in Kosterlinsky's camp."

"Yes, I saw him slip behind a tree last night," said Ben.

"Did you see him this morning?"

"No, I didn't, and I sure looked for him. I'd feel a lot safer if I'd seen him in camp this morning."

"You're like me. If he was in camp, he couldn't be out here watching us through his sights."

"Well, I guess there's no use worrying about him. We're better riders, fighters, and shooters than he is, aren't we?"

"Huh! He won't ride and shoot and fight. He'll lay behind a tree and *venadear* us, stalk us and snipe us like a deer hunter."

"Well, brother, if he shoots at us, maybe he'll miss."

The brothers made a wide circle and found Hoozy's tracks. Hoozy and the VO cowboys had gone east from Kosterlinsky's camp, without Prim Pete. The brothers rode wider and cut for Prim's tracks. They found them in the late afternoon. One of Kosterlinsky's horse-soldiers had taken him south.

CHAPTER 15

Hoozy Briggs was happy because he was finally making a living with his guns. He saw himself as a professional ranger now. With his new job, he was also assuming a respected title that came from other range wars. He was joining the ranks of great gunmen of the west called "regulators."

Hoozy pulled out of the fracas in Medal Canyon with no regret that he was deserting the lumbermen. He felt his responsibility was to keep harassing the Cowdens. He did not care that Thomas and Campana wanted to stay and help the lumbermen drive off the Apaches. The way Hoozy saw it, their job as rangers required that they look out for themselves. The responsibilities of his job also justified his riding away and leaving Whitey dying under his horse. When the cavalry showed up, the regulators took Prim Pete and beat it out of there.

Hoozy could not forget the big arrow either. He could still see it impaling Whitey and his horse. More like a lance than an arrow, it did not soar, loft, and glide in an arc to the target as an arrow should. Whitey was not its first victim, and Hoozy could be its next victim. The big arrow was not like the feather, shaft, and stone an ordinary man might launch, and then hope for it to strike true. It was more like a spear of lightning and seemed so unerring that Hoozy did not ever want to find himself in its country when it flew again.

Instead of being sad about Whitey, Hoozy wanted to celebrate. He was carrying gold coin in his pocket from the sale of Prim Pete. He could now also call himself a full-fledged Indian fighter. He was doing the mischief Vincent hired him to do and earning his wages. The mischief had lost him a brother, but he could be sure big paydays were on the way.

The regulators helped him sell Prim Pete to Kosterlinsky. Thomas and Campana had been drinking with Kosterlinsky in the Crystal Palace when he told them he was in the market for good horses. Now they knew he meant it. They also liked the prompt and rigorous way he paid off, too.

Kosterlinsky did not argue a whit about the price. He took the regulators into his tent, gave them brandy to drink, and counted out their gold. That was the way Hoozy liked to do business.

The regulators were hurrying toward VO headquarters. They had already crossed the Buena Vista range and were on the eastern slope of Saddle Mountain. Thomas stopped at a fork in the trail above the Ray Johnson ranch and said, "We can take the Washington Camp trail here and ride through the mountains to get home, or we can go straight through Ray Johnson's place and be home in time for supper."

"What's wrong with riding straight across?" asked Hoozy.

Campana laughed.

"Johnson warned he would shoot us if we ever rode across his place again," Thomas said. "The other day he caught us driving some Cowden steers across his pasture, and he ran us off. So, take your pick. If we ride through Johnson's outfit, he'll pester us, and if we ride through Washington Camp, we won't make it to the bunkhouse for supper tonight."

"I don't know about you, but I'm not letting any squatter stand in the way of my supper," Hoozy said.

"Have it your way, then. Take the downhill trail."

Hoozy rode out ahead of Thomas and Campana. He drew his pistols and checked their loads. He drew his .4570 and checked its load. The rifle was heavy, and he had to stop his mare and dismount to put it back in the scabbard.

He was riding along, trying to keep his mind off the raw saddle sores inside his knees, when he heard an ax chopping. He turned back and saw Thomas and Campana stop their horses.

"Well, are you stopping because you think that's Johnson's ax we hear?" he asked.

"We're on his place," Thomas said. "It's a good thing we can hear the ax. Gives us a chance to go around him."

"What's the matter, you scared of one squatter?"

"Have at 'er, badguy," said Thomas.

"Huh? You think I won't?" Hoozy was thankful he could sit still, talk a minute, and rest his sore places.

"No, we think you ought to ride up to that big feller, take his ax away from him, and make him move out of our way."

Hoozy shifted in the saddle to ease the pressure on his butt. When he moved, his mare, Patch, thought he wanted to press on, so she started walking down the trail again. Hoozy was not eager to have an argument with Ray Johnson, but he bravely let Patch go on.

A dog started barking as Patch descended into a *cañada*, a pretty glade, where the man was working. A team of horses hitched to a wagon was tied in oak shade on the edge of the glade. Johnson was trimming an oak trunk with a sharp ax, cutting off the big limbs and then cording them to firewood size against the trunk. A woman was sitting in the shade in front of the horses weaving a beargrass basket. A boy about ten was sitting close to her. The boy was watching Hoozy, but the woman kept her head down, her face hidden by a sunbonnet.

Hoozy was surprised at seeing a woman there. He did not know Johnson had a woman. He rode toward the man.

Ray Johnson was tall and husky. His shoulders were broad. The black beard on his jaw looked hard as onyx. The ax looked small in his hands. His eyes were black, and he was giving Hoozy a mean look. The dog stopped barking and began growling and giving Hoozy the same look, as if to say, "That's it. Not one more step." Patch understood him and stopped.

"Afternoon, Ray," said Hoozy.

"Hello, Hoozy." Johnson laid down the ax and picked up a rifle. He walked to the wagon, took a water jug from beneath the seat, and poured himself a drink in a tin cup. Hoozy looked back over his shoulder to see where his partners were. Vincent's other regulators were nowhere in sight.

"Where're your friends?" asked Johnson.

"What friends are you talking about, Ray?"

"Your horse-thieving friends, Thomas and Campana."

"What makes you think they're my friends, Ray?"

"You dumb crook, everybody in the country knows you ran off with A. B. Cowden's horses and got Whitey killed. The Farley twins have been to the bars in Harshaw, and the story's spread through every other bar in the country. Hell, it was even printed in the *Harshaw Bullion*."

Johnson took another drink and put away his cup without offering Hoozy a drink.

"You didn't answer my question, Briggs."

"I never stole any horses. I saw some horses in Medal Canyon a bunch of Apaches were driving when they jumped us and killed Whitey. The Farley twins came up and held them off while me and two VO cowboys got out of range, but those Indians stole the horses, not us."

"Where are Thomas and Campana?"

"I don't know. They headed south. I've been prospecting."

"Prospecting for what, more horses to steal?"

"Well, if you don't believe me, I can't make you, but I thought a man had to be caught with the goods before he could be called a horse thief."

"I think you'd better go back to your partners and get off my place. Now that you've thrown in with the VO, stay away from me, Briggs."

"I will, if that's what you want. I only came down here to ask for a drink of water. You can give me a drink, can't you?"

"Yes, but after you drink, leave."

Hoozy started Patch toward the wagon, but the black dog bristled and planted himself in front of her. Patch stopped and calmly worked her ears. She did not care if she moved any closer to the wagon.

"Well, call off your dog so I can have my drink," said Hoozy.

"Go around him."

Hoozy absolutely craved water now. He had been counting on dismounting, standing a few moments in the shade, and cooling himself with a drink.

He stepped off his mare and walked around the dog. The dog pressed him, growling a mean breath against his pantleg. Hoozy reached for the jug. The dog crouched under the wagon at his feet. The jug was wrapped in a wet gunnysack, and the water was deliciously cool. Hoozy poured himself another measure. The dog's growl was becoming softer and less vicious.

The woman was sitting on a blanket, the family's lunch in a basket by her side. A large butcher knife was also lying there. She looked cool. Her hands were clean and very pretty. The Johnsons had not eaten lunch yet. Hoozy was hungry, but not only for food. He wished he could sit with them and have lunch.

The boy stepped away from the woman and began winging rocks at a tree with a slingshot. He was using an *honda*, a slingshot made of two leather thongs and a leather cradle for the rocks. The boy's target tree was about fifty yards away. The end of the thong popped when he released it, and the rocks hummed and shattered bark off the tree.

The boy kept demonstrating his prowess. He chose his rocks with calm, fit them in the cradle, hefted them for weight and balance, glanced at Hoozy out of the corner of his eye, swung them overhead, and let them fly at the tree.

Hoozy was convinced that a rock from the boy's doodad could kill him as dead as Johnson's rifle bullet or the butcher knife. Hoozy knew what he was up against here. He was puzzled though. He knew the boy's mother was dead. The boy was Ray Johnson's only kid. Who was the woman?

Hoozy put the cup carefully back where it belonged. Johnson was leaning on his rifle, watching him. Hoozy knew he ought to be able to draw both pistols, as he'd practiced, and shoot Johnson before he could take his weight off his rifle. He did not have enough confidence in himself to do anything that audacious, though, so he dismissed the idea before it caused him trouble.

"That's awful good water, Ray; thank you very much," Hoozy said. He did not think he would mind killing the man, but he did not want him to be mad at him.

Johnson turned his back and walked away. Hoozy thought, *Now*, or you'll never be the man you hope to be. He drew his pistol.

"Ray," he called.

"What," said Johnson, but he did not turn to see what Hoozy was doing.

Hoozy thought about the consequences of shooting the man in the back. He was not against it, but he did not want Thomas and Campana to go away telling people he was a coward. After he shot the man, he would certainly have to shoot the woman and the boy too.

That hesitation after he drew his pistol almost cost Hoozy his life. The black dog snatched his gun hand in his jaws and went into a frenzy. The pistol spun away uncocked, and Hoozy let out a wail of pain. The dog was trying to tear his arm off. He jerked Hoozy to his knees and backed under the wagon. Hoozy drew the second pistol he carried in his belt and shot the dog, to no avail. The dog snatched and jerked him so viciously that he lost his voice. His throat seemed paralyzed against all passage of breath and sound.

Johnson was running toward Hoozy with his rifle upraised like a club. The dog banged Hoozy's head against the wagon. Hoozy found some leverage, pulled the dog to him, jammed the pistol into the dog's ear, and pulled the trigger. That time he killed the dog.

"You sonofabitch!" yelled Johnson, swinging the rifle at Hoozy's head. Hoozy raised his hand against the blow, and the cocked pistol went off against Johnson's brisket. Johnson fell on Hoozy like a tree. The top of his head struck Hoozy's nose. The man's blood welled over Hoozy's shirt, and his big body pinned him to the ground.

"Ray!" screamed the woman. She was holding the butcher knife over Hoozy's head with both hands. He scurried out from under Johnson, and the woman swooped at him with the butcher knife. She was no expert attacker and her excitement made her inaccurate, but she bloodied Hoozy's head and hands before he made it to his feet. He grabbed a chunk of oak out of the wagon, knocked the woman down, and searched the ground for his pistols.

The boy sprang over the top of the wagon, landed on Hoozy's head and rode it into the ground. Hoozy wondered briefly if he would smother. The boy's weight made him gasp. He inhaled a gulp of dirt. The boy dug his fingers into his eyes and nostrils and chewed on one ear. The whole kid was on Hoozy's head, pressing it against the ground.

He caught his breath and stood up. He tore the boy off his head, slammed him into the ground, and stomped him.

His boots were inadequate for killing. His eye fell on Johnson's rifle, and he snatched it up, stood back, and shot the boy in the head without a pause. Killing was in his heart now, and he wanted more. He turned to the woman.

She was crippled, moaning, crawling away. She heard Hoozy's step and turned her face to him. He recognized her then. She was Ann Burr, the Kansas girl he brought to Arizona to marry. "Murderer," she said. He shot her and put an end to her.

Thomas and Campana rode up, looking at Hoozy as though they had never seen him before in their lives. They stopped their horses and examined the carnage without dismounting, staying above it and keeping themselves apart.

"Well, we didn't think you'd come down here and kill every man, woman, and child you found," said Thomas. "I only wanted you to talk to them awhile so we could get around them."

Campana stood his horse over the body of Ann Burr. Hoozy was not sorry about killing any of them, especially her. His head was covered with blood from her attack. He was trying to reload a pistol and could barely see. He searched along his belt, but he could not find the rims of the cartridges with his fingers. He looked down and saw his cartridge belt was full. He reached for a cartridge again without looking at it. He could not find the rim with his fingers. He looked at the cartridge he wanted, then looked at his hand and saw he was missing most of the fingers. His forefinger was swinging on a shred of skin. He began wrapping his handkerchief on the hand, then realized the woman had cut nearly all the fingers off, and he fainted.

He thought he was going a lot farther away than the ground, and the sudden leaving wrenched a whimper from him, but then he began to feel so warm and comfortable he did not care. As he revived, he found he was lying comfortably with his body settled from his cheek to his toes against the ground. Patch was across the draw, trailing the reins and grazing. He sat up.

Campana was standing beside him. "Your face is an embroidery," he said.

"How did you lose your ear?" asked Thomas. "Did they shoot it off, or bite it off? That was the fightingest family I ever saw."

Hoozy froze like a man does when he first discovers his wallet is missing. He felt the side of his head for his ear. Then he swiped at it, because he had no fingers to help him find it. He began to weep, held it back, stopped it, and went to the water jug. He moistened his handkerchief, held it against the side of his head, and sat down under a tree. He watched blood drip from various places into the ground between his legs. Thomas dismounted and searched over the battleground, looking for the ear.

"Where did you lose it, Hoozy?" asked Thomas.

"I don't know."

Thomas walked to the wagon. "Here's where most of the fight took place," he said. "Right here, I think. Oh, oh, here it is." He stooped and picked something off the ground. "No, this is a finger. And here's another one. Did you lose your fingers too?"

Hoozy said, "I don't know. Something's wrong with my hand. Come and look, will you, Tom?"

Hoozy unwrapped the hand and made himself look at it while he showed it to Thomas. Thomas drew his sheath knife and trimmed off the dangling forefinger with a daft swipe that Hoozy barely felt. He tore a swath of material off Ann Burr's petticoat and he used the water from the jug to bathe Hoozy's face and hands and take stock of his wounds. The face was disfigured.

Hoozy's right arm was in shreds. He held it up, and the pain shifted and rolled as though he was carrying hot rocks inside the sack of his skin. A sharp bulge in his forearm showed it had been fractured by the dog. His scalp was carved off his skull in places and shaved in other places where the woman grazed it with the blade. The line of his jaw, his brows, and the bridge of his nose had been hacked to the bone by the butcher knife.

"That's the best I can do for you," said Thomas, looking into Hoozy's face and shaking his head. "We'll take you to the doctor in Santa Cruz. We better clear out of here now. Somebody might catch us with these dead people."

"Indians killed these people," Hoozy said. "Let's take the bodies back to their house. That way, nobody will find out where it happened, and it won't matter if somebody finds the ear."

Hoozy piled the boy into the wagon. He straightened. Thomas and Campana were standing still, watching him.

"You're a cowardly son of a buck, but you're tough, I'll say that for you," Thomas said.

"Help me load these people," said Hoozy.

Campana turned his back and walked toward his horse. Thomas was waiting to see what Campana was going to do.

Hoozy levered a cartridge into the chamber of Johnson's Winchester. "Do you want to die too, Campana?" he said. Campana kept walking. "You, Campana—you want to die and be found with these people?"

Campana picked up his horse's reins.

"Don't get on that horse if you want to live," said Hoozy.

Campana turned and led his horse to the tree where Johnson's team was tied. He untied the team and backed it away from the tree. He took the lines and climbed into the wagon. "I'll drive the wagon, if you'll lead my horse," he said.

Thomas stepped up and helped Hoozy load Johnson and Ann. Hoozy climbed on Patch and started riding.

The regulators stripped the bodies and left them in the yard of the Johnson ranch to make it look as if Apaches had killed them. They burned the wagon, house, and barn. While they were there, the Johnson remuda came in to water. They drove the horses with them when they left.

On the way to Santa Cruz, Hoozy began to think he was lucky. He'd done his job for Vincent, covered his tracks well, and acquired a whole herd of horses.

"Well, these horses will pay me for the loss of my ear and fingers," Hoozy said. "The wages I get from Vincent won't ever cover that. Vincent wanted mischief; he got mischief. Kosterlinsky wants horses; he'll get horses."

"You're welcome to the horses as far as I'm concerned," said Thomas. "I don't want a thing out of this. After we've found someone in Santa Cruz to look after you, I hope I never lay eyes on Hoozy Briggs again."

"You feel the same way, Campana?" Hoozy asked.

"What a shame for a man," said Campana in Spanish. "Before this day, he was only stupid, but because of that, he is now disfigured. Then, to finish himself off, he's disfigured his soul with murder."

Hoozy smiled at Campana. Campana smiled back because he knew Hoozy did not understood a word of Spanish.

"Who said the owl-hoot trail was the easy way? I never worked so hard in my life," Hoozy said happily.

"Or enjoyed it less," said Thomas sourly.

"No, or enjoyed it so much," said Hoozy. With that, he swooned and landed on his head under his horse.

His partners tied him over the saddle and took him to Campana's cousin's house in Santa Cruz where the women charitably cleaned him, patched him, and put him to bed. When he revived, his partners told him they were leaving him in good hands, leaving him his saddle and leading Patch back to the VO, so that no one would know where he was. They also wanted him to know they hoped they'd seen the last of him.

CHAPTER 16

The brothers tracked Prim Pete to the Maria Macarena
ranch. They rode into the hacienda from the west and did
not have to ask anyone where their horse was. He was
eating corn in the shade of a cottonwood tree behind the
main building.

The brothers rode around to the front yard and waited.
They sat their horses, on ground that had been swept with
a broom and sprinkled by hand with well water.

Margarita, the young widow of Pedro Elias, came to the
door, and Ben asked to speak to Don Juan. The brothers
knew that Don Juan had not stolen the horse, but they
would not dismount until they were welcomed properly
and were sure of the climate of the Maria Macarena.
Because they were not on a friendly errand, they remained
formally, almost stiffly polite. Margarita received them in
the same way.

Don Juan stepped outside his front door and closed it
behind him. A small boy of five or six came out with him
and stared straight into Les's eyes as he stood close to Don
Juan for protection.

"*Hola, Don Juan Pedro,*" Ben said softly.

Don Juan said, "El Majo is standing in my backyard. I
can't imagine your father selling him to Kosterlinsky, but
that is what I have been told to believe."

"He was stolen, and we're here to get him back. We also want the man who stole him."

"You will find no horse thieves here, youngster."

"We know who stole the horse. The thief left him in Kosterlinsky's camp and went back to the U.S.A. We're surprised Kosterlinsky thought he could send him on to you, Don Juan."

"I am as surprised as you," said Don Juan. "Please dismount and come in. I'll have someone take care of your animals. Go, grandson," he said to the boy. "Ask your father to come and tend to these horses."

The boy broke out from under his grandfather's arm at a run. Ben and Les dismounted and took their rifles, morrals, and blanket rolls off their saddles and carried them to the house.

"Come in," said Don Juan. "Stand your rifles here by the door, if you want to. Come in and rest. I was about to have a *sopa* of rice. It's time for sopa in Sonora, no? It's a pleasure to have you here."

The brothers stepped inside the solid coolness of the adobe building and walked through the entrance hall to the ramada and arbor that sheltered the patio. They shook hands with Don Juan's unmarried daughters. The girls' hands were moist and cool. Their beauty always distracted the brothers so much they were never able to say how many girls Don Juan was raising. The daughters spent every winter, fall, and spring at school in the capital city. Seeing them, Ben was convinced again that Sonora girls must be the most beautiful in the world.

The brothers washed, and a girl brought them a clean towel. The girls took the brothers' blankets to the room where they would sleep. Don Juan led the way to his table and sat them down. They were served mescal and coffee by Margarita. The brothers relaxed a moment with *copitas* of mescal and sips of strong coffee. After the mescal, the girls served the sopa, rice steamed in a covered frying pan with tomato, onion, and tastes of garlic and pepper.

Don Juan said, "You caught me with El Majo before I had time to do my duty. I was about to send a messenger to notify your father that I have his horse. He hasn't been here very long."

"We know. We've been on his trail," said Ben.

"Kosterlinsky's man left him here early yesterday and ordered me to feed him, rest him, cure his sore feet, and notify him when he was ready to travel. I consented. These days, no one refuses Kosterlinsky.

"Nowadays, with the power he has been given in his campaign against the Apaches, Kosterlinsky does as he pleases. This has made him a bigger chief of bandits than even Geronimo. He takes everything he wants in the name of the government. Geronimo kills and runs and leaves us alone awhile. Kosterlinsky kills and makes himself rich and blames it on Geronimo. He is an embarrassing example of the delinquency of authority in this *reign* of Porfirio Diaz. *La delincuencia de autoridad.*"

"Don Juan Pedro, we'll go by Kosterlinsky's camp on our way home so he'll know we took our horse back. He'll have to congratulate us for recovering him, or admit he tried to steal him, but he won't be able to blame you for anything."

"But how can you take the horse anywhere? The poor animal cannot walk. He'll have to grow an inch of hoof before he can even be shod. He should not be forced to do anything now except turn his head from his feed to his water."

"We know he's sore, but we thought he could make it home if we shod him."

"Don't be in a hurry to take him home. I'll take care of him and return him to you in better shape than he was before he was stolen."

"He has to go into training by the middle of August. We're running him in Tombstone on the sixteenth of September."

"You never told me you matched another race," Les said in Spanish.

"I didn't tell anyone," said Ben. "I only want to run this race one time. I didn't want to start blabbing about it a long time before it happened. If I did, by the time we were ready to run, everybody in Arizona would be wanting us to cover their bets."

"Hell, I won't bet against you. Mark won't bet against

you. You could have told us, couldn't you?" Les was trying not to show it, but he was wounded.

"All right, I'll tell you. I've matched Prim Pete against any horse John McClintock can produce, lap and tap, for one quarter of a mile for three thousand dollars."

"Well, this time you overmatched yourself. John'll import a racehorse from Texas or California and bloody your nose."

"Hell, we'll win it. No horse in the Southwest can outrun Prim Pete in a quarter of a mile if we can keep him at home and have him in shape."

"The Maria Macarena will have to be his home for a while," said Don Juan. "I'll accommodate him, even if I have to move my *viejita*, that little old sorrowing lady who sleeps with me, out of my bed to do it."

The brothers rested that night with Don Juan's family and left with the *guia* star the next morning. They found Hoozy's tracks by a spring called Yerba Buena on the Santa Cruz river and camped there that evening. When they rode through the Buena Vista the next morning, they finally became aware that the drouth was upon them.

Springs were dry. All the bloom was burned off the country. The farther they rode, the poorer the country looked. They stopped to talk.

"I sure never realized the country was in this kind of trouble until now," Ben said.

"We'll never be able to ride hard enough to save these cattle from starving unless our horses learn to fly," said Les.

"If we weren't in such a hurry, we could find plenty to do right here. Somebody has to start riding this river and watching for weak cattle."

"I think for today we better forget about catching horse thieves. I'll ride the river to the edge of Romero's country and meet you at George Moore's tonight," Les said.

They rode away from each other. The Santa Cruz River ran into Arizona from Mexico, through the Buena Vista then north to Tucson. The river usually ran high in July, but Ben found no running water in the river. Thirsty cattle bunched at seeps that welled up along the dry river bottom.

The steers from Temporal Canyon were not doing well. Without rain, they would not grow big enough to meet

Walter Jarboe's requirements in the fall. Now a big wind from the southwest was whipping the country, and not a cloud was building on any horizon. Ben rode with his back to the wind toward the camp of his friend George Morris on Saddle Mountain.

George was sweet on Betty Cowden. He was so inept a suitor that Betty often acted as though she did not recognize him when she saw him coming. Even when she opened the door and let him into her father's house, she did not call the poor man by his name.

Thinking of George Moore made Ben smile to himself. George was good at resting. He showed more energy paying long and sporadic suit to Betty than he ever showed working his mine.

Twenty minutes after he and Les separated, Ben heard gunshots and knew his brother was probably in trouble. Another shot sounded, and Ben tied the packhorse to a tree and headed into the wind at a high trot. Passport perked up and flicked his ears in the direction of the shooting and then back at Ben, as though he knew he was headed for excitement.

The wind increased and gusted hard, blowing dust and grit into Ben's and Passport's faces. Ben could not keep his head down so his hat would take the brunt of it; he had to watch for Les.

He was hurrying, but he knew he was so far away the shooters would surely settle the argument before he arrived. The shots came from the mouth of a canyon where it ran into the Santa Cruz. He traveled on the bottoms of washes and draws as much as he could and hurried across the open spaces to keep from being seen.

He was tired of riding. He had anticipated stopping at George Moore's and resting for the day. Now he struck Pop's tracks where he expected them to be and watched the high points for a sniper.

Pop . . . pop—the shots sounded again. Ben figured they were a mile away. He let Passport break into a lope. A half mile from the place he expected to find his brother, he circled under cover of a ridge until he was downwind from the shooting. He stopped to let his horse blow. He was anxious about Les. Les must be down; all the shooting was coming from one place.

The wind was causing great commotion now, snatching everything it caught hanging loose. It snatched at Ben's breath. He turned Passport away from the gusts and rode along the brow of the ridge until he could see the mouth of the canyon and the dry bed of the Santa Cruz.

He saw part of a downed horse and saddle under the near bank of the river. He could not see the head or the tail. He found the tree where the bushwhacker had tied his horse. He saw a tegua track, then found the bushwhacker's empty brass casings. The sniper had probably seen Ben coming and pulled out.

A bullet whined high over Ben's head. He heard the explosion of a pistol from the wash, then three more evenly spaced shots, like a signal.

"Les!" Ben shouted. He waved his hat over the top of his ridge. "Brother!" he shouted. He rode down to the bottom of the canyon and let Passport step out in plain sight of the wash. He followed Top's tracks on a trail and drew no shots and no call.

He went down into the riverbed and around a loamy curve in the bank. Les was sitting there with his back against the bank, pointing his pistol at Ben, his leg pinned under his dead horse.

"Have you been shot, brother?" Ben asked.

"I might as well be," Les said. "The bastard shot Top. I *knew* this was going to happen. I knew that Yaqui wanted to do it, knew he would do it today, and I, by God, picked the best spot for him when I rode down between that ridge and this riverbank."

Ben could tell by the tone of his brother's voice that he was not seriously hurt.

"Was it the Yaqui?" Ben asked.

"Of course it was."

Ben dismounted and knelt by his brother. Top's noble eye was glazed.

"My Lord, did he fall off the bank on you, brother?"

"The bullet just kind of slapped Top behind the ear, and he flipped over backwards, stuck my head down in the well and landed on my leg in this loam."

"It's a wonder the Yaqui didn't come down and finish you off."

"I had my pistol. My rifle's under Top. I could raise up and twist around and shoot over the bank. I couldn't stay that way long, though. Kept him off me, though. I was counting on you hearing the shots."

Ben put the loop of his reata around Top's front legs, mounted Passport, and dragged the horse off his brother. He unsaddled Top while Les walked around to limber up his leg. Les's ankle was so swollen he did not dare take off his boot; he would never get it back on if he did. The side of his face was scraped raw from grazing down the bank in the fall. Ben lit his pipe and waited for his brother to recover so they could go on.

Les did not complain of being hurt, though he was plenty sore. He would not look at Top.

"Sit down, brother," Ben said. "It's all over now."

Les sat. He looked at the ground, his face hidden by the brim of his hat.

"Don't let it eat you. We'll get even," Ben said. Les liked to get even.

"It's not eating me. I've been thinking about it. It seems we can't ever have anything but more work. Country's drying up, cattle dying. I saw the carcasses of two of our cows. People want us in jail. Gunsels try to take our horses. Apaches ransack our home. One minute, the Mexicans we like are grinning at us and giving us brandy. The next minute, they're sending bushwhackers after us. Why didn't he just kill me and take my horse like everybody else tries to do?"

"Kosterlinsky probably didn't want him to."

"Why not?"

"You know Kosterlinsky. He's funny. He likes us."

"Well, he's not funny anymore. He killed my horse. He did it to slow us down from going after Hoozy and to scare us off so we wouldn't go back for Prim. He's got a stake in Vincent's shenanigans again."

"I know, brother."

"I'm not even mad at anybody. I feel too bad. That Top was a real good horse."

"I know."

"Everybody's trying to strip us of our livestock and everything else we've got. They take our stock, then give it back, or give half of it back, or kill it and give nothing back. Everybody figures they can play with us as they damned please."

"I guess they do, Les."

Les stood up, went to the morral hanging on Ben's saddle horn, and took a swallow of mescal from the *amphorita*, a long, clear, thin bottle Ben carried. "I don't know what I'm going to do about it," Les said. "But I'm about to do something indecent for a change, and it'll be so bad, it'll probably even shock me."

Ben was thinking about the amphorita. *Amphora* was the name for a bottle about as big around as a silver doller and about eight inches long in which the Mexicans sold the cheapest tequila and mescal. The amphora was the cheapest measure of strong spirits sold in the country, except for the shot sold across the bar. Yet it had been given an elegant name, *amphora*, as though it was a silver cruet or ancient vase. It was nice to look at, but made a nicer bludgeon, and the spirits it carried were like a bludgeon.

Kosterlinsky was like that, like everything Americans mistakenly liked at first and then learned to dislike about Mexico. People saw Kosterlinsky in his uniform with his clean lines, nice manners, and earthy humor, and they said, "If only all Mexicans were like that." And then he gave them the Mexican *abrazo* with a poniard in his hand and administered the fatal *puñalada* that severed the spine and dispatched a soul—so he could steal a horse.

After that people said, "See? That's what the best of the Mexicans will do to you. What won't the rest of them do if you give them the chance?" The trouble was, the 2 percent of Mexicans that was made up of Kosterlinskys were up front representing the 98 percent who were the finest people in the Americas, bar none. Every day, people like the Cowdens thanked God for 98 percent of the Mexicans and damned to hell the Kosterlinskys who were in authority, but they kept on living with Mexicans and liked it.

Ben and Les rode double on Passport, carried Les's saddle back and loaded it on the packhorse, then went on to George Morris's mine. They found George sitting under a tree reading a book. They figured on staying the night with him, as they usually did when they rode the Buena Vista. They had arranged for Mark to meet them there with fresh horses.

George picked himself up out of the shade of his tree as though he was wearied unto death. He face was freshly shaved, and his hair was neatly combed; George was fastidious. His hat was clean and free of sweatstain. His corduroy trousers were worn only in the seat and showed no other stress; his shirt was open, his sleeves rolled up. Ben could see no line of tan at his wrist or collar to show that he went out in the sun, but then he was a hard-rock miner and could say he spent most of his time down in the dark of his mine.

"Well, George," said Ben. "Here you are, right where you're supposed to be. We were afraid old Yawner might have come by to see you this time."

"Yawner?" George had a soft and gentle voice, and this was so because he did not exert himself. He was a gentleman, though. "Heck, nobody but the VO's been to see me since the last time you were here."

"Maybe you were down in your mine working when old Yawner came by," Les said.

"No, I haven't been down in the hole in two weeks," George said. "I stay out of there when old Yawner's in the country. I know a lot more about what's happening when I can sit out here in the quiet and read a book."

"Doesn't it tire you to sit and read all day?" asked Les.

The ground all the way around the base of George's tree was worn smooth by his butt. The sun that came up and traveled across the sky never had a chance to burn George. He was always ready to shift his butt to stay in the shade.

"You fellows unsaddle your horses," said George. "I put on the coffee when I saw you coming."

Les slid off Passport's hips and limped away a few steps to study the country below him. He could see the whole Buena Vista range from George's camp.

While he was unsaddling Passport, Ben told George about the Yaqui bushwhacking Les. George acted as though he knew such dangers were common, but they did not affect him because he did not associate with bushwhackers.

Ben said, "You sure could see anybody coming from up here and have plenty of time to leave if you didn't want to visit, couldn't you, George?"

"Yes. Nothing happens around here that I don't know about. For instance, did you know the VO's have cattle over here?"

"We haven't seen any, yet," Ben said. "But Vincent's been laying claim to all the grass, so it wouldn't surprise anybody if he moved in on the Buena Vista too."

"I didn't know Vincent had country in Mexico, either," said George. "His cowboys have been driving cattle across the line toward Santa Cruz."

"That's Elias and Romero country over there," Ben said. "Vincent doesn't own anything on the Mexican side."

"I saw his cowboys turn a bunch of cattle over to some Mexican soldiers, too," said George.

"Kosterlinsky," said Ben. "Vincent and Kosterlinsky are conniving again. George, you're the best lookout I ever saw. Were you able to see the brands on the cattle?"

"No, I can only tell you what I saw from here. I never move off this spot."

"Never mind, you've seen plenty. We might come up here and camp with you more often."

"I might not be here much longer," said George. "One of those VO cowboys brought me a letter from Vincent. Says my mine is on his land and I have to get off. Says I have to make an accounting of the ore I've sold and pay him a third of my take. He sent Ray Johnson the same message."

"He can't take your mine, or Ray's ranch. Don't let him bother you," Ben said.

"It does bother me. I'm not a fighter. I won't stay here if it means trouble with people."

"You won't have to fight anybody, George," Ben said.

"I won't fight. I'll leave. Ray'll fight, though. I went over to see him the other day and he greeted me like I was wearing a warbonnet and teguas."

"Vincent won't harm a man with a little boy. He's about half politician, and that would make folks mad at him. He takes everybody to court and breaks them with lawyers' fees. I don't think he'll fight anybody a war."

"Here comes our brother," said Les. "Just in time! Now, that's a cowboy!"

Mark appeared horseback on the flat a half mile below George's camp leading two horses. George went into his cabin to tend to the fire in the stove.

Mark was not smiling when he rode into the camp. He tossed the ends of his lead ropes to Les.

"Ray Johnson and his family have been murdered, and they're saying the Yawner did it," said Mark with no other greeting.

"When did it happen?" Ben asked.

George came to them with tin cups, a coffee pot, and a bowl of sugar.

"The miners at Washington Camp say it must have happened yesterday. Goldwater, the old peddler, found them last evening. They'd been lanced and stripped. I came by there awhile ago. The place is burned to the ground, and the stock's been run off."

"Well, the Yawner didn't do it," Ben said. "He was never over there. Les and I can swear to that."

"How do you know the stock's gone, Mark?" asked Les.

"I looked at tracks. Somebody on shod horses went south with Ray's remuda."

"I bet the VO killed Ray," said George. "I'm pulling up stakes."

"Something else," said Mark. "Annie Burr was killed with Ray and his son."

"Ann? What was she doing with Ray?" asked Les, shocked again.

"They were married in Santa Cruz two or three days ago," Mark said.

"How could that be?" asked Les sorrowfully.

"Well, those girls came out here to get married, and they wanted to get married," Mark said defensively.

Les moaned as though he had been lanced. He turned toward Ben, shook his head, and said, "See what I mean? We can't hope for a damned thing to stay alive for us with all the *sonsabitches* loose in the country."

"Old Goldwater loaded the bodies and took them back to Washington Camp," Mark said. "They were in the schoolhouse while the miners were digging the graves.

Nobody knew Annie's name, though they did know Ray had married. They asked me to see if I could identify her because I knew people in Santa Cruz. They thought she was a Mexican girl. I sure was surprised when I saw it was Annie. She'd been beaten and shot."

"Aw, it couldn't have been Ann," Les said angrily. "How could you be sure, Mark?"

"She had a bruise on her temple, but it was her. She didn't look any different in her face, and that long blond hair was braided her way. Nobody else puts her hair up like that except her sister."

The next day, Mark and George rode as far as the Johnson place with Ben and Les. The feed was green and pretty inside the Johnson fence. A nice shower or two had brought a big spot of green grass to life on the Johnson homestead. Now it marked the graves. The buildings were in rubble and still smoking.

Ben was thinking that if he and Les had kept after Hoozy, they might have helped Ray and his family when the murderers came. People sure were worthless. Everybody at Washington Camp must have heard the shooting, yet they let the peddler go down to find the bodies. Hoozy and his partners must have been close too.

Ben and Les, riding fresh horses, watched Mark and George disappear toward Washington Camp and Durazno. Mark was taking Passport and the packhorse home. George was riding a horse and leading a mule. His camp was packed on his mule, and he was quitting Saddle Mountain.

The brothers followed the trail of the Johnson horses south. The plainest tracks were the ones on top, the ones the riders made driving the horses. Ben recognized the tracks he and Les had followed all the way from the Durazno pasture, but he did not say anything. Les dismounted and examined the ground where a horseman had ridden around a stray horse and turned him back into the herd.

"Here's the track that cinches it for me," he said. "Here's where Hoozy's mare peed. I can always tell it was a mare peed by the tracks. This is Hoozy's mare, all right. See there?"

Ben rode to him and looked at the sign.

"That's her," Les said. "Plain as Hoozy's face. I know it's my imagination, but I even think I smell old Hoozy on this track. He always smells kinda like mare's pee."

The brothers found the Johnson horses in a fenced pasture near the Sonora town of Santa Cruz. Workers were building a large adobe ranch house nearby. They were quitting for the day when the brothers rode up.

"Look at these *vaqueros*, what a miracle!" one of the workers said as he walked out to greet the brothers.

Ben recognized him as Hector Romero, grandson of the old gentleman who had sold the San Rafael ranch to Vincent. Ben and Les shook his hand without dismounting.

"What brings my friends to Santa Cruz?" asked Hector. "They have beer down at the cantina. That's where I'm going."

"Oh, we won't be thirsty till dark," said Les. "A drink from your well would sure be appreciated, though." He looked toward town with serious longing. Ben knew he probably would like to get good and drunk with the misery he felt for losing Ann Burr. He'd been sparking her, and she'd married without his even knowing it, and now she was dead.

"Listen, this is a new well, and the water is sweet," said Hector. "Come on and drink."

"We need to water our horses, too," said Les, looking over Hector's head at the other workers. Ben was already watching them. He was not sure he and Les should be too trusting at the place they found the Johnson horses after the Johnson massacre.

"We can water them out of the well bucket," said Hector. "After all, what's cleaner than a horse?"

The brothers followed Hector around the house to the well and dismounted as he drew a bucket of cool water with new rope on a new windlass. They drank from a cup hanging on a wire by the windlass, and then they slipped the bits out of their horses' mouths and drew water for them until they were full.

"Is your family building a new house?" Ben asked.

"Oh, no, this isn't ours anymore," said Hector. "This piece of land has been appropriated by the government. We're building a garrison here."

"When was this decided?"

"Kosterlinsky confiscated one square league of our ranch here because he wanted land on the river. We dug the well, then we fenced the trap on the river where those horses are. Now we're building the *cuartel*, the living quarters and offices."

"And you have the job of making adobe and hammering nails," said Ben.

"Not a job, an order. We do this free of charge as volunteers in the campaign against the Apaches. We have been told that we're doing this for our country, but we know Kosterlinsky is setting himself up as an *hacendado*, a landlord, and this will be his hacienda."

"How do those horses in the pasture fit into his plan?"

"Those horses?" asked Hector. "All I know is those horses belong to our neighbor, Ramón Johnson, unless he's sold them."

"Who penned them here?"

"Two VO cowboys, Thomas and Campana, and one other rider."

"Who was the other rider?"

"He was riding a mare. I didn't know him. He looked like a miner I've seen over by the Mowry. He was suffering *un desmadre de dolor*, an unmothering of pain. He stayed down by the river, but we heard him moaning and saw him sitting on a log and rocking an arm as though it was a little baby.

"The VO cowboys turned the horses into this pasture and rode away without speaking to us. The one who was suffering rode away with them. The mare was lame and worn-out, too."

"Ramón Johnson was murdered night before last. Those men drove the horses here from Ramon's corrals."

"They killed Ramón for his horses?"

"Whoever killed him also killed his wife and son. Burned his place to the ground. At least that's what the tracks say. We did not read one sign of a tegua around the Johnson ruins."

"*Que Lastima!*" said Hector. "*Muerto con todo y familia!* What a shame, his life and everything gone, and his family too. His new wife was a pretty girl. They married here at the *presidencia* only a few days ago.

"Ramón's tanks were full, and his grass was green. Me and my friends were talking about him today while we were laying adobe. We admired his luck. He just married a pretty wife and gave his little boy a mother. Also, Ramón and his family are the only ones who have been blessed by rain this season."

CHAPTER 17

A. B. and Freddie sat alone at the breakfast table. In the Cowden household the men breakfasted before the women, so they could start work outside early. Freddie and A. B. were the only men home that morning, so they were being given plenty of attention.

Paula Mary was making herself available to help with breakfast for a change because her best friend Maudy was making the work easy for everyone. Maudy was quick to take hold of any kind of work. Now that she was in the house, no one else had to do a thing.

Paula Mary did not like to work. She kept an eye out for the jobs that might be coming up so she would know when to disappear. She possessed an instinct for knowing exactly the moment someone who was doing needful work would look up for help. That instinct enabled her to appear to be busy doing something else, or to hide before she was drafted for a real job.

That morning she assigned herself the chore of buttering hot biscuits for A. B. and Freddie. Her father and her small brother ate one biscuit right after another, and that kept Paula Mary busy doing something she liked.

A. B. and Freddie were half through their breakfast when Danny and Donnie Farley hollered from down the canyon to alert the house. The Cowdens went outside and watched the remuda stream by the front of the house. The horses nickered with joy at being home. They trotted the last yards to the corral and waited for Gordo to open the gate. They were weary and hungry from their adventure, but their heads were up, and they were happy to be home.

The twins penned the horses, hurried to the house, washed on the back porch, and went into the kitchen. They were ready to eat and sat down at the table immediately, but the Cowdens wanted to hear the whole story of the battle with old Yawner's warriors and the recapture of the remuda.

The girls prepared the twins' breakfast carefully, lovingly, as they listened. They knew most of the twins' story would end when they began feeding. When the girls were satisfied the story was complete, they served the breakfast. The twins had been out a week cutting wood, driving teams, sleeping on the ground, and fighting Indians. They proceeded to consume a dozen eggs, a pound of bacon, a pan of biscuits, a half jar of peach jam, a dish of butter, a half-gallon of milk, and a pint of cream for their coffee.

Freddie Lee watched the feeding Farleys the way he watched the old tiger that came to Harshaw with the Mexican circus every year. He laid his chin on the table for a prey's-eye view, and the sight was a new wonder for him. Once, he even looked underneath the table to see what was happening to the Farley bellies into which all that food was piling. He could see no signs of swelling, so he went back to watching the fierce expressions.

The twins were much like feeding tigers—they did not chew, they chomped the food enough to accommodate it to the size of a swallow. They knew their manners well enough not to make offensive sounds or crouch over their food. However, they gave the impression that they caught it when it came in range, and their looks were menacing when the girls did not come close enough, soon enough with food.

When the stream of food being carried to them began to falter, the twins remembered their manners and paused to answer questions. Tragically for them, their appetites were surviving the amount of breakfast drawn that morning from the Cowden larder. They looked the table over as unobtrusively as possible to be sure they had consumed every bite offered them. They glanced anxiously toward the stove when the food stopped coming, then made signs that they might have to leave if they were not offered more. They were not ones to stick around a kitchen table after breakfast was all gone. Their other appetites made it so they had to keep moving.

"We were hungry," said Danny. "Thank you, Aunt Viney."

"Thank you, Aunt Viney," said Donny, who was still slipping covetous looks at the empty platters. His craving for breakfast still bothered him, and he was not sure it would subside by the time he climbed back on his horse.

"It's always a pleasure to have you boys with us," said Viney, laughing. "You do so well at the table."

"Sorry we didn't have hotcakes this morning, boys," said A. B. "Do you think you can make it home for dinner before you fall over in a faint?"

"Oh, yessir," said Donny. "I'm about full."

"Not full yet?" asked Viney. "Would you like more biscuits and jam?"

Donny looked at Danny to see if he would stay for another biscuit. They were standing away from the table, though, and it was too late to sit down again.

"We'd better get home to our folks," said Danny, but he and his brother turned to the bread pan in unison, like a yoke of oxen at the feed-trough, and cleaned out the last of the biscuits on their way out the door.

Paula Mary saw her chance to disappear. It was time to do the dishes. She headed out the door with the twins. "Paula Mary Cowden," said Viney, "you get right back in here and clear off the table. The only thing you did all morning was butter your papa's biscuits."

Paula Mary halted, went limp, and let her legs and arms flop as she fell back into the kitchen.

"Do you want me to help you, Paula Mary?" asked Maudy. "Here, you clear off the table, and I'll wash the dishes. I like to wash dishes."

A light shone way back in Paula Mary's eye. "Do you like to dry them, too?" she asked, recklessly. At that moment she did not care that Maudy was her best friend. When it came time to protect oneself from work, it was every man for himself.

"Sure I do. I like to do everything that has to be done," said Maudy.

"Then you can dry them, too."

"Oh, well, I don't want to take all your chores away from you."

"Oh, that's all right. I do them all the time when you're not here."

That remark quelled all movement and sound in the kitchen. Paula Mary was appalled at the stillness of the room. Then Viney, in a soft and dreadful tone, said, "Oh, today Paula Mary is going to learn to clear the table and wash and dry the dishes all by herself, aren't you, daughter?"

Paula Mary wanted to do something instantly to save herself more embarrassment, but she was paralyzed. She suspected nothing short of working herself to death the rest of her life would save her. The simple lifting of a dirty dish off the table would have saved her, but she had been opposed to such action for so long, she could not move quickly enough to do herself any good.

"Did you hear me, daughter?" asked Viney, softly.

"Yes," said Paula Mary in a tiny voice, knowing she was doomed, for if her shame did not strike her dead in another minute, she would certainly die the lingering death of a kitchen drudge.

Then, to her everlasting gratitude, Maudy saved her by handing her a dirty dish. "Here, Paula Mary," said her friend. "You start by carrying everything to the sink, and I'll take the tablecloth outside and shake it. Then I'll help you get your dishwater ready and show you how to scour your pans. It's easy and fun, you'll see."

Paula Mary took hold of the plate, and that worked for her like a starting gun. In a few moments she cleared the table, and put the dishes in a pan of soapy water to soak, and was so busy she forgot that work could kill. Viney picked herself effortlessly out of her chair and left the room.

The girls were responsible for another important consideration they must show their father every morning. He always went to the barn right after breakfast and gave the girls time to clean up the kitchen. After that, he expected them to clear out of the house for a while.

A. B. had built this house with an indoor toilet, and every single morning of his life, he availed himself of that facility after he came back from his early walk and inspection of the barn and corrals. For this function, he required exclusive use of the entire house.

The only other person allowed inside was Viney, and she served as sentinel. She opened all doors and windows and sat in her sewing rocker while A. B. took comfort inside the indoor toilet. All other indoor activities of the Cowden family were suspended until A. B. Cowden pulled the chain in his privy.

After Paula Mary washed and dried the dishes, she felt a great need to be by herself. She went out behind the house, climbed her white oak tree, and hid in the top. She was awfully close to being unhappy because she had been caught trying to evade work and also because the work had not killed her. She did not want to be seen.

Paula Mary watched the Farley twins ride out of sight toward Harshaw. A. B. was in his privy. Viney was sitting in her sewing rocker, mending trousers. Eileen, Betty, Maudy, and Freddie were in the orchard watering the trees with Freddie's burro.

The burro was packed with a canvas *bota*, a water bag that hung in five-gallon compartments on his sides. The compartments had spouts in their bottoms with wooden stoppers. Freddie and Maudy used a bucket to fill the bota with water from the seep in the creek, then led the burro back and stood him over the tree wells and pulled the stoppers to water the trees. Eileen and Betty cleaned and bordered the tree wells.

Freddie and Maudy were leading the burro with the empty bota back to the creek when they looked up and saw VO steers coming off the road to water in the seep. Freddie tossed the burro's lead rope to Maudy, ran up the bank, and began bouncing rocks off the horns of the leaders to turn them away.

"Here, quit that throwing rocks at those steers," shouted one of the VO cowboys. Freddie recognized him a the one called Ted Broderick who had threatened to draw his pistol on Freddie the day the VO cowboys ran their steers over the Cowdens' dam. The only water in the bottom of the creek now was a puddle from the seep. Freddie emptied it each time he filled the bota, and it took a quarter hour to seep full again.

"I don't want your old steers drinking my seep dry," shouted Freddie, and he ran at the cattle—crowded them, shouted, bounced another volley of rocks off their ribs, and sent the whole bunch running up the road.

Broderick was riding a big bronc. He bailed down the bank and ran along the creek bottom to get ahead of the steers. The burro shied from the bronc and jerked Maudy into Broderick's path. The bronc brushed Maudy violently against the bank. Broderick aimed his horse at Freddie, ran him out of the creekbed, and laughed at him for turning tail. He went on to head the steers and stop them.

"Now, you kids stay out of our way, Gawdammit," said Broderick.

Freddie Lee was not one bit afraid of him. He laid down a barrage of rocks on Broderick and his horse. The rocks were smooth, round, and heavy. The first rock bounced off Broderick's shoulder, the second off his knee, the third off his knuckles, and the fourth off his horse's head. After that, Freddie was not so accurate because the bronc was spinning.

Broderick squalled with anger and tried to talk nice to his horse at the same time to keep from being bucked off. The horse scared the steers into a run. Broderick's partner stayed out in front of them, but did not stop them until they were almost out of sight.

Broderick regained control of his bronc, and this time he jerked his rope down, built a loop, and charged Freddie to rope him. Maudy Jane pelted a handful of gravel at the bronc. Betty raised her shovel and charged out of the orchard.

Broderick was swinging his loop over his head, but Freddie did not turn to run from him. He stood on top the bank, throwing handfuls of dirt in the bronc's face to keep him out of range. Maudy's gravel so unsettled the bronc that Broderick could do nothing but swing his loop and cuss.

The horse finally turned his tail to the volleys of dirt and gravel, and Betty ran along the top of the bank, rang the blade of her shovel off Broderick's head, and unhorsed him. She could have split his skull, but his loop deflected the shovel. His falling off was caused more by his losing his balance when he dodged the shovel than by the force of Betty's blow, but he tangled in the rope as he fell. The horse flinched away in terror when he saw the man was caught underneath him, and he sold out down the wash, dragging the man at his heels.

Maudy was in the wash ahead of the horse. She saw he was dragging the man, and she picked up a dry cottonwood branch, waved it in the bronc's face, and turned him into the bank to stop him.

Eileen burst into the house, shouting, "Mama, I don't care if Papa's on the throne, he has to get off the best way he can and come and shoot a VO cowboy before he kills Freddie Lee."

Viney scattered her sewing basket onto the floor as she jumped up to run outside and gather her children.

The bronc was still dragging Broderick and trying to break away. Maudy kept turning him into the bank with her branch. The horse was trampling the man, but if he broke loose, he would drag him and kick him to death on the run.

Snider, the other VO cowboy, finally saw his partner was in trouble, let the cattle go, and came running to help. He knocked Maudy down with his horse as he tried to take hold of the bronc's bridle reins. The bronc whirled away from Snider and saw the daylight he wanted at the moment Broderick finally untangled himself and stood up. The horse sprang for the open, shied away from Maudy on the ground, and ran over Broderick. Snider launched his horse after the bronc and ran over Broderick, too. The bronc stampeded out of the wash and up the road toward Harshaw with Snider chasing him.

When Broderick made it to his feet, he drew his pistol. "By the holy Lord," said he, spitting blood. "The next sonofabitch who throws a rock, or swings a shovel, or even gives me a dirty look is going to get his head blown off." He looked around for a target.

His eyes met Maudy's. He did not look a bit formidable to her. She figured he must have a bruise on every square inch of his carcass. "Pshaw!" she said. "Count your lumps and remember how you got them." She threw the cotton-wood branch down at his feet and walked to the house. Viney gathered Maudy with her other children and took them inside.

Broderick found himself alone in the creek except for the burro. He ran and cussed at the burro to run him off, but the old burro only trotted a few steps up the bank, stopped, and looked back as if to say, Bad temper never cleared a field. Then he ambled on toward the orchard where he knew of some green and tender grass by the tree wells.

By the time Snider came back with the bronc, Broderick was too angry to do anything right except go home and put himself to bed, but he wanted to get even with the Cowdens. He helped Snider gather the steers and start them up the road again.

"I'm glad that's over," Snider said when they were out of sight of the house.

Broderick rode around the leaders and stopped them.

"What are you doing?" demanded Snider.

"Let's stop a minute," Broderick said. He held the steers until they settled down and began grazing by the side of the road. He stepped down off his bronc, handed the reins to Snider, took his chaps and spurs off, and hung them by their straps on his saddle horn.

"Now what do you think you're going to do?" asked Snider.

"You stay right here and see that these cattle don't walk away," said Broderick. "I'm going to burn that gentleman's barn down."

"Listen, that's going too far. We aren't being paid for that. I wouldn't burn these people's barn for any man."

"I'm not doing this for Vincent, and I don't need your approval. This is for my own satisfaction."

As he sneaked across the wash, Broderick realized again how much he enjoyed watching people blow up when they saw their barn burning. They always reached the fire in time to work themselves half to death, but never in time to put it out. Broderick wanted to put a big black smudge on the Cowdens that would make him happy every time he rode by. If they built themselves a new barn, he would burn that one too.

He skulked through the corrals and stepped inside the barn. This would not be the first barn he'd burned. He crossed to A. B.'s office where he found a kerosene lamp. He went down the row of stalls and sprinkled coal oil on the straw bedding. He went back into the office to see if he could find anything to steal before he burned it all up.

From her tree, Paula Mary saw Broderick walk into the barn. She thought Broderick was Maudy's brother Pete, coming to visit his sister. Paula Mary hoped he would hurry up and come out of the barn. Pete was the handsomest man beside her own brothers she had ever seen in her life.

Paula Mary was sulking when the VO cowboys were causing the commotion in front of the house, so she had not investigated. She figured her sisters would call her if they wanted her. None of the sounds of the commotion alarmed her enough to make her want to climb out of her tree.

Now she was up the tree with her pride. Her fanny was getting tired of pride. She hoped her mother or her sisters would miss her now and start looking for her. She couldn't stay in the tree all day

Finally her butt got so sore from sitting on the same old limb she stopped sulking and climbed down. She had seen the cattle and the VO cowboys go by on the road. She began to think the commotion might have been her family keeping the VO steers out of the orchard, or something like that. She saw the cattle go around the bend, but they had not come back in sight.

She'd recognized the cowboy called Snider. One of his nieces was in school with Paula Mary, and he was a friend of Pete Pendleton's. Pete did not work for the VO, but Paula Mary knew he and Snider were pals. Snider ran a camp for the VO over by the Pendleton homestead at Canelo, where Maudy's brothers camped. He'd even been out sparking Maudy Jane from time to time.

Paula Mary decided she would go talk to Pete. She ran

down and stopped at the big door of the barn. She did not see Pete, but she heard a stealthy sound in her papa's office. Nobody ever went in there unless A. B. was there. Well, if Pete was alone in her papa's office, he was giving Paula Mary a chance to scare his hair stiff on his skull. She grinned and tiptoed to the door. After all, she was the world's best ambusher.

Pete Pendleton was not in her papa's office. The VO hand they called Broderick was bending over A. B.'s desk and quietly snooping through a drawer.

Paula Mary tiptoed backward until she was outside. She turned and tiptoed until she was away from the barn, and then she broke loose and ran back to the house as fast as any girl ever ran in her life. Her papa was in the front room laughing with the girls, listening to Freddie Lee tell about putting the run on the VO cowboys.

"Where have you been, Paula Mary?" asked Eileen. "Did you know that your family has been in the fight of its life?"

"Papa, that Broderick from the VO is in your office going through your desk," said Paula Mary.

A. B.'s smile disappeared so fast that Paula Mary couldn't remember what it looked like. Ice sparkled in his pale blue eyes. He moved out of his chair with the same quickness she remembered seeing when he arrested Whitey Briggs. He picked up his double-barreled shotgun and headed for the door, telling Viney to keep everyone inside.

A. B. walked to his barn and stopped inside the door. He heard the sound of a drawer sliding shut. He smelled the coal oil in his barn. He cocked one hammer on his shotgun. All sound in his office stopped.

Silence on both sides. A. B. heard Broderick's pistol slide from its holster. The sound of A. B. cocking the other hammer was loud and plain.

Silence.

Broderick cleared his throat.

Silence.

"I'm coming out the door and I'm gonna shoot the first man I see, so get ready to die, or say who you are," Broderick said.

Silence.

Broderick shuffled his feet, but he did not move toward the door. Anybody in the world Broderick's age in 1885 knew the sound of a hammer cocking on a shotgun.

Silence.

"Dammit to hell, say who you are, or I'm gonna kill ya," Broderick squalled.

"Yell another cussword on my place, and I won't worry about messing up my office anymore. I'll just go in there and give you both barrels," said A. B.

"Cowden?"

"Keep talking, but don't say any cusswords. My wife and babies might hear you."

"By God, I'm through talking," Broderick bawled.

"You're right, you've blasphemed for the last time in your life," said A. B., and he walked through the door with his finger on the hair trigger of the first barrel. He pointed the gun at Broderick's foot and discharged the first load of double-aught buckshot.

The charge was so compact at that range that it blew a three-inch hole in the floor beneath the curled toe of Broderick's boot. The explosion, the impact of the heavy shot on the floor, and Broderick's reaction tossed him backward across a table and into a wall. A. B. kept walking and poked him in the throat with the end of the barrel. Broderick dropped his pistol without even cocking it.

"Now, repent to the God you blaspheme, because I'm going to blow your bloody head right through the wall," said A. B., his finger on the second trigger.

"Please don't kill me. I cuss a lot, but I don't really mean it."

"You tried to hurt my little babies," said A. B. "You came right up to my house and thought you could piss on my world and laugh. You came back to burn my barn. Why should I let you live?"

Two big tears rolled out of Broderick, but he made no sound and no movement. A. B. stepped back and let him off the table. "Get hold of yourself, now," said A. B. "You'll have to be a man if you are to live. Walk to the front of the barn and call your partner."

Broderick moaned and stumbled out the front door. He could not find his voice to call Snider.

"Speak, you big crybaby, or by hell I'll blow your backbone into Harshaw Creek."

"I'm *trying*," Broderick whimpered.

"All right," A. B. said gently. "Do it right."

Broderick sighed. "All right."

"Call the other bully."

"Snider," Broderick called. "John." His voice broke, but he spoke out clearly and loudly enough.

After a moment, Snider showed at the bend in the road, leading Broderick's horse. He saw Broderick standing in front of the barn by himself.

"Tell him to come here and bring your horse. Don't shout. I don't want them to hear you in the house."

Broderick spoke to Snider again and gestured to him. Snider looked back once at the cattle and came on.

A. B. made Broderick back into the barn so Snider would have to ride to the door to find him. Then he made Broderick lie facedown on the ground.

A. B. disarmed Snider when he rode up and made him unsaddle their horses and put them in the corral. He made both men rake the oil-soaked straw out of the stalls, carry it outside, and burn it. The cowboys tended the fire until it burned out, then A. B. marched them back inside and made them put new straw bedding in the stalls. When that was done, he made them sit on the dirt floor with their backs against a wall.

A. B. addressed Broderick. "This has been a long time building, I guess. I should have done something about it before this. No one should wait to settle scores until he gets as mad as I am. I came awfully close to splattering your head on my wall. My children go in that office from time to time. They would never have forgotten that I killed a man in there."

"Yeah, well, you don't have any right to dam up the water in that creek. You keep our cattle from watering downstream when you do that," Broderick said.

"Shut up, will you, for the love of Pete," Snider said. "You can't stand prosperity, can you?"

"Aside from the fact that the creek doesn't run downstream when it's dry like it is now, I have the right to dam it, because the entire creek is on my land. I've never denied water to a living soul who stopped here to drink. You did not come to drink. You came to bully people. We both know that.

"You're cowards who pick on little boys and girls when their father and brothers are away. Cowards are more afraid of what people think of them than anything else, so I'm going to show you up for all the world to see. When you leave here, you'll have to sneak around for a long time before you find a haven. Take off your boots and socks."

"Now, if *that* ain't something," said Broderick.

"Do what the man says, you damned fool," said Snider as he began pulling off his boots.

"This is silly. I don't think he can make me take off my boots," said Broderick.

"Take off the boots," said A. B.

"Well, I guess not. My boots stay on my feet."

A. B. stepped up and tried to bend the barrels of the shotgun around the side of Broderick's head. He picked the soft side, and if Broderick had not deflected the blow, it would have caved in his skull at the temple. As it was, the barrels made a four-inch gash along the line of his sunburn above his ear.

"Not another word," said A. B. "Get barefooted."

Snider helped Broderick take off his boots. A. B. picked up a can of coal oil and ordered the cowboys to walk ahead of him. They minced along on their bare feet across the creek and up the road until they were with the cattle again and out of sight of the house. A. B. stopped them and looked back over his shoulder to make sure they could not be seen by his family.

"Now take off your clothes," he said.

"Now, Mr. Cowden, I don't blame you for any of this, but I won't take a beating from any man," said Snider. "You'll have to kill me."

"I'm not going to beat you," said A. B.

"What are you going to do?" asked Snider. "I have to tell you, I've never been in favor of this harassment of your family. I don't expect you to believe me, but that's the way it is, and I don't think I ought to be punished for anything."

"You ran your horse over my little friend Maudy Pendleton. Now get your clothes off and shut your mouth, or I'll blow all the toes off your foot and instead of only being Vincent's coward, you'll also be his cripple."

When the two were standing naked in front of him, A. B. made them stack their clothes in a pile. He drenched it with coal oil and struck a match to it. Broderick and Snider did not cuss as the clothes burned. A. B. kept pouring oil and making the cowboys stir the clothes until every stitch was burned.

"Now, you fellers leave the country and start new somewhere else. If Vincent sends somebody for your horses, I'll know you're still with him, and the next time I see you, or my sons see you, you'll certainly wish you left when you had the chance. If you show up in Harshaw, I'll find out and come and get you. I won't ever forget what you tried to do to my babies. Don't ever let me see your faces again. Get going."

CHAPTER 18

Ben and Les Cowden took a room in the hotel in Santa Cruz that evening. They had supper with Hector Romero and his family and then went for a walk in the oldest part of the town. In the time of the Spaniards, the community was called Santa Maria de Suanci. A certain placer gold, world famous for its fineness, beauty, and malleability was sold from there, though no one knew the spot where the rains washed it free of the ground.

Ben knew a goldsmith who made fine jewelry with Suanci gold, and he was in the habit of visiting the goldsmith when he was in Santa Cruz and bargaining for something golden that he could afford. This time he bought a bracelet he thought Lorrie would like. He might not like Lorrie's brother, and he knew his family did not approve of her, but when he remembered her fresh embrace, he wanted more. When he saw the bracelet, he thought it would look nicer on her than it would on anyone else in the world. The bracelet took all the cash Ben and Les could raise between them. They went back to their hotel room and went to bed.

The brothers rode out of town with the *guia* star the next morning. They had lost Hoozy's tracks in the mill of traffic outside Santa Cruz the evening before, but they hoped to find them again at the VO. Santa Cruz was on the stage and freight line most used by Americans as a southern route to California. The traffic was heavy now that old Yawner was harassing people on more solitary routes. The road passed close to the VO headquarters. Ben lit a match and examined the trail near the headquarters corrals. He found the VO cowboys' tracks where he expected to.

Vincent's home looked like a hotel. He had built it out in the open, like a dude. Everybody else in the country preferred building under the lee side of a hill, to shelter against the prevailing southwestern winds. They dug their wells near creeks or rivers and drew their water with buckets and windlass. Vincent could have built on the Santa Cruz River, only a mile away, but he preferred living in a castle high in the wind where everybody could see it and he could survey all the country he hoped to own.

The well that provided water for his stock, bunkhouse, and home had been drilled a hundred feet in the ground. Vincent did not have to go and live near water, in Arizona like other people. He could afford to drill into the top of a high mesa and lift it up out of the bowels of the earth.

Ben and Les stopped their horses in an oak thicket above the VO headquarters an hour before sunup. All the lamps were lit in the bunkhouse, but the main house was still dark.

"You suppose old Vincent and his wife are gone someplace, or do you think they're still in there sleeping?" asked Les, joking.

"Could they still be in bed?" asked Ben. "Nobody could still be in bed this late, could they? What would they *do* in bed at this hour?"

"At this hour, anything they did would have to be shameful."

"Yes, and I'm pretty sure what it is."

"What is it?" asked Les, grinning.

"They're counting their money and hiding it under the bed."

"Les laughed, and a dog started barking near the bunkhouse.

"Did you ever notice the difference between the way Indians and cowboys live and the way bosses and dudes live?" Ben asked. "Have you noticed how city people and cattle barons live differently from people who work their ranches, or hunt and roam outdoors for a living? I'd call Vincent a cattle baron, wouldn't you, brother?"

"He'd call himself one."

"He's one. Tell me how they're different from us."

"Sure, they pump their water farther. That ain't so bad."

"Look down there at their setup. There's Vincent and his wife and little daughter and a servant-woman living in a house they say has ten bedrooms. I've heard it has a parlor *and* a front room. It has a fireplace in *every* room. It has two kitchens and pantries, a firewood room, an Arizona room, screen porches, closets, and no telling what else. All that is for three people and their maid. The maid is Jesusita Romero, and I bet she sleeps in a kitchen closet because they can't spare more room.

"On the other hand, there's probably fifteen cowboys in that one-room bunkhouse. They have a dinky little kitchen stove to keep them warm and cook their chuck. They stuff their warbags under their bunks. They have their meals and card games on one big long table with two long benches. That's it for fifteen men and a cook.

"Why do you suppose Vincent came out here to live? He could live indoors if he was in town, so he probably came out here so he could live in the wide-open spaces. Yet, he doesn't live in the wide-open spaces. You know what I'd say about this setup if I was an Indian?"

"Tell me what you'd say, brother," said Les.

"I'd say, 'Indian goes outside, builds little house, lives outside. White man goes outside, builds big house, lives inside.'"

Les smiled and did not look at his brother. After a while, he asked, "How come you're talking so much this morning?"

"I don't know. I guess I can see the big money companies are going to take over this country and put us out, sooner or later, if we don't have a lot of good luck along with our excellent ability.

"These money people like Vincent can buy in one day what it will take us a lifetime to build by catching wild cattle. We've been spreading our cattle thin on this range to save it. Vincent turns out all the steers money can buy. By the time we build a decent herd, the dudes will have all the land bought up, and we won't have any place to run a herd."

"Hell, Ben, don't get down. He can't buy it all. The country's too big for any one man to own it all."

"Vincent's not one man. A dozen of the richest men in the world are behind him, from England and New York. He's backed by men who buy and sell railroads, mines, oil companies, and whole governments. Vincent is buying our territorial government, too."

"Hell, don't worry about the government. It don't know what we do out here horseback," said Les. "People like Vincent might talk big and get a lot of city folks to listen, but he can't get them to come out here horseback to stop what I do."

"That's how I think, too. That's why someday we won't matter. Someday it won't matter a damned bit that we ride good horses. Vincent can't even ride a horse, but he, or somebody like him, will be running the country. In the long run, our ways won't pay unless we can invent a horse-drawn money machine."

"What brought all this on, Ben? Why are you worrying so much all of a sudden?"

"Ever since *Día de San Juan* we've been kept running one way or the other by a machine, and its headquarters is right down there in front of us. It's using the Apaches as a diversion to pull us away from our business. Vincent looked us up and tried to put the *whoa* on us at the dance. Then he took a run at us with Hoozy and drew us away from our work. He got Kosterlinsky to hold us awhile, and then he sent us off another way and drew us here.

"We've been doing everything but look after our cattle. Old cows are our only way of getting ahead in the world. The whole world wants money, Les. If we don't learn to keep our minds on the money, we're going to dry up and blow away like horseturds."

The brothers watched the VO cowboys at the chores and then saw them go back in the bunkhouse for breakfast. They smelled the VO coffee. They waited and watched and imagined a hot breakfast in a warm bunkhouse. The cowboys came out laughing and talking, caught their horses, and rode out in different directions for the day's work.

Hoozy Briggs was not with the crew, and his mare was not in the corral. Hoozy had slipped away, but Ben did not mind settling for a talk with the chief cattle baron. Now was a good time. Only two thugs were still lolling around the corrals and bunkhouse, probably staying as a bodyguard for Vincent.

Ben and Les rode down to the corrals and dismounted before anyone came out to invite them off their horses. After a while, Thomas stepped to the door and invited them into the bunkhouse for coffee. They turned their horses inside a corral with the saddles on.

The brothers stopped at the washstand, pumped water for each other, washed their faces and hands, and smoothed down their hair. They dried themselves with their bandannas and put their hats back on. This was not a friendly place worthy of their respect. Rules of hospitality only made it neutral ground. They did not take off their spurs and leggings.

Thomas and Campana were in the bunkhouse with the cook. Ben was careful not to sit with his back to a window, even though the VO hands were respectful and polite. Les was the wary one and always good to have along as sentinel, but he itched for contention with the VO, and he was not in that bunkhouse to be polite.

The VO hands seemed to welcome the time to relax and be hospitable to the Cowdens. Campana brought cups and sugar, and Thomas poured them coffee. Ben figured his fight with Thomas at American Boy was the only clean one they would ever have in the war that was coming between the Cowdens and the VO. The venting of Thomas's head had been done in retaliation for blows and insults and was acceptable as settlement of a fight in the society of cowboys. Ben knew that no one would ever show fairness in this fight again; hospitality perhaps, but not fairness.

The differences between the Cowdens and the VO had grown since the venting of Thomas. The Cowdens were through arguing with Vincent, and they were through fighting bare-handed.

"Would you fellers like some breakfast?" Thomas asked. He looked over at the cook.

"Who's going to cook for 'em?" asked the cook. He was an old fellow, bald and pale and cranky.

"Well, I'd think you would, since you're the only one who tries to cook around here," Thomas said.

"Well, don't be so damned quick to invite people to eat unless you're as quick to do the work," the cook said.

"Don't put yourself out for us," Ben said. "This coffee's fine." He could see that Les would have taken anything the VO offered. The brothers had left Santa Cruz too early for breakfast.

Campana brought the coffeepot and filled their cups again.

"Are you fellers here on urgent business?" asked Thomas. "I'm not nosy, but we're supposed to ask questions like that."

"We want a word with your boss," Ben said. "Is he home?"

"Oh, yes. If we're here, he's here. He don't go anywhere without us."

"Is he hiding?" asked Ben. "Or is he too worthless to get out of bed in the morning? Why does he need you big bulls to head off his visitors?"

"He's being careful. He's having trouble taking possession of land he's bought around here. He's not a fighting man. He's never armed, and he don't like trouble."

"And you two are his bodyguards?" asked Les; he laughed.

Thomas looked Les in the eye. "Yes."

"I wish him much good luck."

"The trouble with you is you think one little skirmish like the one I had with Ben puts an end to the war. It usually does, but this time it don't. Men like me and Campana don't quit until we get even."

"You mean terrible old Campana?" Les said, and he laughed at Campana's expression.

"Campana don't forget, and neither do I."

"Want to fight right now and save the bushwhacking?"

"No, we won't fight here. The next time we fight, you won't be so ready."

"Don't worry. I'm learning to watch out for you fellers. All I ask is for you to be out in front of us where we can see you when you're ready, and don't cry when it's over," Les said.

"Sounds all right to me," said Thomas.

Ben looked toward the main house. Vincent's lamps were lit. He and Les went over and knocked on the door.

"Well, well, come in," Vincent said when he recognized Ben. He was cordial. The Cowdens would have also been nice to Vincent if he came and knocked on their door.

"We're having our coffee," Vincent said. "My daughter Dorothy is handy at brewing coffee."

Vincent led the brothers into the kitchen and sat them down. They said hello to Jesusita Romero, who was helping Dorothy set the table for breakfast. Vincent poured their coffee while he talked about the drouth and the way the railroad's high prices made it prohibitive to ship cattle by rail. He avoided talking about Apache killings, horse thieves, and grass wars. Ben also decided not to bring up those subjects until he and Vincent were outside the house. Sitting close to the man in his home, Ben felt no dislike for him. He liked Vincent's face, but then everybody could show a nice face when he was pouring coffee for a visitor at his kitchen table.

Dorothy Vincent was a pale, thin girl about sixteen. She was seldom allowed to attend the dances in Harshaw or Patagonia or to visit other girls in the country. She came to the VO for a few days with her mother every summer when she was let out of school. Ben had never heard her say a word to anybody.

Ben was not surprised Vincent allowed his wife and daughter to stay at the ranch when the Yawner was making trouble. Vincent never changed his schedule for anything. His cowboys carried on with their work like the Cowdens did, whether the Yawner was in the country or not. Cowboys were expected to watch over their own shoulders for Apaches.

Mrs. Doris Vincent made her entrance. Her starched dress and petticoats caused the air to swirl fragrantly in her wake. She smiled for the brothers when they stood to shake her hand. They were glad their faces were washed and their hair smoothed down because she was gracious and pretty.

Mrs. Vincent was never in Arizona more than two months out of the year, but she belonged to every woman's club, Presbyterian church committee, charity organization, and other civic league within two hundred miles of the VO headquarters. She was the daughter of a man who had been in President Lincoln's cabinet. She was on a committee that was trying to form a national society called the Daughters of the American Revolution.

The woman was always stopping at Durazno to recruit Viney for some new mission in which she was engaged. She did not seem to be aware of their husbands' differences. Ben remembered the first time she dropped in on his mother. He had walked into the parlor in the middle of the afternoon, unaware his mother was entertaining visitors. The parlor was full of the hats, fans, feathers, powdered faces, and billowing dresses of Doris Vincent and the wives of the Harshaw mine's chief executives.

Doris Vincent's eyes had locked on Ben with a look so admiring that his mother was not able to hide her amusement. The women from Harshaw giggled with embarrassment at the way she stared at Ben.

Now, she sat down at the table, leaned close to Ben, and looked at him as though she wanted to lay all her needs at his feet. "I'm so delighted you men are here," she said. "I desperately need information from Viney as to how many, if any, ladies in Pima County are from old eastern families. I spent last winter in Washington, D.C., helping organize the Daughters of the American Revolution.

"I can't wait to get back. Summers in the country are so slow. Everything is happening back east. However, this year I'm staying for the sixteenth-of-September fiesta in Tombstone. That is Independence Day for the Mexicans, you know, and is still a traditional holiday in this country.

"Tombstone is such an exciting town. This will be my first Mexican fiesta, and I'm so looking forward to it. Do you men think this trouble with Geronimo will be resolved in time so the fiesta won't be canceled?"

The woman said all this in one breath, drew another, and kept on talking. Ben stopped listening.

Jesusita Romero, the lady who cooked and served them breakfast, was an older sister of Pepe Romero, the man who was killed by the Apaches with Pedro Elias at La Acequia. Ben wondered what she would think if she could understand English. She lived under the same roof as Mrs. Vincent, and all Mrs. Vincent could believe about Apaches was that they might interfere with her traveling to Tombstone for her first Mexican fiesta. Margarita could not even see her family unless she risked being lanced by Apaches.

All of a sudden Mrs. Vincent noticed the golden bracelet on Ben's wrist. "Oh, what a beautiful piece of work," she said. She reached across the table and lifted Ben's hand in both of hers. She beamed at the bracelet at though she was not aware she was holding Ben's hand so close he could feel the warmth of her breath, her hands, and her breast as one.

"What a beautiful contrast between the deep brown of your hands and the freshly pounded gold. The metal looks almost liquid, doesn't it? As though it has been poured on your wrist. I've never seen a man wear a bracelet. It becomes you. Oh, I've seen Indian men wear them, and I can see now why they do. You have the same coloring as an Indian. Do you have Indian blood, Mr. Cowden?"

"Not one blasted drop," Ben said.

"Oh, I can't believe that. You're not ashamed of your Indian blood, are you?"

"I don't guess I would be, if I had any. I don't have any," Ben said.

"What made you wear the bracelet? Are you Mexican?"

"No, I bought it for a friend in Harshaw and decided to wear it instead of carrying it in my pocket where I'd risk losing or bending it."

"Oh, you have a lady-friend in Harshaw?"

"I have a lot of friends."

"And who is this lady-friend?"

Vincent chuckled indulgently. "I believe Ben and Lorrie Briggs are good friends, Doris. You know who she is, don't you?"

Mrs. Vincent's smile froze on her face as she turned to her husband. "I'm afraid I don't know any of the young men and women in Harshaw."

"She's the girl who came to the hotel to take Dorothy to the picnic during the San Juan's Day celebration."

"Oh, yes," said Mrs. Vincent, and she turned back to Ben. She was still holding on to his hand.

"You know, we need to have some kind of get-together this fall." She let go of the hand. "That bracelet is a beautiful gift for a lady," she said.

Ben took the bracelet off. "Here, take it as my gift to you, Mrs. Vincent," he said.

"Oh, no, I couldn't accept it," she said, but she took it deftly from his hand. "But it's so nice of you."

"Well, you appreciate it so much, you should have it. I hope it gives you pleasure," Ben said.

Mrs. Vincent put it on and showed it to her husband.

"That's nice. Thank you, er, Cowden," Vincent said.

"You're very welcome," said Ben.

The brothers stood up from the table, thanked the Vincents for the coffee, picked up their hats, and headed for the door. Outside, Ben asked Vincent to walk with them to the corrals. Vincent stepped back inside the door for his hat, and Mrs. Vincent came out on the veranda with him.

"Ah," said Mrs. Vincent. "What a nice fresh morning breeze." She pirouetted so her hair and skirts would catch the wind of the drouth and then strode back inside the house.

Vincent's bodyguards came and flanked Ben and Les as they walked back to the corrals.

"We ought to go into the bunkhouse so we can have our talk out of the wind," said Vincent.

"We'll talk out here in the open," Ben said.

"That suits me, too," Vincent said.

Ben leaned against the corral with his arms on the top rail. Vincent stood beside him and did the same. Both of them watched the Cowden saddlehorses in the corral. At that moment they were almost friendly to each other, and Ben wanted to settle their differences. Anyone who did not know the tension between them would have thought they were trying to make a friendly horse trade. Les stood by Ben's other side, facing Thomas and Campana and carving a toothpick out of a wood chip with his stock knife.

"Nice horses," said Vincent. "Are they for sale?"

"No," Ben said.

"I'd like to buy them. I need some horses."

Ben did not have any more to say about it.

"I'll tell you what I'll give; then you can tell me whether or not they're for sale."

Ben packed his pipe with tobacco.

"I'll give you five hundred dollars for the two of them. You see, I happen to know the country they've covered in the last several days. Some of my men covered the same country it seems, and they were afoot when they got back last evening. Your horses still look fresh."

Ben did not figure it was to his advantage at all to let Vincent know he and Les had changed horses at George Moore's.

"That Hoozy and these two bodyguards of yours made a big circle," Ben said.

"Hoozy?"

"Your man Hoozy Briggs. The man you sent to steal our horses. The man who turned my racehorse over to Kosterlinsky. The man who stole Ray Johnson's horses and turned them over to Kosterlinsky's place in Santa Cruz. That man and these two standing here looking like fresh turds in their own corral probably murdered Ray Johnson and his family on your orders, Vincent."

"Hoozy Briggs does not work for me. According to my men, he and his brother rode into the same Apache ambush that caught my men in Medal Canyon. I believe two of your own cousins were witnesses to that. The Apaches stole your horses. I guess the Indians still have them, don't they?"

"My brother and I took the horses back."

"From Apaches?"

"Yes."

"Then why are you making me explain what happened? You already know."

"We tracked your men from our pasture to the ambush. The Apaches didn't take our horses. Your men did."

"Are you sure it was your horses you were tracking?"

"Damned sure."

"Did you see your racehorse at Kosterlinsky's?"

"We caught up to him at the Maria Macarena ranch."

"Did my men have the horse?"

"No."

"Where is the horse?"

"Still at the Maria Macarena."

"Some story. I'm not calling you a liar, but where is the evidence that my men stole your horses?"

"I have my brother Les as a witness."

"My men told me a different story."

"I guess they would."

"Do you have any other evidence?"

"We don't need any. We followed their tracks."

"Well, tracks don't prove a thing. You can't take tracks inside a courtroom, so nothing you're saying matters a bit."

The fire in Ben's pipe was going out, and the last puffs did not taste good. "You're right. Our war will be outside the courts, so why talk about it anymore."

"Are you drawing a line here? Do you want a war?" Vincent demanded.

"You've decided to take what you want by murder and theft, so from now on, we'll protect ourselves. The VO hands who came on our range will be leaving your employ, one way or another."

Vincent was still calm. "Listen, I won't stand the blame for the Johnson murders. As I understand it, my men moved the Johnson horses to Kosterlinsky's so they would be safe from Apaches. Kosterlinsky is the closest military protection we have."

"Kosterlinsky is another thief. The plain truth is, if Apaches had killed the Johnsons, they would have taken the horses. Your hoodlums were the only ones who left tracks at the Johnson massacre besides old Goldwater and our brother Mark."

Ben waited a minute for the accusation to sink in, but Vincent's expression did not change, and he did not turn to face Ben.

"Doesn't it bother you that you've become a murderer and a thief?" Ben asked. "You thought you could intimidate us? We have more respect for the poorest barefooted Apaches, and we've been able to hold our own against them for a long time. We even protected you from them when you first came here.

"Think about this. To us, the VO is worse than the

Apaches. We no longer consider you a neighbor and ally against them. You're not Americans, as far as we're concerned. You're just another gang of bandits, Mr. Vincent, and we've been shooting bandits, or hanging them, for as long as we've been fighting Apaches."

"You won't harm me, Cowden. I never carry a weapon, and there's not a man in this country who'll shoot an unarmed man."

"No one but you, Vincent. In your all-out kind of war, women and children die, too."

"Listen, I have a wife and daughter, and I want them kept out of it. I want your mother and sisters kept out of it, too."

"No, my mother and sisters won't stay out of it. They know what you'll do if they make the mistake of trusting you, and they'll fight. Watch out for them. They'll ask no quarter and give none."

Vincent faced Ben. "All right, that's plain enough for me. I'll make you wish you could find a job cleaning slop jars in a whorehouse, or selling hair ribbon on commission before this fight is over. You'll be so sick of land and cattle, you'll change your name from Ben Cowden to Lupe Rodriguez so you can find a place to sleep."

"That's the way I like to hear you talk, killer. Now, we can have at 'er," said Ben.

"How about let's have it out right now, while we're all here," said Les, grinning at the bodyguards. "Let's make it simple and get it over with."

Thomas and Campana spread out and moved away from the Cowdens. Vincent headed toward the house and kept his back to everybody.

Thomas said, "Shall we accommodate these fellers while we still have them in sight, Mr. Vincent?"

"No," said Vincent. "My womenfolk are in the house. There'll be no killing on this place today."

"Dying, you mean," Les said. "Order them not to die, or by hell I'll kill all three of you and leave a nice mess for old Doris and little Dorothy to clean up."

"Clear out, Thomas," Vincent ordered. "Both of you, turn your backs. Go to the bunkhouse. You can fight any other place in the country, but not here and not now."

Ben touched his brother's arm. "Come on, Les. Time to go home."

Viney's washpots were boiling on open fires under the cottonwoods by the creek. The big cast-iron caldrons could stand a lot of fire. Paula Mary's job was to keep stirring the dirty clothes with a long, smooth stick as they boiled in lye soap. Viney and Eileen scrubbed work-clothes on washboards. Betty rinsed the clean articles in pots of clear boiling water. Maudy Jane helped Betty wring the rinse water from the clothes, then carried them to a clothesline behind the house and hung them up to dry.

Maudy carried a basket of wet clothes to the line and set it down, then reached up and unpinned a dry sheet and started taking it off the line. As she gathered the sheet to drape it over her shoulder, she looked squarely into the eyes of John Snider, who was sneaking up on the other side of the sheet, stark naked.

"Oops!" whooped Maudy.

Caught in the open, Snider covered himself with his arms crossed, stooped over so Maudy would not be as likely to see his parts, scampered backward so fast he raised dust with his bare feet, and hid behind the woodpile. "Shh, Maudy!" he said.

"What in the *world* has come over you, Snider?" asked Maudy, laughing.

"Old A. B. burned our clothes. I've been having a *helluva* time. I darned near froze to death last night."

"Well, you must have. You're in an *awful* state."

"Believe me, Maudy, I am."

The thick hair on Snider's bare head was wildly mussed. His marble-white brow, torso, arms, and legs contrasted sharply with the mahogany tan of his face, neck, and hands.

Maudy could not keep from laughing at his bare bones.

"Listen . . . please, listen, Maudy," pleaded Snider.

Maudy composed herself. "All right, I'm listening."

"I have to get back to my camp. I need clothes. I've *got* to get some *sleep*."

"All right, but what can I do?"

"Haven't we always been friends, Maudy?"

"Sure."

"Can you bring my horse to me?"

"No, because Mr. Cowden took your horse and Broderick's bronc to Harshaw and impounded them for damages."

"Nuts. Now what am I going to do?"

"Go to Harshaw and bail him out, I guess."

"I can't do that. Mr. Cowden ordered us to stay out of Harshaw."

"Where's Broderick?"

"He went to Harshaw."

"Why didn't you go with him?"

"I just want to do what Mr. Cowden ordered me to do and go to my camp, get my gear, and leave the country as soon as I can. I couldn't walk any farther barefooted, and I knew you were here, and we've always been friends."

"So, how are you going to leave without a horse, Snider?"

"I don't know. I'm sunk. Aren't there any other horses in the corral?"

"Sure, plenty. Which one of Mr. Cowden's horses you gonna steal?"

"Oh, God, none, I guess. I'm sunk. Unless you'll lend me one of the Cowdens' horses and then back me up and admit to it if I get caught. I promise I'll leave the horse at Canelo on my way out of the country. I only want to get back to my camp, put on my clothes, and leave on my own horse."

"I won't do that."

"There's one other thing you might do, Maudy. I wouldn't ask you if we hadn't always been friends."

"What's that?"

"Loan me your horse. I saw him in the corral."

"*Pshaw*! Loan you Little Buck? The sun got your brain?"

"It's my only chance. It's the only thing you can do, don't you see?"

"I never loan my horse to anybody."

Maudy pulled the sheet off the line.

"Please, Maudy. I'm desperate, and I don't want to have to steal a horse."

Maudy looked him in the eye with her teeth full of clothespins. "All right," she said. "I'll loan you Little Buck.

But if anything happens to him and you don't put him in our corral at Canelo tomorrow, I'll make sure they hang you as a horse thief."

"Believe me, Maudy. On my word of honor. I'll leave him at Canelo tomorrow."

"All right. Get on back behind the hill and wait for me. I'll bring him when I'm finished here."

"Well, Maudy, thank you . . . but, have a little consideration, will you, please?"

"About what?"

"Get me a shirt and some pants, please."

"Oh, no, I'm not stealing these boys' clothes."

"You suppose Bill Knox will lend me some?"

"Gosh, no. He's got a shotgun loaded for the likes of you after you almost burned his barn. Here." Maudy threw him an old dress of Viney's that she was planning to tear up for rags and patches. "They don't need this, and you won't get in as much trouble wearing it as you would if the boys caught you in their clothes."

CHAPTER 19

Paula Mary noticed George Morris always brought walnuts instead of candy when he came calling on Betty. Black walnut trees, the *nogales*, grew at every natural water hole in the country, but there were very few candy stores. George spent a lot of time under the trees everywhere he went.

He had been hanging around the kitchen talking to Viney now for half a day, and Betty would not come out to say hello. Four or five hours was a long time for Betty to stay in her room. George sat in the same chair in the same position the whole time. Paula Mary was in absolute awe over the way that man could sit.

Paula Mary was making fudge and putting George's walnuts in it. The Cowden girls did not know what George thought he would gain by sitting so long, but he always did that when he came to visit. This time he made it plain when he first sat down that he did not have anything else to do for a while. He was not going back to his mine on Saddle Mountain.

George was such a fastidious man. He did not look at all like a hard-rock miner. His hands were always white and clean, his face pale and fleshy, his boots polished, his three-piece suit well worn. Paula Mary never got to see him outside that three-piece suit. Even when he came riding in to Durazno leading his mule, he was in his suit.

Everybody was glad to see George when he first came. His being at Durazno made it so A. B. and Mark could leave the women a few hours and go to Harshaw to tend to business. Bill Knox and Gordo Soto were working in the barn, but the women were glad to have another man around the place when A. B. and the big brothers were gone. Paula Mary was hoping George would leave when her father came home, though. She was ready for him to go.

Paula Mary took the fudge pan out of the oven and set it up on the counter. She let everybody admire it a moment, then took it out to the "Arizona room," a screened-in room along the back of the house. She set it down on the edge of the kitchen step to cool. She did that so people would not start piecing on it. Paula Mary wanted her masterpiece to survive at least until it cooled.

George devoured everything he was offered. If he wanted something and it was not within his reach, he stared at it until someone carried it to him. Paula Mary made the mistake of leaving the mixing bowl with its remnant of fudge by him. He took after it with the wooden stirring spoon and ended by wiping it out with two fingers and licking them clean. He did not leave a smudge in the bowl.

"I knew you'd smell the fudge," Eileen said when Betty finally came out of her room.

"My, my, daughter, I'm glad you finally made your appearance," Viney said. "Here's George to see you."

Paula Mary heard George's chair scrape the floor as he stood up. Betty was not saying a word. Paula Mary could see her plainly through the window over the sink between the Arizona room and the kitchen. Betty took a drink out of the water bucket with the dipper. She looked out the window past Paula Mary and sipped at the water, then turned back to face George as his feet tangled with his chair. He mumbled something, remembered to snatch his pipe out of his mouth, then sat heavily down again.

Betty kept her back against the counter, as far away from George as she could be. She took another swallow of water, floated the dipper in the bucket, and sidled along the counter to the door. She went out to the Arizona room and sat down by Paula Mary.

Sometimes Paula Mary did not think Betty was even human. She hardly ever seemed to care about anybody. A person had to be her sister, or she wouldn't even sit close to her. Paula Mary was reasonably sure Betty loved her family, but she seldom gave them any sign of it. She stayed close to her family when she wanted protection, though.

Betty's face was so flushed she looked feverish. She must be feverish. George could not put color in anybody's face. He came to stand in the door, homing on Betty. He searched her face and was not given even a glance in return. She was looking toward the orchard. He looked away at nothing, too.

All of a sudden, Paula Mary knew that George was about to step in her fudge. She had put the fudge on an end of the step that was longer than the doorway and furnished an extra surface that nobody used.

Paula Mary had not anticipated that George would pause on that step with his big foot beside her fudge. Her family's feet were small and always hurrying right on through that door. George's feet were immense. His big ankle-length shoe covered most of the doorstep. Paula Mary was sure he did not have any idea where his feet were. He did not even know where his pipe was, and he was always occupied with his pipe. Now, even though it was still smoking, he was trying to pocket it, fumbling here and there, trying to poke it in a hole where it would be out of the way.

Paula Mary was paralyzed.

Then Eileen walked up behind George and said, "Excuse me, George, I have to get through here."

George looked back over his shoulder at Eileen, stepped aside, and put his big foot in Paula Mary's fudge.

"Oh, George," said Paula Mary softly.

Betty calmly walked out the screen door. George looked down at his captured foot. The pan was stuck to his shoe. His foot so filled the pan that for a moment he did not know he had stepped in the fudge.

Paula Mary sat still and watched George, waiting for the aftershock. When he realized his foot was in the fudge, he sat down so quickly his butt bounced on the step and he swiped the pan off his foot. He let the fudge and pan scatter over the floor, took out a clean white handkerchief, and wiped the fudge off his shoe. He stood up, inspected the foot, and went back into the kitchen.

"Gosh, George," called Paula Mary. "I hope my fudge didn't hurt your shoe."

A. B. and Mark went to Harshaw in the buggy. Mark held the team while A. B. went to the telegraph office in the hotel lobby. John Porter, one of Viney's brothers, ran the office. He had sent his messenger to Durazno for A. B. He stood up when A. B. walked in.

"A. B., a telegram came for you this morning that I thought should be kept confidential. I didn't send it with the messenger because I didn't think you would want anyone else to know about it."

"My Lord, are we at war with Mexico, or what?"

"This is war, but not with Mexico. The telegram is from the sheriff notifying you that a warrant has been issued for the arrest of Ben Cowden for cattle stealing. You're instructed to apprehend him immediately."

"Did it say who made the complaint?"

"Mr. Duncan Vincent."

A. B. smiled. "I wonder why I even asked."

"The sheriff said he would understand if you wanted to be relieved of this duty. If you do, you are to wire him immediately so he can come down and do it himself."

"Who could make a more peaceful arrest in this case than me? Aren't I supposed to keep the peace? Please notify the sheriff for me that I'll arrest the man as soon as he comes home. That ought to be this evening about suppertime."

"I'm sorry to be the one to tell you this, but I've kept it absolutely quiet. Nobody else in town knows about it."

"I appreciate this, John."

"Is there anything else I can do?"

"Yes, you can tell me if you've seen Mr. Jarboe this morning."

"I saw him in the hotel dining room a few minutes ago."

A. B. asked Mark to take the team and buggy to the Farleys', borrow a horse, and ride out to find his brothers.

He told Mark he wanted him home by suppertime, whether he found them or not.

A. B. found Walter Jarboe sitting by himself at a corner table in the dining room. Jarboe stood, offered A. B. a seat, and ordered coffee for him.

Jarboe said he was still waiting for the San Rafael roundup to start, but Vincent was not disposed to set a date. Jarboe wanted to get in touch with Ben again. A. B. told him about the sheriff's telegram.

"Could the charge be true?" Jarboe asked.

"Absolutely not. You know about the differences that exist between my son and Vincent. Even though the charges are unjust, I will take my son to Tucson to face them. I want an open hearing to bring attention to the issues. A hearing will also help me discover who Vincent's paying in the territorial government. The sheriff is probably a member of his club by now. I'd also like to know where you stand on this."

"I'm only a spectator, Mr. Cowden."

"But I understand you're a U.S. marshal."

"Yes, I am, but I only obtained that commission so I could have the power to reclaim my investment in the Kosterlinsky cattle. I didn't come here to enforce territorial laws."

"But you're sworn to uphold the law, aren't you?"

"I guess I am, but I don't want to take sides in your son's fight."

"Listen, without my son's help, you'll never get your cattle. You better help him. You have authority here. I want your support when I arrest my son. We have to keep him safe so he can stand trial."

"Mr. Cowden, I'm not a law-enforcement officer by profession. For business reasons, I'd like to remain neutral in this."

"Mr. Jarboe, I won't let you do that. I don't think Vincent has bought you, too, or am I mistaken?"

"No, you're not mistaken, Mr. Cowden."

A. B. looked up and saw Will Pendleton walk into the dining room, back from his trip to Tucson.

George Morris took Maudy and all the Cowden girls for a drive to Harshaw. Viney suggested the drive. She could not think of anything else that would take George out of her kitchen. She sent the whole bunch away for an hour or two. One poor lonesome and marriageable miner mixing with three unmarried girls and a cranky child like Paula Mary caused too much confusion in Viney's kitchen.

She kept Freddie Lee home watering the orchard with his burro because he liked to devil George. Viney knew if he went along, he would pester everybody so much they would come home too soon. Being alone with four girls made George nervous enough.

Viney was expecting a visit from her brother Billy Porter. He was coming early and staying the day. He always did what he said he would do. If someone said an Indian was coming to get Viney at 12:00 noon but Uncle Billy Porter said he would be there at 11:59, everybody could feel safe to leave Viney alone at the ranch. Uncle Billy would be there. He was a roper, a fighter, and a wild-horse rider, and he feared no creature of God.

Viney looked out the window to see how Freddie Lee was doing. Snoose the burro was standing over the last tree well, and Freddie was letting the water out of the bota. Freddie was a good worker. He and Snoose were already through watering the peace orchard. Viney decided to go outside and tend to her flowers.

Freddie Lee took Snoose to the barn and saddled him with the kid's saddle that each of the Cowden children had used in learning to ride. He strapped on his birthday hooks, a small pair of Chihuahua spurs Les had given him, and threw his coiled lariat over his saddle horn. He mounted Snoose and reined him away from the barn the way his brothers did their saddlehorses, rolling him back on his heels.

He spurred Snoose to make him lope, even though he knew if he kept it up, he'd make him mad. He galloped out of the barnyard, down into the creek, and back up the bank into the orchard. Viney was digging in a flower bed in front of the house. Freddie hollered *whooaa!* and stopped the burro short of the petunias.

"Now, son, don't ride your burro in my flowers," said Viney, but she laughed at him. He was wearing the same look his brothers used when they were schooling their broncs and showing off their mastery of beasts.

Freddie wheeled the burro and drove his hooks into him, getting wild and showing off. The burro coldjawed and trotted away on a heading of his own, showing Freddie he would not put up with a show-off. Freddie leaned back to pull him around by one rein and stop him. Snoose canted his head over to one side and kept going his own way until he stumbled into the creekbed.

The pool Freddie used to fill his bota had seeped full again. He noticed it was wider and clearer than it had been that morning before he cleaned out all the leaves and sticks and dipped out all the water.

He pulled Snoose away from the pool and made him go back to the orchard. The burro strained to head for the barn. He balked in the orchard. Freddie took down his rope and tied it to his saddle horn the way his brothers did and began roping a stake that had been driven in the ground to brace a young tree. The tree was standing straight now, and the wire stay had been removed.

Freddie roped the stake time after time. His mother was watching. After each throw, she showed her pleasure. Her boy was an unerring roper of iron stakes from atop a burro.

At first, Freddie flipped the loop off without jerking the slack after he caught the stake; he did not want to get off the burro to take the loop off the stake. Then, he decided to practice jerking his slack to close the loop on the horns so the steer would not run through the loop and escape.

He was throwing a flat, wide loop that would someday spread over the long old horns of big wild steers. With each throw he imagined he was coasting up on a steer after a mighty run. He spread his loop over the horns, jerked it closed, and pitched his slack away so his horse would not tangle in it.

Viney could see he had taken himself away into the reckless downhill flight of the cowboy roping the wild bovine. Freddie could see his mother appreciated how expert he was becoming, and he began to add more style and flare to his casts. Finally, he jerked his slack too hard, and his loop tightened on the stake.

To show more style, he spurred Snoose up until he was standing over the stake. Without dismounting, he hooked his left arm through the coils of his rope and reached down with his other hand to take the loop off the stake, the way he'd seen his brothers do.

He was straining to reach the *honda* of his rope when Snoose looked around, saw him hanging upside down on his side, and took a step away in astonishment. With that, the boy's saddle slipped, and he fell on his head beside the stake. His hand broke his fall, but he fell underneath the burro. Further astonished, Snoose shied away and tightened the coils around the boy's arm. The sounds Freddie made as he was dragged under the saddle made the burro swing his rump toward the boy to protect himself. He switched his tail over the rope, and that burned its tender underside and made him jump and straddle the rope. The rope scorched the tender skin between his hams, and he kicked up with both hind feet and bolted away.

Viney was given one shocked instant in which she could see that she might save her son from being dragged when the stake held the burro. Snoose stopped in his tracks, but the coils ran and burned on the saddle horn and jerked Freddie up into his flank. He lunged and kicked Freddie in the head with both hind feet, jerked the stake out of the ground, and stampeded, kicking Freddie with every jump he made down the hill. He tore through the orchard fence, carrying barbwire and posts with him, and ran out into the pool in the bottom of the creek and stopped. Freddie's face was just under the surface of the water.

Viney's terrible lot had been to see her child's helpless little face each time the animal kicked him in the head and ran and ran and ran away from her. The wire held the animal but became a barricade around her child, and the burro's lunging and kicking made it a live trap for Viney and her full skirts. She could not reach her child to lift his face out of the water. She could not hold her son while he died. She had to turn her back on him and run to the house for a knife to cut the rope.

The burro was so mad and tormented that he fell to his knees, laid his head on the ground, and bawled with his mouth wide open. Viney was on her way back with the knife when Uncle Billy Porter came along. He rode straight to the animal's head and snubbed it up against his saddle horn by the bridle reins, tied off, dismounted, and cut Freddie loose.

Viney carried her son to the house and laid him on Mr. Cowden's bed, but he was dead. She had known he was lost when his saddle first slipped and he fell under the burro. No power on earth could have stopped the killing after that.

Uncle Billy left his sister alone with her child and went outside. Bill Knox and Gordo were unsaddling the burro at the barn and doctoring the wire-cuts in his thick hide. Uncle Billy took him from them, led him up a canyon downwind and out of sight of the house, and shot him.

CHAPTER 20

Mark found Ben and Les on the edge of the VO range. They
headed home from there. The brothers were angry because
they saw several of their Temporal steers near Vincent's
headquarters. They were not in any mood to meet visitors
when they arrived at home, but several carriages and
wagons were parked in their barnyard. Neighbors' horses
filled the stalls in the barn.

Bill Knox and Gordo Soto were nowhere in sight. The
brothers unsaddled and grained their horses. They could
not hear a voice on the place.

Maudy Jane walked out to meet them on their way to
the house. Her face was bright, her smile fresh, and she
was all dressed up. "Oh, oh, here comes lovely," Les said.

The girl looked into Ben's eyes, and he saw she was
carrying bad news. "What's the matter, Maudy?"

She put her hands out to the brothers. She was a willing
hand at everything she did, and she was strong enough to
carry bad news, but she began clouding up.

"Take your time," Ben said.

"The burro dragged Freddie," Maudy whispered.

"Is he hurt bad?" Les asked.

"He's gone," Maudy said, and she started crying. Ben
put his arm around her shoulders and walked her back to
the house. Ben and Les paused in the Arizona room to

wash, and Maudy waited for them. "Your mother saw it happen," Maudy said before they went inside.

Freddie's body was lying on A. B.'s bed, bathed, combed, and dressed in his best suit, a purple bruise on his temple. Viney was sitting by the bed. Ben could not remember ever seeing her cry so many tears, but she was not making a sound.

Viney hugged her sons and told them she knew they were hungry, and so they should go eat, their supper was prepared. They turned away from her. Their father was waiting for them at the door. He served their supper himself.

Betty had come home sick from the drive to Harshaw, and she was in bed with a fever. Maudy, Eileen, and Paula Mary were serving supper to the visitors on the family table in the front room. People were coming straight to El Durazno for the wake without stopping for supper at home. Ben saw that Paula Mary was taking hold of the work like an old hand. She made sure she was at the right place at the right time without playing the role of littlest daughter. She and Eileen were not taking time to grieve.

The brothers ate supper and then took themselves to the barn to bathe and change into their best clothes. They returned to the house prepared for an all-night vigil.

Les was grief-stricken and weeping openly. Mark and Betty were alike. They kept their tears wiped away and did not look to other people for solace when they were sorrowing; they felt their grief should stay hidden in their hearts. They could endure the deep pain better if they were not expected to give voice to it. Mark sat by Betty's bed until she fell asleep.

Ben had always felt Freddie Lee was a special treat God sent the Cowdens. That child's being in the family was great good fortune. His loss carried away a vital measure of the family hopes and dreams. Ben mourned the child most because he felt he should have given him more attention. The little fellow had still required the protection of his mother and sisters too much to be a pal to his big brothers. Ben never got enough of him.

All the Cowdens were weepers, but did not weep without trying to hold it back. Ben could not get the little boy off his mind, so he made himself responsible for greeting the visitors. He knew he should take advantage of the gathering to tell his neighbors about the war with Vincent, but he could not separate himself from the bosom of his family to do it.

Danny and Donny Farley came to kiss their Aunt Viney and look at Freddie Lee. They could not stay because it was their turn to take cattle out of a trap they shared with the Cowdens near the Mowry mine. They drew Ben aside before they left.

"Ben, did you hear what they found in Ray Johnson's little boy's mouth?" asked Danny. "They found an ear."

"An *ear*?" said Ben.

"Yessir. When old Goldwater pulled in to Washington Camp with the bodies, he told those miners to look in the boy's mouth. He was sure the boy had bitten off part of a person. They pried him open and found an ear."

"Yessir," said Donny. "It didn't belong to the Johnsons, either. They all had their ears."

"You figure it was the killer's?" Ben said.

"It had to be. One of the killers won't be hard to find at all, will he?"

"Did you tell my papa?"

"Darn right."

John Porter arrived and told Ben about the warrant for his arrest. Ben knew if he let his father take him to jail, he would be out of the fight until Vincent won. He decided to go away after the funeral. He knew A. B. was honor-bound to arrest him. He could not defy his father, so he stayed away from him. He gently informed his mother that he did not intend to be taken into custody, but would be close by if she needed him.

At sunup, Ben and his brothers went outside and talked over their strategy. They agreed Ben should stay at Viney's side throughout the procession and burial. A. B. was not likely to arrest him in her presence. Mark and Les would stay by their father's side and try to distract him if he decided to make the arrest.

Mark packed Ben's bed and provisions on a horse and led him to Harshaw. He left him tied under a tree at the Farleys' and returned quickly before he was missed.

Ben saddled Star to ride in the funeral procession. Carriages, wagons, and horsemen left El Durazno at mid-morning and filed out on the road to Cemetery Hill below Harshaw. Harshaw did not have a minister. The Catholic priest came regularly on a circuit that included Harshaw, but he was not there. Evangelists came from time to time and held tent meetings, but none were there. Will Pendleton read the service at graveside, and the Cowdens buried Freddie Lee with an iron cross Bill Knox made to mark the spot.

Ben kissed his mother good-bye. She encouraged him to leave while A. B. was still preoccupied with the funeral. The sight of his mother going to his father to be by his side, his father holding his hat and bowing his head over the grave of his smallest son, made Ben feel he was disloyal to be leaving. He forced himself to mount his horse, line out for Harshaw, and not look back.

The Farleys' house was deserted. Ben changed to his work-clothes. The two VO hands, Broderick and Snider, were waiting for him when he stepped outside. They had unsaddled Star and turned him into a pen. Snider was leaning against the corral whittling on a stick with his stock knife. Broderick was a few steps away with Ben's rifle in his hands.

Ben's pistol belt was strapped high on his waist. His holster was positioned behind his ribs so it would not interfere when he handled the lead rope of his packhorse. If he tried to reach his pistol, Broderick would shoot him dead.

"Lookee here at the fugitive," Broderick said. "I told Snider you'd show up after they planted your little brother. I knew that packhorse had to be for you. When the deputy came in from Tucson this morning and said he had a warrant for you, I said to myself, Now, wouldn't it be satisfying to catch that man when he comes away grieving from a funeral."

Ben walked on and stopped between the two men. "Where did you fellers find clothes?" he asked.

"Well, now, you're going to find that out. Your old pappy taught us that game, and we're glad to have a chance to teach it to you. You're gonna learn what it's like to strip down jaybird naked in the middle of Harshaw. Start getting 'em off."

"Aw, fellers," Ben said.

"Off with them."

Ben turned to Snider as he unbuckled his pistol belt. He held on to the buckle with both hands and swung it at Snider's chin. He whacked Snider, swung on around, and bashed Broderick in the head. The pistol and holster glanced into the air, and Broderick hit the ground unconscious.

Ben bumped against something sharp on the corral fence before he could turn back to Snider. He cocked his pistol to shoot the man if he had to. Snider threw down the whittling stick and knife, showed Ben the palms of his hands, and ran backward.

"Stand fast, you sonofabitch," Ben said.

"Shit! Are you going to shoot me, Ben? I didn't mean it."

"Lay down on your face by your partner."

Ben used pigging strings to hog-tie Broderick and Snider. He gagged them with their neckerchiefs and dumped one on top of the other, facedown, between a water-trough and the side of the saddlehouse. He saddled Star and led his packhorse east out of town.

He paused to let his horses blow on Harshaw Pass before he started down the other side. He looked back and saw Will Pendleton and his brothers, the first of the funeral horsemen and rigs, coming up the street in front of the saloons. He kept watching until he saw A. B. and his mother and sisters. He was too sentimental about his family that day to go on without a last look.

Ben was conscious of a burning in his back a nail or a sliver of wood had caused when he bumped the fence in the fight. His shoulder was stiffening. The back of his shirt was wet with blood. The scratch or cut was in the muscle along his spine.

He headed south toward Washington Camp on a trail that was used so much he would be hard to track. He stayed on the trail for more than an hour and even stopped and visited with people he met. Then he left the trail and headed east, hiding his tracks under manzanita brush so thick a rider would have to dismount to see the ground.

He rode into the Mowry Camp in the early afternoon. The twins were taking their siesta in a tent in the deep shade of a cliff in a sycamore grove. This camp in canyon and mountain country was one of the most hidden of all the Cowden-Farley camps.

Ben grumbled and lowed like a bull to wake up the twins, but they slept on. He could see the soles of their boots and their hats over their faces. The tent was rolled up and tied off the ground on all sides to let the breezes through. If they made a habit of sleeping that soundly, someday an Apache or a VO would stretch the twins' siesta until it lasted forever.

Ben tied his horses in the sycamores and carried water to them from a spring underneath the cliff. He did not want to leave deep tracks in the wet ground by the spring. He took them a quarter mile farther and tied them in a cedar thicket. He wiped out most of their tracks and went back to the tent.

The twins were not in the boots. The boots were old and useless for wearing. The forms Ben thought were the twins were only rags and worn-out boots lying under old hats. The twins had tricked him and must be laughing at him.

"Yes, he would be dead, brother, because he still doesn't know where we are," Ben heard one twin say. Ben always thought he and his brothers knew this camp better than anyone, but he could not tell where the twins were hiding. They hooted like owls to make fun of Ben, and he started running. He jammed his hat down over his ears and ran until he was sure he was out of sight, then dove inside the roots of a sycamore and lay still.

The twins stopped laughing. "Well, genius," he heard one say. "Where is he now?"

"Yeah, genius. He's gone," said the other.

"Quiet, I don't think he's located us, yet. Let's split up."

Ben located them. They were inside a high fissure in the face of the cliff. He flanked them, climbed to the top of the cliff, and found their entrance. The fissure had always seemed too narrow and dark a place for him to explore. Ben and his brothers never played in it as children because it looked like a good place for snakes, scorpions, and centipedes.

He wriggled on his belly to get inside and saw the twins had cleaned it of loose rock and brush. He moved up behind Danny Farley.

The twin was sitting up with his head bowed against his knees, keeping himself small and quiet. Danny was one who could hide and wait for three days in one spot, like an Indian. Ben knew of caves in the Sierra Madre where the dry mummies of native people had been sitting forever the way Danny was sitting. They made Ben think they were waiting for the time of the world's corruption to be over, so they could stand up, come out, freshen up with a drink of water, and go back to living.

"Is that you, Ben?" Danny asked with his mouth against his knee." 'Cause if it isn't, I'm a skinned rabbit."

"You'd be easy to skin, at that," Ben said. He settled against the cool rock, relaxed, and was instantly asleep. A moment later he was awakened by the sound of men and horses. They passed so close to the top of the cliff Ben could feel the weight of the animals move the walls in the fissure. He felt refreshed, even though the sleep was so short Danny had not moved.

"Hello," someone called.

"Hello," Donny answered from down in the camp.

"Farley, is that you?"

"That's right," Donny said.

"Where's the other one? Aren't you a twin and come in pairs?"

The riders laughed, and Ben slid over to a crack where he could watch them. The first man he recognized was the sheriff, Carl Perkins. Then, he recognized Fitzgerald, Vincent's portly cow boss. The other six men were wearing badges. Hell, this was a sheriff's posse.

"Get off your horses, and I'll make coffee," Donny said.

"Where's the other one?" asked Fitzgerald. He always wore his hat one size too small, and it sat way up on the top of his head. He used a big deep voice to talk big everywhere he went.

"The other what?" asked Donny.

"That other shanty brother of yours. You know what we're looking for, so stand up here and pay attention to what I'm saying," said Fitzgerald.

The sheriff was a small man, very slight and stern. He wore a big gray brush of a mustache. He rode between Donny and Fitzgerald. "There's no use abusing the boy. I'll ask the questions."

"Well, you question him, then," Fitzgerald said.

"Young man, have you seen Ben Cowden?" Sheriff Perkins asked.

Donny did not look up. He banked coals around his coffeepot. "Yessir, I saw him the other day in Medal Canyon."

"You haven't seen him today?"

"He was headed for Mexico when I saw him." Donny looked the sheriff in the eye. "That's the damned truth. If he was here, I'll guarantee he wouldn't run from you."

The sheriff turned to the posse. "Fan out and look around. See what you can find."

My horses, Ben thought. Dammit, they'll find my horses. He moved along the fissure to watch the men who searched toward his cedar thicket. Two riders started that way, but they stopped at the spring and watered their horses. They went back and told the others about the spring. After that, the whole posse rode to the spring when they came back from the search, then went to the fire and availed themselves of Donny's coffee.

Donny kept pouring coffee, but he made the whole posse sip from the same cup. The Cowdens and the Farleys kept plenty of cups in the camp, but Donny only gave the deputies one to use, so they would not think they could stay and have all the coffee they wanted.

"What's Ben done?" Donny asked the sheriff when the last of the posse straggled to the fire.

"What he's done hasn't been decided. He's accused of stealing cattle."

"Who's accusing him of that?"

"That's not important. We want to take him in before somebody starts a war. If you see Ben, you tell him that."

"I sure will. He'll be pleased you came all the way out here from Tucson to put him in jail for Vincent and not start a war."

"Don't get smart with me, youngster. Just tell him what I said."

"Oh, nosir, I won't get smart. I'm really awful dumb. My brother's been telling me that."

The sheriff mounted his horse and rode away through the trees. His posse scrambled out of the camp and followed him.

Ben unloaded and unsaddled his packhorse and turned him loose in a trap with the twins' remuda. He waited for another quarter hour and then followed the posse. He stayed behind until the posse rode out on the open plain of the San Rafael. He stopped in sight of the VO headquarters.

The sheriff had covered only enough country to put him at the VO at sundown and suppertime. After supper he would have a cigar and brandy, count votes, and talk politics with the great man, Duncan Vincent. The sheriff would sleep in a featherbed tonight. That was fine. A peaceful night for the posse meant a peaceful night for Ben. He turned back.

He made a circle across VO range that neighbored the Johnson ranch. The range was covered with green grass that had been made by the same rain that freshened the Johnson place. On the way back to the twins' camp, Ben counted ninety-three of the steers he and his brothers caught on the Temporal. Well, the VO did the Cowdens a service when it moved those cattle off the drouthy Buena Vista. The steers were on green feed. If Vincent was blessed with more rain, they might even grow big enough to be sold to Walter Jarboe in the fall.

Ben got back to the twins' camp after dark. When he tied his horse in the cedars, he could see the glimmer of the twins' fire and hear voices through the trees. They had visitors. Star was so tired he did not nicker to the twins' horses. He needed his morral, but Ben did not even loosen his cinches. He climbed the cliff and crawled into the fissure to see who was in the camp. He sure liked that fissure now.

"We know he's been here, because that's his packhorse your brother's sitting on," somebody was saying. Ben found the crack he used to spy on the camp.

Donny Farley was sitting on Moose, Ben's packhorse, by the fire. His hands were tied behind him. The loop of a reata was around his neck. The reata had been cast over a limb above him and tied to the trunk of the tree. Hoozy Briggs was sitting at the fire with his back to Ben. Danny Farley was sitting on the ground in front of him. Hoozy was poking a stick into the front of Danny's shirt. Broderick, Snider, Thomas, and Campana were at the fire. Someone was behind Moose, outside the firelight, but Ben could not identify him.

"That's not Ben's packhorse," Danny said. "That's old Blaze. He looks like Moose, but he's not Moose."

"The hell he ain't," Broderick said. "I know horses, and that horse was packed with Cowden's gear and standing tied under a tree at your daddy's pens in Harshaw this morning."

"Danny?" said Donny from atop Moose, worried.

"Let my brother down off that horse," Danny said. "At least tell that Indian to quit lurking around behind him. He'll booger the horse and strangle my brother."

The man behind the horse moved into the light, and Ben recognized the Yaqui.

Hoozy kept jabbing the stick into Danny's chest. Danny was crying silently and gently brushing the stick aside. Hoozy's stick made Ben think of his sore back. He suspected Snider had poked him with something sharp during the fight at the Farleys' corral. The ache from the scratch or scrape was spreading up to his shoulder and down into the small of his back.

"You think we're playing?" Hoozy asked Danny.

"No," said Danny in a child's voice.

Ben thought, My God, the twins are only seventeen. The whole family has been thinking these boys are men enough to run these camps by themselves.

"What do you think we're doing here?" Hoozy asked.

Danny narrowed his eyes when he looked at Hoozy. "I don't know."

"We're county rangers with orders to arrest Ben Cowden."

"You want me to tell you where he is?"

"You can if you want to. I'm going to kill you whether you do or not, but I might not hang your brother."

"He was here, and he's coming back," Danny said. "It's likely he's watching you right now."

Thomas and Campana lay back with their hats over their eyes. Broderick poured himself a cup of coffee. Snider stood up and dragged his feet to the woodpile.

"What if he's telling the truth?" Broderick said, scanning the cliff face.

"If Cowden can hear me, he'd better know I'll hang this boy if he doesn't come out where I can see him *right now*," yelled Hoozy.

Ben was not sure he could shoot from his hiding-place. The fissure hid him well but was so narrow at the top he did not think he could raise up high enough to aim and fire at all six men.

Hoozy dropped the stick, stood up, and walked around the fire. "Campana, get your quirt and stand behind that horse." The voice was Hoozy's, but the face was unrecognizable.

Campana came out from under his hat. "What?"

Scabs on Hoozy's face crisscrossed each other like stitches on a quilt. The patches of the quilt were different sizes and colors. He was wearing a purple lump against the side of his head where his ear ought to be. His right arm was in a splint. Hoozy would never be able to hide that face as long as he lived, and it marked him forever as the Johnson family's killer.

"Briggs, I don't like what you're doing," Snider said. "Don't you know any better than to tie a boy on a horse with a noose around his neck like that? Anything could cause that horse to step out from under the boy."

"What do I care if the squatter accidentally hangs? I'm being paid to get rid of squatters, and I'm owed for my ace," said Hoozy.

"Well, you're not owed this boy's life. I'm taking him down before something happens to him."

Ben felt a footfall overhead. The Yaqui was standing on an overhang above him, watching Hoozy and Snider argue.

Snider started toward the tree to untie the reata. Hoozy drew his pistol. Small rocks scuffed away from the Yaqui's eguas and dropped on Ben's back. Ben's face was pressed against the crack. He was breathing through his mouth with his tongue out to keep his breathing quiet, and he could taste the sides of the crack. Thomas and Campana were fascinated by Hoozy. If Hoozy was going to kill Snider and hang the boy, they wanted to watch.

"Snider, if you untie that lariat, you're gonna die," Hoozy said.

Snider ignored him and kept going. Hoozy slapped Moose across the hips with his rifle. Moose was standing shot-hipped and half asleep. He woke up, but did not untrack. Ben wanted to cheer. Thank God for old gentle horses. Moose put his slack foot down and rolled an eye at Hoozy. Hoozy raised his rifle and hit him again, and this time Moose hopped forward a step. Donny was dragged choking over his hips. He clutched Moose's sides with his feet to keep from swinging clear.

Snider untied the reata and let it drop off the tree trunk. Hoozy hit Moose on the tail. Moose lurched out from under Donny, and the boy landed on the ground on his back.

Snider's face was white because he knew he had probably given up his life when he untied the reata.

Hoozy said, "You yellow bastard, I'm gonna kill you for that."

"Go ahead," Snider said.

The Yaqui shifted his feet on the overhang and chuckled softly, enjoying the show. Danny untied Donny. Hoozy began raving and stomping and waving his pistol. Ben started moving out from under the Yaqui.

"I will kill you, you bastard," Hoozy shouted. "I killed a whole family for getting smart with me like you just did. Get over here in the light where I can see you."

"That's fine." Snider could barely find his voice, he was so scared, but he was brave. "If you're going to kill me, I want you to look me in the eye so you'll remember me when they make you pay for it."

Ben moved a few inches each time Hoozy yelled. He needed to be ten feet down the fissure before he could raise up and start shooting. He had never in his life worked so hard or with so much urgency to put himself in the right place at the right time.

When he arrived at the place, he sat up and looked for the Yaqui, but the Yaqui was gone into the night again

Snider was walking toward the fire, and Hoozy was raving and walking backward in front of him. Ben took aim with his pistol to send a round through Hoozy's skull, but Hoozy snagged his heel on a sycamore root and sprawled on his back. Snider ran like a wildman.

Ben aimed low at Hoozy as he scrambled to his feet. He wanted to shoot the man so bad, he jerked the trigger. The bullet only blew Hoozy's bootheel off, but the report scared everybody else a foot off the ground and put them to flight. The shot so surprised old Moose that he bumped into Hoozy and blocked Ben's next shot. Hoozy tripped over backward into a pile of rocks.

The twins split apart and ran for the darkness. Thomas, Campana, and Broderick fired toward Ben as they scattered out of the light. Ben missed two quick shots at Broderick running like a ghost with his shirttail flying and never got another chance to kill Hoozy Briggs. Everybody was gone out of the firelight in the next instant, and nobody was hit. The Briggs gang crashed through the night to their horses.

Ben ran along the top of the hill toward the cedar thicket where Star was tied. He could not fire another shot until he located the twins. He stopped above the thicket and listened to the horses running and the men grunting, whipping and spurring through the brush and the darkness. He waited until he could hear his horse stir in the thicket, and he picked his way down and stopped close to him. He could not see a thing inside the dark cedars.

Ben grumbled softly, like an old bull bellering.

"Ben?" whispered one of the twins.

"Thank God," Ben said. "Where's your brother?"

"Right here."

CHAPTER 21

Paula Mary decided she just had to ride the horse called Colonel. He was Mark's top horse, a tall sorrel. Her brothers usually let her ride any horse she asked for, but her family said Colonel was too much horse for her.

Every animal at El Durazno belonged to Cowden Livestock Company. Each of the girls owned a brand of her own and a start of cows for her dowry. None of the girls owned any horses, though. The boys owned nothing but their saddles.

Even Lemonade belonged to the company. After they learned to ride, A. B. figured his girls did not need horses. They would never do much riding; they could not endure the long circles after cattle. The country was too dangerous for them to ride for pleasure, so A. B. did not encourage them to ride.

The boys were each assigned a string of ten horses. A horse a man broke, trained, and used as a cow horse was considered to be in his string and belonged to him in that sense. A horse was only ridden by the man in whose string he belonged. Nobody dared touch a horse in a stranger's string, not even to lead him to water. Anytime a Cowden girl wanted to ride, unless she was content to ride old Lemonade, she asked one of the boys to loan her a horse from his string. The boys always loaned the girls their pokiest, most dog-gentle old partners.

A. B. tried to teach his girls to know their limitations, so they could protect themselves around high-powered horses. Paula Mary was the only one who was so headstrong she thought she could make a hand on any animal she could climb aboard.

Colonel was snorty about his feet and touchy about small creatures Paula Mary's size. Paula Mary knew how to walk up to snorty horses, climb in the middle of them and make them do what she wanted. She'd been laying for Colonel. Mark was riding him, looking for the broodmares that morning. He would be home for dinner at noon.

The horse was so full of juice all the time that Mark would leave him saddled in the corral at noon. He would use him again all afternoon to work some of the snortiness out of him.

This was one of the days the family was having dinner in shifts. A. B., Viney, and the girls had eaten. Les and Mark would soon be in from the pasture. After they ate dinner, the family would rest for an hour or two. Paula Mary did not take naps anymore. On that day, she planned to take a ride on Colonel during siesta hour.

She had been keeping to herself since Freddie Lee died and Ben was forced to leave home. A. B. was working hard to clear Ben's name. Eileen had taken over all the housework, and Betty was still sick with a fever. Viney spent most of her time in the sewing rocker in the Arizona room, grieving. She had moved it out there so she would not have to look out the window at the front yard where Freddie had been killed.

Paula Mary missed Freddie Lee, but she was mischief-prone because she did not know how to grieve for him the way everybody else did. She was lying on her back on the big limb of the walnut tree that stretched over the road. Young limbs cradled her on both sides. A breeze moved the tree gently. She was half asleep when she heard the murmur of her brothers' voices, the sound of their saddle-leather, and their horses pacing on the road. They would pass directly underneath her.

As they approached, Les said quietly, "Steak, potatoes, gravy, biscuits, and butter, little brother."

"I'm ready," Mark said.

When they were underneath Paula Mary's limb, Les said, "When was the last time we had dinner with Mama's light biscuits and butter?"

Paula Mary could feel the smile in her brother's voice.

"The day before yesterday at the wake when Ben was with us. We had honey, too." Mark sighed.

They rode along.

"We'll probably stay home now, until Ben can come home," Mark murmured. "He wanted to rest awhile, too. He was getting tired."

They rode a little farther, and Paula Mary barely heard him say, "I wonder where he is. I don't wonder what the poor guy's having for dinner, though. Jerky."

Paula Mary gave her brothers time to settle down to their dinner, then she climbed down from the tree and ran to the barn. Bill Knox was in the hayloft, snoring. Gordo lay with his face to the wall by the back door, sound asleep.

Paula Mary picked up a five-gallon bucket and went into the corral. Colonel was snorty, but he was law-abiding. A Cowden horse did not dare run from anybody who wanted to catch him. He let Paula Mary walk up to him, even though every step she took was a new horror for him.

She reached up and patted his shoulder. He was tall. She stood on the bucket to take the bridle off the saddle horn, slipped the reins around his neck, and led him to the fence. She made him stand alongside the fence while she climbed up beside him and bridled him. He quivered and snorted with displeasure, but he stood for it.

Colonel was trained to know the law and to believe he was under sentence of death if he broke it with even the smallest Cowden. The law was clear for horses: Stand still for saddling, bridling, and mounting; opening gates, dismounting, and shoeing.

Paula Mary tightened Colonel's cinches and climbed on his back. She opened the corral gate, rode through, and latched it behind her without dismounting. She crept away at a walk until she passed the house, hoping she would not be seen riding away.

Now *this* was a horse. His shoulders were wider and more powerful than any she had ever seen. His mane was

ner, his ears more delicate. His neck was thick and
rched, and it glinted with copper lights in the sun. He
eined to the slightest touch.

The horse watched to see what Paula Mary wanted him
o do. She felt he was ready to explode to her touch, but
as letting her hold him in the crook of a finger.

Colonel was the kind of horse her father liked most. A
erson could ride him to pen a mean bull, cradle a child
hile a diaper was changed, gather acorns under a tree, or
op a runaway team. Paula Mary gave him slack and let
im coast into the breeze at a lope. Her feet were three feet
ort of the stirrups, but he was so smooth, he made her
el she was part of him. Mark's stirrups didn't even flop
hen he loped. He was as soft-footed as a cat and hardly
ade a sound. She slid him to a stop in the middle of a draw
elow a deep canyon. She sat him a moment, glorying.

The Porter girls all rode sidesaddle. Uncle Billy Porter
orked his girls horseback almost as much as he did his
oys. Maudy Jane Pendleton was the best horsewoman in
e whole country. She was the best rider and made the
rettiest picture on a horse, bar none. She never rode
tride. She even sat one side of the horse when she rode
areback. She could ride that way at a gallop, a trot, or a
ead run. The Mexicans called it, riding *a la Lola*, Lola's
ay. Paula Mary wanted to be able to do that.

She decided to practice riding sidesaddle on Colonel.
e headed up the canyon, swung her leg over the horn
d started him at a lope.

Colonel began to float. Paula Mary was sure no one else
the world ever traveled so fast. The trail was wide and
eep because cattle were using it to come down to the
eps in Harshaw Creek. Colonel carried her so effortlessly
at she did not stop him until she reached the top of the
nyon.

She let him blow, but he was not tired. She turned him
d walked him all the way back to the draw, then turned
m up the canyon and loped him to the top again. When
e reached the top of the canyon the second time, Paula
ary was ready to head for home. The swells and horn on
ark's saddle were too rough to grip with the inside of her
g, and she was getting sore. She started Colonel back
own the canyon.

She realized no Cowden girl had ever ridden alone awa
from the house this far and began to feel a little afraid. Sh
wanted to hurry home, but she was already in trouble fo
taking the horse away from the house. If she loped hi
toward home, she would be in a lot worse trouble. N
Cowden ever gave a horse his head going toward the hous
That made barn-soured horses that ran away with peop
every time they were pointed toward home. She knew sh
must be patient and let Colonel walk and cool down all th
way back to the barn.

She rode around a narrow bend in the trail, and the b
Indian called the Yaqui stepped out of the shade of a cl
and grabbed Colonel's bridle. That maneuver scared Pau
Mary's blood cold.

"Hey!" Her yell sounded loud in the canyon.

The Yaqui grinned and bared his brown teeth, but h
was not looking at her face. He was looking at Mar
saddle, bridle, and blankets. The saddle was better th
new, well used and well oiled. Paula Mary could see th
Yaqui figured he had just taken possession of a valuab
horse and saddle, knew exactly how to dispose of them, a
did not care about the child who was attached to them.

All he needed to do was yank Paula Mary off the hors
leave her afoot, and go back to Mexico. Instead of doi
that, he asked, "Es muy buen caballo? Is this a real go
horse?"

"Ah, no, es muy mañoso. He's a real mean horse."

The Yaqui slid his hand under Paula Mary's leg a
fingered the thickness of the leather in the saddle's skirt
He took a close look at the bridle and reins, open
Colonel's mouth, and examined his teeth. He admired a
wanted all the booty; had the eye of a looter and w
probably a wholehearted thief. He would not have to car
it away on his own back, either.

Someone was chopping wood on a ridge above th
canyon, out of sight. Paula Mary knew every woodcutter
the country.

"Es mi papá," she said, her eyes wide, her mou
smiling, pointing to the ridge. She did not stop to think th
this Yaqui would know that her father and brothers we
not woodcutters. He probably spent as much time watchi

El Durazno to see what he could steal as Paula Mary spent daydreaming in her walnut tree. The Yaqui looked over his shoulder to see if anyone was watching.

Paula Mary noticed he was wearing a thick gold chain around his neck, like the one Guilo Soto wore. Dangling on the chain was Myrtle Farley's ruby ring. Paula Mary knew that ring instantly. She had been blaming herself for losing it, dreaming someday she would find it and give it back to Myrtle. Here it was, hanging on a chain that probably belonged to Guilo. She always knew it was somewhere, but never dreamed she would find it hanging on the neck of a thief and murderer.

The Yaqui caught Paula Mary staring at the ring, and he raised a hand to grab her out of the saddle. Colonel flinched away from him. The Yaqui grabbed for the bridle again and stumbled. Paula Mary spun Colonel toward him. His head collided with Colonel's, and he went down.

Paula Mary spun Colonel like a top toward home, gave him his head, and let him run. The horse already sensed her fear and the Yaqui's anger. When she turned him all the way loose, he panicked. He made five jumps toward home, realized he was completely on his own, and cast himself away on the wind. Not even a grown man could have controlled him.

The runaway horse woke up the whole country. Chris Wilson was driving along half asleep when Colonel clattered onto the Harshaw road in front of his twenty-mule team. In his panic, Colonel did not see the team until he flew up over the bank onto the road and was forced to swerve to keep from smashing into the leaders. All four of his feet flashed out from under him on the hard road when he changed direction, but he righted himself, skidded on each of his feet in turn, regained his momentum, and rattled on up the road. He came so near colliding with the mules and surprised them so much, they caught his panic and bounded off the road with Chris hollering and rearing back on the lines. Chris held them as they crossed the boulders in the stream, then headed them into a willow thicket, tangled them in it, and stopped.

Colonel was so crazed in flight that he opened his and Paula Mary's graves wider with every jump. Every creature within a quarter mile caught his panic. The whole Cowden family heard and understood what was happening at the same moment and ran out of the house as Colonel passed under the walnut trees. Bill Knox and Gordo ran out and shouted and waved their arms to stop the horse as he headed into the barnyard. Paula Mary shrieked with every breath she caught.

Colonel shied and skittered past Bill Knox and Gordo, dove through the open front door of the barn, barreled out the open back door, and braked and slid across the back yard. He glanced off a board fence and loosened Paula Mary's seat. He braked and dodged crazily on his front feet as he saw he was about to crash into the next fence, threw Paula Mary against it, then slammed it headfirst and knocked himself down.

Mark and Les ran up to grab Colonel, but they were not in time to keep him off the girl. He stamped over her as he got up and whirled on her again when he saw the brothers running toward him. Mark cornered him away from the girl and took hold of him.

Les picked up his sister, ran through his family, and banged through the house to her bed. A thick smear of blood covered her face, and little bubbles of her breath were rising through it. He cleared the blood away from her nose with his handkerchief and fainted dead away.

Hoozy was riding with Snider, Broderick, Thomas, and Campana toward Porter Canyon. He did not know how long he would be able to stay around Snider without killing him. He wanted to be rid of him. Snider was soured on his job.

He was sour himself that morning. He had been in so much pain and distress that he rested a few days in the VO bunkhouse, contrary to Duncan Vincent's orders. He needed a place to recuperate and did not want to be seen in Harshaw.

Vincent surprised him by calling him aside and giving him $100 in cash as a bonus for his work and trouble. Then he ordered him to take Thomas, Campana, Broderick, and Snider and stay in a camp on the edge of the Porter range. Vincent did not want Hoozy and his gang to be seen at the VO headquarters. He wanted them doing mischief to the Porters.

Now Hoozy was back on Patch, riding toward Porter Canyon. He did not mind riding with Thomas and Campana, but Broderick was a big whiner, and Snider disapproved of everything the VO was doing on grounds of sin.

The blacksmith at the VO had shod Patch, but she was still lame. Hoozy was finding out how tiring riding a crippled horse could be. A fresh horse might be all he needed. Now, if he could get rid of Snider, he could have Little Buck. That would rest him considerably, to ride a fresh horse as pretty as Little Buck.

Hoozy suspected Snider was about to quit. Cowboys seldom saddled their personal horses unless they intended to leave an outfit. Hoozy had to ride Patch because Vincent didn't want anyone to know he worked for the VO. Hoozy figured if he didn't kill Snider for being so sour, he could kill him for the buckskin.

Vincent had made him feel good and given him new purpose when he rewarded him with $100, but he was having second thoughts about taking on the Porters. The Porters were five grown men who would rope the devil just so they could listen to him squeal.

Vincent complained that every time he looked out his window, he saw a Porter cow. The Porters were not making way for Vincent at all. Porter probably owned as many native cows as Vincent owned steers. Besides that, every time Vincent saw an old common Porter bull, he was putting the run on blooded VO sires and covering purebred VO cows.

Hoozy and his gang stopped on a bluff at the junction of Porter Canyon Creek and the Santa Cruz River. Below them, three vaqueros were branding calves in a set of pens. A band of mares and their foals were grazing nearby,. The stud moved out and nickered to Hoozy's horses, and the vaqueros looked up and saw the VO cowboys.

"Who's that down there working?" asked Hoozy.

Nobody answered him.

"That's Mexicans, ain't it? That's not the Porters. Who're those Mexicans, Campana?"

Campana cleared his throat but kept his peace.

"Why do you always have to know who everybody is?" asked Snider. "Did you ever stop to think it might not be any of your business?"

"Shut up. Who're those Mexicans, Campana?"

Campana cleared his throat again. "Romeros from Santa Cruz."

"What are they doing working cattle on this side of the line? Whose horses are those?"

"Don't you know those horses?" asked Thomas.

"Why should I? They're saddlehorses belonging to those Mexicans in the pens, aren't they?"

"Any horseman would know that's a band of mares and not a remuda of saddlehorses, even from this far away. You've never seen nursing colts in a remuda, have you."

The whole gang could see Hoozy was thinking fast to avoid showing his ignorance. "Those mares? I was about to ask you if that didn't look like the bunch we took from the Johnsons."

"Hoozy, what kind of a horse thief are you? You stole the Johnson horses for yourself. Now you think the first bunch of horses you see are yours. When you steal a horse, you better learn to remember what he looks like, or someday you'll hang for a horse you don't even know. There weren't any baby colts in the Johnson horses. What's the matter with you?"

"Now I've heard it all. You murdered the Johnsons so you could steal their horses, you damned butcher?" Snider said.

Hoozy turned to Snider with his pistol in his hand. Snider said softly, "I guess I'm not surprised."

"I'll give you another chance to be surprised, then," said Hoozy. "You're gonna get off that buckskin and give him to me."

"I'm gonna do what?" asked Snider. "I guess you think you can make me. You've still got an ear left."

"I guess I'll kill you *before* you get off the horse."

"You want the horse? You've got him. No horse is worth a man's life." Snider jumped off Little Buck and backed away from him. "There he is. Take him."

Hoozy watched Snider a moment and speculated.

"There he is. What more do you want?" asked Snider.

"Don't kill him, Hoozy," said Thomas. "He's on our side."

"All right, Snider, unsaddle my mare," said Hoozy.

Hoozy stepped off Patch. Snider unsaddled her and turned her loose. She walked away a few steps and looked back. She put her head down and took several quick, ravenous bites of grass. She raised her head, stopped chewing, and froze. Grass stuck out both sides of her mouth as she stared at the band of mares. The stud nickered to her, and the whole band trotted out a few steps in greeting. They were a half mile away, but they could smell her.

"Leave that saddle on the buckskin," said Hoozy. "I like it better than my old kak."

Snider stepped away, exasperated. "You're going to leave me afoot?"

"What would you ride?" asked Hoozy.

"Well, your old mare can get me to my supper at least."

"She needs a rest."

"You better let me catch her, or you'll lose her to that Porter stud," said Thomas.

"Let her go. I'll tell you what we're going to do about that bunch of mares in a minute," said Hoozy, staring at Snider. "After I kill somebody."

"So, you're leaving me afoot," Snider said quickly, acting resigned to it. He preferred being afoot to being dead.

Hoozy sighted his pistol on Snider's eye. "You don't have to worry," he said. "You won't wear out any shoe-leather."

"Now, Hoozy, don't kill the man," said Thomas. "We won't have it. We don't quit our partners, and we don't kill them. We didn't quit you at Santa Cruz, did we?"

"I only want to kill this one," said Hoozy.

"Turn around and get going, Snider," said Thomas. "Walk away." Snider turned his back and started walking.

"Leave the pistol, too," said Hoozy.

Snider dropped his pistol on the ground and kept going.

Hoozy picked it up, examined it, and stuck it in his belt. He dragged his Sharps rifle and its boot out from under his saddle and mounted Little Buck. He looked down at the horse approvingly while he slung the Sharps on his saddle horn. He rode off the bluff toward the pens where the vaqueros were working. Halfway down the hill he yelled back, "Come on, you're paid to help me."

Broderick turned to Thomas. "Are we going to keep on riding with that sonofabitch?"

"What the hell, we'll never have a chance to see him shot if we quit him now," said Thomas.

"Do you know those Mexicans, Campana?" Broderick asked.

"Oh, sí," said Campana. "All their lives."

"Then you'd better hurry and warn them to look out for that rabid sonofabitch."

"Oh, he tell them," said Campana. "Look."

Hoozy was stepping off Little Buck with his big Sharps. He was down in a deep wash that protected him and hid the horse. He raised the rifle over the bank, rested it on the ground, cocked it, aimed it, and killed the horse under a vaquero who was opening a gate to let cattle out of the pens.

The other two vaqueros drew their pistols and ran toward their downed partner, firing at Hoozy. He was completely out of their range.

The Porter mares trotted up the draw away from the shooting and stopped. Patch ran to catch up, and the stud called to her, encouraging her. The cattle streamed out the gate in a hurry.

Hoozy's Sharps launched another round. The bullet shattered a bundle of firewood the vaqueros were using for branding inside the pen. The downed rider was pinned under his horse in the open gate. He yelled at his companions to stay back and fired at Hoozy with a pistol. The vaqueros did not have rifles. Their pistols were no defense against Hoozy's Sharps. Hoozy did not even look up when they fired at him; they were a thousand yards away.

Snider sat on a rock on the top of a hill and watched. Thomas, Campana, and Broderick were still sitting their horses on the bluff. The two vaqueros came out from behind the pens horseback and ran along the river toward Hoozy to shorten the range. They came fast, using the riverbank, cottonwoods, and brush for cover. Thomas and Campana rode off the bluff at a walk toward Hoozy.

Broderick stayed on the bluff. He waved to Snider, shook his head, and grinned. Thomas and Campana spurred their horses into a lope. Broderick shrugged, waved to Snider again, drew his rifle, and followed them.

The vaqueros hesitated before riding out of the riverbed into the open in front of the Sharps. When they saw the other VO hands dismount by Hoozy with their rifles, they pulled back and headed downriver.

Thomas and Campana fired at them but could not tell where their bullets were striking in the brush and trees. Hoozy aimed and fired his Sharps again. The bullet stuck sandstone by one of the horses and blasted rock and grit into the side of his head. The horse recoiled, kicked up behind, twisted like a fish, and landed dead on his feet, stunned. He was so addled that Hoozy's gang stopped shooting to laugh. The horse hung his head, cocked it, and waved it back and forth over the ground as though he was hit in the eye.

The man slumped over the swell of his saddle, head down. He took out his handkerchief and held it against his cheek while he urged his horse to move on. The animal shambled with his head down until he was close under the riverbank with the other horse. After that, the vaqueros stayed out of sight.

Hoozy came down off the bank, caught Little Buck, and holstered his Sharps. "Well, boys, two got away, but I got one," he said cheerfully.

Campana was looking at the downed rider.

"Who is he, Campana?"

"Hector Romero."

"Tell him we're coming over there to see how bad he's hurt."

Campana laughed. "You tell him."

"Why? I can't talk Mexican."

"Maybe he'll believe you. He won't believe me."

"Why?"

"He's no fool. You shoot his horse, then you want me tell him you going to hold his hand?"

"All right, tell him to throw his weapon out where we can see it. He's under arrest."

The Briggs gang climbed out of the wash. Campana

stepped forward and shouted, "*Rindete, Romero!* Surrender! The gringo says he wants to take you to jail. Throw away your pistol. *Avienta la pistola.*"

Romero aimed high enough so the next three shots he fired from his *pistola* made the Briggs gang dive on their bellies back into the wash.

John Snider walked to the Porter headquarters to see if he could buy a horse and saddle. Two cavalry mounts were resting in the shade of a quince tree by the main house. Uncle Billy Porter came out the front door chewing on a bite of his dinner.

"Where's your horse, Snider?" asked Uncle Billy.

"Hoozy Briggs took him and my saddle," said Snider.

"Wash here and come in."

Uncle Billy's wife and daughters were serving dinner to Lieutenant Little and his sergeant, a big Irishman named O'Kane. Two of Uncle Billy's sons, Jim and Bud Porter, were also at the table. He introduced Snider and told him to sit down and eat.

"Mr. Snider, I'm glad you're here," said Lieutenant Little. "You'll save us a ride to your headquarters. As soon as possible, we'd like you to hurry back and tell your boss we need his help.

"Lieutenant Hughes and his troop of Buffalo soldiers from Fort Grant are driving the Yawner east toward Long Mountain. Kosterlinsky's making a drive from the south. We hope to make contact with the Yawner from this side tomorrow. If we can crowd him enough, he might make a stand.

"Tell Mr. Vincent to send us every man and saddlehorse he can spare. We need fresh animals so we can tree the old Yawner. Maybe he won't get away this time."

Everybody was looking at Snider, decent people expecting his enthusiastic cooperation.

Snider said, "You better send somebody else to the VO. I'm headed for El Paso."

Lieutenant Little looked to Uncle Billy for support and tried once again to impress Snider with the importance of the errand. "You don't understand. We want you to drop what you're doing and ride back to the VO for us."

"Mister, I don't work for the VO anymore. Furthermore, if you think Vincent will help you, you're crazy. He'll only see this as a chance to cause his neighbors more grief so he can blame it on the Yawner. He's hoping Yawner'll kill the nice folks so he can have their country.

"When I left his hoodlums this morning, they were down at the river pens shooting at one of the Romero brothers. As soon as they get him out of their way, they'll probably run off the Porters' broodmares. Vincent's doing worse things to people than the Yawner ever thought of doing."

"Will you at least stay and help us?" asked Lieutenant Little.

"I sure would like to," said Snider. "But I'm leaving the country today. If the Porters will sell me a horse and saddle and an old pistol, I'll make some miles before dark. If there's anything I can do for you on the way to El Paso, name it and I'll do it or die trying, but don't ask me to stay in this country another day."

"Well, no, we don't need anything done in El Paso," said Lieutenant Little. "We need brave men to help us tree the Yawner, though."

No one said anything for a few moments. The silence was polite, but the men were uncomfortably quiet. The women left the room. Snider leaned back and laid down his fork. "Mr. Porter, I want you all to set easy, so I'll just wait outside until you can let me know if you can help me." He made a move to leave the table.

"Sit still," said Uncle Billy. "Finish your dinner. I thank you for walking all the way over here and telling us about this. We'll sell you a horse and saddle, and I have a rifle I'll give you. We know how a man feels when he's made up his mind to leave a country. Nobody on this outfit will ever blame a man for wanting to make a new start."

"Mr. Porter, right now I want to put the VO behind me and find decent work in a new country. I didn't like being in the wrong, and Vincent is sure doing wrong."

"That's all right, young man, you don't have to explain."

"Just let me tell you what his regulators have been doing."

CHAPTER 22

The cut on Ben's back bothered him all the time now. He rode to the camp he shared with Will Pendleton at La Noria, hoping Juan Heredia could doctor the wound. Juan ran the camp and kept his family there.

Ben saw Maudy's sidesaddle on a horse standing in the corral. He unsaddled his horses and walked to the house. Maudy was feeding clabbered milk to chickens outside the front door. Ben noticed how tiny her bodice was, how full her bust. Her waist was as high off the ground as his. She was long-legged and high behind, like a good racehorse. She smiled at him, called to tell her father he was there, and stepped up to hug him. She took him in, cooked his breakfast, and fed him sourdough biscuits.

Will Pendleton was keeping Maudy at La Noria with the Heredias now. He could not leave her alone at Canelo.

"Did your intended bring Little Buck back yet, Maudy?" Ben asked, kidding her. "I guess we'll be calling you Snider pretty soon, won't we?"

"*Posh*," Maudy said. "I'll never get my horse back."

"Oh, well, he's still in the family, isn't he? Or, at least he will be when you and Snider get married."

"What makes you think I'd marry that billy goat?"

"Well, you wouldn't lend your top horse to him unless you were sweet on him, would you? Snider's kind of a good-looking young blade. You did save him from a life of shame by covering his nakedness with your kimono, then made sure he'd come back when you loaned him your horse."

Maudy stopped what she was doing. "I'll never marry a man like that. He flat did me out of my horse. I *loved* Little Buck."

Maudy was not taking the kidding well. Ben looked to Will for an explanation. Will kept his eye on Maudy and said, "She sets great store by Little Buck. I'd hate to be the one that made off with him."

"What are you doing here, Ben?" That was not the kind of question little Maudy ever asked, but she was not so little anymore. Ben even thought he saw an inhospitable glint in her eye.

"Oh, I'm wandering around. Eventually, I guess I'll head for Porter Canyon. I want to see if the mesas made any feed. We're out of grass on the Buena Vista."

"You mean you're on the run and don't know where to hide?"

Ben could not think of an answer to that until Maudy smiled to show she was teasing him to get even.

Will was grinning. "She got you, didn't she?" he said.

"You both did," Ben said.

"The sheriff came by day before yesterday, looking for you." Maudy said. "I told him you ran off down to Mexico."

"Yes, I'm a wanted man, Maudy." Ben grinned. "I didn't think you knew."

"Everybody in the country who was at Freddie Lee's funeral knew, and they went home and told everybody else."

"You know I haven't stolen any cattle, don't you?"

"I know you're in a fight with Duncan Vincent, and Father says he sicced his sheriff on you. Who is *your* sheriff, Ben? That sounds like the thing to do, get your own sheriff."

"I do have my own sheriff. My papa. He wants to arrest me, too."

"I suppose you're saying they're false charges. We all believe you, of course, but false or not, you're practically a jailbird, now. I guess I won't have much trouble choosing between you and Snider. He has a good job with a great man, a real empire builder. And you? Your own papa wants to put you in jail."

"You know how to hurt a feller, Maudy Jane."

"Well, now we're even. Anyway, what made your shirt bloody in the back?"

"Oh, that? I scratched it on the fence the other day. I think I need doctoring."

"Let's see, then. Take it off."

"My shirt?"

"Of course your shirt. I didn't say your BVDs."

Juan Heredia came to the back door and said, "Here come the Porters."

Maudy took the shirt. "Filthy," she said. "That's the end of that shirt. *Now* drop your BVDs."

"Maudy! Can't you doctor me through the hole in my underwear?"

"Wouldn't that be something? Drop the top."

Ben unbuttoned the top of his long johns and let it hang under his waist.

Maudy examined the wound. "My lord! That looks *terrible*. Who knifed you?"

Through the open door Ben could see the Porters crossing the Santa Cruz. Army Sergeant O'Kane was with them. Ten kids aged three to ten were riding in front of the group on Indian ponies, some riding double. All were brown-faced and towheaded. Infants, yearlings, and two-year-olds were being carried in the arms of their mothers and aunts.

Ben's grandfather and grandmother, William and Mary, were with them, and so was Uncle Billy's wife and daughters and his sons, James and Bud. Uncle Billy's three brothers were there with two of their sons and all their wives and daughters. Ben's maiden great-aunt Emily who lived with his grandparents was up on a big gray horse. Everybody was horseback, the women riding sidesaddle. All the grown men and women were armed with rifles, pistols, and knives. The men were leading the remuda tied head-to-tail together and driving packhorses. Bedding and clothing was wrapped in tarps and hitched on the pack horses.

Maudy put a quart bottle of mescal and a pile of clean rags on the table. Her touch felt good as she explored the wound. Her fingertips always looked clean, cool, and rosy. He liked relaxing while Maudy fixed him, so he did not jump right up to go out and greet his relatives.

The Porters dismounted at the barn, and Juan Heredia and Will helped them unsaddle and pen their horses. One of the packhorses was carrying a body rolled in a tarp. The Porters took it down and carried it into the barn.

"How you doing, Maudy? I need to go down and help those people," said Ben. She was causing sharp pains in his back. "Why are you skinning me?"

"I'm sorry. It looks like somebody took a carving knife to you. A slab of your skin was laid back and it's been trying to heal. It needs to be reopened and drained and cleaned out. It's infected."

"It's nothing bad, is it? All I did was back into a fence."

"You did more than that. It looks like somebody tried to slice a steak off your loin."

"Hell, am I gonna die, or what?"

"Not if I clean it out and pour it full of mescal."

Maudy made thick suds with warm water and lye soap, then washed his back and rinsed it with mescal. She put her palms on both sides of the wound and tore it open as she would a seam that was badly sewn. That brought tears to Ben's eyes. She cleaned out the wound, doused it with mescal again, dressed it, covered it with a clean undershirt and a work-shirt of Will's, and turned him loose.

"How did you really get that cut?" asked Maudy. "Did somebody knife you?"

"I ran into a sharp sliver or a nail sticking out of a board in the Farley fence." Ben hurried out the door before Maudy asked more questions.

The body in the tarp belonged to Hector Romero. The Porters found him hanging in a cottonwood at the river pens. Hoozy's gang had driven the Porter broodmares past La Noria toward Santa Cruz, and the Porters were following their tracks.

"I did not like my family seeing Hector Romero hanging in a tree," said Uncle Billy when the Porter women had gone to the house with Maudy. "I'll probably have to be the one to tell his mama and daddy he's dead."

"This fight with Vincent will have to stop now," said Grandfather Porter. "The Yawner is giving both sides enough to contend with."

The Porters planned to leave their womenfolk and children with a few of the older boys at La Noria while they helped the soldiers corner the Yawner. Every family along the Santa Cruz was trying to find a safe place before the battle.

Lieutenant Little had telegraphed Harshaw for help before he left Fort Huachuca. An hour after the Porters arrived at La Noria, Mark and Les Cowden and the Farley twins rode into the Pendleton yard. Each man was leading three extra saddlehorses. Mark and Les took Ben aside.

Les's face was haggard. "I've got some more bad news, Ben."

"What's wrong?" Ben asked, alarmed. "What's happened, now?"

"Paula Mary snuck off on that Colonel horse while we were having dinner day before yesterday. He had a runaway and hurt her pretty bad."

Les choked and stopped talking.

Without any expression, Mark said, "Yeah, knocked her colder'n a fart and gave her a nosebleed."

"That's all?" asked Ben. He had been expecting to be laid low by a new catastrophe.

"That's all. Scared old Colonel out of his mind."

"Well, we don't really know how bad she was hurt, but I'll tell you, I was scared to death," Les said. "I'm still so scared my spit dries up every time I think about it."

"The Yaqui stepped out on the trail and scared Paula Mary so bad she gave old Colonel his head," Mark said. "The poor old horse thought he had a banshee on his back and stampeded. I would have done the same thing. He bounced off the back corral and threw Paula Mary into the fence. She's so light it didn't hurt her very much. Les was in worse shape than she was. He had a runaway carrying her to the house and then fainted on top of her and damned near smothered her. Then Eileen and Mama went to bawling and swooning. I'll tell you, me and Betty and Papa had a time with four Cowdens taking turns going into a coma.

"While that was going on, John Porter's messenger arrived with Lieutenant Little's telegram. That straightened everybody up. Paula Mary took a nap and got all right."

"Are you and the twins the only ones coming from Harshaw to help fight the Yawner?" Ben asked.

"I don't know if anybody else is coming. We came on so we could find the twins and bring them with us. We didn't waste time hunting help in town."

"What about the sheriff and his posse?"

"The sheriff's in Harshaw. He told Papa he would bring his posse to reinforce Lieutenant Little later if he thought it was necessary, but in the meantime he thought it was more important to help the citizens defend their property."

"Where's Papa?"

"He was at home when we left. Mama and the girls are still grieving for Freddie Lee, so he thought he'd better stay there."

"Maybe Mark should have stayed home."

"Papa wouldn't have it. He sent us here and told us to be sure and tell you to help Lieutenant Little. He said it will help him have that warrant for your arrest lifted. Uncle John Porter is watching the telegraph, and he promised to go out to the ranch and help Papa if the Yawner headed that way."

"Look, there," Grandfather Porter said. The Porters were watching a column of dust rising in the wind and moving east toward Long Mountain. "That might be old Yawner."

"You suppose he'd be raising a dust like that?" Uncle Billy said.

"He is if he's got a troop of those Negro soldiers after him. If that is his dust, he's doing what the soldiers want him to do."

"Well, if that's him, we better get ready," Uncle Billy said.

The Porters and Cowdens checked their weapons and saddled fresh horses. They hung morrals full of corn on their saddle horns for their horses and went to Maudy's kitchen for food. Juan Heredia's wife gave them fried beans, beef cooked in red chile, and white Sonora cheese rolled in tortillas. They wrapped the fat burros in cornhusks and put them away in their morrals.

Ben replenished his amphorita with mescal from Will's jug. He hung a canteen of water on his saddle horn and tied it down with his saddle strings. He never carried water when he was working cattle, but no cowboy work ever made a man as dry as a firefight. He led Moose out and tied two of the Cowden horses head-to-tail behind him to lead to battle. He was riding Star.

Everybody watched the dust, and when a new column appeared behind it, Grandfather Porter said, "Sergeant O'Kane says that new dust is the army chasing the Yawner and it's time to go."

The men mounted, and the women came out to see them off. Three teenaged Porter boys and Juan Heredia's two young sons were left behind to defend the families. Nobody gave orders. The riders spread out so they could sweep the country and stay out of each other's way. They headed toward Long Mountain.

If army strategy was working, Lieutenant Hughes' buffalo soldiers were making that dust behind the Yawner. Kosterlinsky would be hazing the Yawner from the south. The Cowdens and Porters would help Lieutenant Little make a drive from the north toward Long Mountain. Lieutenant Little's troop was east of the Cowdens and Porters, waiting to hit the point of the Yawner's column and drive it against Long Mountain.

That was the plan. Ben knew the Yawner could not be too worried. If a battle ever took place, Kosterlinsky would be his fire exit. Before the sun went down, Kosterlinsky was bound to throw off on everybody.

As the Porters drew near Lieutenant Little's position, Grandfather Porter and Sergeant O'Kane sent Ben ahead to ride point. Three miles from Long Mountain, Ben rode over a knoll, started down into a broad wash, and flushed an Apache patrol. Four Apaches were squatting in the bottom of the wash looking back toward the Yawner's column. Ben was riding along the bank above and downwind from them when he surprised them and they surprised him.

Every one of the warriors was already holding an arrow
on the string of his bow. Ben fired at the middle of them
and spurred his horse back toward his own people as the
flight of arrows came after him. They all missed, and he
kept going without looking back. He kept a vivid picture of
the Apaches running lean and quick as ocelots as they
scattered away from each other and left the spot where his
bullet hit. They did not leave more than a puff of dust
hanging to show where they had been.

The Porters and Cowdens barely got a look at them but
opened fire immediately. The Apaches were not good
targets. By the time Ben was out of arrow range and turned
to shoot at them, they were gone. The instant the Porters
and Cowdens took their eyes off the Apaches to look for
cover for their horses, the Apaches disappeared.

Not a man in the Porter clan was foolish enough to jump
out and chase them. In the brush, Apaches could outmaneuver
any horseman. Their bows were more effective than
firearms at close range and they were quiet.

Grandfather Porter did not want to press from his side
until he joined Lieutenant Little. He was content to drive
the Apaches ahead of him, the way he kept wild cattle in
front of him in a drive. He could do that because the range
of his weapons was longer. When the Apaches saw that the
Porters and Cowdens were not pursuing them, they came
out in plain sight, yipping and taunting. Grandfather Porter
ordered his sons and grandsons to stand fast. He left the
extra horses behind a ridge with the Farley twins. He and
Sergeant O'Kane spread the sons and grandsons in a
skirmish line atop the ridge and watched for a chance to
enter the fight.

Ben sat his horse beside his grandfather and Sergeant
O'Kane and watched the battle develop with the sergeant's
spyglass. A thick cloud of dust was being raised by the
Yawner's horses in the center of his column. The Apache
war chief sent a strong force of foot soldiers to stop Little's
push at the base of Long Mountain. These warriors were his
fleetest and made a good buffer for his column.

The Yawner's column swung north, away from Koster-
lasky. He made an oblique run across Little's front toward

the Huachuca Mountains, as though he wanted to make a
stand on the high ground. He ran up to the foot of the
Huachucas at the Copper Glance mine where Little was
waiting for him.

Little ran his cavalry at the Yawner's point. The Apache
foot soldiers let the horsemen charge in deep toward the
main body and then tried to isolate them. The soldiers
fought to stay together. Their bugler sounded *Recall*, and
they managed to regroup and pull back to the Copper
Glance.

The point of Lieutenant Hughes's buffalo soldiers hurried from the west to help Little. The Yawner's rear guard
was in flight ahead of them. Kosterlinsky was galloping up
and making dust from the south, hoping to present his
troops for the kill.

The Yawner set up an ambush of riflemen for the buffalo
soldiers below an Indian burial ground called Los Metates
and unhorsed half the point with his first volley. His
warriors formed a wedge and ripped through the middle of
Kosterlinsky's rumpled troopers as they galloped in to help
the buffalo soldiers. A volley of Apache rifle fire downed
several of the Mexican horses, and a small group of those
soldiers took cover afoot on a burial mound. The rest rallied
to their guidon and galloped back to Mexico.

The Yawner's point withdrew, and his flankers were in.
All his forces massed in the column. Little's and Hughes's
soldiers were all together, moving to fight the Yawner
against Long Mountain as planned. The fight would begin
in a few minutes. The Porters and the Cowdens gave their
horses their heads to run in and fill the gap between Little
and the buffalo soldiers.

The wind from the west was strong, constant, and heavy
with dust as it swiped and buffeted Ben and his horse. Ben
and his brothers were on the left flank of their group
watching to make contact with Little to the east. Ben was
the man closest to Little's troop. He saw an Apache hiding
in chaparral brush with his face turned away from the wind
toward the Copper Glance.

The Apache did not move or look toward the Cowden
brothers. Ben thought there might be more Apaches in the
chaparral and they wanted the Porter line to go by. The

were gambling the brothers would go on without seeing them. The Apache Ben caught in the open was pure ladino. Sometimes when a ladino was surprised by a cowboy in the brush like this, he would turn his head away and remain stock-still to keep from attracting attention with a look.

Ben screamed and reined Star in so tight the horse crouched and his hind feet plowed long furrows in the ground. The scream was so squeaky, it made Ben laugh. He spurred Star toward the Apache. The Apache grinned at Ben as though shamefaced and ran in a crouch toward a cover of rocks. Les and Mark heard Ben's shout and turned with him to back him up. Ben stood in his stirrups and fired into the chaparral. A half-dozen Apaches jumped up from their hiding places and ran across a draw toward the rocks. Ben and his brothers braked their horses and dismounted on the run. They steadied their rifles on the ground, picked their targets, and fired. Ben's only shot made a man cartwheel as though he had been overtaken and lifted from behind on the horns of a bull. Ben did not get a chance to draw another bead. He and his brothers ran for cover to get out of the line of fire as Little's men laid down a volley at the Apaches in the rocks.

Ben and his brothers had run across Little's front. Soldiers yelled at them to get out of the way, and they mounted their horses and ran to catch up with the Porters.

Bud Porter met them and Ben rode with him to a hill where Grandfather Porter and Sergeant O'Kane were watching the burial mound at Los Metates with the spyglass.

"Kosterlinsky thinks he's got old Yawner by the ear," William Porter said, handing the glass to Ben. "But he can't decide whether to bite it and hold on, or whisper in it and lay down."

Ben looked through the glass and saw the Yawner's column heading south. Only Kosterlinsky's handful of Sonorans on the burial mound were opposing him, but their rifles had stopped him.

The Apaches moved separately and quickly to envelop the mound. The Sonorans would not be able to hold it or even stay alive, unless Kosterlinsky hurried back to help them.

Ben saw Kosterlinsky's guidon flying above a ridge safely beyond the mound. Then the troop came in sight, circling at a high trot toward Lieutenant Hughes's troops. Kosterlinsky was leaving the gate open so the Yawner could escape to the Sierra Madre. Ben and his grandfather and Sergeant O'Kane watched the Yawner's warriors overrun the squad on the burial mound in twenty minutes, killing every man and picking at the bodies on the run. They had to hurry to catch up with the Yawner's main column, for it was leaving. The Apaches slid back into Mexico without raising any more dust. They sent happy yelps of derision over their shoulders when they were out of sight.

The Porters and Cowdens hurried to join Hughes's pursuit of the Yawner. Lieutenant Hughes was ready to go, but Kosterlinsky's troop was blocking the way. Kosterlinsky was proclaiming that he would defend Mexico against any invasion by U.S. troops.

Ben rode to the head of the column to see if he could help Hughes. Kosterlinsky was bareheaded, his hair blowing in the wind. He looked as though he had just broken away from hand-to-hand combat. His sword was drawn, and his sword hand was bandaged, as though it might have been damaged in dealing killing thrusts to the indigenous savage. Ben figured the loss of his hat and that old wind mussing his hair were the only hardships he could have suffered all day, hard as he fought to stay clear of the battle.

Hughes's Spanish was terrible, but Kosterlinsky refused to speak to him in English. Kosterlinsky needed to show some kind of valor in front of his troops after letting the Yawner go, so he was making a brave political stand against the U.S. Army. This political battle would save his reputation. He had already carefully seen to the preservation of his skin by deserting the men on the burial mound of Los Metates.

"Sir," the lieutenant said to Ben. "Can you speak this man's language?"

Ben said, "I'm one of the few who can."

"He doesn't seem to understand my Spanish, or else he doesn't want to."

"He can understand your English better."

"I tried that," said the Lieutenant.

"Why did you open the gate on the Apaches and ride over here and close the gate on these real soldiers, Gabriel?" Ben asked Kosterlinsky.

"El Bostezador is a Mexican problem now. We will deal with him." Kosterlinsky looked at Ben as though he did not know him at all.

"Why don't you run on back to Santa Cruz and take your bath if you want to, but let these soldiers fight," Ben said. "They still have two hours of daylight left."

"Listen, these gringos lost the day for us. I turned El Bostezador north, and they retreated. He then turned back and cut me to pieces because this gringo and his *negros* cowarded and deserted my flank. Tell them to go home and learn military strategy. They are not soldiers. Me and my soldiers will take over this fight. We are Indian fighters here, not parade ground specialists."

"Tell the man to move his unit aside, or I will overrun him," said Hughes.

"Hear that, Gabriel?" Ben said.

Kosterlinsky wheeled his horse dramatically and faced his troop. "*Sargento*, prepare the troop for battle," he commanded.

The sergeant turned and faced the troop. "*Tropa, preparese.*" The look on his face was not enthusiastic. The troop did not even shift its weight on its stirrups.

"You might as well pull in your horns, Lieutenant Hughes," Ben said. "Kosterlinsky won't let you go after the Yawner. It's more important for him to defy you. He's a politician, not a soldier. Rest your troops."

The lieutenant was spent, but his heart was still in the fight. His sergeant rode up beside him and handed him a canteen. The lieutenant took a long drink, handed it back, and glared at Kosterlinsky.

"Lieutenant," the sergeant said softly. His skin was ebony, his hair silver at the temples. He was a professional accustomed to squandering himself in a fight, but he knew about political battles too. He knew that politics took over and somebody else took the credit after his fighting was done. His buffalo soldiers were as able as any cavalry in the world and had just finished a job. Now talks would be held and policies made. "We've been hard at the old Yawner's heels for five days and nights. Don't you think he deserves a little rest? He's probably *tired*."

"Yes, I guess he does, Sergeant." The lieutenant smiled. "We'll let him go, this time."

"I think that's a good idea," said the sergeant. "He's the only Indian we got left to fight."

Ben rode back to the Porters. They were sitting in the shade in a wash, waiting for orders.

"Fight's over, fellers," Ben said. "Kosterlinsky won't let us go into Mexico. He's afraid we'll make him look bad."

"We sure don't want him to look bad," Grandfather Porter said. "If the old savage'll make him look good, he can have him."

"The Yawner'd rather be down in Mexico, anyway," Sergeant O'Kane said. "Mexicans don't bother him much. We can't lick him, either, but we bother him. I think he wanted some fun, so he made a sashay, raised some dust, and shot some soldiers for drill. You can't keep a wolf in one place very long if he doesn't have anything to bite."

Ben said, "Old Yawner taught me a lesson. We're making a good fighter out of him. He's a true ladino. Every time we let him get away, he gets stronger, wiser, and meaner. Every time we try to catch him, he tears down more fence. He should have been run down and whipped good the first time, before he got any training. That ought to teach us how we should treat our other enemies. We're letting them get away with too much."

"Did you see that little Che Che up there with Kosterlinsky, brother?" asked Les.

"I haven't seen one Indian I could call by name all day," Ben said.

The Porters laughed quietly.

"No, I mean just now when you were up there talking to Kosterlinsky, didn't you see Che Che with him?"

"You mean the Apache kid who ran off with our horses?" Ben asked.

"That one," said Les. "I saw him at the head of Kosterlinsky's column when you were on the way up to help Lieutenant Hughes. I'm sure it was him. I told Grandfa-

her. He was on the same sorrel dink he was riding San
Juan's Day."

"My lord," Ben said.

"Yes. You suppose he hired on to scout for Kosterlinsky,
but still belongs to the Yawner?"

"You mean he's a spy? Wouldn't that be something?"
Ben and his brothers sat in the shade and ate their beef and
bean burros. He tried to rest in the sand. His wound hurt.
He was feverish. He laid his head on his arm and slept.

The Porters awakened Ben when they were ready to
ride. Ben told his grandfather that he and his brothers were
going after Hoozy Briggs. "He's more trouble to us than the
Yawner, Grandfather. All the Yawner ever did to us was
steal Papa's top hat and Mama's drapes."

"Where will you start?" asked Uncle Billy. "We need to
know where we can find you. You know your papa will be
looking for you, to serve that warrant."

"Uncle Billy, Hoozy and his *compañeros* won't keep us
from our appointments. As soon as we're finished with him,
I'll go home and give myself up."

"I want to know where you'll be."

"We're going to Santa Cruz first."

"In that case, we'll ride along with you and bring our
mares back, if by chance we find them. I have to tell
Epifanio Romero his son is dead."

Kosterlinsky's troop pulled out for Santa Cruz as the
Porter clan mounted their horses. The Porters rode parallel
to the Mexican troop for a while, but Kosterlinsky doubled
his pace and pulled away. Che Che was riding by his side.

As the Porters and Cowdens were fording the Santa
Cruz near the new hacienda, a group of Mexican soldiers
came around the buildings driving the Porter and Johnson
horses. The soldiers let the horses go, and they trotted
down and watered in the ford. Uncle Billy waved to the
soldiers, and the soldiers waved and turned back. The
Porters waited for the horses to water before starting them
back to La Noria.

Uncle Billy stood his horse beside Ben before he rode
on to the Romero hacienda with the bad news about
Hector. "You have a whole bunch of Porters here who
would like to help you deal with Hoozy Briggs, Ben," he

said. "We don't need everybody to drive a few mares home. They're already anxious to be home. Let some of us go with you and outnumber them."

"We already outnumber them, Uncle Billy," said Ben. "Me and my brothers are enough. If we had a .410 shotgun and a bicycle, we would have more power than we need. I'm not even sure they're here. We don't need the whole Porter clan. We don't want to start a war with Mexico. I only want Hoozy Briggs to get what he's been giving."

"All right, but we'll meet at La Noria for supper. We'll stay there tonight."

"We'll be there, Uncle Billy."

CHAPTER 23

Ben Cowden and his brothers watched Kosterlinsky ride away toward Santa Cruz with his sergeant and his valet. When he was gone, the brothers rode to the new garrison and looked for Jacinto Lopez, their friend who was an army conscript.

Ben found him in the bivouac, down on his knees driving a stake into the ground. Ben greeted him and waited.

"*Qué tal?*" Lopez finally said, without looking up. "What do you want?"

Ben could tell by his tone that he did not want an answer. He watched him unfold a tent.

"Are we still friends, or have the Apaches taken your smile?" Ben asked.

Lopez turned to Ben. "They took my friends today, and the lieutenant who would be president took my pride."

"The Cowdens have always been your friends."

"How can you be the friends of a Mexican? Didn't you see what we did? Our leader sent my squad to its death and then quit the battlefield. To our disgrace, we followed him."

"You obeyed orders, and you're alive, Lopez. You'll fight another day."

"You didn't see us when we attacked the ridge. We were

cheering ourselves when we turned the Yawner back. We thought we beat him. We put ourselves in perfect position to stop him, but Kosterlinsky ordered retreat. Everyone in my squad was afoot when the Apaches counterattacked. How could we retreat? All we could do was stand and die. Kosterlinsky sacrificed my squad so he could run away.

"That was my squad that fought on the burial mound. My squad leader sent me back to Kosterlinsky with my comrades' horses while the squad dug in to defend the burial mound. Kosterlinsky took me with him when he deserted the field. He did not even let me go back to see if anyone was alive, or to retrieve the bodies after the killing was over. The burial detail has not even been dispatched yet." Lopez sat down and wept.

"You did your best, Lopez."

"I'll never live it down."

"Listen, forget it and tell me what that Che Che was doing with Kosterlinsky."

Lopez wiped his eyes and was quiet a moment, looking at the ground. "I don't know. Sometimes they're close as twins."

"I thought the Yaqui was his scout."

"Him too. He uses other Yaquis, but those others come and go from Colonel Bustamante's headquarters."

"Where did Che Che go?"

"*Quien sabe*? Who knows? Nobody keeps track of Kosterlinsky's Indians."

"Did you see the men who brought my racehorse, El Majo, to Kosterlinsky?"

"You mean Hoozy, Thomas, and Campana? Of course I saw them."

"Then, you know them, Lopez?"

"Of course I do. Kosterlinsky is courting Hoozy's sister. I often get drunk with Thomas. Campana and I went to the same church when we were boys."

"Have you seen them here?"

"Yes, they're in Santa Cruz."

"And the Yaqui? Have you seen him too?"

"No, Ben. I won't tell you a lie. I haven't seen the Yaqui in several days."

"That Yaqui shot my brother's horse out from under him."

"*Bueno*, I'm not surprised. Kosterlinsky often uses the Yaqui to *venadear*, serve as his sniper. You have to understand, Benjamin, Kosterlinsky's a politician. You don't have to be his enemy for him to have you killed."

"Thank you for telling me."

"I'll tell you another thing, Benjamin. Kosterlinsky has El Majo at Campana's sister's house in Suanci. You know the three Campana sisters who live in the old pueblo on the other side of the river?"

"How could they be Campana's sisters? They're pretty girls. He's uglier than cowdung on a new hat."

"They're his sisters. How come you didn't know?"

"The girls don't keep brothers around when I'm there."

"They have a good reason. Campana and his older brother have been in prison most of their lives. He was released about six months ago. The older brother is still caged, and of course you must know about the other brother they keep chained in the backyard."

"*Que bonito!* That's pretty! Why did Hoozy have to pick the Campana place to hole up? I want to make a mess of him."

"Those girls are his friends. They're everybody's friends."

Ben led his brothers away from the bivouac. He stopped to inspect his weapons. He was feverish now and seeing everything extraordinarily clear. The sight of his pistol barrel made him smell gunpowder. The shine of the brass on the smooth cartridges made him feel the concussion of a round exploding against his eardrums. He remembered he enjoyed the kick of his pistol when it went off, he knew he was about to smell gunpowder and know the smoke again. He took his extra pistol out of his saddlebag and stuck it in his belt. He and his brothers did not speak.

The brothers crossed the river and rode along the outskirts of the old town of Santa Maria de Suanci. The Campana place was built like a fort. An adobe wall, or *tapia*, encircled a courtyard behind the main building. Ben stopped on a hill behind it. Maudy's Little Buck, Prim ete, the big snorty bay Campana rode, two other horses branded with the VO, and Hoozy's tender-footed mare were in a corral inside the tapia.

The brothers dismounted in a grove of giant cottonwoods and waited for sundown. They wanted to go in and do their business at twilight. They could see into the courtyard, lush with broad-leaved trees and shrubs the sisters kept watered, a nice oasis for their visitors.

Ben said, "Of all the places in Suanci, I know this place the best. I know these girls well, but I didn't know they were Campana's sisters."

"I know them, too." Les laughed. Ben was too feverish to ask how well he knew the sisters. Les said, "So does Mark."

"It's time to fight. Do either of you know a reason why we shouldn't?" Ben said.

"Not me," Les said.

"No," Mark said.

"All right, since we've never been there together, let's talk about what we have to do and make sure we all have the same knowledge of the place. See that small house in the center of the courtyard? The family madman is chained in there. The chain is long enough so he can move out to the yard and sit under the shade of that tree in front of the door. The other house inside the courtyard is a guesthouse. I've been in there. It's one room. Hoozy, Thomas, or Broderick, or all three might be in there.

"The big house, as you both probably know since you say you've been there, is one long room. The kitchen is partitioned off on the right. Bedrooms are partitioned on the left. They use the middle space for a receiving room, dining room, and playroom for their kids. The girls have two or three little toddlers in there, so be careful of them.

"I think we best try to scare whoever is indoors out into the courtyard, if we can. Mark, you knock on the front door. Les and I will be in the courtyard when the girls let you in. I'll stand by the door of the guesthouse while Les goes and teases the loco, the madman. That loco has the loudest mouth in the state of Sonora. When Les riles him he'll cause both houses to turn inside out, and we'll see who is there to shoot at. How does that sound?"

"Sounds good," Les said. "But I know that loco. I wish we didn't have to fool with him."

"Believe me, brother, if you can cause him to make that sound he makes like a *sireen*, everybody in the house will come arunning. Besides that, the loco's noise will keep the town away while we're schooling Hoozy and his gang."

Mark's face could have belonged to a twelve-year-old, he looked so young and trusting at that moment. His breast swelled with a deep sigh.

Ben said, "Mark, just come through the front door and stop in the vestibule. You won't be there long. I guarantee everybody'll run to the courtyard when Les starts teasing the loco. All you have to do is draw your pistol and come toward the maniac when everybody is out of the house."

"Don't worry about me, brother," Mark said.

"That's fine. If we do this right, we'll cut out this batch of VO cutthroats and be rid of them for good. All we'll have to do then is take Little Buck and Prim Pete home."

Mark rode his horse around to the street in front of the house. Ben and Les left their horses tied in the cottonwoods and slipped through the back door of the tapia into the courtyard. Les went to the back of the house of the maniac, and watched Ben. Ben went to the guesthouse, the *cabaña*, as the Campana girls called it. He heard Mark knock on the front door.

"*Quien?*" called one of the girls in a high, keening voice. "Who is it?"

Mark answered softly.

Ben heard male voices laughing in the main house and the quiet voices of a man and a woman passing their time in peace and comfort in the cabaña. He gave Les the signal to show himself to the maniac.

Les stepped to the rear window and rang his pistol barrel off the bars. He pressed his face between them, stuck out his tongue at the maniac, and said, "Yah, yah, yah!"

"Yiii!" screamed the maniac, and he collided with the inside of the bars with such force adobe dust puffed out of the window frame. Les jumped back as though flinching away from a charging bull, but he recovered in time to catch the loco by the hair and jerk him to the bars.

The maniac snatched the front of Les's shirt, banged him against the bars, and screamed in his face.

Broderick rushed out of the cabaña, his face covered with shaving lather, wearing no shirt and no shoes, brandishing his pistol. Ben's friend Euphemia followed him out with a straight razor in her hand.

Campana, unarmed, ran out of the main house straight to the maniac's house. Thomas came out behind him and stopped in the courtyard. He was carrying a muzzle-loader shotgun Ben knew the girls kept for their protection. They charged the old musket with every nail, screw, nut, and bolt they could find rusting on the ground.

The crazy man keened like a siren as he and Les rattled each other's bones against the bars. Les was tiring because he was the less crazy of the two.

Ben stepped around the corner so Broderick and Thomas could see him. Thomas saw him and raised the musket. Ben aimed and sent a bullet through him.

A hot shaft of rusty nuts and bolts and crooked nails from the musket tore through the boughs of a tree over Ben's head and showered him with particles of leaf and stem. Ben swiveled his pistol arm like a cannon to bear on Broderick. Broderick whirled to face Ben, wild-eyed from seeing what Ben's bullet had done to Thomas.

"Don't—" he said, but he raised the pistol.

Ben shot him. He did not shoot Broderick because he was forced to do it in self-defense. He would have done the same if the man were unarmed. He did it for the same reason he shot Thomas because he had promised himself he would stop him the next time he saw him.

Ben hurried into the crazyman's house to help Les. Campana was choking the loco from behind to pull him off Les. The maniac was handling Les like a child, cramming his face against the bars and clawing at it. Les had dropped his pistol and was too tired to defend himself. Ben tried to split the maniac's head open with his pistol barrel. As the maniac slumped into Campana's arms, Ben stepped back and split Campana's head open too.

Ben went outside again. Thomas and Broderick were still down, their weapons lying untended. Thomas wa moaning. Les came around from behind the loco's house and picked up Broderick's pistol.

Kosterlinsky came out of the main house with his sergeant, his valet, and another man. Euphemia and her sisters tried to comfort Thomas. Broderick lay apart from everyone, unmoving.

Ben rushed through the door of the cabaña looking for Hoozy. He pushed over an upright cabinet, and the weight of the stuff inside burst its every seam. He picked up one side of a bed and threw it against the wall. Hoozy was not there.

Euphemia came to the door, angry, pale, and shaking. She backed away when Ben turned to her but kept looking into his eyes to see if he recognized her. "Benjamin, do you know what you did? You killed them," she said.

"Where is he?" Ben growled through his teeth.

"He's gone," Euphemia said.

"His mare's in the corral."

"He went on the stage, Ben. He was very tired and sore."

"Where did he go?"

"I don't know. He got a message from Tombstone."

"Why didn't these other *cabrones* go with him?"

"They quit. *Renunciaron el trabajo*, Ben. They renounced their jobs."

Ben remembered Kosterlinsky was in the courtyard. He and his companions were standing fast because Mark was behind them with his rifle. Les was holding a pistol in each hand, guarding the door of the loco's house in front of Kosterlinsky, wiping the blood off his face with his sleeves.

Euphemia covered her face with her hands and started to cry. The razor was dangerously close to her cheek. Ben took it gently from her hand, folded it, dropped it on the ground, and headed for Kosterlinsky.

"Are you happy, now, Ben?" asked Euphemia from behind him. "You killed them for nothing."

Kosterlinsky stood very still and aloof. An official-looking gent in a dark suit was standing frightened beside him with the sergeant and the valet. The official was talking, but nobody was listening.

"Why this killing, Ben?" asked Kosterlinsky. He wore

the expression of a man who believed he was about to be stood against the wall and shot.

"Give Kosterlinsky his pistol, Mark," Ben said.

Mark walked around in front of Kosterlinsky and tried to hand him his pistol.

"No, no pistol." Kosterlinsky sidled behind his valet and kept sidling. He raised his hands and showed their empty palms. "I won't duel with you, Ben."

"Don't try to scurry away from me now, you sonofa-bitch," Ben told him in English. "Give him his pistol, Mark."

Kosterlinsky would not raise his hands to take the pistol.

Mark hung it around his neck by the lanyard and stepped away. "Is that good enough?"

"That's fine. He can defend himself now, and I can kill him."

"Kill me, then." Kosterlinsky's lips stiffened, his chin wrinkled. "But I don't know why. We've always been friends."

"You're a liar. You stole my horse. You sent your Yaqui to potshot my brother. You sacrificed a squad of good Sonorans so you could save yourself and wave your sword at people who were trying to help you. You ungrateful, cowardly son of a bitch, how can you call anyone your friend?"

"I don't know, Ben. I guess I can't, but you don't hate me enough to kill me, do you?"

Ben cussed himself, but he knew he had already relented and could not shoot the man. He might have been able to do it before he started talking, but he couldn't do it now. "All right, Gabriel, get away from me before I do it, and from now on stay away from me. You are not my friend anymore."

"Kill me, then, if I'm not worthy of being your friend." Kosterlinsky was vehement, now. "I invite you to make sure I'll never be your enemy. Kill me!" He grabbed his pistol and waved it over his head to put on a brave show; he knew his danger was past. "Why spare me?" He splayed his fingers so Ben could see none of them was near the trigger.

"Now you're reverting, Gabriel. Don't revert with me.

I'm not sparing your life so you can use your two faces on me again."

The Porters had all gone home when Ben and his brothers returned to La Noria that night. Ben left his brothers unsaddling their horses, and led Little Buck to the house.

"We're back, Maudy," he called, hiding Little Buck in the dark behind his horse.

The girl seemed glad enough to see him when she came out, but she looked toward the corrals for something more.

"Well, this is grand, Ben," she said. "Me and the Heredias are the only ones here. Father went to Canelo, and your grandmother took her whole family home, so I have a mess of steak and potatoes, biscuits and gravy, already cooked. Tell your brothers to get ready for supper."

She paused. "Did you see that worthless John Snider down in Mexico?"

"No, I guess he left the country, Maudy," Ben said. "Was he kind of worthless?"

"He sure was. Did you see anything of my Little Buck? Uncle Billy told me Snider's partners took him down to Mexico."

"No, and I didn't think to ask about him either, Maudy. I'm sorry."

"Don't be sorry. It wasn't your worry. I let myself get bamboozled into that deal. Well, get ready for supper. I have a big platter of steaks and a big pan of biscuits."

Maudy backed into the house to close the screen door.

"We did run on to a friend of yours, Maudy," Ben said. "He sure would like to say hello."

"Who could that be?"

Ben turned Little Buck into the lamplight so Maudy could see him.

Maudy pushed open the screen door for a better look, recognized her horse, and ran and hugged him around the neck.

"Is this the friend you've been so worried about?" Ben asked.

Maudy hugged her horse around the chest and patted his shoulders. "He's lost fifty pounds. Nothing but a darned fool could've been riding him, because nothing but a fool owns him, I guess."

She did not have a tear in her eye or in her voice. She was another one of the kind who could handle happiness and livestock without bawling.

"I'm glad to see we brought the right horse," Ben said.

"Well, you sure did," she said.

"However, I thought you'd shed at least one tear for your friend Snider."

"Oh, *posh*. I didn't care anything about Snider. His elbows were dirty. I didn't know what I was going to do without Little Buck, though."

Maudy handed the horse's lead rope back to Ben. "I'm glad to see him. I'll get your supper now."

Ben did not think he could make it back to the barn. The pain in his back had spread all the way up to his ears and jaws and all the way down into his groin. He was hot, and a terrible aching stiffness had settled inside him. He stepped off Star at the water-trough, took off his hat, and stuck his head under the water. He wiped his face with his handkerchief and led Star to the barn.

Mark and Les bustled in and out of the saddlehouse.

Ben stopped outside the door, sat down, and passed out.

CHAPTER 24

Maudy heard the screen door slam and looked up as Mark and Les carried Ben through the door.

"He's passed out, Maudy. He's awful sick," Les said.

Ben's face was flushed with fever. The brothers stretched him out on her father's bed and pulled off his boots. She laid her hand on his forehead and cheek.

"You might as well take off his clothes," Maudy said. "I think I know what's the matter with him. I bet that cut on his back is infected. If I'm right, he'll be here awhile."

The brothers stood and looked at Maudy.

"Well, get amoving," Maudy demanded. "What's the matter with you?"

"We don't know how Ben will take it if we undress him before it's time to go to bed," Les said. "He'll probably want to head for Tombstone as soon as he wakes up."

"Listen, he's not going to Tombstone today, I'll guarantee it. I hate to tell you this, but he might have blood poisoning."

The brothers started unbuttoning Ben's clothes. Maudy brought in a pan of hot water and lye soap and ordered them to bathe him from head to toe. She went out again and brought back a quart of 100-proof mescal that was clear as a mountain stream. She told the brothers to sponge Ben with the mescal after they rinsed off the soap.

Ben still had all his clothes on. The brothers washed his face and neck. They each picked up a hand to wash. They washed right up to the cuffs of his shirt.

"What are you doing?" Maudy asked. "How can you give a man a bath if you don't take off his clothes?"

"Everything's all right, Maudy," Les said. "Don't worry, we'll undress him as soon as you stop coming in here."

"So that's it," said Maudy. "You're afraid I'll see him. Listen, you might as well strip him naked in front of me now while you can help me. I'll have to do it all by myself every day until he gets well."

"But Maudy," Les said, disturbed. "He don't have to be naked in front of us and you too, does he?"

"I want those filthy clothes off him. What are you thinking? Do you think I ought to swoon at the sight of a naked man? I've handled every inch of my brothers' carcasses through knifings, shootings, broken necks, gray back lice, crabs, and an attack by a lion. How do you think I'll handle Ben when you're not here? You two aren't figuring on staying here to carry out his chamber pot, give him his bath, and change his sheets every day, are you?"

"We have to get on home," said Les. "Our mama has to know we're all right, and we have to get back to work."

"That's what I thought. I'll tell you what, to save your delicate sensibilities, I'll go out while you strip him and wash him and sponge him with that mescal. When you're through, leave him on his side so I can dress the wound."

Les picked up the bottle of mescal. An absolutely beatific look passed over his face.

"And don't you drink one drop of my spirits," said Maudy. "All I have to keep your brother from putrifying is that mescal, some unguent, and a few drops of carbolic. Now, get him naked."

Ben was swelling out of his world. The place in which his body was suffering the death was too small for him, too confining. His flesh was too small. He was leaving his body but it still held a tiny grip on him.

Then, his clay grew numb, and he began to leave behind like a residue, a waste. The numbness scared him. He felt so loyal to his poor body and was so sad he was deserting it that he began to weep.

His own cry awakened him, and he did not know where he was. He was unable to move. He could be in his tomb. He was back inside his body, but he could see no light, feel nothing but pain, hear nothing at all. He could not locate the place in which his flesh had settled because his pain had no borders.

He was awake in the dark to all the scariest realizations a man could have. He was thirsty and did not know how to find a drink, unable to stir, and that kept him from finding his limbs. He was so scared, his mind was sliding along the edge of a black place where he could fall into panic.

"Oh, God," he said softly. Immediately he heard a live rustle beside his bed. He saw the flare of a match against a wall and watched a small person light a lamp, then stand by his bed. The person was a girl, clean and spare as starch; cool, friendly, and near. She put a soft hand on his forehead, then pulled the covers off him. She left the sheet over him. The air cooled it and bathed him in the wetness of his own sweat. She wrung out a cloth from a pan of water by the bed and wiped his face and neck, arms and chest. He still was not sure where he was.

He wanted to see the girl's features, but the lamp was behind her and they were in shadow. A smoldering halo surrounded the little head. She picked the wet rag off his brow and laid her hand on his forehead again. He wondered if his skull would burn her hand as it did the skin on his face.

"Everything's so hot. It was like a *mauguechi*, a brush-clearing fire, inside those blankets," he said.

"Ben, do you know me?" Maudy asked.

"I think your name is Snider. Do you know your hair's burning, Snider?"

"You had a chill, and I covered you up. Now your fever's back again." Maudy laid the wet cloth on Ben's face.

"Thanks. I've never seen it so hot this time of year."

Maudy rinsed the fever out of the cloth again, straightened it, fanned it over his forehead, and let it float onto his face. A breeze cooled the room through the windows.

"Helluva time to play baseball. We ought to have musicians, Snider," Ben said, and Maudy knew he was unconscious. A few minutes later, his skin turned cold, and she piled on the covers. When he seemed comfortable, she went to sleep with her head on the edge of the bed. . . .

She kept watch on him without respite for the next three days and nights. She warmed him when he chilled, cooled him when he was feverish. She steadied him during his delirium and helped him to and from the chamber pot when he was conscious. Ben did all the rest of the fighting, and his fever diminished.

After five days, the wound began to heal, the infection to abate. Maudy and Ben were visited by Uncle Billy Porter. He went on to Santa Cruz and telegraphed A. B.

One morning A. B. came driving up with Paula Mary at his side and Les and Mark and the Farley twins for an escort. Maudy saw them coming when they were still a mile away, a tight cavalcade made up of two stout black horses on the buggy and four big horsemen leading, flanking, and trailing close by. The sight made Maudy thankful for strong friendships.

A. B. and Paula Mary carried in food and clean bed-clothes while the boys unhitched the team, unsaddled and fed the horses, and unrolled their beds in the barn. Maudy met everyone at the door with a smile, but she would not let anyone past the kitchen. Everybody had to sit down in the kitchen and be quiet.

"Well, can't the boy even talk?" asked A. B.

"A week ago I didn't think he would live, Mr. Cowden," Maudy said.

"You mean my son almost died?"

"He did. He's still fighting, though I think he's winning now. I sure don't want a relapse. I don't think he's strong enough to survive one, and I'm not going to take any risks."

"Can I go to the door and look at my son, young lady?"

"You can all go, but only as far as the door."

The family crowded to the door. Ben's black hair looked thick and alive, his face emaciated. A. B. thought his bare shoulder looked thin as a woman's. He took Paula Mary by the shoulders and turned back into the kitchen.

"He's lost a hundred pounds," he said.

Maudy was sitting at the table resting her head on her arm. A. B. thought she looked like a little old woman.

"You've just been through hell, haven't you, Maudy Jane?" he said.

"I'll be all right as soon as I can sleep a whole night," she ̲said.

Mark was grieving. "What are we going to do? He's not ̲making it. Ben's the best man in the whole world. What'll ̲e do if he dies?"

Les and the twins looked at each other as if to say, Well, ̲at's it; we've lost him. They went outside.

Paula Mary had been told her brother was sick, but no ̲ne ever told her sickness could do so much harm. Even ̲e dead people she had seen looked better than that.

A. B. sat down at the table again. Maudy poured coffee ̲r them all. The Cowdens were so stunned by the sight of ̲en, they retreated into their own thoughts.

Maudy could see the Cowdens were demoralized, and ̲at was the reason she gave them coffee, but she was not ̲ing to put up with any grieving, moaning, or emotional ̲vastation in her kitchen. She was too tired and busy to ̲ke on the care of more casualties. "Ben's better, and he's ̲ing to make it," she said.

Paula Mary sighed as though her heart would break, ̲d that put an end to Maudy's patience. "I think you all ̲tter go home now. I haven't got time for you. I already ̲ve Ben to take care of."

"I guess you're right. We better get out of your way," ̲. B. said.

Maudy was looking at Paula Mary when she said, "Next ̲me you come, leave your deep sighs and your sad displays ̲El Durazno. I'm having enough trouble helping Ben get ̲ell. I don't need a bunch of Cowdens hanging around who ̲t sick at the sight of a sick person."

That gentle rebuke strengthened them. A. B. went out ̲the buggy to get a quart of his good whiskey for Ben. He ̲nsidered his poison an effective antidote for all the other ̲isons of life. A. B. also brought Maudy a quarter of beef, ̲d the boys went to work carving it into jerky. Maudy told ̲em she wanted it cut into broad, thin sheets and gave ̲em salt and black pepper for it.

When Maudy went back inside, Paula Mary was sitting ̲ Ben. Maudy placed Paula Mary's hand on Ben's fore-̲ad. "You watch him now, Paula Mary. If he gets hot, pull ̲e covers down, but leave the sheet over him. If he wakes up, talk to him. He'll be glad to see you. After he cools off cover him again."

Maudy lay down on a cot nearby and slept. Paula Mary sat as still as she could for the longest time in her life. Her brother was still as a post. No, a post would be harder to move than her brother. He only looked as still as a feather could be. He looked so wasted, a puff of wind could move him. She put her hand on his forehead exactly as Maudy did. Ben stirred and opened his eyes. He closed them again.

"Hello, Ben," said Paula Mary. "It's me."

He opened them again and looked at her. The Cowdens sometimes frowned a little before they said something that was difficult to say, a family trait they got from A. B. It was more pronounced in young, sick, and sad Cowdens and seldom appeared when they were whole and sane.

Ben frowned and said, "Can I please have a drink of water, Paula Mary?" Paula Mary felt clumsy as an old cow backing off a cattle car as she hurried to fetch it. With both hands she lugged the whole water bucket back to the bed, dipped out a cupful, and helped her brother drink. She made sure he got all the water he wanted before she took back into the kitchen. When she returned, wide-eyed, to find more ways to serve, he was asleep again. She had never seen anybody so sick.

The Cowdens stayed so Maudy could sleep the whole night through. The next morning after breakfast she wanted them to leave. They knew she was right. If they stayed, she would feel she had to wait on them.

Paula Mary offered to stay but did not argue when she was refused. She was grownup enough to know Maudy needed peace and quiet at La Noria with no visitors camping on her.

The Cowdens pulled out at sunup. They did not form so compact a cavalcade on the way home. Maudy felt lightened of another burden after they were gone.

A. B. felt more burdened. The warrant for his son's arrest was heavy in his pocket. He vowed to be rid of it, but not by serving it on Ben. U.S. Marshal Walter Jarboe possessed all the muscle necessary to relieve A. B. of the weight of that warrant.

Paula Mary promised God that if Ben did not die, she would try to show everybody how much she sorrowed for Freddie Lee. She had been feeling very guilty for not knowing how to mourn for Freddie Lee, and now she was afraid God was punishing her for not showing more grief over his loss.

"Do you think Ben is going to die, Papa?" she asked.

"I hope and pray he doesn't, don't you, little daughter?"

"I sure do. He seems to be going away by himself already."

"He's in an awful spot, that's the whole truth of it."

"Does everybody start going away by themselves like that when they die?"

"That's a good way of putting it, Paula Mary."

"The livestock does that too, doesn't it, Papa?"

"Yes it does. Everything does."

"The culls do it the same as the good stock, don't they?"

"Yes."

"And sometimes they call for help?"

"Sometimes they scream because it hurts so much."

"Why isn't Ben calling for help if he might die? Doesn't he want his family to help him?"

"I don't think Ben is the kind who needs help for that. If he needs anybody, he has Maudy. His family would only be in the way, right now."

Paula Mary thought about that a moment. "How would a person like me know when it was time to die, Papa?"

"Hardly anyone ever gets to know that, daughter."

"I guess when you get to know that, it's too late and you don't get to tell anyone, huh?"

"I think that's right."

"You've gone away all alone when that happens."

"Yes, that's so."

"Freddie Lee had to face that all alone, didn't he?"

A. B. saw his little girl was crying. "Yes, honey, but maybe only for a tiny second," A. B. said. "It happened so fast."

"Do you think he was afraid, Papa?"

"I don't think that little boy was ever afraid of anything."

"Do you think I'll be afraid when I die, Papa?"

A. B. put his arm around Paula Mary's shoulders and

hugged her close. "Little daughter, I know without any
doubt at all, that you will be the bravest of the brave."

A week later, Ben was able to dress and sit outside in
the morning sun. Maudy left him alone because she was
aware he was troubled. He needed to be by himself awhile,
so his mind and thoughts could heal. His appetite for food
was returning, but his appetite for life was not.

One windy morning he came back into the kitchen
earlier than usual and sat down at the table. Maudy gave
him coffee.

"Darned wind comes up earlier every day," Ben said
sourly. "The whole world's drying up, not just me."

"*Posh*. What do you mean you're drying up?"

"Nothing."

"What is it, now? You think you're getting drouthy
too?"

"I'm all dried up inside and out. Look." Ben pulled up
his sleeve and laid his forearm on the table. His arm and
hand were shrunken from the fever. "I'll never get my body
back, nor my soul, after all the corruption I had in me."

"*Pshaw*! You're stronger and healthier every day, Ben."

"You think so because you're good, Maudy."

"Oh, I guess you're bad? Is that what you're trying to
say?"

"I'm all dried up for good and forever."

"Why do you feel that way? You're eating good. Your
fever's gone. You're even smoking your pipe again. You're
almost well, Ben."

"I'm sick of this war with Vincent. If I told you how bad
everything turned out in Santa Cruz, you'd probably regret
nursing me through this terrible time."

"What are you talking about? Are you afraid to tell me
you shot those hard cases of Vincent's? I already know about
that."

"I killed two men, Maudy."

"Well, Ben, I know you did what you thought was
right."

"I never thought killing anybody was right."

"Les and Mark told me those men killed the Johnsons.
I don't think they would have treated you much different.
You were probably next on their list."

"I killed Broderick in cold blood and let Thomas bleed
to death on the ground."

"Ben, face facts," said Maudy. "Those men were killers.
I've been telling you and telling you, that wound in your
back was not done by a nail or a sliver on a fence."

"I guess that's so, and I ought to hate Snider for doing it,
but I don't. I didn't think that boy could stab anybody."

"Well, I'm glad you finally got that through your head.
He viciously stabbed you, and his partners killed some
good people."

"That doesn't make me feel any better. I wouldn't have
killed Snider for what he did, but I turned right around and
killed those two in Santa Cruz. What came over me?"

"You were mad, Ben. I don't see how you men can
declare war on one another and then be surprised when you
have to kill one another to settle it. Declaring war is bad
because you have to kill to back it up. Then you always have
to live it down if you're still alive after you declare peace.
I'd rather you were the one who spent his life living it down
than the one who got killed."

"I'm glad Snider wasn't in Santa Cruz, Maudy. I know
you like him."

"He was a friend," Maudy said. "But he's no part of a
man. He's a backstabber and a horse thief, and I'm glad he's
gone."

Ben laughed at that, and then Maudy did. They looked
straight into each others' eyes. Maudy was the most decent
girl he knew. If she liked him, he could quit crying about
having to shoot people in a war.

"Him losing my horse was bad enough, but I could
shoot him dead for hurting you," Maudy said. "I know how
close you came to kicking the bucket. What if I lost you?
What would I tell your mama?" She was trying to joke, but
the look she gave Ben was grave.

"But Maudy, that's Snider you're talking about, the man
you almost married," Ben said, trying to help her.

"Listen, I don't think I'll ever have to marry a jackass. I
know the man I want."

"You're too young to know who you want. How old are
you? Fourteen?"

Maudy looked away when he said that, but then she

turned back to him. "Not too young to know what I want, and not too young to get what I want," she said. "I'm fifteen, Ben. I'll be sixteen in September."

"Don't pick somebody who's too old for you, or somebody who's done things he's ashamed of, Maudy."

"Ben, do you think you're too old and worldly for me and somebody like Snider isn't?"

"Well, Snider is a lot younger, and he hasn't made the mistakes I've made."

"Who loves Snider, Ben? I can't name one person who'd miss him, now that he's gone."

"All any man needs is one lady like you to love him, Maudy, nobody else."

"All I need is for you to love me like I love you."

That was that. Maudy's feelings were in the open. Ben respected her and appreciated her courage, so he had to answer her. "I love you, too, Maudy, but you've always been like another little sister to me. You've always been more Paula Mary's little friend than mine. You're giving me a big surprise. Don't you want to be wooed?"

"Wooed? That's hypocritical. It's too late for wooing. I traded wooing for your chamber pot. I gave you baths instead of kisses. You whispered in my ear a lot, though. You said all kinds of crazy things to me when I held you in my arms to make you well. If wooing would have brought us close, your being sick and my nursing you brought us a lot closer. I know you awful well, now, Ben, and that includes a lot you would not have wanted me to know you'd been wooing me. What's wooing worth compared to this test we had to pass together?"

Ben had never given Maudy more than a brotherly kiss, but he was as happy as he would have been if he was sleeping in the same bed with her. That last little peck on her cheek happened so long ago, he could not remember whether it was for hello or good-bye. Now he could feel the touch of her thigh against his, even though she was standing clear across the room from him.

He liked being with her, but if he was thinking about sleeping in the same bed with her, he should be healed enough to move on. Soon, she would realize they were in a bad spot. They were alone together all the time. Jua

Heredia's wife had taken their small children to Santa Cruz. They would be staying there until the trouble with the Yawner was over for good. Juan and his sons were sleeping in the barn. Ben knew he should leave, or go sleep in the barn too. He didn't because he wanted to be alone with Maudy. He found it hard to even leave her alone to do her chores. He was jealous of anything that kept her away. They had such an easy way with each other he caught himself sighing for her when he was alone in bed at night.

One morning Ben stayed in his chair out on the sunny side of the house longer than usual, and Maudy went to see how he was doing. She walked up beside him and did not say anything. His head lay back against the wall. He seemed to be asleep. She rustled her skirts a little so he would open his eyes. He did not.

She shuffled her feet, and when he still did not move, it scared her. She bent close to his face.

"Ben?"

No answer.

"Oh, Lord." She put her hand on his forehead, it was hot again, the black hair smooth with moisture. She opened his collar and found an accumulation of sweat at his throat, a sure sign of the fever.

"Ben," she said, and she began to cry because she did not think she could beat a relapse of the infection. She hugged him, afraid her strength and love would not be enough to beat the sickness again. She had not recuperated enough to go to battle with that fever again. She was still afraid and tired from the last fight.

Ben growled in the voice he used to make old mean cows hunt their bulls, breathing on Maudy's neck. He took her around the waist and sat her on his lap. She tightened against him to keep him from seeing her face, but she accommodated herself quickly on his lap.

"Kiss," Ben said. "Not hug."

"*Posh,*" she breathed, with her lips against his neck. "I thought you were trying to die on me again."

"I'd *die* for you, Maudy Jane Pendleton . . . Snider."

"No."

"*Kiss,* then."

CHAPTER 25

Will Pendleton returned to La Noria on the day Ben was leaving. When he learned Ben was headed for Tombstone, he decided to send Maudy with him. He wanted Maudy to stay with her brother Bob and his family in Tombstone until the Yawner was caught and the ranches were safe.

Ben and Maudy rode to El Durazno to see Viney. Mark and Les were working on the Buena Vista, and A. B. was in Tucson. Ben and Maudy stayed the night. He told his mother he wanted to take Prim Pete and put him in training for the sixteenth of September race in Tombstone, and while he was at it, he would see Maudy safely to her brother's house.

The next day Ben and Maudy loaded Prim and Star on the train in Patagonia and rode in the caboose with the freight to Tombstone. Tombstone's silver mines were pouring out precious ore, and the New Mexico and Arizona Railroad hauled it away and brought back more miners. The town was brimful of money, and that was why Ben and McClintock wanted to run their matched horserace there Ben's private reason for going to Tombstone was to find Hoozy Briggs.

Ben left Maudy and Prim Pete at Bob Pendleton's Alfredo Heredia, a brother of Juan's, would serve a *caballerango*, trainer, for Prim Pete. Alfredo worked for Bob and would train the horse at his place.

Ben stopped to leave Star in a livery close to his hotel. As he led him into the barn, his father's team of blacks raised their heads over the boards of their stalls and nickered to him. A. B.'s surrey was parked in the yard. Ben saw Star to his stall and walked out on the main street to see what he could provide for himself.

He bought new clothes and went to the barbershop for a bath, shave, and haircut. When he came out, he bought a bottle of whiskey, went to the Silver Crown Hotel, and registered for a room. Walter Jarboe stopped him in the lobby.

"I've almost given up hope of ever returning to Kansas," Jarboe said. "I'm about to do something drastic to get Vincent's attention and make him deliver my cattle."

"I apologize for not being more help to you," Ben said.

"You have helped me. Your father's been very attentive, too. In fact, I just came from a long meeting with him. I'm driving his rig and team."

"I thought he was here when I saw his black horses at the livery. I sure don't want to see him right now. He has a warrant for my arrest, and I don't want to go to jail."

"You were the subject of our talk. He told me about the warrant and enlisted my help. Consider yourself to be in my custody for the time being. Better still, you can be my deputy and help me if Vincent starts trouble. He's here in Tombstone, and I'm about to roll his fat in the fire."

"Can you deputize me that easy?"

"Hell, I don't know much about the power of a U. S. Marshal, but Vincent deputizes anybody he wants, and he isn't even a sheriff. I ought to be able to do the same. If somebody questions that, we'll bluff it."

"I'm glad Vincent's here. I hope his *pistolero*, Hoozy Briggs, is with him. I have a lot to settle with those two gentlemen."

"Listen, Vincent's on his own over here. The law's not on his side, and the people are mad at him. A lot of it has to do with an editorial that came out in the *Epitaph* this morning. It's based on information I gave the editor. The people in this county are ready to hang Vincent for some land and mining schemes that went sour."

Ben stretched and stood up. "Mr. Jarboe, I think I'll rest awhile. I've been down with an infection, and that caboose wore me out. If you need me for anything, come and knock on my door. I'm in Room twenty-three."

"Go and rest. I know you've been down sick. I'll stay here and watch for Vincent. If I'm not badly mistaken, he's about to be run up a tree, and I want to watch."

Ben went to his room and drank half a glass of whiskey. He pulled off his boots and lay down on the bed in his new duds.

Tombstone was always full of strangers. Ben did not know a hundred people here, but he knew the best people. Hoozy and Vincent probably felt safe here. All the other crooks in the country did because half the law was crooked. Hoozy probably thought he could come out in the open and do anything he wanted to. All he needed to do to make Ben happy was come out in the open. Ben wanted to put an end to Hoozy. After that, maybe Vincent would give up.

Ben was awakened in midafternoon by someone in the next room making a speech. Stentorian tones reverberated through the dry lumber of the hotel. Ben was used to solid, soundproof adobe shelter. The man's voice made the hotel vibrate like a drum. Every once in a while a woman's voice piped in to ask for the speaker's approval of some new foofaraw she had acquired in the shops that day. The man would answer peremptorily and then go back to the serious intonation of his speech.

Ben stretched, let his bones settle in comfort, and listened. The orator sounded familiar, like Duncan Vincent. Ben was sure it was Vincent. Lucky. Hoozy might be coming to see him. All Ben might have to do was lie still and wait.

This was not such a coincidence. Ranchers and other people from the country stayed at the Silver Crown because it was the quietest hotel in Tombstone. Every other hotel was in the screaming middle of the saloons and gambling, fights and cussing, yelling and shooting that went on day and night in the town.

Ben lifted his bones and sat on the edge of the bed. Vincent finished practicing his speech.

"That was wonderful," the woman said. Her voice was husky and mature. "Now come over here and see me."

The bed in Vincent's room was on the other side of the wall by Ben's bed. The springs squeaked with Vincent's weight, only two feet away.

"Closer," said the woman.

The springs squeaked a little more.

"I'll swear, for a big man, you sure are bashful. I thought you always just grabbed what you wanted. Don't you even want to touch me?"

"Yes, girl, but let's at least . . ."

"At least what?"

"At least wait until after my speech and . . . at least until after dark."

"Ooo," she crooned. That was Lorrie's voice, Lorrie Briggs in there with Vincent.

"Wait, don't go," the girl said. "Now what are you doing? It's too early for you to go."

"I have to give my speech."

"I know you do, Dunky, but you don't have to go right now. Sit back down here."

The springs were practically playing a tune with Vincent's ups and downs.

"Don't you want to take off your shoes and shirt, and lie down awhile? I won't bother you, much." Lorrie giggled cutely.

Ben heard the first shoe hit the floor. He did not stay to hear the second.

He was crossing the lobby when Doris Vincent came in the front door. She glanced at him but went straight past him to the desk without speaking. Ben knew he was standing between Duncan Vincent and perdition, but he liked Doris Vincent. He did not think she deserved the humiliation she would suffer if she caught Vincent with Lorrie, his shoes on the floor and his shirt on the chair.

Ben waited for Doris. The clerk was bound to know who she was, and knew her husband was upstairs with another woman. When Doris asked for the key to Room 25, the man found a lot to do that kept his head under the counter.

"Hello, Doris," Ben said.

The woman turned to Ben with a wild and vulnerable look, the expression of one who did not know how to fight but would try to learn as soon as she got her hands on the key to Room 25.

"Hello, Ben. I'm looking for my husband. You know who he is? He's the one trying to run Arizona and get rich."

"I haven't seen him, Doris. I'd like to, though. I want to talk to him."

"I bet you're not as mad at him as I am." She stepped away from the desk. "Are you sure you haven't seen him?"

"I sure haven't, and I've been here several hours."

"He has you in trouble with the law, doesn't he? I am every bit as angry at him as you are."

Doris Vincent sat down in an easy chair, and Ben sat near her on the end of a sofa. Doris's eyes were moist, but she was too angry to cry. "You're such a gentleman, Ben Cowden. I doubt you'd tell me you're mad enough at my husband to kill him."

Ben laughed and looked away. "Would you like a cup of coffee?" He wanted to take her out of the lobby before Vincent and Lorrie sashayed out into the open.

"No, thank you. I'll sit here with you a minute and see if I can calm down. Have you seen what the *Epitaph* printed about Duncan?"

"No, I haven't."

Doris showed Ben a copy of the newspaper. An editorial accused Vincent's hired constables of "Hanging Hector Romero, a member of a prominent Santa Cruz, Sonora family, and a mere boy." The editorial also listed the "depredations" of the Yawner and balanced them against a list of the "depredations" of the VO syndicate of railroad, land, mining, and cattle speculators. The VO was found to be a more successful, ruthless, and dangerous predator than the Yawner. Vincent had run a full-page advertisement in the same newspaper, promising to tell his side of the story at the city park that evening.

Ben was glad someone besides the Cowdens, Porters, and Pendletons could see what the son of a bitch was doing to the country. He handed the paper back to Doris.

"How can anyone print lies like that?" she said. "All the

old fool ever did was bring in blooded stock to improve the herds. He's responsible to a large respectable company for every single thing he does. I'm mad at him, but right is right, and Duncan Vincent is no murderer." Doris's voice wavered with that last statement and she glanced wildly at Ben again.

Ben pretended he did not read the look. The woman was scared to death she was losing her old Duncan. How could any decent person love the son of a bitch? "I'm sure you know him better than anyone," he said.

"I know he's not the best of men. He's not gentle, and he's not affectionate, but I've always thought he was honest. If all these accusations are true and some other stories of his deeds that have just come to my attention are true, then he's been deceiving me, too. If he's been making a fool out of me, by God, he's going to pay for it."

"Well, Doris, I'm sure he'll clear everything up to your satisfaction as soon as you see him," Ben said. "I'm going out to look for him, so why don't you come on and walk with me. When we find him, you can have the first slice of his hindquarters. I'll take whatever's left. How's that?"

Doris stood up. "That's fine with me."

"Good." Ben walked the woman out of the lobby, relieved he was finally getting her out of range of a public confrontation with her husband that would mean certain humiliation for her. She stopped on the veranda. A crowd was gathered in front of a dress shop across the street.

"Your country girl is making quite a sensation over here, isn't she?" Doris said.

"What country girl?"

"Little Maudy Pendleton is on display in that window as Sleeping Beauty. Haven't you seen her?"

"No, I haven't. The last time I saw her, she was sitting at her sister-in-law's kitchen table."

"It's a stunt the dressmaker's pulling to draw customers. She brought in some sort of wizard who hypnotized Maudy, and they laid her out in that window dressed as Sleeping Beauty."

Ben hurried across the street and pushed people aside to reach the window. Maudy was lying in a complete coma on a bed of scarlet satin. Her hands were holding a tiny bouquet of posies at her breast. She was dressed in white, with golden rings on her fingers and flowers in her hair, beside her, a sign read, Sleeping Beauty awaits her Prince at Carter's Dress Shop.

"Howdy, Ben. Hey, it's Ben Cowden." Ben recognized the man as a miner from Harshaw named Creswell. He was drunk and he walked up and leaned on Ben and smirked in his face. Ben tried to step away, and the man stumbled closer.

"Look at that purty little thing," Creswell said. "Gives a feller ideas, don't it? I'd buy that dress if they'd leave her in it and let me take it off."

Ben shoved him away. He tried the door, but it was locked. He looked at his watch. The place had been closed for an hour.

"How long are they going to leave her like that?" he asked another man. The man looked away and did not answer. "Who has the key to this lash-up?" Ben looked over the heads of the crowd to Doris Vincent for help. She turned away from him.

Creswell came back and crowded Ben and said, "What the hell, Ben, let's have a drink."

"Listen, who's got the key to this place?"

Ben looked into the faces of the crowd. They were only idle and curious townspeople, indifferent to strangers like Ben and Maudy. Ben took hold of Creswell's shoulders. "Who's got the key to this place, Crez?" he demanded.

"Hell, Miz Carter has it, who the hell else'd have it?"

"Dammit, where is she?"

"Hell, she lives in Fairbanks, don't she?"

"How long before she comes back and opens the place?"

"Hell, far as I know the girl's there for tonight and most of tomorrow. They said her prince was coming tomorrow, or something. Big opening show for the store."

"Who did this to her?"

"The guy's a hypotist, or something."

"A hypnotist?"

"Yeah, something like that."

"Where is he?"

"Hell, I don't know. He's usually in the saloons when he can afford to play poker."

Ben headed for the nearest saloon.

"Hell, what you wanta do, wake her up?" Creswell shouted. "What you wanta do that for?"

Ben searched the saloons until the bartender in the Bird Cage pointed to a man sitting at a poker game under an old top hat. Ben walked up behind him, grabbed him by the head the way he would pick up a bowlful of clabber, lifted him out of his chair, and stood him on his feet. He knocked off the hat, grabbed a handful of hair with one hand, and twisted his arm with the other. He drove him out of the saloon, down the street, and through the crowd in front of the store.

He did not pause. He used the dude's head as a battering ram. He failed to break through the door the first time, so he backed him up again, took a better run at it, and rammed him through the second time.

Inside, Ben held the man and ripped the curtains and gauze away from the bier where Maudy was lying. "Wake her up," he ordered.

"This kind of thing is not done in a hurry," the dude countered. "I need time and quietude."

Ben tried to wrench the man's arm out of its socket. The man squealed.

"Listen to me," Ben said calmly. "If you're alive after this, you can go on telling lies to other little girls, storekeepers, and poker players, but now is not the time for you to lie. If that girl remains unconscious one more minute, your life is over."

"Maudy, do you hear me? Yes, you hear me, don't you? Tell me you hear me," the man intoned softly.

Maudy slept on with a gentle smile on her face.

"Maudy," the man repeated.

A fly landed on Maudy's forehead and walked across her nose, and she did not move. Her face could have been made of plaster, it was so lifeless. The color on her face was only makeup and a rosy light off the scarlet satin. She did not seem to be breathing.

"This girl hasn't been hypnotized," Ben said. "She's drugged. What did you give her, you piece of shit."

"Nothing. I . . . uh . . . it was the laudanum. I gave her a few drops to soften her up before I hypnotized her."

"Wake her up."

"All right, but stop hurting me." Ben released his arm. "Maudy? It's time for you to wake up. You've been asleep long enough. I'll start counting. When I reach the count of five, you will open your eyes and awaken. One . . . two . . . three . . . four . . . *five!*"

Maudy opened her eyes and said softly, "That was a nice dream."

Ben jerked the man away from Maudy's side and took her in his arms. The man was sitting flat on the floor, rubbing his shoulder.

"This little girl better not be hurt," Ben said. "The next time I see you, I'm going to punch you cross-eyed so you'll keep your evil eye to yourself from now on."

He carried Maudy through the crowd and down the street to the Pendletons'. "So nice," said Maudy as he carried her through the front door.

The women took her into a bedroom. The doctor came and went in to examine her. After a while, the door opened, and he came out. "I don't think the girl's been harmed, but I would like to know who it is that goes around giving laudanum to children," he said.

Ben went in to see Maudy.

She still looked lifeless, wraithlike.

"I have to return the clothes," Maudy said.

"Boy, you really know how to do the town, Maudy," Ben said.

"Tell me what they gave you to put you out, girl," the doctor said. "How did that happen?"

Maudy said, "Well, I went in that shop to look for some dress material, and my friend Lorrie Briggs was there. We got to visiting, and she said she was offered a job. She didn't want it, but she said I could have it."

"What was the job?"

"Well, it was to dress up like Sleeping Beauty and let myself be hypnotized for a picture."

"Why did you have to be hypnotized?"

"They said I must lie absolutely still for the picture, and then I'd be awakened and I'd give the clothes back and they'd pay me, or I could take payment in the material I wanted."

"You laid in the window of that store for hours with people staring at you," Ben said.

"In the window? No, they set up a satin couch in the back room for me."

"Did you change into the store's clothes yourself?"

"Well, Lorrie helped me. She chaperoned the whole thing."

"Lorrie stayed right there, did she?"

"Well, yes. I wouldn't have undressed and changed clothes and let them hypnotize me without being sure she was going to be there through the whole thing."

"How much did they say they'd pay you?"

"They said a ten-spot."

"Ten dollars?"

"What did I do wrong?" Maudy asked.

Ben was gone. He went straight to the hotel, crossed the lobby, went up the stairs to the corner room, and pounded on the door.

"Oh," Lorrie Briggs said when she came to the door and saw Ben.

"Hello, Lorrie," Ben said.

Lorrie looked down as though she was not too sure of her footing as she moved out into the hallway. She had the prettiest lower lip Ben had ever seen. She was not much older than a child. She held the door half closed behind her and did not smile at him when she finally looked at him. "My Gosh, Ben, do you know Sheriff Perkins is looking for you?"

"That's what I hear." Ben moved her aside and walked into the room. "Leave the door open."

Vincent's razor and shaving mug were on the dresser. His carpetbag and a pair of his lace boots were under the bed. New dresses, ladies hats, and underclothes were spread over the bed. Boxes and wrappings from the shops were in a neat pile on the floor.

Lorrie closed the door, leaned against the wall, and waited for Ben to finish examining her toiletries on the dresser with Vincent's. Ben took a chair by a window.

"Don't get comfortable; you can't stay," Lorrie said. "What in the world are you doing in Tombstone? I thought you were away in the wilderness chasing your neighbors' cattle. I honestly never expected to see you again."

"Well, I didn't expect to see you way over here either, Lorrie." Ben was trying to be a gentleman. He was not here to torment the girl, but he wanted to know what had been done to Maudy in the dress shop.

"Well, this hotel is my world, now. I live here. What are you doing here?"

"I came to put my horse in training, to look up Duncan Vincent and put knots on his head after my fashion, and to shoot Hoozy Briggs. I was tired, so I came to this hotel to rest awhile. In fact, I took the room right on the other side of your wall. Imagine my pleasure when I awoke from a nice rest and heard His Magnificence practicing another speech. I went out when I heard you order him to take off his shirt and shoes. In the lobby, I was, by God, gladdened to see Doris Vincent come in the front door at the very moment Duncan Vincent's shoes were thumping under your bed."

"His *wife* is here?"

"Yes. Imagine how glad I was to see her, the one person who could hurt Vincent more than I could, even if I shot him dead."

"I can imagine."

"All I had to do was point the way to this room when she asked me if I had seen her husband. Instead, I started worrying because I've been taught to respect women. damned sure respect Doris Vincent. Foolish as she is, she' loyal to her husband."

"So what? You don't respect me? You think I care You're mad because Duncan Vincent is my friend? I wa ready to elope with you. How long did you think I woul wait?"

"I knew you'd run off with the first male who'd take you Lorrie. I never considered running away with you. wouldn't drop my work and my family to do things with yo in the night that other people would buy tickets to see That's all you wanted to do, make a show."

"Oh, it was?" Lorrie walked up to Ben and put he hands on his shoulders, spread his legs with her knees, an moved in between them. "You sure?"

"Which brings me to the reason I'm here bothering you. How much money do you and that hypnotist want for those pictures of Maudy?"

Lorrie stepped back and laughed. "What pictures are you talking about?"

"Don't try to tell me you didn't strip her and take pictures while she was unconscious in that dress shop."

"What a dirty mind you have, Ben Cowden. What makes you think I'd do a thing like that? I didn't stay in that shop long enough to see her head hit the pillow. The last time I saw her, she was still wearing clothes. I'll tell you one thing, though. Whatever happened, she asked for it by being so dumb. Can you imagine me letting a pair of perverts put me to sleep on a bed?"

"She's not dumb. She's innocent. Nobody can blame her for trusting you. I would have trusted you, too."

"You're a fool, then. I don't trust anybody that much."

"She only did it because she thought you would stay with her. You fooled us all, the way you threw off on everybody who liked you."

"You're damned right I did. And now I've got Dunky to eat out of my hand, keep me in good style, and give me everything I want."

Ben headed for the door.

"You're not leaving, are you? You haven't seen everything my Dunky bought me. Have you seen my gold bracelet?"

Lorrie reached into a box on her dresser and held up the bracelet Ben had given Doris Vincent.

"Well," he said. "It finally landed where it belonged."

"What do you mean? You like it on me?"

"Didn't Dunky tell you? I gave that bracelet to his wife. I bought it down in Santa Cruz for you, but Doris Vincent admired it so much, I gave it to her. I thought it would look good on you when I bought it. I see it does."

Lorrie laughed. "Why, you rat, you gave my bracelet to Vincent's frumpy wife? You're a real rat."

"Small world, Lorrie. Watch out, someone else might turn up wearing it." Ben walked out.

He stopped on the veranda of the hotel with Walter Jarboe in time to watch fifty angry men drive Duncan

Vincent and Hoozy Briggs up the street toward the hotel. Vincent was in full flight, and Hoozy was earning his wages by keeping the leaders of the mob from grabbing him. Hoozy's face was so jagged and terrible, it was enough to scare the leaders back when the mob pushed them too close to Vincent.

As Vincent reached the hotel and started up the steps, the crowd engulfed him and lifted him off his feet. He panicked and floundered like a drowning man striking for a beach. Ben hurried down and helped him regain his feet on the first landing of the stairs. Vincent was so afraid he drew blood from Ben's arm as he clutched it for support.

Vincent stumbled past Jarboe, lurched on into the lobby, and started up the stairs. He stopped face-to-face with Lorrie Briggs who was coming down the stairs with her suitcase. She blocked his flight, so he turned to face the crowd.

The mob carried Ben into the lobby. He stepped behind the front desk to keep from being trampled. Someone threw a brick through the window glass that hummed by Vincent's ear.

Hoozy came through the door on the next wave. He saw Ben and scurried away through the crowd as fast and slick as a louse.

Two men hung an effigy of Vincent on the mezzanine. Pinned to its breast was a sign: Duncan Vincent, Assassin.

Somebody in the crowd yelled, "Why hang a dummy? Hang the bigshot himself!" A rock whistled by Vincent and bounced up the stairs to Lorrie's feet. Vincent ducked his head and ran up the stairs to Lorrie. Lorrie stood her ground, but she looked for a way to get by him. The lobby was filling with men who were wild to hurt him.

Vincent started around Lorrie and saw his wife at the head of the stairs. He sobbed, "Oh, Doris, dear, thank God you're here."

Lorrie left Vincent to his wife. She held up her head and looked men in the eye as she walked out of the place.

Vincent sobbed, "Oh, Doris, dear, thank God."

Doris stared down her nose at her husband. Vincent took a step toward her, and she brought a big six-shooter from behind her back and pointed it at his head. The mob

tampeded out the doors and windows. Doris brought up
her other hand and showed Vincent her bracelet.

"Look, Duncan," she said. She waited for the place to
empty and quiet to descend. "I found my nice bracelet.
Guess where it was." She loosed a round from the six-
shooter. The explosion sounded like a piano had been
dropped in the middle of the lobby. The powder flash sent
Vincent stumbling backward, but the bullet missed flesh
and bone and shattered the wall above Ben's head. Vincent
huddled at the foot of the stairs with his arms covering his
head. When he uncovered it to see what Doris was doing,
his hat was over his ears.

"My bracelet was on the wrist of that other little trinket
you had in your room." Doris reached up with the hand that
held the bracelet and cocked the pistol again. Her grip was
so tight on the trigger that the hammer fell immediately.
The ball ripped through the ceiling. Slabs of plaster came
down on men who were trying to burrow into a crowd
under a table. They flounced, scrambled, and flattened in
the calcimine dust as Doris loosed another bullet.

The men who fled the lobby toward the street with the
first shot had run into the face of the mob that was still
jostling in. The fear on their faces and the sound of the
second shot caused a panic in the street. Ben drew his pistol
and fired through a window over the head of the mob to
make sure it ran all the way home. He walked up the stairs
and reached Doris as her last bullet shot through the
ceiling. She cocked the pistol and let the hammer fall on an
empty cartridge, then sat down on the stairs and leaned
against the bannister. Ben gently took the pistol away from
her.

Vincent raised his head again and saw that his wife was
no longer shooting. He gathered himself and stood up
straight. He looked shamefully into many faces, including
Ben's, as he found his legs, but he did not look at Doris.
Then, without looking to the right or to the left, he strode
slowly across the lobby and out the back door.

Ben helped Doris into his room, laid her on the bed,
and covered her with a blanket. He went out and asked the
clerk at the desk to send for a doctor to look after her.

Walter Jarboe was standing in the center of the lobby with a stocky, dark-complexioned man.

"Did you instigate that show, Mr. Jarboe?" Ben asked. "You really meant it when you said you wanted to see if Vincent would tree, didn't you?"

"That was sure a crowd of mean citizens, wasn't it?" Jarboe said, laughing.

"That was a put-up job, wasn't it? It had to be."

"Meet my friend, George Giragi, editor of the *Epitaph*," Jarboe said. Ben shook hands with the dark, stocky man. " gave Mr. Giragi the story of Hector Romero's hanging and then hired ten good men to hang Vincent in effigy, heckle him during his speech, and then chase him off the platform. I did it to take his mind off his own importance and to get even with him. The good citizens of Tombstone caught the fever and did all the terrorizing."

"They were damned mean," Ben said.

"For a while there, I worried they were out of control," Giragi said. "Nothing incites a pack more than the sight of a running fox. It's a good thing Mrs. Vincent cut loose with her six-shooter when she did."

"Well, the fox is limping now. Maybe he'll hobble all the way back to New York," Ben said.

"I don't care where he goes. I have the legal means to gather my cattle and take them home, and I don't think he'll try to hinder me anymore," Jarboe said.

Ben excused himself and headed for the back door.

"Where are you going? I thought we'd have a drink," Jarboe said.

"I just remembered I still have a few things to do." Ben hurried out into the alley. As he expected, Vincent and Hoozy were gone.

CHAPTER 26

Viney was at her early chores for the first time since Freddie Lee died. Both water buckets in the kitchen were empty, so she went out to the well in the orchard to fill them. She had not been to the well since Freddie Lee was killed.

Viney knew she was too much affected by memories. She accused herself of that all the time. It sometimes made her feel bad when she remembered something good. It always made her feel bad to remember something bad, but she still wanted her memories. She decided she must put a stop to her grief over Freddie Lee. She had to think of something else besides that little boy, no matter how much he was reminded of him everywhere she turned.

The rope was gone from the windlass on the well. It had probably finally worn out. Betty and Eileen had been trying to manage the household since Viney began spending whole days in her sewing rocker in the Arizona room. They had not replaced the old rope on the windlass. Viney was forced to go down to the creek to fill her buckets at the seep.

Going down to the seep was like walking into hell. She would always accuse herself of not being courageous enough to run through the wire and the kicking burro to pull her son's face out of the seep. Her son might have survived if she had tried harder to save him.

Viney filled her buckets, but when she started back toward the house, her legs were shaking and her breath was shallow. She set the full buckets on the sand, took a few steps to the creek-bank, and sat down. She was losing consciousness. She laid back into a young, soft, and fragrant clump of arrowweed, and her head came to rest comfortably.

Viney took some deep breaths and recovered her senses. She hoped her grief had not affected her heart. She had never been prone to swooning. During her grief, though, her heart had begun to hurt. Well, she would have to live through this and carry the water back to the house. She had other children, so her heart would probably have to endure a whole lot more hurt before it quit.

She raised her head, looked to see what had been cushioning it so nicely, and found Freddie Lee's boot. Her head had been lying on the soft boot-top. The boy's birthday spur was crammed down tightly on the bottom of the heel, evidence of the awful forces that exerted themselves on him the moment he was killed. Viney lifted the boot, and the spur tinkled as it departed the ground, a tiny ring in the stillness of the canyon. Viney hugged the boot and sank to the ground.

A. B. came down the road in his buggy a few minutes later and saw Viney lying in the creek-bed. He laid the buggy whip across the horse's hips and drove him at a run to the barnyard and through the front barndoor. Gordo and Bill Knox were working at the forge. They stopped the horse and held him. A. B. jumped down and ran like a boy to Viney.

Her face was composed, her eyes were closed, and she was not moving. He sat down dejectedly beside her, saw the boot, took it from her, and recognized it. He looked back at Viney's face. She still had not moved, but her eyes were open, and she was looking at him. He reached for her and she took his hand and sat up. He held the boot away from his side as though it might cause more misery.

"I never even missed that boot," Viney said. "It was the last thing I wanted to find down here this morning."

"Darling, I thought . . ." A. B. cleared his throat. "I ought you were . . . sleeping."

"No, I had a little spell of faintheartedness."

"I'll go find the other boot and get rid of them both."

"No, Mr. Cowden. That would be a waste. This family n always use its boots and spurs. Someday they'll fit mebody again."

The fierce old Apache called the Yawner stood in a high ddle of a mountain smelling a moist wind off the Califor-a gulf. A wind like that should have brought rain. From is saddle the Yawner could look down on the sunset. He atched the failed storm clouds dying over the Sierra adre to the south. The saddle was just below the peak of t. Wrightson, in the Santa Rita Mountains of Arizona.

The wind gusted, and he smelled cattle. Cattle stirred ore dust than game did, and with the dust's rising, the nolesome odor of cud was on the wind. Those cattle might at the spring of the *javalí*, the water hole he would pass morrow. With luck he would find cows in the traps of the ree brothers, the ones the Yawner's band called *los etes*, the horsemen.

The Yawner rubbed the back of his shoulder against the ank of a pine tree to scratch an itch. The summer sun ade him itch, but he felt good when he scratched. He felt fit as a wolf. He remembered the soreness he suffered in ; heavy legs during the first week he ran from San Carlos. ey were light as a deer's now. The prosperity of a band in the pace the leader was able to set and sustain. The wner seldom quickened his steps, but he was always able lengthen a lead on a pursuer.

When the buffalo soldiers had stopped to blow at Los etates, the Yawner jogged south to the Santa Barbara ountains. He doubled back and hid his tracks at the Santa uz River and then jogged north. No one pursued him. hen he reached the top of the Santa Ritas, he stopped to nt and recuperate. The soldiers thought he was deep in nora. The Yawner smiled. They probably thought he was Sahuaripa drinking *bacanora* mescal, or even at Mulatos. ey thought he was drinking *tesguino* on the Mulatos ver.

Mountains were the avenues of the Apache. No oth
man and no horse or mule could keep up with an Apach
walking in mountains. The Yawner had left no trail now f
twenty-five days.

The country would suffer from the drouth. Dust ro
easily and hung over the ground a long time, then lay heav
on the oak leaves. The killing dryness was deep inside th
ground. The days were hot, and the nights were cold in th
high places. The grass was not growing.

The Yawner's band would eat cattle. They would k
cows and make jerky before the cattle began to wither
the grass was withering. The band must soon go to th
Sierra Madre. In the Sierra they did not have to be
vigilant. They could grow corn, squash, pumpkin, bean
and tobacco along the rivers of Sonora.

Four of the younger men were out coursing for game
the eastern foothills of the Santa Ritas, where the feed w
still good. Four were on the western slope. The two olde
Apaches were watching from the high points. The Yawne
kept the fiercest and wisest of his fighters with him. H
strongest fighters were posted in a perimeter around h
camp.

He must head south, soon.

Hoozy and the Yaqui were headed for Nogales to jo
Kosterlinsky. Hoozy was sure Kosterlinsky would hav
something for him to do.

The Yaqui had been staying close to Hoozy. He ha
roamed Tombstone while Hoozy was there and was on han
with the horses when Hoozy ran from the mob.

Now, the Yaqui was balky. As they climbed the foothi
of the Santa Ritas, he kept stopping to examine the countr
He stopped so much Hoozy became impatient and bega
worrying about pursuit.

Finally, Hoozy asked the Yaqui why he kept looki
back, like a coyote. The Yaqui said, "*El Jinete.*" We
Hoozy did not know a "*Heenaytay*" from a "*Gatto.*"

The Yaqui made a sign of a man forking a horse, point
with his chin at their backtrail, and said, "*Benjami*
Hoozy became more nervous and impatient to reach M
ico.

As they climbed the side of a long, high ridge on the slopes of the Santa Ritas, the Yaqui balked again. A draw below them afforded thick mesquite cover for an ambuscade. The side of the ridge afforded them no cover. Anyone could watch them, shoot them, or even knock them over with a rock from the top of the ridge.

The Yaqui was sitting very still on his horse. Hoozy could see he was worried. The Yaqui usually smiled when others expected him to be worried, but now his face was serious, and he was sweating.

"What now?" asked Hoozy impatiently.

The Yaqui said, *"Apache."* He pronounced it clearly, the Yaqui way, and then pointed to a stand of cedars on top of the ridge. He pointed to the mesquite thicket below them. *"Nos va llevar toda la chingada!"* he muttered. "We're screwed!"

Hoozy could not understand the man, and he did not see a thing wrong with the cedars or the mesquites. But he drew his .4570 and rode ahead of the Yaqui, to clear the way.

The Yaqui sat his horse and did not move. Hoozy stopped and turned back to him. He might be impatient, but he knew better than to go on without the Yaqui.

The Yaqui looked past him at the cedars on top the ridge. All of a sudden he saw something he did not like. He drove his big spurs into his horse's flanks and fled downhill.

An Apache brave walked out of the mesquites in front of the Yaqui. Laughing softly, he drew his bow and drove an arrow into the Yaqui's chest. Hoozy saw the point come all the way through without piercing the back of his shirt. The arrow made a peak, like a tent, inside the shirt and brought the blood through.

The Yaqui braced up straight as a tree on his horse. His horse pivoted and changed direction. The Yaqui stopped him. He was standing stiff in his stirrups over his horse with a death grip on the reins. The horse wavered in his tracks, uncertain of his direction, no longer guided by the Yaqui's rigid hand. Then an arrow big as a lance, its feathers cutting the silence, rushed past Hoozy and shocked the Yaqui dead off his horse.

Hoozy spurred downhill to get away, but two mounted Apaches came out of the mesquites in front of him. One of them caught his rein and jerked his horse to a stop so abruptly that Hoozy almost fell off. He dropped his rifle as he caught hold of his horse's mane with both hands.

Hoozy knew one of the horsemen, but that Apache showed him no friendship. "Che Che, my friend," Hoozy said. Che Che was carrying a bow and a quiver of arrows over his shoulders, a lance in his hands. Hoozy realized the enemy Apache was upon him.

"My God, I bet you don't recognize my *face*," Hoozy said, and he smiled so the savage would remember their friendship.

Che Che positioned his horse by Hoozy's side, waggled the point of his lance against Hoozy's chest, and said, "*Ay, que feo!* How ugly!" Hoozy was still smiling and looking down at the sharp head of the lance when Che Che thrust it into his solar plexus. Che Che found the soft pit of the stomach with the point, shoved again to sever the spine, then leaned forward and screamed in Hoozy's ear as he died.

Ben Cowden was having no trouble tracking Hoozy across the country, but he was in no hurry to catch him. Hoozy was such a greenhorn any kind of predator could eat him whenever he ventured out of doors. Apaches, the law, or the soldiers might get him any minute. He might fall off his horse and break his neck, or a bear might run him off a cliff, or he might lie down beside his other brother, the coontail rattlesnake. Being with the Yaqui was no insurance that Hoozy would escape. The Yaqui might just decide Hoozy was too helpless to go on living.

Ben rode down from the Canelo Hills above the Vaca ranch. He could see new feed sprouting on a strip of the Vaca five miles wide and ten miles long. At the base of the Canelos, Hoozy's tracks turned west across the Vaca range. Ben dismounted in a campground on the Santa Cruz River, a place where teamsters tested their harness and rested their horses before climbing the hills. He hobbled Star to let him graze and ate fried chicken Maudy had packed in his morral.

This was the middle of August, not too late for the country to revive if it caught some general rain. The growing season was gone, but cattle might recuperate. Ben and his brothers might still be able to sell some big steers if the rains started right away.

Cattle were still strong enough for Ben or organize a drive and move them to California where rain was falling and the climate would be good through the winter. A. B. loved California. The Cowden brothers might lease new range out there and let this country rest through the drouth.

Ben would enjoy seeing new country. He knew only the balmy winds and climate of southern Arizona and Sonora. He would like to cowboy on the green grass of Wyoming and know the chinooks of the Montana winter. He wanted to know the market for cattle in the goldfields of Alaska where the Arctic snows made cattle scarce. By seeing how creatures grazed on the tundra of Alaska or on the seacoast of California, he would learn more about how to husband his stock in Arizona.

Later, Ben headed up Rosa del Monte Canyon on Hoozy's tracks. He sensed the Apaches only an instant before he saw the track of a rawhide shoe. He searched until he found the place in the mesquites where the three braves had hidden to ambush Hoozy.

He was about to run away and head for home when he saw a pile of naked flesh on the side of the ridge. He rode toward it and on the way stumbled over the darkening remains of the Yaqui. He saw how the two well-placed arrows, one of them twice the size of the other, had killed the Yaqui an extra time. He rode on and found Hoozy's lanced and stripped carcass.

Ben shook his head. Now, instead of the privilege of making Hoozy pay for all the grief he's caused, Ben had the duty of burying him.

He almost decided not to do it. He was the only person in the world who knew Hoozy needed burying. Nobody would know if he didn't do it. He did not want to do it. Hoozy would be stinking by the time Ben returned for him with a packhorse.

The Apaches were not far away. The evidence of the ambush was still fresh. They must have watched Hoozy for quite a while, so they probably knew Ben had caught up.

They must have taken their time killing Hoozy and the
Yaqui, stripping their bones, lancing them again for good
measure, talking about it, and catching the loose horses
They would be watching Ben now.

Well, he could outrun them if he saw them in time. He
could outrun an arrow if he saw it coming far enough away
He rode to the top of the ridge and stopped in the cedar
thicket to look around. He saw the spot at the base of a tree
where the Apache who manned the big bow must have
been sitting when he launched the arrow that practically
buried the Yaqui. He looked down into the next draw and
saw four Apaches sitting their horses and waiting for him
He realized they had relinquished the high ground to him
on purpose when they saw him coming.

"*Jinete!*" growled one of them, softly. "Horseman!"

The Apaches could see him in the thicket, and they
were close enough to kill him with an arrow or speak to him
in a low voice. Ben rode out into the open. When they saw
he was not going to run, three of the braves moved aside
and waited with their backs to him.

Ben did not recognize the Apache who faced him.

"*Jinete!*" the Apache said again. He was Apache and did
not look Ben full in the face. This was a courtesy he
extended so he would not offend Ben with the direct gaze
of the predator.

As always, Ben felt privileged to be given a close look at
an Apache, the way he felt when he got to see a lion,
jaguar, a wolf, or a mustang. He was seldom given time to
examine the Apache seat on a horse, the jaunty way he
carried his weapons, or the way he dressed himself. This
one was wearing A. B.'s top hat. He was also wearing
green toga over one shoulder that was probably made of
Viney's velvet drape.

"I guess I ought to give you something for killing my
enemies, but you've already adorned yourself with my
father's best hat and my mother's best curtain," Ben said in
Spanish. "What are you called?"

The warrior waited a moment before he answered, as
though offended that Ben did not know him. "Che Che," he
growled. This made Ben pause. Then he recognized the
Apache who had posed as a Mexican, consorted with Hoozy

Briggs, stolen the Cowden remuda, and ridden side-by-side with Kosterlinsky's guidon.

"You fooled us all. You are a brave man. What can I do to return your favor?" Ben said.

"Return this for me to the little *reyezuela*, the little wren, who perches in the walnut tree." Che Che held up Myrtle Farley's ring on the Yaqui's golden chain and hung it carefully on a cedar tree. Then, he reined his horse around and rode after his partners.

About the author of
THE ARIZONA SAGA

Joseph Paul Summers Brown—J.P.S. to the readers of his books and Joe to his friends—was born in Nogales, Arizona, and raised on a sprawling 185-section ranch; he is a fifth-generation Arizona cattleman. He attended the University of Notre Dame majoring in journalism. At the same time, he joined the U.S. Marine Corp Reserve. At Notre Dame, he won the middleweight boxing championship in 1951; the following year, he won the light-heavyweight championship there.

Brown returned to the family ranch after college and began a career in journalism, working as a general assignment reporter on two weekly newspapers, *The Apache County Independent News* and *The Holbrook Tribune News*, where he wrote a popular column called "Highway 66." He later went to work for the *El Paso Herald-Post* as general assignment reporter and farm and ranch page editor. One of his duties was to write a weekly farm feature. His paper won the Scripps Howard Award for best farm feature page in 1954.

That same year, Brown enrolled in the U.S. Marine Corps Officer Candidate School in Quantico, Virginia, and was commissioned a 2nd Lieutenant. Released from active duty in 1958, he returned to the cattle business in Mexico and Arizona.

It wasn't until 1965, during a bout with hepatitis, that Brown began to write. His first novel, published to critical acclaim, was *Jim Kane*, in 1971, which became the basis for the movie *Pocket Money* with Paul Newman and Lee Marvin.

A stint as a cowboy gathering maverick cattle provided the inspiration for his second novel, *The Outfit*, which is now considered a Southwestern classic. Brown is also a cattle rancher and furnishes livestock for the motion picture industry.

In 1974, his third novel, *The Forests of the Night*, was published; 1986 saw the publication of *Steeldust*. In 1990, Bantam Books began publishing his original series, *The Arizona Saga*.

The author and his wife, Patsy, currently make their home in Tucson, Arizona.

J.P.S. Brown

has been one of the most respected writers of
the American Southwest for the past two
decades. If you enjoyed THE ARIZONA
SAGA Book 1: THE BLOODED STOCK, you
will want to read the second book in this
exciting new series by J.P.S. Brown

THE ARIZONA SAGA
Book 2:
THE HORSEMAN

Turn the page for a dynamic preview
from THE HORSEMAN, on sale this fall
wherever Bantam Books are sold.

Ben Cowden rode into Patagonia leading a packhorse loaded with the carcasses of two of his worst enemies, Hoozy Briggs and the Yaqui. This was Hoozy's home town and people did not receive him as though he was at the head of a parade. Everybody knew one of the corpses under the tarp was Hoozy's, because Ben had told them Hoozy was dead when he came in to borrow the packhorse.

Now all he wanted to do was turn the bodies over to Dick Martin, return the packhorse, and go home. Because of Hoozy Briggs, Ben had not been home much lately. For some time before he got himself killed by Apaches, Hoozy had been doing mischief to Ben Cowden and his family. Hoozy and his Yaqui partner were running away from Ben when the Apaches caught and lanced them.

Ben did not like it that Dick Martin, a friend of Hoozy's, was the new constable of Patagonia. Martin was not quite as sorry as Hoozy, but he would do for sorry when Hoozy was not around. Ben paraded the packhorse all over town by every saloon and could not find Martin. He wanted Martin to be the one to turn the body over to Hoozy Briggs's parents. He finally saw he would have to take Hoozy home himself.

Not a sign of a Briggs was showing when Ben stopped his horse at the Briggs house in the middle of town. Rather than shout for them to come out for their son, he dismounted, tied his horses to a tree, and knocked on the front door.

He heard no sound inside the house. He went around to the back and was about to knock when he heard metal strike metal behind him. He turned and saw an elderly man lift an ax out from under a plowshare.

Ben knew the man did not intend to use the ax as a tool, but as a weapon. Anytime a Briggs was near a Cowden these days both sides dropped tools and picked up weapons. The trouble was, there weren't many Briggses left. This man was the father, but he was hardworking and not prone to mischief. His two mean sons, Whitey and Hoozy, were dead. His daughter Lorrie was somewhere on her way to a new adventure after being caught in a hotel room with Pima County's self-styled leading citizen by that citizen's leading wife.

Ben knew a teenaged brother of Whitey and Hoozy still lived with his parents. He looked around for him. Everybody said the poison of young snakes was the most potent. The Briggs offspring were mean as snakes, but Ben always thought the mother and father were decent people because they worked so hard.

"Good evening, Mr. Briggs," Ben said.

Briggs did not even nod.

Ben made himself walk toward the man. Some men would rather stand away at a distance to tell bad news, but Ben thought it hurt people worse when they were told that way. He did not like the Briggses, but he did not have anything against this man who had lost two sons in the last month and a half.

"My name's Ben Cowden," Ben said when he was decently close.

"I know who you are."

"I'm here on sad business, Mr. Briggs."

"I know why you're here. They came and told me you borrowed a horse to bring in the body of my son."

"Yes, sir. I found him in Rosemont Canyon lanced by Apaches."

"You're one of the sonsabitches that found Whitey's body, too, aren't you?"

Ben did not answer. He did not want to fight. He only wanted to hand the man his son's body.

"Now you bring me the mess that's left of another son. You're kinda rubbing my nose in it, aren't you?"

"No, Mr. Briggs. Hoozy and I weren't friends, but I thought you'd want his body back."

"No, you goddamned murdering Cowden, you wanted to parade my son's body back here so everybody'd know you finished him."

"Sir, I've done the decent thing. Will you help me take him down off the horse?"

"I will not. I won't help clean up your mess. Get it away from here before his mother comes home."

Ben went back to the front of the house. Lorrie Briggs, Hoozy's sister, was coming through the front gate with her mother and Ted, the younger brother. Mrs. Briggs hurried into the house. Lorrie and the boy stared at Ben as though he was to blame for Hoozy's killing. That was all right for the father, the mother, and the brother , but Lorrie had no right to blame him. She was Hoozy's boss's mistress. Ben and Hoozy's boss were at war.

"You've got a lot of nerve, you son of a bitch," Lorrie said. "Killing my brother and then trying to dump him on our doorstep."

Ben wanted to get on his horse and go somewhere and wash. He was not handling Hoozy's corpse because he liked it. He should have let Hoozy rot on the side of the hill where he found him. "Lorrie, I didn't kill your brother. I found him in Rosemont Canyon and I thought your folks would want him home."

"Yeah, and where's Rosemont Canyon, you bastard?"

"You know where it is, Lorrie."

"Yes, I know where it is. It's way out in the most desolate corner of the county where even God won't go. You're trying to tell me you just "found" my brother there? How was that? What were you doing there? Much as you hated each other how come you just happened to find him dead in a place where nobody else in the world ever goes?"

"I was after him, Lorrie. You knew that."

"Yeah, you were after him and you killed him the way you did his partners in Santa Cruz, but you're so high and mighty you think you'll get away with it."

Ben stared at Lorrie. She was so damned pretty and she used to be his best girlfriend. Now she'd like to kill him. He was a damned fool for packing the carcass through the country where people could see him with it and accuse him of the killing.

Lorrie glanced past him at something and Ben turned and saw old Briggs come around the corner of the house with the ax.

"Mr. Briggs, please put that down," Ben said, and drew his pistol.

Briggs kept coming.

"Get him, Teddy," Lorrie said. The boy charged Ben with a pocket knife. Lorrie was wearing a joyful look. Ben fired over Mr. Briggs's head and stopped him. The boy came on as though he would collide with Ben, slashed at him from a safe arm's length before he reached him, and ran away. He might wish he was mean and tough, thought Ben, but he'll never be a Hoozy Briggs.

Ben walked past Lorrie toward his horses. She hit him a heavy blow on the side of the head with her purse. The purse hurt so much he thought it must be full of rocks. He recovered and warded off the next swing of the purse, but it wrapped around his head on its drawstrings and bloodied his ear. He took it and threw it into the yard as he walked to his horse.

"That's right, run, you sonofabitch," screamed Lorrie. "And don't try to dump your rotted carcasses in our front yard. Take them home and bury them in your mother's flower bed."

Ben climbed on his horse, ducked his head under the tree, untied the packhorse and rode toward Harshaw. He would turn the bodies over to the coroner there and be rid of them legally.

"Turn tail, you bastard," yelled Lorrie. "Tell your sister Betty to throw away her teddy bear and take my brother's carcass to play with. My brother was too good a man for her when he was alive, but he's just right now."

That made Ben feel sad. Hoozy had once come sparking after Ben's sister Betty.

A.B. Cowden did not know much about the Interior Department of Arizona, but he knew most employees of the territorial government were incompetent and corrupt as hell. The way Frank Marshall lolled behind the desk and looked at A.B. out of the side of his face was enough to make A.B. distrust him wholeheartedly.

The man leaned forward as though he might stand up to shake A.B.'s hand, then slumped back on his tailbone when A.B. did not offer it across the desk. He kept his face profiled to A.B., pretending he was interested in something outside the window.

"Nice place you've got here, Cowden," Marshall said.

Dick Martin winced. People in that country called A.B. Cowden "Mister." Calling him by his last name as though he was some clerk in a bureau in the basement of the Interior Department was a mistake. Any fool should be able to see A.B. was a dignified man, respected by everyone who knew him. He was a leader who exerted a good influence on people. Martin did not want A.B. to think he approved of Marshall's insulting manner. He stood up to leave the room.

"Where are you going?" asked Marshall.

"Outside to see about our horses," Martin said.

"Just squat back down there. I want you to hear this."

"Aw, you can handle it without me." Martin went out.

"Come back here, mister." Marshall uncoiled, reached the door in one stride and threw it open, but the constable was already gone.

Marshall was a tall man. A.B. figured he was six foot six. He carried himself with a grace that only came with prime strength in a mature man. A.B. only knew two other men who moved like that: his sons Ben and Les. Mark would someday be as graceful, but he was still a gangly boy. This Marshall might be a bureaucrat, and he probably was a martinet and a bully, but he was big and powerful. His hands were well shaped and big. His head was large as a lion's, his hair thick and curly, his face handsome. His arms and legs were long, his shoulders wide, his stomach flat.

He sprawled in A.B.'s chair again. "Have a seat and let's talk," he said.

"What can I do for you, Captain Marshall?" asked A.B.

"Well, Cowden, I'll tell you, I'd consider it a great kindness if you'd send to the house for some coffee and maybe a little something nice to eat. I've been riding several days and I haven't had one proper meal since I left Tucson."

"Of course." A.B. stepped to the door and asked Gordo Soto, his stableboy, to go to the house and ask the girls to send coffee and cakes for Constable Martin and

Captain Marshall. He closed the door and stepped back to the center of the room. "Anything else?"

"Have a seat. We have quite a lot to talk about."

A.B. stayed where he was. Marshall levelled his authoritative gaze on him. "Listen, old man, I can't talk with you standing over me like that. I'm ordering you to have a seat."

"Mr. Marshall, I'm sure you can say all you have to say and be on your way before I get tired of standing here. Speak up and be done with it."

"Well, all right, I hope you can stand what I have to say. The governor has put me in charge of doing away with cattle theft and title fraud in Arizona Territory. I understand a warrant has already been issued for your son Ben Cowden by the county for cattle theft. You were supposed to enforce it, but it's still outstanding.

"A new federal warrant has been issued for him for the crime of murder. He recently killed two Americans in the town of Santa Cruz in Sonora. I'm here to find him and take him in. Tell me where he is and I'll be gone."

"He's not here and I don't know where he is."

"Old man, I'm going to camp right here on the Peach Tree Ranch until he comes home and then I'm gonna put knots on his head and take him to jail."

"Let me see your warrant, Captain Marshall."

"Now there you have me for the time being, Cowden. We should be notified of the issuance of our warrant by telegram sometime tomorrow. I came a little early because the Tombstone marshal notified us Ben Cowden was headed this way."

"I don't abide by telegraphed warrants," said A.B. "Any crooked bureaucrat can issue a warrant that way. When I see the real document signed by Judge Black in Tucson, my son will wear irons. Until then, go find someplace else to park."

A.B. was not carrying his pistol, and his double-barreled shotgun was in the house behind the kitchen door. At that moment he felt he might need a weapon.

Marshal drew his revolver. "You will not impede this arrest. I always know when old villains like you are about to pull a gun. Raise your hands and face the wall."

A.B. opened his coat to show he was unarmed. Marshall crossed the room, turned him to the wall and frisked him expertly. As he straightened and stood back, Betty tapped on the door and came in with a tray of coffee and rolls.

Betty was so beautiful almost every man, woman and child who saw her was forced to turn and give themselves another look. Frank Marshall was no exception. The girl was in bloom. Her curly black hair, blue eyes, fairness and carriage stopped hearts when she walked by. Frank Marshall quivered to his full height as though a cockroach had run up his leg. He put the pistol away so fast Betty never saw it. A.B. was always being reminded and was thankful for the good looks of his daughters, but at that moment Betty's served him better than a pistol or a double-barreled shotgun. He would rather have subdued Marshall and driven the meanness out of him some other way, though. Now he might never be rid of him.

"Papa, here's coffee and cinnamon rolls," Betty said, setting the tray on the desk. She paused near Marshall long enough to allow her father to introduce him. When A.B. did not make the introduction she headed for the door.

"Pardon me, young lady. I'm Frank Marshall, Special Agent for the Interior Department of the Territory." Marshall stretched up to the last inch of his six and a half foot frame, rocked on his toes for more, showed his broad white teeth in a smile and puffed up like a pouter pigeon.

Betty glanced at him with the same consideration she would give a broken pitchfork handle and left him standing with his teeth bared. If her father would not introduce the fellow, he must be awfully common.

"Is that creature *your* daughter, Cowden?" Marshall asked when she was gone.

A.B. poured Marshall a cup of coffee and said, "If you're satisfied you don't need to search me anymore, young man, here's the collation you asked for."

"Say, listen. I'm sorry about that. It seemed to me our talk had broken down. I don't mind telling you, I'm a careful man."

A.B. went to the door and called for Dick Martin. When he came into the office, A.B. turned to Marshall. "Our talk did not break down, Captain Marshall. You said everything you needed to say. You didn't need to pull a gun on me when I didn't tell you what you wanted to hear, though. I don't pull guns on my visitors. When a visitor pulls a gun on me, his visit is over. Have your coffee and leave."

"Listen, I'm really sorry about this," Marshall said. "Won't you please forget it? I'd like to call on your daughter. What's her name?"

A.B. walked out of the office.

"Martin, tell me the name of that girl who brought the coffee," Marshall demanded.

"That is Betty Cowden," Martin said.

"Geez. Are there any more like her? Of course not. There couldn't be another girl that beautiful anywhere else in the world."

Ben was riding up to the barn. A.B. called to Gordo and Bill Knox when he saw the packhorse. Ben dismounted and hugged his father.

"Son, what are you carrying on the packhorse?" A.B. asked.

"It's the bodies of Hoozy Briggs and that Yaqui who ran with him, Papa. I brought them here because I didn't know what else to do. I took them to the Briggses first because I thought that was the most decent thing to do, but Hoozy's folks had a fit and ran me off. I sent a wire to Harshaw asking Judge Dunn to meet us here for an inquest. I guess I should have taken the bodies on to Harshaw. I can still do it."

"No, son, we'll wait for Judge Dunn and have the inquest here. You can rest."

"Thanks, Papa."

Frank Marshall and Dick Martin came out of the barn.

"Hello, Dick," said Ben. "I looked all over Patagonia for you when I heard you'd been made the constable. I wanted to turn these carcasses over to you."

Dick Martin lifted the tarp on the packhorse and looked at the bodies. "Who is it, Ben?"

"Hoozy Briggs and his Yaqui," Ben said.

"You kill them?"

"No, the Yawner's people killed them in Rosemont Canyon."

"What do you have there, a couple of dead men?" Marshall moved his coat aside and showed his badge. "You say you found them in Rosemont Canyon? What were you doing there, Cowden?"

"I was on my way home."

"From Tombstone? Wasn't Rosemont out of your way?"

Ben turned to A.B. "Who is this, Papa?"

"He probably has the right to question you, son. He says he's a special agent for the Department of the Interior."

"That's right, Mr. Cowden," Martin said. "He showed me his credentials before I ever brought him here. I wouldn't bring anyone here that wasn't legitimate. I hope you know that."

"I know, Dick," A.B. said. "You identified him when

you introduced him. I don't need to see his credentials if you vouch for him."

"I wouldn't try to lie to anyone," Martin said.

"Well, I want to see his credentials," Ben said.

Marshall rolled his shoulders and rocked on his toes, trying to intimidate Ben.

"Well, let's see them," Ben said.

"Fella, I don't have to show you a damned thing. I'm about to arrest you with the authority vested in my good right arm."

Ben was happy the man was a talker and a bully. He would have worried about a quiet man that big. "Well, get after it if you think you're man enough," he said.

"Oh, I'm man enough, but I'd rather be nice to you I feel a great sweetness for your sister Betty."

This brought the very blood into Ben's eye. He hit Marshall in his left eye and knocked him down. Marshall pulled his gun even as he sprawled on the ground. Ben took a step and kicked it out of his hand. It bounced off the side of the barn and Ben skipped closer to Marshall, intending to land his next step in the man's face. Marshall's good eye widened and he scampered backward like a spider on his hands and feet and butt. A.B. and Martin jumped in and stopped Ben from stomping him.

Marshall jumped up and examined his hurts. Ben emptied the cartridges out of the pistol and dropped it on Marshall's toe. Marshall made no sound as he holstered his pistol.

"Load it when you're ready to use it," Ben said.

"You shouldn't have done that, Ben," Martin said.

"The *hell* you say," said A.B. "He did just right. The man's been asking for a punch in the eye ever since you brought him here."

A buggy rattled up the canyon and Judge Charles Dunn, deputy coroner from Harshaw, appeared. John

Porter, the telegraph operator and Ben's first cousin, was riding with him. John often served as Judge Dunn's recorder. They crossed the creek and pulled up in the yard, their horses shying at the bodies on the pack horse. Judge Dunn stepped down from his rig and ordered the bodies unloaded so he could establish their identities and determine the cause of their deaths.

"Carry them inside for this business," A.B. said. "I don't want my family or people who pass on the road to see them."

Frank Marshall drew the judge aside as the bodies were being carried in. Judge Dunn was an old friend of A.B.'s and an honest man. He looked away while he listened to Marshall. He was hard of hearing and when Marshall was through filling his deafest ear with secret intelligence, he spoke out in his most strident and judicial voice. "Why do you keep holding your hand over your eye, young man?"

Marshall mumbled something nobody else could hear.

"What's that you say, you have foreign matter in the orb?"

Marshall mumbled again, turning his head to make sure no one read his lips.

"Ah, 'twas a fist, you say," announced the judge. "I understand that. Ofttimes fists fly on this outfit, especially when officious bureaucrats like yourself try to assert the law over the best lawman in Arizona Territory."

Marshall puffed out his chest, jutted his jaw and said, "That old man's been fooling everybody long enough. I'm the best lawman this state will ever see."

"Young man, take my advice and don't try to prove that by fist fighting. You'll only disprove yourself again. Out here people admire the Cowdens because they never start a fight or try to end one with words."

"I've not yet been in a fight," Marshall said loftily. "He sundayed me."

Ben laughed.

"Enough of this," the judge said. "Remove the garments from this poor clay and let us make the necessary decisions so we can bury it."

**FROM THE PRODUCER OF WAGONS WEST
AND THE KENT FAMILY CHRONICLES—
A SWEEPING SAGA OF WAR AND HEROISM
AT THE BIRTH OF A NATION**

THE WHITE INDIAN SERIES

This thrilling series tells the compelling story of America's birth against
the equally exciting adventures of an English child raised as a Seneca.

☐	24650	White Indian #1	$4.50
☐	25020	The Renegade #2	$4.50
☐	24751	War Chief #3	$3.95
☐	24476	The Sachem #4	$3.95
☐	25154	Renno #5	$4.50
☐	25039	Tomahawk #6	$3.95
☐	25589	War Cry #7	$3.95
☐	25202	Ambush #8	$3.95
☐	23986	Seneca #9	$3.95
☐	24492	Cherokee #10	$3.95
☐	24950	Choctaw #11	$3.95
☐	25353	Seminole #12	$3.95
☐	25868	War Drums #13	$3.95
☐	26206	Apache #14	$3.95
☐	27161	Spirit Knife #15	$4.50
☐	27264	Manitou #16	$4.50
☐	27841	Seneca Warrior #17	$3.95
☐	28285	Father of Waters #18	$3.95
☐	28474	Fallen Timbers #19	$4.50

Bantam Books, Dept. LE3, 414 East Golf Road, Des Plaines, IL 60016

Please send me the items I have checked above. I am enclosing $_____
(please add $2.00 to cover postage and handling). Send check or money
order, no cash or C.O.D.s please.

Mr/Ms _____

Address _____

City/State _____ Zip _____

LE3 -9/90

Please allow four to six weeks for delivery.
Prices and availability subject to change without notice.